By William Dietrich

Fiction
BLOOD OF THE REICH
THE BARBARY PIRATES
THE DAKOTA CIPHER
THE ROSETTA KEY
NAPOLEON'S PYRAMIDS
THE SCOURGE OF GOD
HADRIAN'S WALL
DARK WINTER
GETTING BACK
ICE REICH

Coming Soon in Hardcover
THE EMERALD STORM

Nonfiction
ON PUGET SOUND
NATURAL GRACE
NORTHWEST PASSAGE
THE FINAL FOREST

WILLIAM DIETRICH

NAPOLEON'S PYRAMIDS

AN ETHAN GAGE ADVENTURE

HARPER

NEW YORK · LONDON · TORONTO · SYDNEY

HARPER

A hardcover edition of this book was published in 2007 by HarperCollins Publishers.

HarperCollins books may be purchased for educational, business, or sales promotional use. For information please write: Special Markets Department, HarperCollins Publishers, 10 East 53rd Street, New York, NY 10022.

FIRST HARPER PAPERBACK PUBLISHED 2012.

Library of Congress Cataloging-in-Publication Data is available upon request.

ISBN 978-0-06-219148-9 (pbk.)

12 13 14 15 16   RRD   10 9 8 7 6 5 4 3 2 1

To my daughter, Lisa

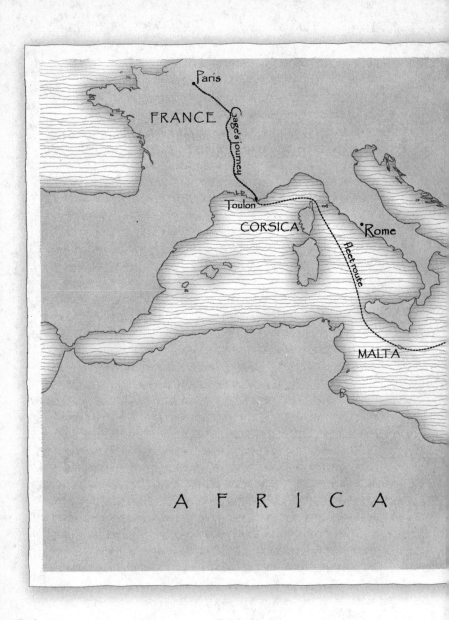

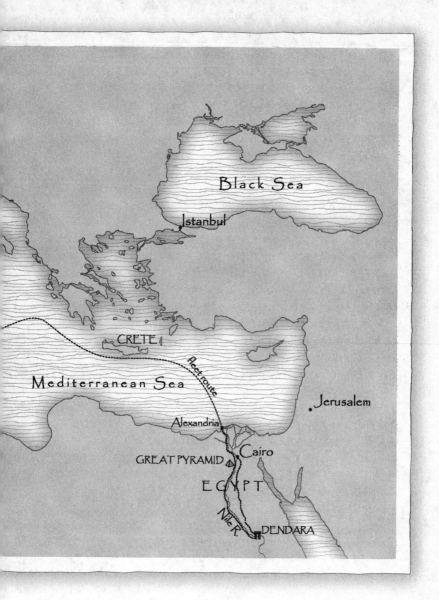

Chambers of the
Great Pyramid
Explored by Napoleon
Looking East (Not Drawn to Scale)

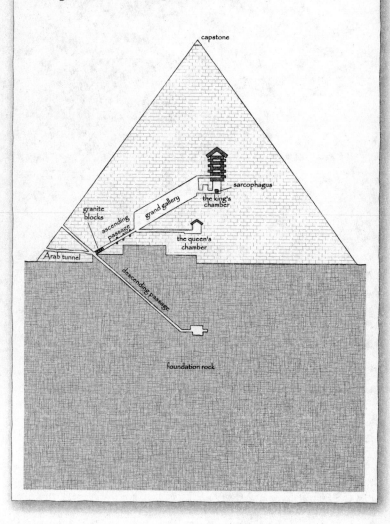

capstone

sarcophagus

the king's chamber

grand gallery

granite blocks

ascending passage

Arab tunnel

the queen's chamber

descending passage

foundation rock

NAPOLEON'S
PYRAMIDS

CHAPTER ONE

I t was luck at cards that started the trouble, and enlistment in mad invasion that seemed the way out of it. I won a trinket and almost lost my life, so take lesson. Gambling is a vice.

It's also seductive, social, and as natural, I would argue, as breathing. Isn't birth itself a roll of the dice, fortune casting one babe as peasant and another as king? In the wake of the French Revolution the stakes have simply been raised, with ambitious lawyers ruling as temporary dictators and poor King Louis losing his head. During the Reign of Terror the specter of the guillotine made existence itself a matter of chance. Then, with the death of Robespierre came an insanity of relief, giddy couples dancing on the tombs of St.-Sulpice Cemetery to a new German step called the *waltz*. Now, four years later, the nation has settled into war, corruption, and the pursuit of pleasure. Drabness has given way to brilliant uniform, modesty to *décolletage,* and looted mansions are being reoccupied as intellectual salons and chambers of seduction. If nobility is still an offense, revolutionary wealth is creating a new aristocracy. There's a clique of self-proclaimed "wonderful women" who parade Paris to boast of their "insolent luxury amid public wretchedness." There are balls that mock the guillotine, where ladies wear red ribbons at their throat. The city counts four thousand gambling houses, some so plain that patrons carry in their own folding stools, and others so opulent that *hors d'oeuvre* are served on sacramental plate and the privy is indoors. My American correspondents find both practices equally scandalous. The dice and cards fly: *creps, trente-et-un, pharaon, biribi.* Meanwhile armies tramp on France's borders, inflation is ruinous, and weeds grow in the deserted courtyards of Versailles. So to risk a purse in pursuit of a nine in *chemin de fer* seemed as natural and foolish as life itself. How was I to know that betting would bring me to Bonaparte?

Had I been inclined to superstition, I might have made note that the date, April 13, 1798, was a Friday. But it was springtime in revolutionary Paris, meaning that under the Directory's new calendar it was the twenty-fourth day of the month of Germinal in the Year Six, and the next day of rest was still six days distant, not two.

Has any reform been more futile? The government's arrogant discard of Christianity means that weeks have been extended to ten days instead of seven. The revision's intent is to supplant the papal calendar with a uniform alternative of twelve months of thirty days each, based on the system of ancient Egypt. Bibles themselves were torn up to make paper gun cartridges in the grim days of 1793, and now the biblical week has been guillotined, each month instead divided into three *decades* of ten days, with the year beginning at the autumn equinox and five to six holidays added to balance idealism with our solar orbit. Not content with regimenting the calendar, the government has introduced a new metric system for weight and measure. There are even proposals for a new clock of precisely 100,000 seconds each day. Reason, reason! And the result is that all of us, even I—amateur scientist, investigator of electricity, entrepreneur, sharpshooter, and democratic idealist—miss Sundays. The new calendar is the kind of logical idea imposed by clever people that completely ignores habit, emotion, and human nature and thus forecasts the Revolution's doom. Do I sound prescient? To be honest, I wasn't used to thinking about popular opinion in such a calculating manner yet. Napoleon would teach me that.

No, my thought was focused on counting the turn of cards. Had I been a man of nature I might have left the salons to enjoy the year's first blush of red bud and green leaf, perhaps contemplating the damsels of the Tuileries Garden, or at least the whores of the Bois de Boulogne. But I'd chosen the card cozies of Paris, that glorious and grimy city of perfume and pollution, monument and mud. My spring was candlelight, my flowers courtesans of such precariously suspended cleavage that their twin advertisements teetered on the brink of escape, and my companions a new democracy of politician and soldier, displaced nobleman and newly rich shopkeeper: citizens all. I, Ethan Gage, was the salon's American representative of frontier democracy. I had minor status thanks to my earlier apprenticeship to the late, great Benjamin Franklin. He'd taught me enough about electricity to let me amuse gatherings by cranking a cylinder to impart a frictional charge to the hands of the prettier ones and then daring the men to try a literally shocking kiss. I had minor fame from shooting exhibitions that demonstrated the accuracy of the American longrifle: I had put six balls through a pewter plate at two hundred paces, and with luck had cut the plume from a skeptical general's hat at fifty. I had minor income from trying to forge contracts between war-pressed France and my own infant and neutral nation, a task made damnably difficult by the revolutionary habit of seizing American ships. What I didn't have was much purpose beyond the amusement of daily existence: I was one of those amiably drifting single men who wait for the future to start. Nor did I have income enough to comfortably support myself in inflationary Paris. So I tried to augment it with luck.

Our host was the deliberately mysterious Madame d'Liberté, one of those enterprising women of beauty and ambition who had emerged from revolutionary anarchy to dazzle with wit and will. Who had known females could be so ambitious, so clever, so alluring? She gave orders like a sergeant major, and yet had seized on the new fad for classical gowns to advertise her feminine charms with fabric so diaphanous that the discerning could detect the dark triangle pointing to her temple of Venus. Nipples peeped over the top of her drapery like soldiers from a trench, the pair of them rouged just in case we might overlook their boldness.

Another mademoiselle had her breasts exposed entirely, like hanging fruit. Was it any wonder that I'd taken the risk of returning to Paris? Who cannot love a capital that has three times as many winemakers as bakers? Not to be outdone by the women, some of the male peacocks sported cravats reaching as high as their lower lip, cod-tailed coats that descended to the back of their knees, slippers as dainty as kitten's paws, and golden rings that glittered on their ears.

"Your beauty is eclipsed only by your cleverness," one drunken patron, an art dealer named Pierre Cannard, told Madame after she cut off his brandy. It was her punishment for his having spilled on her recently acquired oriental carpet, which she'd paid ruined royalists too much for in order to acquire that impossible-to-imitate threadbare look that proclaims the penny-pinching ancestry of the rich.

"Compliments will not clean my rug, monsieur."

Cannard clutched his heart. "And your cleverness is eclipsed by your strength, your strength by your stubbornness, and your stubbornness by your cruelty. No more brandy? With such feminine hardness, I might as well buy my spirits from a man!"

She snorted. "You sound like our latest military hero."

"You mean the young general Bonaparte?"

"A Corsican pig. When the brilliant Germaine de Staël asked the upstart what woman he could most admire, Bonaparte replied, 'The one who is the best housekeeper.'"

The gathering laughed. "Indeed!" Cannard shouted. "He's Italian, and knows a woman's place!"

"So she tried again, asking who is the woman most distinguished among her sex. And the bastard replied, 'The one who bears the most children.'"

We roared, and it was a guffaw revealing our uneasiness. Indeed, what was a woman's place in revolutionary society? Women had been given rights, even of divorce, but the newly famous Napoleon was no doubt just one of a million reactionaries who would prefer repeal. What, for that matter, was a man's place? What had rationality to do with sex and romance, those great French passions? What had science to do with love, or equality with ambition, or liberty with conquest? We were all feeling our way in year six.

Madame d'Liberté had taken as an apartment the first floor above a millinery shop, furnished it on credit, and opened so hastily that I could smell wallpaper paste alongside the cologne and tobacco smoke. Couches allowed couples to entwine. Velvet drapes invited tactile sensation. A new piano, far more fashionable than the aristocratic harpsichord, provided a mix of symphonic and patriotic tunes. Sharps, ladies of pleasure, officers on leave, merchants trying to impress the gossips, writers, newly pompous bureaucrats, informers, women hoping to marry strategically, ruined heirs: all could be found there. Those ranked around the game's shoe included a politician who had been in prison just eight months before, a colonel who had lost an arm in the revolutionary conquest of Belgium, a wine merchant getting rich by supplying restaurants opened by chefs who'd lost their aristocratic employers, and a captain from Bonaparte's Army of Italy, who was spending his loot as quickly as he'd nabbed it.

And me. I'd served as a secretary to Franklin for his last three years in Paris just before the French Revolution, returned to America for some adventures in the fur trade, made some living as a shipping agent in London and New York at the height of the Terror, and now had returned to Paris in hopes my fluent French might help me cement timber, hemp, and tobacco deals with the Directory. There's always a chance to get rich during war. I also hoped for respectability as an "electrician"—a new, exotic word—and by following up on Franklin's curiosity about Masonic mysteries. He'd hinted they might have some practical application. Indeed, some claimed the United States itself had been founded by Masons for some secret, as yet unrevealed, purpose, and that ours was a nation with a mission in mind. Alas, Masonic lore required tedious steps toward degree advancement. The British blockade impeded my trade schemes. And one thing the Revolution had not changed was the size and pace of France's implacable bureaucracy: it was easy to get an audience and impossible to get an answer.

Accordingly, I had plenty of time between interviews for other pursuits, such as gambling.

It was a pleasant enough way to spend one's nights. The wine was agreeable, the cheeses delectable, and in candle-light every male face seemed chiseled, every woman a beauty.

My problem that Friday the thirteenth was not that I was losing, but that I was winning. By this time the revolutionary *assignats* and *mandats* had become worthless, paper rubbish and specie rare. So my pile consisted of not just gold and silver francs but a ruby, a deed to an abandoned estate in Bordeaux I had no intention of visiting before unloading on someone else, and wooden chips that represented promises of a meal, a bottle, or a woman. Even an illicit gold louis or two had found their way to my side of the green felt. I was so lucky that the colonel accused me of wanting his other arm, the wine merchant lamented he could not tempt me to full drunkenness, and the politician wanted to know who I'd bribed.

"I simply count cards in English," I tried to joke, but it was a poor joke because England was reportedly what Bonaparte, back from his triumphs in northern Italy, was trying to invade. He was camped somewhere in Brittany, watching the rain and wishing the British navy would go away.

The captain drew, considered, and blushed, his skin a proclamation of his thought. It reminded me of the story of the guillotined head of Charlotte Corday, which reportedly reddened with indignation when the executioner slapped it before the crowd. There has been scientific debate since about the precise moment of death, and Dr. Xavier Bichat has taken corpses from the guillotine and tried to animate their muscles with electricity, in the same manner that the Italian Galvani has done with frogs.

The captain wanted to double his bet, but was frustrated by his empty purse. "The American has taken all my money!" I was the dealer at the moment, and he looked at me. "Credit, monsieur, for a gallant soldier."

I was in no mood to finance a betting war with a gambler

excited about his cards. "A cautious banker needs collateral."

"What, my horse?"

"I've no need of one in Paris."

"My pistols, my sword?"

"Please, I would not be complicit in your dishonor."

He sulked, peeking again at what he held. Then the kind of inspiration struck that means trouble for everyone within range. "My medallion!"

"Your what?"

He pulled out a large and heavy trinket that had hung, unseen, inside his shirt. It was a gold disc, pierced and inscribed with a curious tracery of lines and holes, with two long arms like twigs hanging beneath. It seemed crude and hammered, as if forged on Thor's anvil. "I found it in Italy. Look at its weight and antiquity! The jailer I took it from said it came from Cleopatra herself!"

"He knew the lady?" I asked dryly.

"He was told that by Count Cagliostro!"

This piqued my curiosity. "Cagliostro?" The famed healer, alchemist, and blasphemer, once the darling of the courts of Europe, had been imprisoned in the Pope's Fortress of San Leo and died of madness in 1795. Revolutionary troops had subsequently overrun the fortress last year. The alchemist's involvement in the affair of the necklace more than a decade ago had helped precipitate the Revolution by making the monarchy look greedy and foolish. Marie Antoinette had despised the man, calling him a sorcerer and a fraud.

"The Count tried to use this as a bribe to escape," the captain went on. "The jailer simply confiscated it and, when we stormed the fort, I took it from him. It has power, perhaps, and is very old, passed down for centuries. I will sell it to you for . . ."—he eyed my pile—"a thousand silver francs."

"Captain, you jest. It's an interesting bauble but . . ."

"It comes from Egypt, the jailer told me! It has sacred value!"

"Egyptian, you say?" Someone spoke with the purr of a

big cat, urbane and lazily amused. I looked up to see Count Alessandro Silano, an aristocrat of French-Italian descent who'd lost a fortune to the Revolution and was rumored to be trying to build another by turning democrat, plying devious roles in diplomatic intrigues. Rumor had it that Silano was a tool of the recently reinstated Talleyrand himself, France's minister of foreign affairs. He also professed himself a student of the secrets of antiquity, on the model of Cagliostro, Kolmer, or Saint-Germain. A few whispered his rehabilitation in government circles owed something to the black arts. He thrived on such mystery, bluffing at cards by claiming his luck was augmented by sorcery. He still lost as often as he won, however, so no one knew whether to take him seriously.

"Yes, Count," the captain said. "You of all men should recognize its value."

"Should I?" He took a seat at our table with his usual languid grace, his strong features saturnine, his lips sensual, his eyes dark, his brows heavy, exhibiting the handsomeness of a Pan. Like the famed hypnotist Mesmer, he put women under a spell.

"I mean your position in the Egyptian Rite."

Silano nodded. "And my time at studies in Egypt. Captain Bellaird, is it not?"

"You know me, monsieur?"

"By reputation as a gallant soldier. I closely followed the bulletins from Italy. If you will honor me with your acquaintance, I would join your game."

The captain was flattered. "But of course."

Silano sat and women gathered, drawn by his reputation as adept lover, duelist, gambler, and spy. He was also reputed to adhere to Cagliostro's discredited Egyptian Rite of Freemasonry, or fraternal lodges that inducted female adherents as well as male. These heretic lodges played at various occult practices, and there were juicy tales of dark ceremonies, naked orgies, and lurid sacrifice. Perhaps a tenth of it was true. Still, Egypt was reputed to be the source of ancient wisdom, and more than one mystic had claimed to have discovered mighty secrets in mysterious pilgrimages there. As a result, antiquities were in vogue from a nation closed to most Europeans since the Arab conquest eleven centuries before. Silano was reputed to have studied in Cairo before the ruling Mamelukes began harassing traders and scholars.

Now the captain nodded eagerly to cement Silano's interest. "The jailer told me the arms on the end could point the way to great power! A man of learning such as you, Count, might make sense of it."

"Or pay for a piece of nonsense. Let me see it."

The captain lifted it off his neck. "Look how odd it is."

Silano took the medallion, exhibiting the long, strong fingers of a fencer, and turned it to examine both sides. The disc was a bit larger than a communion wafer. "Not pretty enough for Cleopatra." When he held it to a candle, light shone through its holes. An incised groove extended across its circle. "How do you know it's from Egypt? It looks as though it could be from anywhere: Assyrian, Aztec, Chinese, even Italian."

"No, no, it's thousands of years old! A gypsy king told me to look for it in San Leo, where Cagliostro had died. Though some say he still lives, as a guru in India."

"A gypsy king. Cleopatra." Silano slowly handed it back. "Monsieur, you should be a playwright. I will trade you two hundred silver francs for it."

"Two hundred!"

The nobleman shrugged, his eye still on the piece.

I was intrigued by Silano's interest. "You said you were going to sell it to me."

The captain nodded, now hopeful that two of us had been baited. "Indeed! It is from the pharaoh who tormented Moses, perhaps!"

"So I will give you three hundred."

"And I will trade you five," Silano said.

We all want what the other wants. "I will trade you seven hundred and fifty," I responded.

The captain was looking from one to the other of us.

"Seven-fifty and this *assignat* note for one thousand livres," I amended.

"Which means seven-fifty and something so worthlessly inflated that he might as well use it on his ass," Silano countered. "I'll trade you the full thousand, captain."

His price had been reached so quickly that the soldier looked doubtful. Like me, he was wondering at the count's interest. This was far more than the value of the raw gold. He seemed tempted to slip it back inside his shirt.

"You've already offered it to me for a thousand," I said. "As a man of honor, consummate the exchange or leave the game. I'll pay the full sum and win it back from you within the hour."

Now I'd challenged him. "Done," he said, a soldier in defense of his standard. "Bet this hand and the next few and I'll win the medallion back from *you*."

Silano sighed hopelessly at this *affaire d'honneur*. "At least deal me some cards." I was surprised he'd given up so easily. Perhaps he only wanted to help the captain by bidding me up and reducing my pile. Or he believed he could win it at table.

If so, he was disappointed. I couldn't lose. The soldier drew into an eleven, and then lost three more hands as he bet against the odds, too lazy to track how many face cards had been dealt. "Damnation," he finally muttered. "You have the devil's luck. I'm so broke I'll have to go back on campaign."

"It will save you the trouble of thinking." I slipped the medallion around my own neck as the soldier scowled, then stood to get a glass and display my prize to the ladies, like an exhibit at a rural fair. When I nuzzled a few the hardware got in the way, so I hid it inside my shirt.

Silano approached.

"You're Franklin's man, are you not?"

"I had the honor of serving that statesman."

"Then perhaps you'll appreciate my intellectual interest. I'm a collector of antiquities. I'll still buy that neckpiece from you."

Alas, a courtesan with the fetching name of Minette, or Pussycat, had already whispered about the handsomeness of my trinket. "I respect your offer, monsieur, but I intend to discuss ancient history in the chambers of a lady." Minette had already gone ahead to warm her apartment.

"An understandable inquiry. Yet may I suggest you need a true expert? That curiosity had an interesting shape, with intriguing markings. Men who have studied the ancient arts . . ."

"Can appreciate how dearly I hold my new acquisition."

He leaned closer. "Monsieur, I must insist. I'll pay double."

I didn't like his persistence. His air of superiority rankled my American sensibilities. Besides, if Silano wanted it that badly, then maybe it was worth even more. "And may I insist that you accept me as the fair winner, and suggest that my assistant, who also has an interesting shape, supplies precisely the kind of expertise I require?" Before he could reply, I bowed and moved away.

The captain, now drunk, accosted me. "It isn't wise to turn Silano down."

"I thought you told us it had great value, according to your gypsy king and papal jailer?"

The officer smiled maliciously. "They also told me the medallion was cursed."

CHAPTER TWO

It was a pathetic attempt at verbal revenge. I bowed to Madame and made my leave, coming outside to a night made dimmer by the era's new industrial fogs. To the west was a red glow from the rapidly expanding mills of the Paris suburbs, harbinger of the more mechanical age at hand. A lantern bearer was near the door and hoping for hire, and I congratulated myself on my continued luck. His features were obscured by a hooded cape but were darker than a European's, I noticed: Moroccan, I guessed, seeking the type of menial employment such an immigrant might find. He bowed slightly, his accent Arabic. "You have the look of a fortunate man, monsieur."

"I'm about to get even more fortunate. I would like you to guide me to my own apartment, and then to a lady's address."

"Two francs?"

"Three, if you keep me out of the puddles." How wonderful to be a winner.

The light was necessary since revolution had produced fervor for everything except street cleaning and cobblestone repair. Drains were clogged, street lanterns half-lit, and potholes steadily enlarging. It didn't help that the new government had renamed more than a thousand streets after revolutionary heroes and everyone was continually lost. So my guide led the way, the lantern hung from a pole held by two hands. The staff was intricately carved, I noticed, its sides scaled for a better grip and the lantern suspended from a knob in the shape of a serpent's head. The reptile's mouth held the lantern's bail. A piece of artistry, I guessed, from the bearer's native country.

I visited my own apartment first, to secrete most of what I'd won. I knew better than to take all my winnings to the chamber of a trollop, and given everyone's interest I decided it best to hide the medallion as well. I took some minutes to decide where to conceal it while the lantern bearer waited outside. Then we went on to Minette's, through the dark streets of Paris.

The city, glorious though it remained in size and splendor, was, like women of a certain age, best not examined too closely. Grand old houses were boarded up. The Tuileries Palace was gated and empty, its dark windows like sightless sockets. Monasteries were in ruins, churches locked, and no one seemed to have applied a coat of paint since the storming of the Bastille. Except for filling the pockets of generals and politicians, the Revolution had been an economic disaster, as near as I could see. Few Frenchmen dared complain too boldly, because governments have a way of defending their mistakes. Bonaparte himself, then a little-known artillery officer, had spattered grapeshot on the last reactionary uprising, earning him promotion.

We passed the site of the Bastille, now dismantled. Since the prison's liberation, twenty-five thousand people had been executed in the Terror, ten times that had fled, and fifty-seven new prisons had been built to take its place. Without any sense of irony, the former site was nonetheless marked with a "fountain of regeneration": an enthroned Isis who, when the contraption worked, streamed water from her breasts. In the distance I could see the spires of Notre Dame, renamed the Temple of Reason and reputedly built on the site of a Roman temple dedicated to the same Egyptian goddess. Should I have had a premonition? Alas, we seldom notice what we're meant to see. When I paid off the lantern bearer I took little note that he lingered a moment too long after I stepped inside.

I climbed the creaking, urine-scented wooden stairway to

Minette's abode. Her apartment was on the unfashionable third floor, right below the attic garrets occupied by servant girls and artists. The altitude gave me a clue to the middling success of her trade, no doubt hurt by the revolutionary economy almost as much as wig makers and gilt painters. Minette had lit a single candle, its light reflected by the copper bowl she'd used to wash her thighs, and was dressed in a simple white shift, its laces untied at the top to invite further exploration. She came to me with a kiss, her breath smelling of wine and licorice.

"Have you brought my little present?"

I pulled her tighter to my trousers. "You should be able to feel it."

"No." She pouted and put her hand on my chest. "Here, by your heart." She traced where the medallion should have lain against my skin, its disc, its dangling arms, all on a golden chain. "I wanted to wear it for you."

"And have us risk a stabbing?" I kissed her again. "Besides, it's not safe to carry such prizes around in the dark."

Her hands were exploring my torso, to make sure. "I'd hoped for more courage."

"We'll gamble for it. If you win, I'll bring it next time."

"Gamble how?" She cooed, in a professionally practiced way.

"The loser will be the one who gains the summit first."

She let her hair drift along my neck. "And the weapons?"

"Any and all that you can imagine." I bent her back a little, tripping her on the leg I had wrapped against her ankles, and laid her on the bed. "*En garde.*"

I won our little contest, and at her insistence for a rematch, won a second and then a third, making her squeal. At least I think I won; with women you can never truly tell. It was enough to keep her sleeping when I rose before dawn and left a silver coin on my pillow. I put a log on the fireplace to help warm the room for her rising.

With the sky graying and the lantern bearers gone, common Paris was getting out of bed. Garbage carts trundled through the streets. Plankmen charged fees for temporary bridges laid over stagnant street water. Watermen carried pails to the finer houses. My own neighborhood of St. Antoine was neither fine nor disreputable, but rather a working-class place of artisans, cabinetmakers, hatters, and locksmiths. Rent was kept down by a confusion of smells from the breweries and dye works. Enfolding all was the enduring Parisian odor of smoke, bread, and manure.

Feeling quite satisfied with my evening, I mounted the dark stairs intending to sleep until noon. So when I unlocked my door and pushed inside my dim quarters, I decided to feel my way to my mattress rather than bother with shutter or candle. I wondered idly if I could pawn the medallion—given Silano's interest—for enough to afford better habitation.

Then I sensed a presence. I turned to confront a shadow among the shadows.

"Who's there?"

There was a rush of wind and I instinctively twisted sideways, feeling something whistle by my ear and collide with my shoulder. It was blunt, but no less painful for that. I buckled to my knees. "What the devil?" The club had made my arm go numb.

Then someone butted me and I fell sideways, clumsy from agony. I was not prepared for this! I kicked out in desperation, connecting with an ankle and drawing a yowl that gave some satisfaction. Then I skidded on my side, grabbing blindly. My hand fastened around a calf and I pulled. The intruder fell on the floor with me.

"*Merde*," he growled.

A fist hit my face as I grappled with my assailant, trying to get my own scabbard clear of my legs so I could draw my sword. I was awaiting a thrust from my opponent, but none came. Instead, a hand groped for my throat.

"Does he have it?" another voice asked.

How many were there?

Now I had an arm and a collar and managed to land a blow on an ear. My opponent swore again. I yanked and his head bounced off the floor. My thrashing legs flipped a chair over with a bang.

"Monsieur Gage!" a cry came from down below. "What are you doing to my house?" It was my landlady, Madame Durrell.

"Help me!" I cried, or rather gasped, given the pain. I rolled aside, got my scabbard out from under me, and started to draw my rapier. "Thieves!"

"For Christ's sake, will you help?" my assailant said to his companion.

"I'm trying to find his head. We can't kill him until we have it."

And then something struck and all went black.

I came to with a mind of mutton, my nose on the floor. Madame Durrell was crouched over me as if inspecting a corpse. When she rolled me over and I blinked, she jerked.

"You!"

"*Oui*, it is I," I groaned, remembering nothing for a moment.

"Look at the mess of you! What are you doing alive?"

What was *she* doing leaning over me? Her flame-red hair always alarmed me, erupting in a wiry cloud like escaping watch springs. Was it time for rent already? The warring calendars kept me in constant confusion.

Then I remembered the assault.

"They said they were reluctant to kill me."

"How dare you entertain such ruffians! You think you can create a wilderness here in Paris as in America? You will pay for every sou in repairs!"

I groggily sat up. "Is there damage?"

"An apartment in shambles, a good bed ruined! Do you know what my kind of quality costs these days?"

Now I began to make sense of the muddle, scraps pulsing through the gong that was my head. "Madame, I am a victim more than you." My sword had disappeared with my assailants. Just as well, since it was more for show than utility: I'd never been trained to use the thing and it banged annoyingly on the thigh. Given a choice, I'd rely on my longrifle or Algonquin tomahawk. I'd adopted the hatchet during my fur-trading days, learning from the Indians and voyageurs its utility as weapon, scalper, hammer, chopper, shaver, trimmer, and rope cutter. I couldn't understand how Europeans did without one.

"When I pounded on the door, your companions said you were drunk after whoring! That you were out of control!"

"Madame Durrell, those were thieves, not companions." I looked about. The shutters were now open, admitting full morning light, and my apartment looked like it had been struck by a cannon ball. Cabinets were open, their contents spilled like an avalanche. An armoire was on its side. My fine feather mattress was flipped and torn, bits of down floating in the air. A bookcase was toppled, my small library splayed. My gambling winnings were gone from my hollowed copy of Newton's treatise on optics that Franklin had bestowed as a gift—surely he hadn't expected me to read the thing—and my shirt was ripped open to my belly button. I knew it hadn't been torn to admire my chest. "I've been invaded."

"Invaded? They said you invited them!"

"Who said?"

"Soldiers, ruffians, vagabonds . . . they had hats, capes, and heavy boots. They told me there'd been an argument over cards and you would pay for damages."

"Madame, I was almost murdered. I was away all night, came home, surprised thieves, and was knocked unconscious. Though I don't know what I had to steal." I glanced at the wainscoting and saw it had been pried loose. Was my hidden rifle safe? Then my eye strayed to my chamber pot, as rank as before. Good.

"Indeed, why would thieves bother with a shabby fellow like you?" She looked at me skeptically. "An American! All know your kind has no money."

I set a stool upright and sat down heavily. She was right. Any neighborhood shopkeeper could have told robbers I was behind on my debts. It must have been my winnings, including the medallion. Until the next game, I'd been rich. Someone from the cozy followed me here, knowing I'd leave shortly for Minette's. The captain? Silano? And I'd caught them with my dawn return. Or had they waited because they hadn't found what they were looking for? And who knew of my amorous plans? Minette, for one. She'd pressed herself against me quickly enough. Was she in league with a scoundrel? It was a common enough ploy among prostitutes.

"Madame, I take responsibility for all repairs."

"I would like to see the money to back that up, monsieur."

"As would I." I stood unsteadily.

"You must explain to the police!"

"I can best explain after questioning someone."

"Who?"

"The young woman who led me astray."

Madame Durrell snorted, and yet showed a glimmer of sympathy. For a man to be made a fool by a woman? Very French.

"Will you allow me the privacy to right my furniture, repair my clothes, and dress my bruises, madame? In spite of what you think, I'm modest."

"A poultice is what you need. And keeping your breeches belted."

"Of course. But I am also a man."

"Well." She stood. "Every franc of this goes on your rent, so you'd better get back what you lost."

"You can be certain of it."

I pushed her outside and closed the door, setting the big pieces to right. Why hadn't they just killed me? Because they hadn't found what they were looking for. What if they returned, or a snoopy Madame Durrell decided to do her own cleaning? I put on a new shirt and fully pried open the wainscot by my washbasin. Yes, my Pennsylvania longrifle was safe: it was too obvious to carry about in a Paris street and too conspicuous to hock, since it might be identified with me. My tomahawk was also there, and this I tucked into my favorite place, the small of my back beneath my jacket. And the medallion? I went to the chamber pot.

There it was under my own sewage. I fished it from its hiding place, washed myself in my basin, and threw waste and soiled water out the window to the night garden.

As I'd expected, it was the one place a thief wouldn't look. I slipped the cleansed medallion around my neck and set off to confront Minette.

No wonder she'd let me win our sexual contest! She was expecting to get the medallion another way, by distracting me!

Back I went the way I'd come, buying bread with the few coins I had left in my pocket. With full morning, Paris had erupted with people. Entrepreneurs accosted me with brooms, firewood, brewed coffee, toy windmills, and rat traps. Gangs of young louts lounged near fountains, where they extorted money for water. Children marched in uniformed troops to school. Draymen unloaded barrels into shops. A pink-cheeked lieutenant stepped from a tailor's shop, resplendent in the uniform of the grenadiers.

Yes, there was her house! I galloped up the stairs, determined to question her before she awakened and stole away. Yet even as I came up to her landing I sensed something was wrong. The building seemed curiously empty. Her door was slightly ajar. I rapped, but there was no answer. I looked down. The knob was askew, the stop splintered. When I swung it wide a cat darted out, its whiskers pink.

A single window and the coals of the fireplace gave adequate light. Minette was on the bed as I had left her, but with the sheet pulled from her naked body and her belly cut through with a knife. It was the kind of wound that killed slowly, giving its victim time to plead or confess. A pool of blood had formed on the wooden floor beneath the bed, and the cat had been lapping.

The slaying made no sense.

I glanced around her room. There was no sign of robbery. The window, I saw, was unlatched. I opened it to peer out at the muddy yard behind. Nothing.

What to do? People had seen us whispering together at the cozy, and it had been plain I'd intended to spend the night with her. Now she was dead, but why? Her mouth was agape, her eyes rolled back.

And then I spied it, even as I heard the heavy boots of men

pounding up the stairs. The tip of her forefinger was bright with her own blood, and with it she had drawn something on the planks of pine. I tilted my head.

It was the first letter of my last name, the letter *G*.

"Monsieur," a voice said from the landing, "you are under arrest."

I turned to see two gendarmes, a police formed by the revolutionary committees in 1791. Behind was a man who looked as if his suspicions had been confirmed. "That's the one," the swarthy fellow said with an Arab accent.

It was the man I'd hired as lantern bearer.

If the Terror had abated, French revolutionary justice still had a tendency to guillotine first, investigate later. Better not to be arrested at all. I left poor Minette by springing to her chamber window, vaulting its frame, and dropping lightly to the muddy patch below. Despite the long night I hadn't lost my agility.

"Halt, murderer!" There was a bang, and a pistol shot sizzled by my ear.

I bounded over a picket fence to the alarm of a rooster, kicked my way past a territorial dog, found a passageway to an adjoining street, and ran. I heard shouts, but whether of alarm, confusion, or commerce I cannot say. Fortunately, Paris is a maze of six hundred thousand people and I was soon lost under the awnings of the markets of Les Halles, the damp earthiness of wintered apples, bright carrots, and shiny eel steadying my senses after the fantastic shock of the butchered body. I saw the heads of two gendarmes hurrying by the cheese aisle, so I went the other way.

I was in the worst kind of trouble, meaning I was not entirely sure what the trouble is. That my apartment had been ransacked I could accept, but who had killed my courtesan—the thieves I thought she was in league with? For what? She had neither my money nor my medallion. And why would Minette implicate me with a bloody fingertip? I was as baffled as I was frightened.

I felt especially vulnerable as an American in Paris. Yes, we'd depended on French aid to achieve our independence.

Yes, the great Franklin had been a witty celebrity during his years as our nation's diplomat, his likeness reproduced on so many cards, miniatures, and cups that the king, in a rare display of royal wit, had him painted inside one ardent female admirer's chamber pot. And yes, my own connection to the scientist and diplomat had won me a few well-placed French friends. But relations had worsened as France interfered with our neutral shipping. American politicians who welcomed the idealism of the French Revolution became disgusted by the Terror. If I had any usefulness in Paris, it was trying to explain each nation to the other.

I'd first come to the city fourteen years before, age nineteen, as a means for my shipping merchant father to disentangle my emotions (and his fortune) from Annabelle Gaswick and her socially ambitious parents. I didn't know for certain that Annabelle was with child, but I'll allow it was theoretically possible. It was not a match my family desired. A similar dilemma had reportedly driven young Ben Franklin from Boston to Philadelphia, and my father gambled that the ancient statesman might sympathize with my plight. It helped that Josiah Gage had served in the Continental Army as a major and, more importantly, was a third-degree Mason. Franklin, a longtime Freemason in Philadelphia, had been elected to the Paris Lodge of the Nine Muses in 1777, and the following year was instrumental in getting Voltaire initiated into the same august gathering. Since I'd made early trading trips to Quebec, spoke passable French, and was reasonably gifted with letters (I was in my second year at Harvard, though I'd already grown impatient with musty classics, the scholarly self-absorbed, and debates over questions for which there is no answer), my father suggested in 1784 that I might be an assistant to the American ambassador. In truth Franklin was seventy-eight, declining in vigor, and had no need of my naïve counsel, but he was willing to help a fellow Mason. Once I was in Paris the old statesman took an odd liking to me, despite my lack of clear ambition. He introduced me to both Freemasonry and electricity.

"In electricity is the secret force that animates the universe," Franklin told me. "In Freemasonry is a code of rational behavior and thought that, if followed by all, would do much to cure the world of its ills."

Freemasonry, he explained, had emerged in England at the dawn of our eighteenth century, but traced its origins to the guild of masons who wandered Europe building the great cathedrals. They were "free" because their skills allowed them to find employment wherever they wanted and demand a fair wage when doing so—no small thing in a world of serfs. Yet Freemasonry dated itself even older than that, finding its roots in the Knights Templar of the Crusades, who had their headquarters at Jerusalem's Temple Mount and later became the bankers and warlords of Europe. The medieval Templars became so powerful that their fraternity was crushed by the king of France and their leaders burned at the stake. It was the survivors who reputedly were the seed of our own order. Like many groups, Masons took a certain pride in past persecution.

"Even the martyred Templars are descendants of yet earlier groups," Franklin said. "Masonry traces its ancestry to the wise men of the ancient world, and to the stone workers and carpenters who built Solomon's temple."

Masonic symbols are the aprons and leveling tools of the stonemason, because the fraternity admires the logic and precision of engineering and architecture. While membership requires belief in a supreme being, no creed is specified, and in fact its fellows are forbidden to discuss religion or politics in the lodge. It is a philosophical organization of rationality and scientific inquiry, founded in freethinking reaction to the religious wars between Catholics and Protestants in earlier centuries. Yet it also plays with ancient mysticism and arcane mathematical precepts. Its emphasis on moral probity and charity, instead of dogma and superstition, make its commonsense teachings suspect to religious conservatives. Its exclusivity makes it a subject of jealousy and rumor.

"Why don't all men follow it?" I asked Franklin.

"Too many humans would gladly trade a rational world for a superstitious one if it calms their fears, gives them status, or gains them an advantage over their fellows," the American philosopher told me. "People are always afraid to think. And alas, Ethan, integrity is always a prisoner of vanity, and common sense is easily eclipsed by greed."

While I appreciated my mentor's enthusiasm, I was not a notable success as a Mason. Ritual tires me, and Masonic ceremony seemed obscure and interminable. There were a good deal of long-winded speeches, memorization of tedious ceremonies, and vague promises of clarity that would come only when one advanced in Masonic degree. In short, Freemasonry was a bore, and took more effort than I was willing to give. It was with some relief that I left with Franklin to the United States the following year, and his letter of recommendation and my proficiency in French caught the attention of a rising New York fur trader named John Jacob Astor. Since I was advised to keep some distance from the Gaswick family—Annabelle had been married to a silversmith in hurried circumstance—I leapt at the chance to experience the fur business in Canada. I rode with French voyageurs to the Great Lakes, learning to shoot and hunt, and at first thought I might find my future in the great West. Yet the farther we got from civilization the more I missed it, and not just that of America, but Europe. A salon was a refuge from swallowing vastness. Ben said the New World was conducive to plain truth, and the Old to half-forgotten wisdom just waiting to be rediscovered. He was torn his whole life between the two, and so was I.

So I descended the Mississippi to New Orleans. Here was a miniature Paris, but hot, exotic, and newly decadent, a crossroads of African, Creole, Mexican, and Cherokee, of whores, slave markets, Yankee land speculators, and missionary priests. Its energy whetted my appetite for a return to urbanized comforts. I took ship to the French sugar isles, built on the back of restive slave labor, and had my first real introduction to the horrid inequity of life and the soothing blindness of societies built atop it. What sets our species apart is not just what men will do to other men, but how tirelessly they justify it.

Then I rode a sugar ship to Le Havre in time to hear of the storming of the Bastille. What a contrast were the Revolution's ideals to the horrors I'd just seen! Yet the growing chaos forced me out of France for years, while I made a living as a trade representative between London, America, and Spain. My goal was uncertain, my purpose suspended. I'd become rootless.

I finally returned to Paris when the Terror subsided, hoping to find opportunity in its chaotic, feverish society. France boiled with an intellectual sophistication unavailable at home. All of Paris was a Leyden jar, a battery of stored-up sparks. Perhaps the lost wisdom that Franklin longed for could be rediscovered! Paris also had women with considerably more charm than Annabelle Gaswick. If I lingered, fortune might find me.

Now the police might instead.

What to do? I remembered something Franklin had written: that Freemasonry "made men of the most hostile feelings, the most distant regions, and diversified conditions, rush to the aid of each other." I was still an occasional participant because of its social connections. France had thirty-five thousand members in six hundred lodges, a fraternity of the able so powerful that the organization had been accused of both fomenting the revolution and conspiring to reverse it. Washington, Lafayette, Bacon, and Casanova had all been Masons. So had Joseph Guillotin, who invented the guillotine as a way to alleviate the suffering of hanging. In my country the order was a pantheon of patriots: Hancock, Madison, Monroe, even John Paul Jones and Paul Revere, which is why some suspect my nation is a Masonic invention. I needed advice, and would turn to my fellow Masons, or to one Mason in particular: the journalist Antoine Talma, who had befriended me during my irregular lodge visits because of his bizarre interest in America.

"Your red Indians are descendants of ancient civilizations now lost, who found serenity that escapes us today," Talma liked to theorize. "If we could prove they are a tribe of Israel, or refugees from Troy, it would show the path to harmony."

Obviously he hadn't seen the same Indians I had, who'd seemed cold, hungry, and cruel as often as they were harmonious, but I could never slow his speculations.

A bachelor who didn't share my interest in women, Antoine was a writer and pamphleteer with lodgings near the Sorbonne. I found him not at his desk but at one of the new ice-cream cafés near the Pont Saint-Michel, nursing a lemonade he claimed had curative powers. Talma was always faintly ill, and continuously experimenting with purgatives and diets to achieve elusive health. He was one of the few Frenchmen I knew who would eat the American potato, which most Parisians regarded as fit only for pigs. At the same time, he was always lamenting that he'd not lived life fully enough and longed to be the adventurer he imagined me to be, if only he didn't have to risk a cold. (I'd somewhat exaggerated my own exploits and secretly enjoyed his flattery.) He greeted me warmly as always, his young features innocent, his hair unruly even after being cut short in the new Republican fashion, his day coat rose-colored with silver buttons. He had a broad forehead, wide, excited eyes, and a complexion as pale as cheese.

I nodded politely at his latest remedy and asked instead for a wickeder drink, coffee, and pastry. The black brew's addictive powers were periodically denounced by the government to obscure the fact that war made the beans hard to come by. "Could you pay?" I asked Talma. "I've had something of a mishap."

He took a closer look. "My God, did you fall down a well?" I was unshaven, battered, dirty, and red-eyed.

"I won at cards." I noticed Talma's table was littered with half a dozen failed lottery tickets. His luck at gambling didn't match my own, but the Directory relied on his kind of dogged optimism for much of its financial support. Meanwhile the café's gilt-bordered mirrors, reflecting endlessly, made me feel entirely too conspicuous. "I need an honest lawyer."

"As easy to find as a scrupulous deputy, vegetarian butcher, or virginal prostitute," Talma replied. "If you tried lemonade, it might help correct such fuzzy thinking."

"I'm serious. A woman I was with has been murdered. Two gendarmes tried to arrest me for the deed."

He raised his eyebrows, not certain whether I was joking.

Once more, I had trumped his voyeuristic life. He also wondered, I knew, whether this was a tale he could sell to the journals. "But why?"

"They had as witness a lantern bearer I'd hired. It was no secret her chamber was my destination: even Count Silano knew."

"Silano! Who'd believe that rascal?"

"Perhaps the gendarme who discharged a pistol ball past my ear, that's who. I'm innocent, Antoine. I thought she'd been in league with thieves, but when I went back to confront her, she was dead."

"Wait. Thieves?"

"I surprised them tearing apart my own apartment and they clubbed me. I won some money at the tables last night, and an odd medallion, but . . ."

"Please slow down." He was patting his pockets looking for a scrap of paper. "A medallion?"

I took it out. "You can't write about this, my friend."

"Not write! You might as well say not breathe!"

"It would only make my situation worse. You must save me with secrecy."

He sighed. "But I could expose injustice."

I put the medallion on the marble table, shielding it from the view of the other patrons with my torso, and slid it to my companion. "Look: The soldier I won it from said it was from ancient Egypt. Silano was curious. He bid on it, and even wanted to buy it, but I wouldn't sell. I don't see that it's worth killing over."

Talma squinted, turned it over, and played with its arms. "What are all these markings?"

I looked more closely for the first time. The furrow across the disc, as if marking its diameter, I have already described. Above, the disc was perforated in a seemingly random way. Below were three series of zigzag marks, the way a child might draw a mountain range. And beneath them, scratches like hash marks that formed a little triangle. "I have no idea. It's extremely crude."

Talma spread the two arms that hung down to make an upside-down V. "And what do you make of this?"

He didn't need to explain. It looked like the Masonic symbol for a compass, the construction tool used to inscribe a circle. The order's secret symbolism often paired the compass with a carpenter's square, one overlying the other. Spread the medallion arms apart to the limit of their hinge and they would draw the circumference of a circle about three times the size of the disc above. Was this some kind of mathematical tool?

"I don't make anything of it," I said.

"But Silano, of the heretical Egyptian Rite of Freemasonry, was interested. Which means that perhaps this has something to do with our order's mysteries."

Masonic imagery was said to be inspired by that of the ancients. Some were commonplace tools such as the mallet, trowel, and trestleboard, but others were more exotic such as the human skull, pillars, pyramids, swords, and stars. All were symbolic, and meant to suggest an order to existence I've found hard to detect in everyday life. In each degree of Masonic advancement, more such symbols were explained. Was this medallion some ancestor of our fraternity? We hesitated to speak of it in the ice-cream café because lodge members are sworn to secrecy, which of course makes our symbolism all the more intriguing to the uninitiated. We've been accused of every kind of witchcraft and conspiracy, while mostly what we do is parade around in white aprons. As one wit declared, "Even if that is their secret—that they have no secret—still, it is an achievement to keep that a secret."

"It suggests the distant past," I said as I put it back around my neck. "The captain I won it from claimed it had come with Cleopatra and Caesar to Italy and was owned by Cagliostro, but the soldier thought so little of it that he gambled it away in *chemin de fer*."

"Cagliostro? And he said it was Egyptian? And Silano took interest?"

"It seemed casual at the time. I thought he was simply bidding me up. But now . . ."

Talma pondered. "All this is coincidence, perhaps. A card game, two crimes."

"Perhaps."

His fingers tapped. "Yet it could also be connected. The lantern bearer led the police to you because he calculated that your reaction to the ransacking of your apartment would be to unwittingly plunge yourself into the scene of a horrific murder, making you available for interrogation. Examine the sequence. They hope to simply steal the medallion. Yet it is not in your apartment. It has not been given to Minette. You are a foreigner of some standing, not assaulted lightly. But if charged with murder and searched . . ."

Minette had been killed merely to implicate me? My head was whirling. "Why would anyone want this so badly?"

He was excited. "Because great events are in motion. Because the Masonic mysteries you irreverently mock may at last have an effect on the world."

"What events?"

"I have informants, my friend." He loved to be coy, pretending to know great secrets that somehow never made their way into print.

"So you agree I'm being framed?"

"But naturally." Talma regarded me gravely. "You have come to the right man. As a journalist, I seek truth and justice. As a friend, I presume your innocence. As a scribe who writes about the great, I have important contacts."

"But how can I prove it?"

"You need witnesses. Would your landlady attest to your character?"

"I don't think so. I owe her rent."

"And this lantern bearer, how can we find him?"

"Find him! I want to stay away from him!"

"Indeed." He thought, sipping lemonade. "You need shelter, and time to make sense of this thing. Our lodge masters may be able to help."

"You want me to hide in a lodge?"

"I want you safe while I determine if this medallion could give both of us an unusual opportunity."

"For what?"

He smiled. "I've heard rumors, and rumors of rumors.

Your medallion may be timelier than you think. I need to speak to the right people, men of science."

"Men of science?"

"Men close to the rising young general Napoleon Bonaparte."

CHAPTER THREE

The chemist Claude-Louis Berthollet was, at age forty-nine, the most famous student of the guillotined Lavoisier. Unlike his master, he'd ingratiated himself to the revolution by finding a nitrate soil substitute for saltpeter, so necessary to gunpowder. Rising to leadership of the new National Institute that had succeeded the Royal Academy, he'd shared with his mathematician friend Gaspard Monge the task of helping loot Italy. It was scholars who advised Bonaparte on which masterpieces were most worthy of being carted back to France. This had helped make both scientists the confidants of the general and privy to strategic secrets. Their political expediency reminded me of an astronomer who, when making surveys for the new metric system, had been forced to replace his white survey flags, seen as a symbol of King Louis, with the tricolor. No profession escapes the Revolution.

"So you're not a murderer, Monsieur Gage?" the chemist asked with the barest hint of a smile. With a high forehead, prominent nose, stern mouth and chin, and sad, lidded eyes, he looked like the weary lord of a rural manor, regarding science's growing alliance with governments the same dubious way that a father contemplates the suitor of his daughter.

"I swear by God, by the Great Architect of the Masons, or by the laws of chemistry."

His eyebrows barely elevated. "Whichever I happen to worship, I presume?"

"I'm only trying to convey my sincerity, Doctor Berthollet. I suspect the killer was an army captain or Count Silano,
who had an interest in a medallion I'd just won."

"A fatal interest."

"It seems strange, I know."

"And the girl wrote the initial of *your* name, not theirs."

"If *she* wrote it."

"The police claim the width of her final calligraphy
matched her fingertip."

"I'd just slept with her and paid. I had no motive for killing
her, or she of accusing me. I knew where the medallion was."

"Hmm, yes." He took out a pair of spectacles. "Let me
see it."

We examined it while Talma watched us, clutching a
handkerchief in case he could find some reason to sneeze.
Berthollet turned it as Silano and Talma had done and finally leaned back. "Aside from the modicum of gold, I don't
see what all the fuss is about."

"Nor do I."

"Not a key, not a map, not a symbol of a god, and not particularly attractive. I find it hard to believe that Cleopatra
wore this."

"The captain said it simply belonged to her. As
queen . . ."

"She'd have as many objects attributed to her as chips of
wood and vials of blood are attributed to Jesus." The scientist shook his head. "What easier claim to make to inflate
the price of clumsy jewelry?"

We were sitting in the basement of the Hôtel Le Cocq,
used by a branch of the Oriental Lodge of Freemasonry because of the cellar's east-west orientation. A table with a
cloth and closed book rested between two pillars. Benches
were lost in the gloom under the arches of the vault. The
only illumination was candlelight, flickering on Egyptian
hieroglyphics that no one knew how to read and Biblical
scenes of the raising of Solomon's temple. A skull rested on
one shelf, reminding us of mortality but contributing nothing to our discussion. "And you vouch for his innocence?"
the chemist asked my Masonic friend.

"The American is a man of science like you, Doctor," Talma said. "He was apprenticed to the great Franklin and is an electrician himself."

"Yes, electricity. Lightning bolts and flying kites and sparks in a salon. Tell me, Gage, what *is* electricity?"

"Well." I did not want to exaggerate my knowledge to a renowned scientist. "Doctor Franklin thought it a manifestation of the basic power that animates the universe. But the truth is, no one knows. We can generate it by turning a crank and store it in a jar, so we know it *is*. But who knows *why?*"

"Precisely." The chemist considered, turning my medallion over in his hand. "And yet what if people did know, in the distant past? What if they controlled powers unattainable in our own time?"

"They knew electricity?"

"They knew how to erect extraordinary monuments, did they not?"

"It is interesting that Ethan finds this medallion and comes to us at this particular point of time," Talma added.

"And yet science does not believe in coincidences," Berthollet replied.

"Point of time?" I asked.

"However, one must recognize opportunity," the chemist allowed.

"What opportunity is that?" I was beginning to hope.

"To escape the guillotine by joining the army," Berthollet said.

"What!"

"At the same time, you can be an ally of science."

"And Freemasonry," Talma added.

"Are you mad? Which army?"

"The French army," the chemist said. "See here, Gage, as a Mason and man of science, can you swear to keep a secret?"

"I don't want to be a soldier!"

"No one is asking you to. Can you swear?"

Talma was looking at me expectantly, his handkerchief to his lips. I swallowed and nodded. "Of course."

"Bonaparte has left the channel and is preparing a new expedition. Even his own officers don't know the destination, but some scientists do. For the first time since Alexander the Great, a conqueror is inviting savants to accompany his troops to research and record what we see. This is an adventure to rival those of Cook and Bougainville. Talma has suggested that you and he accompany the expedition, he as journalist and you as an expert on electricity, ancient mysteries, and this medallion. What if it is a valuable clue? You go, contribute to our speculations, and by the time you return, everyone will have forgotten the unfortunate death of a whore."

"An expedition where?" I've always been skeptical of Alexander, who may have done a great deal in a short time but was dead one year younger than my own age, a fact which didn't recommend his career in the slightest.

"Where do you think?" Berthollet said impatiently. "Egypt! We go not just to seize a key trade route and open the door to our allies fighting the British in India. We go to explore the dawn of history. There might be useful secrets there. Better we men of science have the clues than the heretical Egyptian Rite, no?"

"Egypt?" By Franklin's ghost, what possible interest did I have there? Few Europeans had ever seen the place, shrouded as it was in Arab mystery. I had a vague impression of sand, the pyramids, and heathen fanaticism.

"Not that you're much of a scientist or a Freemason," Berthollet amended. "But as an American and frontiersman, you might offer interesting perspective. Your medallion may also be a stroke of luck. If Silano wants it, it could have significance."

I hadn't heard much past the first sentence. "Why aren't I much of a scientist or Mason?" I was defensive because I secretly agreed.

"Come, Ethan," Talma said. "Berthollet means you've yet to make your mark."

"I am saying, Monsieur Gage, that at the age of thirty-three, your achievement is well short of your ability, and your ambition is shy of diligence. You've not contributed reports to the academies, advanced in Masonic degree, accumulated a fortune, started a family, owned a home, or produced writing of distinction. Frankly, I was skeptical when Antoine first suggested you. But he thinks you have potential, and we rationalists are enemies of the mystic followers of Cagliostro. I don't want the medallion slipping from your guillotined neck. I greatly respect Franklin, and hope you might someday copy him. So, you can seek to prove your innocence in the revolutionary courts. Or you can come with us."

Talma grasped my arm. "Egypt, Ethan! Think of it!"

This would completely overturn my life, but then how much life did I have to overturn? Berthollet had made an annoyingly accurate assessment of my character, though I was rather proud of my travels. Few men had seen as much of North America as I had—or, admittedly, done as little with it.

"Doesn't somebody already own Egypt?"

Berthollet waved his hand. "It is nominally part of the Ottoman Empire but is really under the control of a renegade caste of slave warriors called the Mamelukes. They ignore Constantinople more than they pay tribute to it, and they oppress the ordinary Egyptians. They are not even of the same race! Ours is a mission of liberation, not conquest, Monsieur Gage."

"We won't have to do the fighting?"

"Bonaparte assures us we'll take Egypt with a cannon shot or two."

Well, that was optimistic. Napoleon sounded like a general who was either a shrewd opportunist or blind as a stone. "This Bonaparte, what do you think of him?" We'd all heard his praise after his early victories, but he'd spent little time in Paris and was largely unknown. Word was that he was something of an upstart.

"He's the most energetic man I've ever met, and will either succeed spectacularly or fail spectacularly," Talma said.

"Or, as is the case with many ambitious men, do both,"

Berthollet amended. "There's no denying his brilliance, but it is judgment that makes greatness."

"I will be abandoning all my trade and diplomatic contacts," I said. "And run as if I'm guilty of murder. Can't the police find Count Silano and the captain who lost the card game? Put us all in a room and let the truth come out?"

Berthollet looked away. Talma sighed.

"Silano has disappeared. There's word that the foreign ministry has ordered his protection," my friend said. "As for your captain, he was fished from the Seine one night ago, tortured and strangled. Naturally, given your acquaintance and the fact that you have disappeared, you are a prime suspect."

I swallowed.

"The safest place for you now, Monsieur Gage, is in the middle of an army."

It seemed prudent that if I was going to join an invasion, it would be wise to go with a weapon. My costly longrifle, dating from my sojourn in the fur business, was still cached in the wall of my apartment. Made in Lancaster, Pennsylvania, its maple stock nicked and stained from hard use, the firearm remained remarkably accurate, as I'd demonstrated occasionally on the Champ de Mars. Equally important, the curve of its stock was as graceful as the limbs of a woman, and the filigree on its metalwork as comforting as a purse of coin. It was not just a tool but a steady companion, uncomplaining, smooth, the iron blue-hued, its scent a perfume of powder grains, linseed, and gun oil. Its high velocity gave its small caliber better killing power at greater range than a big-bore musket. The criticism, as always, was the awkwardness of a firearm that came up to my chin. Reloading took too long for the quick, mass volleys of European combat, and it wouldn't fit a bayonet. But then the whole idea of standing in a line, waiting to be shot, was foreign to us Americans. The great disadvantage of any gun was the need to reload after one shot, and the great advantage of an accurate rifle was that you might actually hit something with that first shot. The first order of business, I thought, was to fetch my firearm.

"Your apartment is exactly where the police will look for you!" Talma objected.

"It's been more than two days. These are men paid less than a potter and corrupt as a judge. I think it unlikely they're still waiting. We'll go tonight, bribe a neighbor, and pry at the wall from his side."

"But I've got tickets for the midnight stage to Toulon!"

"Plenty of time, if you help."

I deemed it cautious to enter the building as I'd left Minette's, by a back courtyard window. Even if the police were gone, Madame Durrell would still be lurking, and I was no closer to paying repairs and rent. That evening, Talma reluctantly boosted me up a downspout so I could peek into my own apartment. It was unchanged, the mattress still torn, feathers spotting my abode like flakes of snow. The latch was shiny, however, meaning the lock had been changed. My landlady was trying to make sure I'd settle my debt before getting my things. Given that my floor was her ceiling, I'd decided an oblique attack would be best.

"Keep a lookout," I whispered to my companion.

"Hurry! I saw a gendarme down the alley!"

"I'll be in and out without a peep of noise."

I sidled on the sill to my neighbor Chabon, a librarian who each evening tutored the children of the newly striving. As I'd hoped, he was gone. The truth was that I had no hope of bribing a man of his rigid and rather dull rectitude, and was counting on his absence. I broke a pane and opened his window. He'd be disturbed to find a hole in his wall but I was, after all, on a mission for France.

His room smelled of books and pipe smoke. I dragged a heavy chest away from the wall opposite my own place and used my tomahawk to pry at the wainscoting. Did I mention the hatchet could work as wedge and lever, too? I'm afraid I splintered a few boards, but I'm no carpenter, either. I was making more sound than I'd promised, but if I was quick it wouldn't matter. I saw my powder horn and the butt of my gun.

Then I heard the click of the lock on my own door, and footsteps in my apartment. Someone had heard the noise! Hastily, I shouldered the horn, grabbed the rifle, and started to slowly draw it out the wall, fighting the awkward angle.

I just about had it free when someone grabbed the barrel from the other side.

I peered through the hole. Facing me was the visage of Madame Durrell, her red hair seemingly electrified, her hideously rouged mouth pursed in triumph. "You think I don't know your tricks? You owe me two hundred francs!"

"Which I'm traveling to earn," I whispered hoarsely. "Please let go my gun, Madame, so I can satisfy my debts."

"How, by murdering another? Pay, or I shout for the police!"

"I haven't murdered anyone, but I still need time to put things to right."

"Starting with your rent!"

"Be careful, I don't want to hurt you. The rifle is loaded." It was a frontier habit acquired from the voyageurs.

"Do you think I'm afraid of the likes of you? This gun is collateral!"

I pulled, but she tugged back ferociously. "He's here, come to steal his things!" she shouted. She had a grip like the jaws of a terrier.

So in desperation I abruptly reversed movement and bulled forward through the hole I'd made in the wall, bursting more boards as I drove through to my own apartment. I landed atop my landlady along with gun, splinters, and wall dust. "Sorry. I wanted to do this quietly."

"Help! Rape!"

I staggered to the window, dragging her as she clung to one leg.

"It will be the guillotine for you!"

I looked outside. Talma had disappeared from the muddy yard. A gendarme stood in his place, staring up at me in surprise. Damnation! The police had not been half so efficient when I had once complained to them about a pickpocket.

So I lurched the other way, Madame Durrell's attempt to

gnaw on my ankle somewhat foiled by her lack of more than a few teeth. The door was locked, its key no doubt in my landlady's pocket, and I had no time for niceties. I uncapped my horn, primed my pan, pointed, and fired.

The report was a roar in the room, but at least my landlady let go my leg as the lock shattered. I kicked the door open and plunged into the hallway. A hooded figure on the stairs blocked my way, armed with a snake-headed staff, his eyes startled from the gunshot. The lantern bearer! Smoke hung in the landing's air.

There was a click, and a fine sword point emerged from the snake's head. "Give it up and I let you go," he whispered.

I hesitated, my gun empty. My opponent had the skilled stance of a pikeman.

Then something flew out of the darkness below and banged off the lantern bearer's head, staggering him. I charged, using the barrel of my rifle like a bayonet to thrust against his sternum, knocking his wind out. He lurched and tumbled down the stairs. I clattered after, vaulted his sprawled body, and stumbled outside, colliding with Talma.

"Are you mad?" my friend asked. "Police are coming from every direction!"

"But I got it," I said with a grin. "What the devil did you hit him with?"

"A potato."

"So they're good for something after all."

"Stop them!" Madame Durrell was shouting from a streetside window. "He tried to have his way with me!"

Talma looked up. "I hope your gun was worth *that.*"

Then we were flying down the street. Another gendarme appeared at the end of the lane, so Talma jerked me into the doorway of an inn. "Another lodge," he whispered. "I sensed we might need this." We burst inside and quickly pulled the proprietor into the shadows. A quick Masonic handshake and Talma pointed to a door leading to the cellar. "The order's urgent business, friend."

"Is he a Freemason too?" The innkeeper pointed at me.

"He tries."

The innkeeper followed us down, locking the door behind us. Then we stood under stone arches, catching our breath.

"Is there a way out?" Talma asked.

"Past the wine barrels is a grate. The drain is big enough to slip through and leads to the sewers. Some Masons escaped that way in the Terror."

My friend grimaced, but did not quail. "Which way to the leather market?"

"Right, I think." He stopped us with his hand. "Wait, you'll need this." He lit a lantern.

"Thanks, friend." We scampered past his barrels, pried off the grate, and skidded thirty feet down a tunnel of slime until we popped out into the main sewer. Its high stone vault disappeared into darkness in both directions, our dim light illuminating the scurrying of rats. The water was cold and stinking. The grate clanged above as our savior locked it back into place.

I examined my smeared green coat, the only nice one I had. "I admire your fortitude in coming down here, Talma."

"Better this and Egypt than a Parisian jail. You know, Ethan, every time I'm with you, something happens."

"It's interesting, don't you think?"

"If I die of consumption, my last memories will be of your shouting landlady."

"So let's not die." I looked right. "Why did you ask about the leather market? I thought the stage left near the Luxembourg Palace?"

"Exactly. If the police find our benefactor, he'll misdirect them." He pointed. "We go left."

So we arrived: half wet, odiferous, and me without baggage except for rifle and tomahawk. We washed as best we could at a fountain, my green traveling coat hopelessly stained. "The potholes are getting worse," Talma explained lamely to the postman. Our standing wasn't helped by the fact that Talma had purchased the cheapest tickets, economizing by perching us on the open rear bench behind the enclosed coach, exposed and dusty.

"It keeps us from awkward questions," Talma reasoned.

With my own money mostly stolen, I could hardly complain.

We could only hope the fast stage would get us well on the way to Toulon before the police got around to querying the stations, since our odd departure would likely be remembered. Once we reached Bonaparte's invasion fleet we'd be safe: I carried a letter of introduction from Berthollet. I masked my identity with the name Gregoire and explained my accent by saying I was a native of French Canada.

Talma had his own valise delivered before accompanying my adventure, and I borrowed a change of shirt before it was hoisted to the coach roof. My gun had to go in the same place, with only the tomahawk keeping me from feeling defenseless.

"Thanks for the extra clothing," I said.

"I've far more than that," my companion boasted. "I've got special cotton for the desert heat, treatises on our destination, several leather-bound notebooks, and a cylinder of fresh quills. My medicines we will supplement with the mummies of Egypt."

"Surely you don't subscribe to such quackery." The crumbled dust of the dead had become a popular remedy in Europe, but selling what looked like a vial of dirt encouraged all kinds of fraud.

"The medicine's very unreliability in France is the reason I want a mummy of my own. After recovering our health we can sell the remainder."

"A glass of wine does more good with less trouble."

"On the contrary, alcohol can lead to ruin, my friend." His aversion to wine was as odd for a Frenchman as his fondness for potatoes.

"So you'd rather eat the dead?"

"Dead who were prepared for everlasting life. The elixirs of the ancients are in their remains!"

"Then why are they dead?"

"Are they? Or did they achieve some kind of immortality?"

And with that illogic we were off. Our companions in the coach proper were a hatter, a vintner, a Toulon cordage maker, and a customs officer who seemed determined to sleep the length of France. I'd hoped for the companionship of a lady or two, but none boarded. Our passage was swift on the paved French highways, but tedious, like all travel. We slept much of the rest of the night, and the day was a numbing routine of brief stops to change horses, buy mediocre fare, and use the rural privies. I kept looking behind but saw no pursuit. When I dozed I had dreams of Madame Durrell demanding rent.

Soon enough we grew bored, and Talma began to pass the time with his tireless theories of conspiracies and mysticism. "You and I could be on a mission of historic importance, Ethan," he told me as our coach clattered down the valley of the Rhône.

"I thought we were merely running from my troubles."

"On the contrary, we have something vital to contribute to this expedition. We understand the limits of science. Berthollet is a man of reason, of cold chemical fact. But we Freemasons both respect science yet know the deepest answers to the greatest mysteries are in the temples of the East. As an artist, I sense my destiny is to find what science is blind to."

I looked at him skeptically, given that he had already swallowed three nostrums against the filth of the sewers, complained of stomach cramps, and thought the fact that his leg had gone asleep signaled final paralysis. His traveling coat was purple, as military as a slipper. This man was journeying to a Muslim stronghold? "Antoine, there are diseases in the East we don't even have names for. I'm astounded you're going at all."

"Our destination has gardens and palaces and minarets and harems. It is paradise on Earth, my friend, a repository of the wisdom of the pharaohs."

"Mummy powder."

"Don't scoff. I've heard of miracle cures."

"Frankly, all this Masonic talk of Eastern mysteries hasn't really made sense to me," I said, twisting to stretch my legs. "What's to be learned from a heap of ruins?"

"That's because you never really listen at our meetings,"

Talma lectured. "The Freemasons were the original men of learning, the master builders who constructed the pyramids and great cathedrals. What unites us is our reverence for knowledge, and what distinguishes us is our willingness to rediscover truths from the distant past. Ancient magicians knew powers we cannot dream of. Hiram Abiff, the great craftsman who built Solomon's temple, was murdered by his jealous rivals and raised from the dead by the Master Mason himself."

Masons were required to play out some of this fantastic story upon initiation, a ritual that had left me feeling foolish. One version of the story suggested resurrection, while another mere recovery of the body from a dastardly murder, but neither tale had any point to it that I could see. "Talma, you can't really believe that."

"You're just an initiate. As we climb the ranks, we will learn extraordinary things. A thousand secrets are buried in old monuments, and the few with the courage to uncover them have become mankind's greatest teachers. Jesus. Muhammad. Buddha. Plato. Pythagoras. All learned secret Egyptian knowledge from a great age long lost, from civilizations that raised works we no longer know how to build. Select groups of men—we Freemasons, the Knights Templar, the Illuminati, the followers of the Rosy Cross, Luciferians—all have sought to rediscover this knowledge."

"True, but these secret societies are often at odds with each other, as mainstream Freemasonry is with the Egyptian Rite. The Luciferians, if I understand it, give Satan a status equal to God."

"Not Satan, Lucifer. They simply believe in the duality of good and evil, and that gods exhibit a dual nature. In any event, I'm not equating these groups. I'm simply saying they recognize that the lost knowledge of the past is as important as scientific discovery in the future. Pythagoras himself spent eighteen years studying with the priests of Memphis. And where was Jesus for a similar time during his life, on which the gospels are silent? Some contend he studied in Egypt as well. Somewhere there is the power to remake the world, to restore harmony and recapture a golden age, which is why our slogan is 'Order out of Chaos.' Men like Berthollet go to examine rocks and rivers. They are hypnotized by the natural world. But you and I, Gage, we sense the supernatural one that underlies it. Electricity, for example! We do not see it, and yet it is there! We know that the world of our senses is but a veil. The Egyptians knew, too. If we could read their hieroglyphs, we would become masters!"

Like all writers, my friend had a fervent imagination and not a lick of sense. "Electricity is a natural phenomena, Antoine. It is lightning in the sky and a shock at a parlor party. You sound like that charlatan Cagliostro."

"He was a dangerous man who wanted to use Egyptian rites for dark purposes, but no charlatan."

"When he practiced alchemy in Poland they caught him cheating."

"He was framed by the jealous! Witnesses say he healed sick people that ordinary doctors despaired of. He consorted with royalty. He may have been centuries old, like Saint Germain, who was actually Prince Ragoczy of Transylvania and who personally knew Cleopatra and Jesus. Cagliostro was a student of this prince. He . . ."

"Was mocked and hounded and died in prison after being betrayed by his own wife, who had the reputation of being the greatest whore in Europe. You said yourself his Egyptian Rite is occult nonsense. What proof is there that any of these self-proclaimed sorcerers are centuries old? Listen, I don't doubt there are interesting things to learn in Muslim lands, but I was recruited as a scientist, not a priest. Your own revolution has scorned religion and mysticism."

"Which is why there's so much interest in the mystical today! Reason is creating a vacuum of wonder. Religious persecution has created a thirst for spirituality."

"Surely you don't think Bonaparte's motive is . . ."

"Hush!" Talma nodded toward the coach wall. "Remember your oath."

Ah, yes. Our expedition leader and ultimate destination was supposed to be secret, as if any fool couldn't guess it from our conversation. I dutifully nodded, knowing that given the wheel rumble and our position to the rear, they could hear little anyway. "Are you saying these mysteries are our true purpose?" I said more quietly.

"I'm saying our expedition has multiple purposes."

I sat back, staring moodily at the grim hills of stumps created by the insatiable hunger the new factories had for wood. It seemed like the forests themselves were being recruited for the wars and trade spawned by revolution. While industrialists grew rich, the countryside grew bare and cities became shrouded in stinking fogs. If the ancients could do things by clean magic, more power to them.

"Besides, the knowledge to be sought *is* science," Talma went on. "Plato brought it to philosophy. Pythagoras brought it to geometry. Moses and Solon brought it to law. All are different aspects of Truth. Some say it was the last great native pharaoh, the magician Nectanebo, who lay with Olympias and fathered Alexander the Great."

"I've told you I don't want to emulate a man who died at thirty-two."

"In Toulon you will meet the new Alexander, perhaps."

Or perhaps Bonaparte was simply the latest momentary hero, one defeat away from obscurity. In the meantime, I'd milk him for a pardon for a crime I hadn't committed by being as ingratiating as I could tolerate.

We left the devastation, the highway entering what once was aristocratic parkland. It had been confiscated by the Directory from whichever noble or church official had owned it. Now it was open to peasants, poachers, and squatters, and I could glimpse crude camps of the poor set amid the trees, wisps of smoke drifting from their fires. It was getting near evening, and I hoped we'd reach an inn soon. My bottom ached from the pounding.

Suddenly there was a shout from the coachman, and something crashed ahead. We reined to a halt. A tree had fallen and the horses had bunched, neighing in confusion. The tree's butt looked chopped through. Dark figures were emerging from the wood, their arms pointing at the coachman and footman above.

"Robbers!" I shouted, feeling for the tomahawk I still

wore under my coat. While my skill had rusted, I felt I could still hit a target from thirty feet. "Quick, to arms! Maybe we can fight them off!"

But as I bounded off the coach I was met by the napping customs officer, who had suddenly come wide awake, jumped nimbly off, and met me by aiming an enormous pistol at my chest. The mouth of its barrel seemed as wide as a scream.

"*Bonjour,* Monsieur Gage," he addressed. "Throw your savage little hatchet on the ground, if you please. I am to take either you or your bauble back to Paris."

CHAPTER FOUR

The thieves, or agents—they were too often the same in revolutionary France—lined us up like pupils in a schoolyard and began to strip us of valuables. With the addition of the supposed customs officer, there were six of them, and when I studied them in the dim light, I started. Two looked like the gendarmes who had first tried to arrest me in Paris. Was the lantern bearer here too? I didn't see him. Some held pistols aimed at the coachmen, while the others focused on us passengers, taking purses and pocket watches.

"The police have devised a new way of levying taxes?" I asked caustically.

"I'm not certain he really *is* a customs officer," the hatter spoke up.

"Silence!" Their leader aimed his weapon at my nose as if I'd forgotten he carried it. "Don't think I'm not acting for people in authority, Monsieur Gage. If you don't surrender what I want, you'll meet more police than you care to, in the bowels of a state prison."

"Surrender what?"

"I believe his name is actually Gregoire," the hatter added helpfully.

My interrogator cocked his pistol. "You know what! It must go to scholars who can put it to proper use! Open your shirt!"

The air was cold on my breast. "See? I have nothing."

He scowled. "Then where is it?"

"Paris."

The muzzle swung to Talma's temple. "Produce it or I blow your friend's brains out."

Antoine blanched. I was fairly certain he'd never had a gun aimed at him before, and I was becoming truly annoyed. "Be careful with that thing."

"I will count to three!"

"Antoine's head is hard as a rock. The ball will ricochet."

"Ethan," my friend pleaded.

"One!"

"I sold the medallion to finance this trip," I tried.

"Two!"

"I used it to pay the rent." Talma was swaying.

"Thr . . ."

"Wait! If you must know, it's in my bag atop the coach."

Our tormentor swung the muzzle back to me.

"Frankly, I'll be happy to be rid of the trinket. It's been nothing but trouble."

The villain shouted up to the coachman. "Throw his bag down!"

"Which one?"

"The brown one," I called, as Talma gaped at me.

"They're all brown in the dark!"

"By all the saints and sinners . . ."

"I'll get it."

Now the pistol muzzle was pressed to my back. "Hurry!" My foe glanced down the road. More traffic would be coming soon, and I had a pleasant mental picture of a hay wagon slowly and deliberately crushing him under.

"Can you please ease the hammer down? There're six of you and one of me."

"Shut your trap or I'll shoot you right now, rip open every bag, and find it myself!"

I climbed to the luggage rack on the coach roof. The thief stayed close below.

"Ah. Here it is."

"Pass it down, Yankee dog!"

I dug and closed one hand around my rifle, tucked under

the softer luggage. I could feel the small brass door of its patch box where I'd stuffed a cartridge and ball, and the curl of its nestled powder horn. Pity I hadn't loaded it since shooting my apartment door: no voyageur would make that mistake. The other hand grasped my friend's bag. "Catch!"

I heaved, and my aim was good. The bag's weight hit the pistol and there was a bang as the cocked hammer came down, shooting Talma's laundry to flinders. Stupid sod. The coach horses reared, everyone shouting, as I tumbled off the coach roof on the side away from the thieves, pulling the rifle as I fell and landing on the highway margin. There was another shot and a splintering of wood over my head.

Instead of lurching into the dark forest, I rolled under the carriage, dodging the grinding wheels as the coach rocked back and forth. Lying in its shadow, I feverishly began to load my rifle while prone, a trick I'd learned from the Canadians. I bit, poured, and rammed.

"He's getting away!" Three of the bandits ran around the rear of the coach and plunged into the trees on the side I'd leaped, assuming I was escaping that way. The passengers looked ready to bolt as well, but two of the thieves commanded them to stand where they were. The fake customs inspector, cursing, struggled to reload his pistol. I finished my own ramming, poked my rifle barrel out, and shot him.

The flash was blinding in the darkness. As the bastard buckled I got a startling glimpse of something that had been hanging inside his own shirt, now dangling free. It was a Masonic emblem, no doubt expropriated by Silano's Egyptian Rite, of crossed compass and square. There was a familiar letter in the middle. So that explained it!

I rolled, stood, and swung my weapon by the barrel as hard as I could, clubbing another thief with my gun butt. There was a satisfying crack as eleven pounds of maple and iron trumped bone. I scooped up my tomahawk. Where was the third rascal? Then another gun went off and someone howled. I started running toward the trees in the opposite direction from where the first three had gone. The other passengers, including Talma, scattered as well.

"The bag! Get his bag!" the one I'd shot was shouting through his pain.

I grinned. The medallion was safe in the sole of my boot.

The woods were dark and getting darker as night fully descended. I trotted as best I could, alone, my rifle a makeshift prod to keep me from running into trees. Now what? Were the robbers in league with some arm of the French government, or entirely imposters? Their leader had the correct uniform and knowledge of my prize and position, suggesting that someone with official connections—an ally of Silano, and a member of the Egyptian Rite—was tracking me.

It wasn't just the thief's readiness to cock a pistol in my face that disturbed me. Inside his Masonic symbol, I'd been reminded, was the standard letter said to represent God, or gnosis, knowledge, or perhaps geometry.

The letter *G*.

My initial, and the same letter which poor Minette had scrawled in her own blood.

Was such an emblem her last sight on earth?

The more anxious others were for my trinket, the more determined I was to keep it. There must be some reason for its popularity.

I stopped in the woods to reload, ramming down the ball and listening after I did so. A branch snapped. Was someone following? I'd kill them if they got close. But what if it was poor Talma, trying to find me in the gloom? I hoped he'd simply stay with the coach, but I dared not shoot, shout, or tarry either, so I went deeper into the forest.

The spring air was cool, the nervous energy of escape evaporating and leaving me chill and hungry. I was debating circling back to the road in hopes of finding a farmhouse when I saw the steady glow of a lantern, then another lamp and another, amid the evening trees. I crouched and heard the murmur of voices in a language distinctive from French. Now here was a way to hide myself! I'd stumbled upon an encampment of the Rom. Gypsies—or, as many pronounced the word, Gyptians, reputed to be wanderers from Egypt. Gypsies did nothing to discourage this belief, claiming they were descended from the priests of the pharaohs, even though others considered them a plague of nomadic rascals. Their assertion of ancient authority encouraged lovers and schemers to pay money for their augury.

Again, a sound behind me. Here my experience in the forests of America came into play. I melted into the foliage, using a shadow cast by the lantern light to cloak myself. My pursuer, if that's what he was, came on oblivious to my position. He stopped after spying the glow of the wagons, considered as I had, and then came ahead, no doubt guessing I'd sought refuge there. When his face came into the light I didn't recognize him as either an assailant or a passenger, and now was more confused than ever.

No matter, his intentions were plain enough. He, too, had a pistol.

As the stranger crept toward the nearest wagon, I slid noiselessly behind him. He was looking at the multicolored marvel that was the nearest gypsy *vardo* when my muzzle eased over his shoulder and came to rest on his skull.

"I don't believe we've been introduced," I said quietly.

There was a long silence. Then, in English, "I'm the man who just helped save your life."

I was startled, uncertain whether to reply in my native tongue. *"Qui êtes-vous?"* I finally demanded.

"Sir Sidney Smith, a British agent fluent enough in the tongue of France to recognize that your accent is worse than mine," he replied again in English. "Get the gun barrel off my ear and I'll explain everything, friend."

I was stunned. Sidney Smith? Had I encountered the most famous prison fugitive in France—or a mad imposter? "Drop your pistol first," I said in English. Then I felt something poke my own back, pointed and sharp.

"As you will drop your rifle, monsieur, when you are at my home." In French again, but this time with a distinctive Eastern accent: A gypsy. A half-dozen more emerged from the trees around us, their heads covered in scarves or broad-brimmed hats, sashes on their waist, and boots to their knees, looking raffish and tough. All had knives, swords, or clubs. We stalkers had become the stalked.

"Be careful," I said. "There may be other men chasing me." I laid my rifle on the ground as Smith surrendered his pistol.

A handsome, swarthy man came around to my face, sword in hand, and gave a grim smile. "Not anymore." He drew a finger across his throat as he collected the rifle and pistol. "Welcome to the Rom."

When I stepped into the light of the gypsy campfires, I stepped into another world. Their barrel-roofed wagons with paint-box colors created an elfin village amid the trees. I smelled smoke, incense, and cooking spicy enough to be exotic, heavy with garlic and herbs. Women in colorful dresses, with black lustrous hair and golden hoops in their ears, glanced up from steaming pots to evaluate us with eyes as deep and unfathomable as ancient pools. Children crouched by the colored wheels like watching imps. Shaggy gypsy wagon ponies stamped and snorted from the shadows. All was cast in amber by the glow from their lamps. In Paris all was reason and revolution. Here was something older, more primitive, and free.

"I am Stefan," said the man who'd disarmed us. He had dark, wary eyes, a grand moustache, and a nose so shattered in some past fight that it was as rumpled as a mountain range. "We do not care for guns, which are expensive to buy, costly to maintain, noisy to use, tedious to reload, and easy to steal. So explain yourselves, bringing them to our home."

"I was en route to Toulon when our coach was accosted," I said. "I'm fleeing from bandits. When I saw your wagons I stopped and heard him"—I pointed to Smith—"coming up behind me."

"And I," said Smith, "was trying to speak to this gentleman after helping save his life. I shot a thief who was about to shoot him. Then our friend ran like a rabbit."

So that had been the other shot I'd heard. "But how?" I objected. "I mean, where did you come from? I don't know you. And how could you be Smith? Everyone assumes you escaped to England." In February, the flamboyant British naval captain, scourge of the French coastline, had with female help escaped from Paris's Temple Prison, built from a former castle of the Knights Templar. He'd been missing since. Smith had originally been captured while trying to steal a French frigate from the mouth of the Seine, and was so bold and notorious a raider that the authorities had refused to ransom or exchange him. Engravings of his handsome likeness were sold not just in London, but in Paris as well. Now, here he claimed to be.

"I was following in hopes of warning you. That I came upon your coach shortly after the moment of ambush was no coincidence; I'd been trailing all day at a mile or so behind, with plans to contact you at your inn tonight. When I saw the brigands I feared the worst and crept up on the group. Your work at getting away was brilliant, but you were outnumbered. When one of the villains took aim, I shot him."

I remained suspicious. "Warn me of what?"

He glanced at Stefan. "People of Egypt, can you be trusted?"

The gypsy straightened, his feet planted as if ready to box. "While you are a guest of the Rom, your secrets stay here. As you protected this fugitive, Englishman, in like manner we protected you. We, too, saw what unfolded, and we make a distinction between criminals and their victims. The thief who attempted to follow the pair of you will not return to his fellows."

Smith beamed. "Well, then, we are all fellow men at arms! Yes, I did escape from Temple Prison with royalist help, and yes, I fully intend to soon reach England. I'm simply waiting for the necessary documents to be forged so I can slip out of a Normandy harbor. New battles wait. But while held in that hideous edifice I whiled away some of my time talking with the prison governor, who was a student of the Templars, and was told all kinds of stories of Solomon and his masons, of Egypt and its priests, and of charms and powers lost in the mists of time. Pagan nonsense, but interesting as all hell. What if the ancients knew of powers now lost? Then, while I was in hiding after my escape, royalists brought rumors that French forces are being gathered for some expedition to the East, and that an American had been invited to join them. I'd heard of you, Mr. Gage, and your expertise in electricity. Who would not have heard of a confederate of the great Franklin? Agents reported not only your departure south, but also that rival factions in the French government had a special interest in you and some artifact you carried: something to do with the same legends I'd heard from my warden. Factions within the government hoped to seize you. It seemed we might have common enemies, and the idea of enlisting your help before we both departed France occurred to me. I decided to discreetly follow. Why would an American be invited on a French military expedition? Why would he accept? There were stories of Count Alessandro Silano, a wager in a gambling hall . . ."

"I think you know entirely too much about me, sir, and are entirely too quick to repeat it aloud. What is your purpose?"

"To learn yours, and enlist your service for England."

"You *are* insane."

"Hear me out. My new friend Stefan, might we share some wine?"

The gypsy agreed, snapping an order to a comely lass named Sarylla who had swirling dark hair, liquid eyes, a figure fit for museum statuary, and a flirtatious manner. I suppose it's to be expected: I *am* a bit of a handsome rogue. She fetched a wineskin. Christ, I was thirsty! Children and dogs squatted in the shadows by the wagon wheels while we drank, watching us intently as if we might soon sprout horns or feathers. Quenching his own thirst, Smith leaned forward. "Now, there's some jewel or instrument you hold, is there not?"

Good heavens, was Smith interested in my medallion too? What had the poor strangled French captain found in Italy? Was I, too, going to end up throttled and in some river because I'd won his trinket? Was it truly cursed? "You are misinformed."

"And others want it, is this not so?"

I sighed. "You, too, I suppose."

"On the contrary, I want to ensure you dispose of it. Bury it. Lock it away. Throw it, melt it, hide it, or eat it, but just keep the damned thing out of sight until this war is over. I don't know if my Temple jailer knew more than fairy tales, but anything that tips this contest against Britain threatens civilized order. If you think the piece has monetary value, I will get the Admiralty to compensate you."

"Mr. Smith . . ."

"Sir Sidney."

His knighthood was from mercenary service to the king of Sweden, not England, but he *did* have a reputation of being vain and self-aggrandizing. "Sir Sidney, all we share is language. I'm American, not British, and France sided with my own nation in our recent revolution against yours. My country is neutral in the present conflict, and on top of that I have no idea what you're talking about."

"Gage, listen to me." He cocked forward like a falcon, the very picture of anxious intensity. He had a warrior's build, straight and broad-shouldered, a sturdy chest tapering to a hard waist, and now that I thought about it, maybe Sarylla was being solicitous to *him*. "Your colonial revolution was one of political independence. This one in France is about the very order of life. My God, a king guillotined! Thousands sent to slaughter! Wars unleashed on every French border! Atheism enshrined! Church lands seized, debts ignored, estates confiscated, rabbles armed, riots, anarchy, and tyranny! You have as much in common with France as Washington has with Robespierre. You and I share not only a language but a culture and political system of law and justice. The madness that has seized France is going to unhinge Europe. All good men are allies, unless they believe in anarchy and dictatorship."

"I have many French friends."

"As do I! It's their tyrants I can't abide. I'm not asking you to betray anyone. I'm hoping you still go wherever this young Napoleon chap leads. All I'm asking is that you keep this talisman secret. Keep it for yourself, not for Boney, or this Silano, or anyone else who asks. Consider that your nation's commercial future is inevitably with the British Empire, not a revolution bent on ruin. Keep your French friends! Make me your friend as well, and perhaps we'll someday aid each other."

"You want me to spy for England?"

"Absolutely not!" He looked hurt, glancing at Stefan as if the gypsy should support his protestations of innocence. "I simply offer help. Go where you must and pay attention to what you see. But if you ever tire of Napoleon and are looking for aid, contact the British navy and share what any man could have observed. I'm giving you a signet ring inscribed with a symbol of a unicorn, my coat-of-arms. I'll notify the Admiralty of its authenticity. Use it as a token of safe passage."

Smith and Stefan looked at me expectantly. Did they think me a fool? I could feel the lump of the object in the false sole of my boot.

"First, I don't know what you're talking about," I lied again. "Second, I'm allies with nobody, neither France nor England. I am merely a man of science, recruited to observe natural phenomena while some legal trouble I have is sorted out in Paris. Third, if I did have what you speak of, I wouldn't admit it, given the lethal interest everyone seems to display. And fourth, this entire conversation is useless, because whatever I may once have had, even though I never had it, I have no longer, since the thieves plundered my baggage when I fled." There, I thought. That should shut them up.

Smith grinned. "Good man!" he shouted, slapping my arm. "I knew you had the instincts! Fine show!"

"And now we feast," Stefan said, also apparently approving of my performance. "Tell me more of your lessons from Temple Prison, Sir Sidney. We Rom trace our origins to the pharaohs, and to Abraham and Noah. We have forgotten much, but we remember much as well, and we can still sometimes tell the future and bend the whims of fate. Sarylla there is a *drabardi*, a fortune-teller, and maybe she can cast your future. Come, come, sit, and let us talk of Babylon and Tyre, Memphis and Jerusalem."

Was everyone but me lost in the ancient world? I slipped on Smith's ring, reasoning it couldn't hurt to have another friend.

"Alas, I threaten all of you the longer I stay," Smith said. "To tell the truth, a troop of French dragoons has been on my own trail. I wanted this quick word, but must be on my way before they encounter the robbery, hear the story of my timely shot, and look in these woods." He shook his head. "I don't know what to make of this fascination with the occult, frankly. My jailer, Boniface, was the worst kind of Jacobin tyrant, but he constantly hinted at mystic secrets. All of us want to believe in magic, even if we adults have been told we shouldn't. A learned man would dismiss it, and yet sometimes too much learning makes us blind."

It sounded like what Talma had said.

"The Rom have kept the secrets of our Egyptian ancestors for centuries," Stefan said. "Yet we are mere children in the ancient arts."

Well, their Egyptian connection seemed dubious to me— their very name suggested Romania as a more probable homeland—but then again it was a dusky and colorful group, of vests and shawls and scarves and jewelry, including an ankh here and a figurine of dog-headed Anubis there. Their women might not be Cleopatra, but they certainly had an alluring beauty. What lovemaking secrets might they know? I pondered that question for some moments. I am, after all, a scientist.

"Adieu, my new friends," Smith said. He gave Stefan a purse. "Here is payment to conduct Monsieur Gage and the talisman he doesn't have to safety in Toulon. He will escape detection in your slow wagons. Agreed?"

The gypsy regarded the money, flipped and caught it, and laughed. "For this much I would take him to Constantinople! But for a man pursued, I would also take him for free."

The Englishman bowed. "I believe you would, but accept the Crown's generosity."

Going with the gypsies would separate me from Talma until we reached Toulon, but I reasoned this would be safer for my friend as well as me. He'd worry, but then he always worried.

"Gage, we will meet again," Smith said. "Keep my ring on your finger; the frogs won't recognize it—I kept it out of sight in prison. In the meantime, keep your wits about you and remember how quickly idealism can turn to tyranny and liberators can become dictators. You may find yourself, eventually, on your mother country's side." Then he melted into the trees as quietly as he'd come, an apparition no one would believe I'd encountered.

Meet again? Not if I had anything to say about it. I didn't dream how Smith would eventually re-enter my life, a thousand miles from where we stood. I was simply relieved the fugitive was gone.

"And now we feast," said Stefan.

The term "feast" was an exaggeration, but the camp did serve us a rich stew, sopped with thick and heavy bread. I felt safe amid these strange nomads, if a little astonished at their ready hospitality. They seemed to want nothing from me but my company. I was curious if they might really know anything about what was in the sole of my boot.

"Stefan, I'm not admitting that Smith was right about this pendant. But if some such trinket did exist, what about it would make men so covetous?"

He smiled. "It would not be the necklace itself, but the fact that it is some kind of clue."

"A clue to what?"

The gypsy shrugged. "All I know are old stories. The standard tale is that ancient Egyptians at the dawn of civilization caged a power that they deemed dangerous until men had the intellectual and moral quality to correctly harness it, but left a key in the form of a neckpiece. Alexander the Great reputedly received this when he made his pilgrimage to the desert oasis of Siwah, where he was declared a son of Amon and Zeus before his march into Persia. He subsequently conquered the known world. How did he accomplish so much so quickly? Then he died a young man in Babylon. Of disease? Or murder? The rumor is that Alexander's general, Ptolemy, took the key back to Egypt, hoping to unlock great powers, but he couldn't understand what the token meant. Cleopatra, Ptolemy's descendant, took it with her when she accompanied Caesar to Rome. Then Caesar was assassinated too! On it goes through history, great men grasping and coming to their doom. Kings, popes, and sultans began to believe it cursed, even as wizards and sorcerers believed it could unlock great secrets. Yet none remembered anymore how to use it. Was it a key to good or to evil? The Catholic Church takes it to Jerusalem during the Crusades, again in futile quest. The Knights Templar become its custodians, hiding it first in Rhodes, then in Malta. There are confusing quests for a holy grail, obscuring the truth of what was sought. For centuries the medallion lay forgotten until someone recognized its significance. Now perhaps it has come to Paris . . . and then walked into our camp. Of course, this you have denied."

I didn't like this medallion bringing death to all. "You really think an ordinary man like me could stumble across the same key?"

"I've pawned a hundred pieces of the True Cross and scores of fingers and teeth of the great saints. Who is to say what is real and what is false? Just be aware that some men are in earnest about this trinket you claim not to carry."

"Maybe Smith is right. Supposing I had it, I should throw it away. Or give it to you."

"Not me!" He looked alarmed. "I'm not in a position to use or understand it. If the stories are true, the medallion will only make sense in Egypt where it was crafted. Besides, it brings bad luck to the wrong man."

"I can testify to that," I confessed gloomily. A beating, murder, escapes, a holdup . . . "Yet a savant like Franklin would say it's all superstitious nonsense."

"Or maybe he would use your new science to investigate it."

I was impressed with Stefan's seeming lack of greed, particularly since his tales had helped fuel my own avarice. Too many other parties wanted this medallion, or wanted it buried: Silano, the bandits, the French expedition, the English, and this mysterious Egyptian Rite. This suggested it was so valuable that I should be determined to keep it until I could either unload it at a profit or figure out what the devil it was for. That meant going on to Egypt. And, meanwhile, watching my back.

I glanced at Sarylla. "Could your lass, here, tell my fortune?"

"She is a mistress of the Tarot." He snapped his fingers, and she fetched her deck of mystic cards.

I'd seen the symbols before, and the illustrations of death and the devil remained disturbing. In silence she dealt some before the fire, considered, and turned some others: swords, lovers, cups, the magician. She looked puzzled, making no forecast. Finally she held one up.

It was the fool, or jester. "He is the one."

Well, I had it coming, didn't I? "That's me?"

She nodded. "And the one you seek."

"What do you mean?"

"The cards say you will learn what I mean when you get where you must go. You are the fool who must find the fool, becoming wise to find wisdom. You are a seeker who must find the first to seek. Beyond that, it is better you don't know." And she'd say nothing more. That's the knack of prophecy, isn't it: to be vague as a fine-written contract? I had more wine.

It was well past midnight when we heard the tread of big horses. "French cavalry!" a gypsy sentry hissed.

I could hear their clink and rattle, branches snapping under the hooves. All but one lamp was extinguished and all but Stefan melted toward their wagons. Sarylla took my hand.

"We must get these clothes off you so you can pretend to be Rom," she whispered.

"You have a disguise for me?"

"Your skin."

Well, there was an idea. And better Sarylla than Temple Prison. She took me by the hand and we crept into a *vardo,* her lithe fingers helping me shed my stained clothing. Hers slipped off as well, her form luminescent in the dim light. What a day! I lay in one of the wagons next to her warm and silken body, listening to Stefan murmur with a lieutenant of cavalry. I heard the words "Sidney Smith," there were growled threats, and then much tramping about as wagon doors were jerked open. When ours had its turn, we looked up in feigned sleepiness and Sarylla let our blanket slip off her breasts. You can trust they took a good long look, but not at me.

Then, as the horsemen moved off, I listened to what she suggested we do next. Curse or no curse, my journey to Toulon had taken a decided turn for the better.

"Show me what they do in Egypt," I whispered to her.

three hundred certificated washerwomen expected to provide other morale-building services, and hundreds more smuggled wives and concubines. Aboard as well were four thousand bottles of wine for the officers as a whole and eight hundred choice ones from Joseph Bonaparte's personal cellar, brought to help his brother entertain. Our commander had also packed a fine city carriage with double harness so he could survey Cairo in style.

"We are a French army, not an English one," he'd told his staff. "We live better on campaign than they do in a castle."

The remark would be remembered with bitterness in the months ahead.

I'd come to Toulon after a meandering gypsy journey on their slow wagons. It had been a pleasant interlude. The "priests of Egypt" showed me simple card tricks, explained the Tarot, and told me more tales of treasure caves and temples of power. None had ever been in Egypt, of course, or knew if their stories had a grain of truth, but story spinning was one of their chief talents and source of income. I watched them cast optimistic fortunes for milkmaids, gardeners, and constables. What they couldn't earn with fantasy, they stole, and what they couldn't steal, they did without. Accompanying the band to Toulon was a far more enjoyable way to complete my escape from Paris than the highway coach, despite knowing that my separation and delay would cause anxiety for Antoine Talma. It was a relief not to have to listen to the journalist's Masonic theories, however, and I left the warmth of Sarylla with regret.

The port had been a madhouse of preparation and excitement, crammed with soldiers, sailors, military contractors, tavern keepers, and brothel madams. One could spot the famous savants in their top hats, excited and apprehensive, clumping in sturdy boots still stiff from newness. The officers were bright as peacocks in their resplendent uniforms, and ordinary soldiers were excited and cheerfully fatalistic about an expedition with no announced destination. I was reasonably anonymous in such a crowd, my clothes and green coat more stained and worn than ever, but to be safe I swiftly boarded *L'Orient* in order to stay out of the reach of bandits, antiquarians, gendarmes, lantern bearers, or anyone else who might offer me harm. It was on board that I was finally reunited with Talma.

"I feared I was entering into peril and adventure in the East without a friend!" he exclaimed. "Berthollet has been concerned as well! *Mon dieu,* what happened?"

"I'm sorry I had no way to get word to you. It seemed best to travel quietly. I knew you'd be worried."

He embraced me. "Where's the medallion?" I could feel his breath at my ear.

By this time I was cautious. "Safe enough, my friend. Safe enough."

"What's that on your finger? A new ring?" He was looking at the token from Sidney Smith.

"A gift from gypsies."

Talma and I briefed each other on our separate adventures. He said the surviving brigands had scattered in confusion after my escape from the coach. Then cavalry came, on the hunt for some other fugitive—"it was all bewildering in the dark"—and the horsemen plunged into the woods. Meanwhile, the coachmen used their team to drag the blocking tree out of the way and the traveling party finally pushed on to an inn. Talma decided to wait for the next day's stage in case I emerged from the forest. When I didn't, he went on to Toulon, fearing me dead.

"Gypsies!" he now cried, looking at me in wonder. "You do have talent for finding mischief, Ethan Gage. And the way you just shot that man! I was astounded, exultant, frightened!"

"He almost shot you."

"Of course you have been among the Red Indians."

"I've met a lot of people in my travels, Antoine, and learned to keep one palm open in greeting and the other on a weapon." I paused. "Did he die?"

"They carried him away bleeding."

Well, one more thing to wonder about in the dark hours of the night.

"Are the gypsies scoundrels, like their reputation?" Talma asked.

"Not in the least, if you watch your pockets. They saved my life. Their spicing awakens senses that their women satisfy. No home, no job, no ties . . ."

"You found your own kind! I'm surprised you came back!"

"They think they're descended from the priests of Egypt. They've heard legends of a lost medallion, saying it is a key to some ancient secret there."

"But of course, that would explain the interest of the Egyptian Rite! Cagliostro saw himself in competition with ordinary Freemasonry. Perhaps Silano believes this could give his branch an advantage. But to openly rob us? The secret must be potent indeed."

"And what word of Silano? Doesn't he know Bonaparte?"

"The word is that he's gone to Italy—to look for clues to what you won, perhaps? Berthollet has told our general about the medallion and he seemed quite interested, but Bonaparte has also called Masons imbeciles, consumed by fairy tales. His brothers Joseph, Lucien, Jerome, and Louis, who are all in our fraternity, argue the point. Napoleon said he's as interested in your opinions of Louisiana as your choice of jewelry, but I think he's flattered an American is along. He appreciates your ties to Franklin. He hopes you may someday help explain his schemes to the United States."

Talma introduced me as a celebrity fugitive to the fellow savants who had boarded the flagship. We were part of a group of 167 civilian professionals whom Bonaparte had invited to accompany his invasion. The number included nineteen civil engineers, sixteen cartographers, two artists, one poet, an orientalist, and a grand assortment of mathematicians, chemists, antiquarians, astronomers, mineralogists, and zoologists. I met Berthollet again, who had recruited most of this group, and in due course was introduced to our general. My nationality, my slim connection to the famed Franklin, and the story of how I'd escaped ambush all impressed the young conqueror. "Electricity!" Bonaparte exclaimed. "Imagine if we could harness your mentor's lightning bolts!"

I was impressed that Napoleon had won the leadership of so ambitious an expedition. The most famous general in Europe was lean, short, and disconcertingly young. At twenty-nine he was junior to all but four of his thirty-one generals, and while the difference between English and French measures meant that British propagandists had exaggerated his lack of height—he was actually a respectable five-six—still, there was so little to him in terms of breadth that he seemed swallowed by boots and dragging sword. The tittering ladies of Paris had nicknamed him "Puss-n-Boots," a teasing he never forgot. Egypt would make this young man into the Napoleon who would take the world by storm, but on the decks of *L'Orient* he was not quite Napoleon yet; he was viewed as much more human, more flawed and striving, than the later marble titan. Historians invent an icon, but contemporaries live with a man. In fact, Napoleon's rapid ascent during the Revolution was as annoying as it was breathtaking, and it made more than one of his seniors hope he would fail. Yet Bonaparte himself was confident to the point of vanity.

And why not? Here at Toulon, he had risen from captain of artillery to brigadier general in days after situating the cannon that drove the British and the royalists from the city. He had survived the Terror and a brief stint in prison, married a social climber named Josephine whose first husband had been guillotined, helped slaughter a counterrevolutionary mob in Paris, and led the ragtag French army to a series of astounding victories over the Austrians in Italy. His troops had warmed to him as if he were Caesar, and the Directory was delighted by the tribute he sent their bankrupt treasury. Napoleon wanted to emulate Alexander, and his civilian superiors wanted his restless ambition out of France. Egypt would serve both just fine.

What a hero he looked then, long before his days of palaces and cream! His hair was a shock of black across his forehead, his nose Roman, his lips pursed like a classical statue's, his chin cleft, and his eyes a dark, excited gray. He had a flair for addressing troops, understanding the human thirst for glory and adventure, and carried himself in the way we all imagined heroes should stand: torso erect, head high, eyes on a mystic horizon. He was the kind of man whose manner, as much as his words, persuaded that he must know what he is doing.

I was impressed because he'd clearly risen by merit, not birth, which fit the American ideal. He was, after all, an immigrant like us, not really French, having come from the island of Corsica to the barracks of a French military school. He'd spent the early years of life wanting nothing more ambitious than his homeland's independence. By all reports he was a middling student in all but mathematics, socially awkward, lonely, without a mentor or powerful patron, and faced upon graduation with the daunting upheaval of the Revolution. Yet while so many were bewildered by the turmoil, Bonaparte thrived on it. The intelligence that had been smothered by the rigidities of military school erupted when the need was for improvisation and imagination, when France was under siege. The prejudice he'd encountered, as a rustic islander from third-rate nobility, melted away when his competence at meeting crises was demonstrated. The diffidence and hopelessness of adolescence had been shed like a clumsy cloak, and he'd worked to turn awkwardness to charm. It was the unlikely Napoleon who'd come to embody the idealism of the Revolution, where rank was won by ability and there was no limit to ambition. Though conservatives like Sidney Smith couldn't see it, this is where the two revolutions, American and French, were alike. Bonaparte was a self-made man.

Yet Napoleon's relationship to individuals was one of the strangest I've ever seen. He'd developed undeniable charisma, but it was always practiced—shy, removed, wary, tense—as if he were an actor playing a role. When he looked at you it was with the brilliance of a chandelier, energy emanating from him like a horse radiates heat. He could focus with an intensity both flattering and overwhelming—he did it to me a dozen times. Yet a moment later he'd swing his entire attention to the next person and leave you feeling as if a cloud had passed in front of the sun, and seconds after that he might disappear into himself even in a crowded room, staring just as intently at the floor as he had at you, eyes downcast, lost in thought and a world of his own. One Parisian female had described his brooding countenance as the type one dreaded meeting in a dark alley. There was a thumb-stained copy of Goethe's *The Sorrows of Young Werther* that he carried in his pocket, a novel of suicide and hopeless love that he'd read six times. I would see his dour passions play out at the Battle of the Pyramids, in triumph and in horror.

It took eight hours for the last ship to parade by, the tricolor streaming from every mast. We'd reviewed a dozen ships of the line, forty-two frigates, and hundreds of transports. The sun was already low when our flagship finally set out like a mother duck after her brood. The fleet covered two square miles of water, the larger warships shortening sails to let the smaller merchant tubs keep pace. When the other convoys joined us we covered four square miles, plodding at little more than three knots.

All but the veteran sailors were miserable. Bonaparte, knowing he was prone to seasickness, spent much of his time in a wooden bed suspended by ropes that stayed level during the ship's rolls. The rest of us were queasy whether standing or trying to sleep. Talma finally didn't have to imagine sickness, he had it, and confided several times that he was almost certainly near death. Soldiers didn't have time to reach the upper deck and lee rail to heave out their guts, so buckets filled to overflowing, every ship reeking of vomit. *L'Orient*'s five decks were crammed with two thousand soldiers, one thousand sailors, cattle, sheep, and so many supplies that we squeezed, rather than walked, from bow to stern. Ranking savants like Berthollet had cabins of red damask, but they were so small it was like occupying a coffin. We lesser intellectuals made do with closets of damp oak. When we ate, we were packed so tightly on benches we barely had room to raise hand to mouth. A dozen stabled horses stamped, whinnied, and pissed in the hold, and every bit of clothing was damp. The lower gun ports had to be closed against the swells, so it was dim below, making reading impossible. We preferred to stay topsides anyway, but the sailors working to drive the ship would periodically become exasperated at the crowding and order us back down. Within a day everyone was bored; within a week we all prayed for the desert.

Added to the discomfort was the anxiety of watching for British ships. A firebrand named Horatio Nelson, already missing an arm and an eye but no less enthusiastic for it, was reputed to be hunting us with his squadron. Since the Revolution had stripped the French navy of many of its best royalist officers, and since our lumbering transports and gun decks were jammed with army supplies, we dreaded any naval duel.

Our chief distraction was weather. A few days out we had a squall, complete with flashes of lightning. It set *L'Orient* rolling so badly that the cattle bawled in terror and anything unsecured became a slurry of debris. Within hours it was calm again, and a day later it was so hot and stifling that pitch bubbled from the deck seams. The wind was inconstant and the water stale. My memory of the voyage is of tedium, nausea, and apprehension.

As we sailed south, Bonaparte had the habit of inviting the scholars on board for after-supper discourses in his great cabin. The scientists found the rambling discussions a welcome diversion, while his officers used them as an excuse to nap. Napoleon fancied himself a savant, having used political connections to get himself elected to the National Institute, and liked to claim that if he were not a soldier he would be a scholar. The greatest immortality, he claimed, came from adding to human knowledge, not winning battles. No one believed his sincerity, but it was a nice sentiment to express.

So we met, in a low-beamed chamber with jutting stern cannon that waited on their carriages like patient hounds. The canvas-covered floor was a black-and-white checkerboard like that of a Freemason lodge, based on the old tracing board of the Dionysian architects. Was a French naval designer a member of the fraternity? Or had we Masons simply appropriated every common symbol and pattern we could find? I knew we had taken stars, moon, sun, scales, and geometric shapes, including the pyramid, from ancient times. And the borrowing could go two ways: I suspect Napoleon's later adoption of the industrious bee as his symbol was inspired by the Masonic symbol of the hive that his brothers would have told him about.

It was here that I observed the scientific fellowship I'd enlisted in, and I couldn't blame the brilliant assembly for regarding my own membership somewhat dubiously. Mystic secrets? Berthollet told the assembly I'd encountered an "artifact" I hoped to compare to others in Egypt. Bonaparte announced I had theories about ancient Egyptian mastery of electricity. I said vaguely that I hoped to bring a fresh eye to the pyramids.

My colleagues were more accomplished. Berthollet I have already mentioned. In terms of prestige he was matched only by Gaspard Monge, the famed mathematician who, at fifty-two, was the oldest of our group. With his great shaggy brows that shaded large, bagged eyes, Monge had the look of a wise old dog. Founder of descriptive geometry, his scientific career was superseded by a ministerial one when he was asked by the Revolution to rescue the French cannon industry. He promptly had church bells melted down to make artillery and wrote *The Art of Manufacturing Guns*. He brought an analytical mind to everything he touched, from creating the metric system to advising Bonaparte on what art to steal from Italy. Sensing, perhaps, that my own mind was not as disciplined as his, he adopted me like a wayward nephew.

"Silano!" Monge exclaimed when I explained how I'd come to be on the expedition. "I crossed his path in Florence. He was on the way to the Vatican libraries, and muttered something about Constantinople and Jerusalem as well, if he could get leave from the Turks. Just why, he wouldn't say."

Also famed was our geologist, whose name, Deodat Guy Silvain Tancrede Gratet de Dolomieu, was longer than my rifle barrel. Renowned in sedate academic circles for having killed a rival in a duel at age eighteen when he was apprenticed to the Knights of Malta, Dolomieu at forty-seven had become independently wealthy, professor of the school of mines, and discoverer of the mineral dolomite. A devoted wanderer with a great mustache, he couldn't wait to see the rocks of Egypt.

Etienne Louis Malus, a mathematician and expert in the optical properties of light, was a handsome army engineer of twenty-two. The sleepy-eyed, booming-voiced Jean Baptiste Joseph Fourier, thirty, was another famed mathematician. Our orientalist and interpreter was Jean-Michael de Venture, our economist was Jean-Baptiste Say, and our zoologist was Etienne Geoffrey Saint-Hilaire, who had the peculiar idea that the characteristics of plants and animals could change over time.

The most raffish and mechanically ingenious of our group was the one-eyed balloonist, forty-three-year-old Nicolas-Jacques Conte, who wore a patch over the orb destroyed in a balloon explosion. He was the first man in history to use balloons in military reconnaissance, at the battle of Fleurus. He'd invented a new kind of writing instrument called a pencil that didn't require an inkwell, and carried it around in his waistcoat to sketch out machines constantly occurring to his inventive mind. He had already established himself as the expedition's tinkerer and inventor, and had brought along a supply of sulfuric acid that would react with iron to make hydrogen for his silk gasbags. This element, lighter than air, was proving far more practical than the earlier experiments of lifting balloons with heat.

"If your plan to invade England by air had made sense, Nicky," Monge liked to joke, "I wouldn't be vomiting my guts out on this rolling bucket today."

"All I needed were enough balloons," Conte would counter. "If you hadn't hogged every sou for your cannon foundries, we'd both be having tea in London."

The age was alive with ideas for warfare. I remembered that my own countryman, Robert Fulton, had just in December been turned down by French authorities after proposing an idea for an underwater warship. There were even proposals to dig a tunnel under the English Channel.

These learned gentlemen and staff officers would gather for what Napoleon called his *instituts,* in which he would pick a topic, assign the debaters, and lead us in rambling discussions of politics, society, military tactics, and science. We had a three-day debate on the merits and corrosive jealousies of private property, an evening discussion on the age of Earth, another on the interpretation of dreams, and several on the truth or utility of religion. Here Napoleon's internal contradictions were plain; he would scoff at the existence of God one moment and anxiously cross himself with a Corsican's instinct the next. No one knew what he believed, least of all he, but Bonaparte was a firm proponent of the usefulness of religion in regulating the masses. "If I could found my own religion I could rule Asia," he told us.

"I think Moses, Jesus, and Muhammad got there before you," Berthollet said dryly.

"This is my point," Bonaparte said. "Jews, Christians, and Muslims all trace their origins to the same holy stories. They all worship the same monotheistic god. Except for a few trifling details as to which prophet had the last word, they are more alike than different. If we make plain to the Egyptians that the Revolution recognizes the unity of faith, we should have no problem with religion. Both Alexander and the Romans had policies of tolerating the beliefs of the conquered."

"It's the believers who are most alike who fight most fervently over differences," Conte warned. "Don't forget the wars between Catholics and Protestants."

"Yet are we not at the dawn of reason, of the new scientific age?" Fourier spoke up. "Perhaps mankind is on the verge of being rational."

"No subject people are rational at the point of a gun," the balloonist replied.

"Alexander subdued Egypt by declaring himself a son of both Zeus the Greek and Amon the Egyptian," Napoleon said. "I intend to be as tolerant of Muhammad as of Jesus."

"While you cross yourself like the pope," Monge chided. "And what of the atheism of the Revolution?"

"A stance doomed to fail, its biggest mistake. It is immaterial whether or not God exists. It simply is that whenever you bring religion, or even superstition, into conflict with liberty, the former will always win over the latter in the people's mind." This was the kind of cynically perceptive political judgment Bonaparte enjoyed making to hold his intellectual weight against the learning of the scientists. He enjoyed provoking us. "Besides, religion is what keeps the poor from murdering the rich."

Napoleon was also fascinated in the truths behind myth.

"Resurrection and virgin birth, for example," he told us one night as the rationalist Berthollet rolled his eyes. "This is a story not just of Christianity, but of countless ancient faiths. Like your Masonic Hiram Abiff, right, Talma?" He liked to focus on my friend in hopes the writer would flatter him in newspaper articles he sent back to France.

"It is so common a legend that one wonders if it was not frequently true," Talma agreed. "Is death an absolute end? Or can it be reversed, or postponed indefinitely? Why did the pharaohs devote so much attention to it?"

"Certainly the earliest stories of resurrection go back to the legend of the Egyptian god Osiris and his sister and wife Isis," said de Venture, our scholar of the East. "Osiris was slain by his evil brother Seth, but Isis reassembled his dismembered parts to bring him back to life. Then he slept with his sister and sired her son, Horus. Death was but a prelude to birth."

"And now we go to the land where this was supposedly done," Bonaparte said. "Where did these stories come from, if not some grain of truth? And if they are somehow true, what powers did the Egyptians have to accomplish such feats? Imagine the advantages of immortality, of inexhaustible time! How much you could accomplish!"

"Or at least benefit from compounding interest," Monge joked.

I stirred. Is this why we were really invading Egypt—not

just because it could become a colony but because it was a source of everlasting life? Is this why so many were curious about my medallion?

"It's all myth and allegory," Berthollet scoffed. "What people doesn't fear death, and dream of surmounting it? And yet they are all, including the Egyptians, dead."

General Desaix peeked from his slumbers. "Christians believe in a different kind of everlasting life," he pointed out mildly.

"But while Christians pray for it, the Egyptians actually packed for it," de Venture countered. "Like other early cultures, they put into their tombs what they'd need for the next journey. Nor did they necessarily pack light, and there lies opportunity. The tombs may be stuffed with treasures. 'Please send us gold,' rival kings wrote the pharaohs, 'because gold to you is more plentiful than dirt.' "

"That's the faith for me," General Dumas growled. "Faith you can grasp."

"Maybe they survived in another way, as gypsies," I spoke up.

"What?"

"Gypsies. Gyptians. They claim descent from the priests of Egypt."

"Or they are Saint-Germain or Cagliostro," added Talma. "Those men claimed to have lived for millennia, to have walked with Jesus and Cleopatra. Perhaps it was true."

Berthollet scoffed. "What's true is that Cagliostro is so dead that soldiers dug up his grave in a papal prison and toasted him by drinking wine out of his skull."

"If it was really his skull," Talma said stubbornly.

"And the Egyptian Rite claims to be on the path to rediscovering these powers and miracles, is this not so?" Napoleon asked.

"It is the Egyptian Rite that seeks to corrupt the principles of Freemasonry," Talma responded. "Instead of pledging themselves to morality and the Great Architect, they look for dark power in the occult. Cagliostro invented a perversion of Freemasonry that admits women for sexual rites. They would use ancient powers for themselves, instead of for the good of mankind. It's a shame they've become a fashion in Paris, and seduced men such as Count Silano. All true Freemasons repudiate them."

Napoleon smiled. "So you and your American friend must find the secrets first!"

Talma nodded. "And put them to our uses, not theirs."

I was reminded of Stefan the Gypsy's legend that the Egyptians might be waiting for moral and scientific advancement before yielding their secrets. And here we came, a thousand cannon jutting from our hulls.

The conquest of the Mediterranean isle of Malta took one day, three French lives, and—before we arrived—four months of spying, negotiation, and bribery. The three hundred or so Knights of Malta were a medieval anachronism, half of them French, and more interested in pensions than dying for glory. After the formalities of brief resistance, they kissed their conqueror's hands. Our geologist Dolomieu, who had been drummed out of the Knights in disgrace after his young duel, found himself welcomed back as a prodigal son who could help in the surrender negotiations. Malta was ceded to France, the grand master was pensioned to a principality in Germany, and Bonaparte set himself to looting the island's treasures as thoroughly as he had sacked Italy.

He left to the Knights a splinter of the True Cross and a withered hand of John the Baptist. He kept for France five million francs of gold, a million of silver plate, and another million in the gem-encrusted treasures of St. John. Most of this loot was transferred to the hold of *L'Orient*. Napoleon also abolished slavery and ordered all Maltese men to wear the tricolor cockade. The hospital and post office were reorganized, sixty boys from wealthy families were sent to be educated in Paris, a new school system was set up, and five thousand men were left to garrison the island. It was a preview of the combination of pillage and reform that he hoped to accomplish in Egypt.

It was at Malta that Talma came to me excited with his latest discovery. "Cagliostro was here!" he exclaimed.

"Where?"

"This island! The Knights told me he visited a quarter-century ago, in the company of his Greek mentor Alhotas. Here he met Kolmer! These wise men conferred with the grand master and examined what the Knights Templar had brought from Jerusalem."

"So?"

"This could be where he discovered the medallion, deep in the treasures of the Knights of Malta! Don't you see, Ethan? It's as if we're following in its footsteps. Destiny is at work."

Again I was reminded of Stefan's tales of Caesar and Cleopatra, of crusaders and kings, and a quest that had consumed men through time. "Do any of these Knights remember the piece or know what it means?"

"No. But we're on the right path. Can I see it again?"

"I've hidden it for safekeeping because it causes trouble when it's out." I trusted Talma, and yet had become reluctant to show the medallion after Stefan's dire tales of what happened to men through history who grasped it. The savants knew it existed, but I'd deflected requests to share it for examination.

"But how are we to solve the secret when you keep it hidden?"

"Let's just get it to Egypt first."

He looked disappointed.

After a little more than a week our armada set sail again, lumbering eastward toward Alexandria. Rumors flew that the British were still hunting us, but we saw no sign of them. Later we would learn that Nelson's squadron had passed our armada in the dark, neither side spying the other.

It was on one of these evenings, the soldiers gambling for each other's shoes to relieve the tedium of the passage, that Berthollet invited me to follow him to *L'Orient*'s deepest decks. "It is time, Monsieur Gage, for us scholars to start earning our keep."

We descended into murk, lanterns giving feeble light, men in hammocks swaying hip to hip like moths in cocoons, coughing and snoring and, in the case of the youngest and most homesick, weeping the night away. The ship's timbers creaked. The sea hissed as it rushed past, water dripping from caulked hull seams as slowly as syrup. Marines guarded the magazine and treasure room with bayonets that gleamed like shards of ice. We stooped and entered Aladdin's Cave, the treasure hold. The mathematician Monge was waiting for us, seated on a brass-bound chest. Also present was another handsome officer who had listened to most of the philosophical discussions in silence, a young geographer and mapmaker named Edme François Jomard. It was Jomard who would become my guide to the mysteries of the pyramids. His dark eyes shone with a bright intelligence, and he had brought on board a trunk full of books by ancient authors.

My curiosity at his presence was distracted by what the cabin contained. Here was the treasure of Malta and much of the payroll of the French army. Boxes brimmed with coin like combs of honey. Sacks held centuries of jeweled religious relics. Bullion was stacked like logwood. A fistful could remake a man's life.

"Don't even think about it," the chemist said.

"*Mon dieu!* If I were Bonaparte, I'd retire today."

"He doesn't want money, he wants power," Monge said.

"Well, he wants money, too," Berthollet amended. "He's become one of the richest officers in the army. His wife and relatives spend it faster than he can steal it. He and his brothers make quite the Corsican clan."

"And what does he want of us?" I asked.

"Knowledge. Understanding. Decipherment. Right, Jomard?"

"The general is particularly interested in mathematics," the young officer said.

"Mathematics?"

"Mathematics is the key to war," Jomard said. "Given proper training, courage does not vary much from nation to nation. What wins is superior numbers and firepower at the point of attack. That requires not just men, but supply, roads, transport animals, fodder, and gunpowder. You need precise amounts, moving in precise miles, to precise places. Napoleon has said that above all, he wants officers who can count."

"And in more ways than one," Monge added. "Jomard here is a student of the classics and Napoleon wants him to count in new ways. Ancient authors such as Diodorus of Sicily suggested that the Great Pyramid is a mathematical puzzle, right, Edme?"

"Diodorus proposed that in its dimensions the Great Pyramid is somehow a map of the earth," Jomard explained. "After we liberate the country, we will measure the structure for proof of that contention. The Greeks and Romans were as puzzled by the purpose of the pyramids as we moderns, which is why Diodorus proposed his idea. Would men really slave so long on a mere tomb, particularly when no bodies or treasures have ever been found in it? Herodotus claims the pharaoh was actually entombed on an island in an underground river, far beneath the monument itself."

"So the pyramid is just a tombstone, a marker?"

"Or a warning. Or, because of its dimensions and tunnels, a kind of machine." Jomard shrugged. "Who knows, when its builders left no records?"

"Yet the Egyptians *did* scatter the world with clues that none of us can yet read," Monge said. "And this is where we come in. Look at this. Our troops captured it in Italy and Bonaparte has brought it along."

The chemist whisked away an embroidered cloth, revealing a tablet of bronze the size of a large dinner platter, its surface coated with black enamel etched by silver. Incised were intricately beautiful depictions of Egyptian figures in the ancient style, spaced in a series of rooms atop one another. The gods, goddesses, and hieroglyphs were bound by a border of fantastic animals, flowers, and trees. "It's the Tablet of Isis, once owned by Cardinal Bembo."

"What does it mean?" I asked.

"That's what the general wants us to answer. For centuries, scholars have suspected there is some message in this tablet. Legend has it that Plato was initiated into the greater mysteries in some kind of chamber under Egypt's biggest pyramid. Perhaps this is a plan, or map, of such chambers.

Yet there is no report of such rooms. Could your medallion be a key to understanding?"

I doubted it. The markings on my neckpiece seemed crude compared to this work of art. The figures were stiff but graceful as angels. There were towering headdresses, seated baboons, and striding cattle. Women had wings on their arms like hawks. Men had the heads of dogs and birds. Thrones were supported by lions and crocodiles. "Mine is cruder."

"You're to study this for clues before we reach the ruins outside Cairo. Many of the characters hold staffs, for example. Are they rods of power? Is there any connection to electricity? Could this advance the Revolution?"

The men asking these questions were eminent figures of science. I'd won my trinket in a card game. Yet solving such a puzzle might lead me to any number of commercial rewards, not to mention a pardon. As I counted the figures, I was struck that some seemed to have grander headdresses. "Here's something," I offered. "The number of primary characters here, twenty-one, coincides with those of the Tarot that the gypsies showed me."

"Interesting," Monge said. "A tablet to forecast the future perhaps?"

I shrugged. "Or just a pretty platter."

"We've made an etching of it that you can take back to your cabin." He reached into another chest. "Another peculiarity is this, which our troops found in the same fortress where Cagliostro was imprisoned. I sent for it when Berthollet told me of you." It was a round disc the size of a dinner plate, its center empty and its edge made by three rings, each fitting inside the other. The rings had symbols of suns, moons, stars, and signs of the zodiac. They rotated, so that symbols could be realigned with one another. Why, I had no idea.

"We think it's a calendar," Monge said. "The fact that you can align the symbols suggests it might show the future or indicate a certain date. But what date, and why? Some of us think it may refer to the precession of the equinoxes."

"The procession of what?"

"Precession. Ancient religion was based on study of the sky," Jomard said. "The stars formed patterns, moved across the heavens in predictable ways, and were believed alive, in control of the fate of men. The Egyptians divided the vault of the sky into the twelve signs of the zodiac, extending each downward to twelve zones on the horizon. At the same time each year—say, March 21, the spring equinox, when the length of day and night are equal—the sun rises under the same zodiacal sign."

I decided not to point out that the officer had chosen to use the traditional Gregorian date, not the new revolutionary ones.

"Yet not *precisely* where it started. Each year the zodiac falls just slightly short of making the full circuit, because the earth wobbles on its axis like a spinning top, the axis making a circle in the sky over a period of twenty-six thousand years. Over long periods of time the position of the constellations seems to shift. At March 21 of this year, the sun rose in Pisces, as it has since Christ was born. Perhaps this is why early Christians chose the fish as their symbol. But before Jesus, the March 21 sunrise was in the constellation of the ram, an age which lasted 2,160 years. Before the ram was the bull, when the pyramids may have been built. Next to come, after the 2,160 years of Pisces, is the age of Aquarius."

"Aquarius had special meaning for the Egyptians," Monge added. "Many people think these signs were Greek, but they are really far older, some dating from Babylon and others from Egypt. The poured pitchers of water of Aquarius symbolized the annual rising of the Nile, vital for fertilizing and watering Egypt's annual crops. Man's first civilization rose in the strangest environment on earth: a Garden of Eden, a strip of green amid inhospitable desert, a place of constant sun and rare rain, watered by a river that rises from sources still unknown to this day. Isolated from enemies by the Sahara and Arabian Deserts, fed by a mysterious annual cycle, roofed with a cloudless canopy of stars, it was a stable land of extreme contrasts, an ideal place for religion to evolve."

"So this is a tool for calculating the cycle of the Nile?"

"Perhaps. Or perhaps it suggests a propitious time for different actions. That's what we hope you will help decipher."

"Who made it?"

"We don't know," Monge said. "Its symbols are different from anything we have seen, and the Knights of Malta have no record of where it even came from. Is it Hebrew? Egyptian? Greek? Babylonian? Or something entirely different?"

"Surely this is a puzzle for your mind, not mine, Dr. Monge. You're a mathematician. I struggle to make change."

"Everyone struggles to make change. Listen, we don't know what all this means yet, Gage. But the interest in your medallion suggests to me that your pendant is a piece of some momentous puzzle. As an American, you are privileged to be on a French expedition. Berthollet here has extended legal protection to you. But this is not an act of charity—it is a hire of your expertise. There are a dozen reasons Bonaparte wants to go to Egypt, but one of them is that there may be ancient secrets to be learned: mystic secrets, technological secrets, electrical secrets. Then you, Franklin's man, appear with this mysterious medallion. Is it a clue? Keep these artifacts in mind as we advance into the unknown. Bonaparte is seeking to conquer a country. All you must conquer is a riddle."

"But a riddle to what?"

"To where we came from, perhaps. Or how we fell from grace."

I returned to the cabin I shared with Talma and a lieutenant named Malraux, my mind both dazzled by treasure and stupefied by the mysteries I was to wrestle with. I could see no connection between the medallion and these new objects, and nobody seemed to have any idea what the puzzle was I was supposed to solve. For decades, charmers and charlatans like Cagliostro had toured the courts of Europe claiming to know great Egyptian secrets, without ever explaining precisely what those secrets were. They had started a craze for the occult. Skeptics had scoffed, but the idea that there must be *something* in the land of the pharaohs had taken root. Now I found myself in the middle of that mania. The more science advanced, the more people longed for magic.

At sea I'd adopted the sailor practice of going barefoot, given the summer's heat. As I prepared to lie in my bunk, my mind swirling, I noticed that my boots were missing. This was disturbing, given how I'd used them as a hiding place.

I poked anxiously around. Malraux, already in bed, muttered something in his sleep and swore. I shook Talma.

"Antoine, I can't find my shoes!"

He came awake blearily. "Why do you need them?"

"I just want to know where they are."

He rolled over. "Maybe some bosun gambled them away."

A quick search of late-night card and dice circles did not locate my boots. Had someone discovered the hollow compartment in my heel? Who would dare violate the possessions of the savants? Who could even have guessed my hiding place? Talma? He must have wondered about my calm when asked the whereabouts of the medallion, and probably speculated where I might be hiding it.

I came back to the cabin and looked across at my companion. Once more he slept like an innocent, which made me all the more suspicious. The more the medallion grew in importance, the less I trusted anyone. It was poisoning my faith in my friend.

I retreated to my hammock, depressed and uncertain. What had seemed a prize in the card salon was feeling like a burden. A good thing I hadn't kept the medallion in my shoe! I put my hand on the touch-hole of the twelve-pounder next to my hammock. Since Bonaparte had forbidden target practice to conserve powder and keep our passage quiet, I'd wrapped my prize in an empty powder bag and used tar to stick it to the inside of the muzzle plug. The plug would be removed before combat, and my plan had been to retrieve the medallion before any sea battle, but meanwhile not risk having it stolen from my neck or boot. Now, with my shoes gone, my distance from the prize made me nervous. Come the morrow, when the others were on deck, I'd fish it from its hiding place and wear the thing. Curse or charm, I wanted it round my neck.

The next morning, my boots were back where I had left them. When I inspected them, I saw the sole and heel had been pried at.

CHAPTER SIX

I almost drowned in the surf of Alexandria because of Bonaparte's fear of Admiral Nelson. The English fleet prowled like a wolf somewhere over the horizon, and Napoleon was in such a hurry to get ashore that he ordered an amphibious landing. It wasn't the last time I'd be wet in the driest country I'd ever seen.

We arrived off the Egyptian city on July 1, 1798, staring in wonder at minarets like reeds and mosque domes like snowy hillocks, all shimmering under the brutal summer sun. There were five hundred of us crowded on the main deck of the flagship, soldiers, sailors, and scientists, and for long minutes it was so quiet you could hear every creak of rigging and every hiss of wave. Egypt! It wavered in distortion like a reflection in a curved mirror. The city was dust brown, dirty white, and looked anything but opulent, almost as if we'd arrived at the wrong address. The French ships slowly wallowed in a rising wind from the north, each Mediterranean swell a topaz jewel. From the land we could hear blowing horns, the boom of signal cannon, and the wails of panic. What must it have been like to behold our armada of four hundred European ships which seemed to fill the entire sea? Households were stuffed onto donkey wagons. Market awnings deflated as the valuables they shaded were secreted in wells. Arab soldiers strapped on medieval armor and mounted cracked parapets with pikes and ancient muskets.

Our expedition artist, the Baron Dominique Vivant Denon, began drawing furiously: the walls, the ships, the epic emptiness of North Africa. "I'm trying to capture the form of the solid buildings against the desert's peculiar volume of light," he told me.

The frigate *Junon* came alongside to make a report. It had arrived at the city a day earlier and conferred with the French consul, and the news it brought jolted Napoleon's staff into a frenzy of activity. Nelson's fleet had already been at Alexandria, hunting for us, and had left just two days before! It was pure luck they hadn't caught us unloading. How long before the English returned? Rather than risk running the gauntlet of the forts at the entrance to the city's harbor, Bonaparte ordered an immediate amphibious landing with longboats at the beach of Marabut, eight miles to the west. From there, French troops could march along the beach to seize the port.

Admiral Brueys vehemently protested, complaining the coast was uncharted and the wind was rising toward a gale. Napoleon overruled him.

"Admiral, we've no time to waste. Fortune grants us three days, no more. If I don't take advantage of them, we're lost." Once ashore, his army was beyond the reach of the British warships. Embarked, it could be sunk.

Yet ordering a landing is easier than accomplishing it. By the time our ships began anchoring in the heavy swells off the sand beach, it was late afternoon, meaning the landing would continue through the night. We savants were given a choice of remaining on board or accompanying Napoleon to watch the assault on the city. I, with more adventure than sense, decided to get off *L'Orient*. Its heavy roll was making me sick again.

Talma, despite his own queasy misery, looked at me as if I were mad. "I thought you didn't want to be a soldier!"

"I'm simply curious. Don't you want to watch the war?"

"The war I can observe from this deck. It's the bloody details you need to be on the beach to see. I'll meet you in the city, Ethan."

"I'll have picked us out a palace by then!"

He smiled wanly, looking at the swells. "Perhaps I should hold the medallion for safekeeping?"

"No." I shook his hand. Then, to remind him of ownership: "If I drown, I won't need it."

It was dusk by the time I was called to take my place in a boat. Bands had assembled on the larger ships and were playing the "La Marseillaise," the strains shredded by the rising wind. Toward land, the horizon had turned brown with sand blowing from the desert. I could see a few Arab horsemen dashing this way and that on the beach. Clinging to a rope, I took the ladder down the warship's side, its tumble-home shape swollen like a bicep and its guns bristling like black stubble. The longrifle I carried across my back, its hammer and pan wrapped in oil skin. My powder horn and shot pouch bounced against my waist.

The boat was heaving like a bucking saddle. "Jump!" a boatswain commanded, so I did, striving for grace but sprawling anyway. I quickly clambered to a thwart as told, clinging with both hands. More and more men dropped aboard until I was certain we could hold no more without swamping, and then a few more piled in as well. We finally pushed away, water sloshing over the gunwale.

"Bail, damn you!"

Our longboats looked like a swarm of water beetles, crawling slowly toward shore. Soon nothing could be heard above the thunder of the approaching surf. When we dipped into the wave troughs, all I could see of the invasion fleet were the mast tops.

Our helmsman, in normal life a French coastal fisherman, at first steered us expertly as the waves mounded toward the beach. But the boat was overloaded, as hard to maneuver as a wine wagon, and it barely had freeboard. We began to skid in the rising surf, the stern slewing as the helmsman shouted at the rowers. Then a breaker turned us sideways and we broached and flipped.

I didn't have time to take breath. The water came down like a wall, driving me under. The roar of the gale was cut to a dim rumble as I skipped along the bottom, tumbling on the sand. My rifle was like an anchor, but I refused to let it go. The submersion seemed like a black eternity, my lungs near to bursting, and then at a lull in the surge I sank enough to crouch on the bottom and push off. My head broke the surface just before I was ready to swallow, and I gasped with desperation before another wave broke over me. Bodies bumped in the dark. Flailing, I fastened onto a loose oar. Now the water was shallow, and the next wave carried me in on my belly. Sputtering, choking on seawater, nose draining, eyes stinging, I staggered onto Egypt.

It was flat and featureless, not a tree in sight. Sand had impregnated every crevice of my body and clothes, and the wind pushed so hard that I staggered.

Other half-drowned men were lurching out of the waves. Our overturned longboat grounded and the sailors rallied us to flip it upright, emptying out the water. Once they found enough oars the seamen pushed out again, to get more troops. The moon had risen, and I saw a hundred similar scenes playing out along the beach. Some boats managed to glide in as intended, grounding neatly, while others foundered and tumbled like driftwood. It was chaotic, men tying themselves to each other with line to wade back out and rescue comrades. Several drowned bodies had washed to the sea's edge, half buried in the sand. Small artillery pieces were sunk to their hubs. Equipment floated like flotsam. A French tricolor, raised as a rallying point, snapped and rattled in the wind.

"Henri, remember the farms the general promised us?" one sodden soldier said to another, gesturing at the barren dunes ahead. "There's your six acres."

Since I had no military unit, I began asking where General Bonaparte was. Officers shrugged and cursed. "Probably in his great cabin, watching us drown," growled one. There had been resentment at the spaciousness he had appropriated for himself.

And yet, far down the beach, a knot of order had begun to form. Men were assembling around a familiarly short and furiously gesticulating figure, and as if by gravity other troops were drawn to their mass. I could hear Bonaparte's voice giving sharp commands, and ranks began to be drawn up. When I neared I found him bareheaded and soaked to the waist, his hat having cartwheeled away in the wind. His scabbard dragged on the beach, cutting a little line behind him. He acted as if nothing was amiss, and his confidence reinforced others.

"I want a skirmish line in the dunes! Kleber, get some men up there if you don't want to be picked off by Bedouin! Captain? Use your company to free that cannon, we'll need it at dawn. General Menou, where are you? There! Get your standard planted to form up your men. You infantry there, stop standing like drowned rats and help those others right that boat! Has a little water knocked the sense out of you? You are soldiers of France!"

The expectation of obedience worked wonders, and I began to recognize Bonaparte's talent for command. A mob gradually became an army, soldiers forming columns, organizing equipment, and dragging away the drowned for quick, unceremonious burial. I heard the occasional pop of skirmish fire to keep roving tribesmen at bay. Boatload after boatload made it ashore and thousands of men assembled in moon and starlight, the trampled sand shining silver where water pooled in our boot prints. Equipment lost in the surf was retrieved and redistributed. Some men found themselves wearing hats too small that perched on their crowns like chimneys, and others with headgear that came down around their ears. Laughing, they traded back and forth. The night wind was warm, drying us rapidly.

General Jean-Baptiste Kleber, who I'd heard was another Freemason, came striding up. "They poisoned the well at Marabut and the men are getting thirsty. It was madness to sail from Toulon without canteens."

Napoleon shrugged. "It was commissary incompetence we can't correct now. We'll find water when we carry the walls of Alexandria."

Kleber scowled. He looked far more the general than Bonaparte: Six feet tall, thick, muscular, and boasting a mane of thick, curly hair that gave him the majestic gravity of a lion. "There's no food, either."

"Which is also awaiting us in Alexandria. If you will look to the sea, Kleber, you will also see there is no British navy, which is the whole point of striking quickly."

"So quickly we come ashore in a gale and drown dozens of men?"

"Speed is everything in war. I will always spend a few to save many." Bonaparte looked tempted to say more; he did not like to have his orders second-guessed. But instead he said to his general, "Have you found the man I told you about?"

"The Arab? He may speak French, but he's a viper."

"He's a tool of Talleyrand and gets a livre for every ear and hand. He'll keep the other Bedouin off your flank."

We set off down the beach, the surf rumbling to our left, thousands of men tramping in the dark. The foam seemed to glow. Occasionally I could hear a pistol shot or the pop of a musket off in the desert to our right. A few lamps shone ahead, marking Alexandria. None of the generals were mounted yet, and walked like common soldiers. General Louis Caffarelli of the engineers stumped along on a wooden leg. Our gigantic mulatto cavalry commander, Alexandre Dumas, walked bowlegged, a head higher than any of his troopers. He had the strength of a giant, and to amuse himself at sea he'd hang from a beam in the horse stalls and grip a mount with his legs, lifting the terrified animal off the deck with sheer thigh strength. Detractors said he had muscles between his ears.

Not being attached to any unit, I walked with Napoleon.

"You enjoy my company, American?"

"I just reason that the commanding general will be safer than most. Why not stand next to him?"

He laughed. "I lost seven generals in a single battle in Italy, and led charges myself. Destiny alone knows why I was spared. Life is chance, is it not? Fate sent the British fleet away and a gale in its place. Some men drowned. Do you feel sorry for them?"

"Of course."

"Don't. Death comes to all of us, unless the Egyptians indeed found immortality. And who's to say one death is better than another? My own could come this dawn, and it would be a good one. Do you know why? Because while glory is fleeting, obscurity is forever. Those men who drowned will be remembered by their families for generations. 'He died following Bonaparte to Egypt!' Society unconsciously knows this, and accepts the sacrifice."

"That's a European calculus, not an American one."

"No? We'll see when your nation is older. We're on a great mission, Ethan Gage, to unify east and west. Compared to that, individual souls mean little."

"Unify by conquest?"

"By education and example. We will defeat the Mameluke tyrants that rule these people, yes, and by so doing we will liberate the Egyptians from Ottoman tyranny. But after that we will reform them, and the time will come when they bless this day that France stepped on their shore. We, in turn, will learn from their ancient culture."

"You're a very confident man."

"I'm a visionary one. A dreamer, my generals accuse. Yet I measure my dreams with the calipers of reason. I've calculated how many dromedaries it would take to cross the deserts to India. I have printing presses with Arabic type to explain that I come on a mission of reform. Do you know that Egypt has never seen a press? I've ordered my officers to study the Koran, and ordered my troops not to loot or molest Arab women. When the Egyptians understand that we're here to liberate, not oppress, they'll join us in the fight against the Mamelukes."

"Yet you lead an army with no water."

"I lack a hundred things, but I'll rely on Egypt to provide them. That's what we did when invading Italy. That's what Cortez did when he burned his ships after landing in Mexico. Our lack of canteens makes clear to our men that our assault must succeed." It was as if he were addressing Kleber, not me.

"How can you be so certain, General? I find it hard to be certain of anything."

"Because I learned in Italy that history is on my side." He paused, considering whether to confide more, whether he

could add me to his political seductions. "For years I felt
doomed to an ordinary life, Gage. I, too, was uncertain. I
was a penniless Corsican from the shabbiest kind of back-
water royalty, a colonial islander with a thick accent who
had spent my childhood enduring snobs and taunts at French
military school. I had no friend but mathematics. Then the
Revolution came, opportunities arose, and I made the best
of them. I prevailed at the siege of Toulon. I drew notice in
Paris. I was given command of a losing, threadbare army in
northern Italy. A future at least seemed possible, even if everything could be lost again in a single defeat. But it was at
the battle of Arcola, fighting the Austrians to liberate Italy,
when the world truly opened up to me. We had to carry a
bridge down a murderous causeway, and charge after charge
had failed, carpeting the approaches with bodies. Finally I
knew that the only way to win the day was to lead a last
charge myself. I've heard you're a gambler, but there is no
gamble like that, bullets like hornets, all the dice cast in a
smoky rush for glory, men cheering, banners snapping in the
wind, soldiers falling. We carried the bridge and carried
the day, nothing scratching me, and there is no orgasm like
the exultation of watching an enemy army run. Whole French
regiments crowded around me afterward, cheering the boy
who had once been a rube Corsican, and it was at that moment that I saw that anything was possible—anything!—if
I merely dared. Don't ask me why I think fate is my angel, I
just know that she is. Now she has led me to Egypt, and
here, perhaps, I can emulate Alexander as you savants emulate Aristotle." He clasped my shoulder, his gray eyes burning into me in the pale, predawn light. "Believe in me,
American."

But first he had to fight his way into the city.

N apoleon had hoped that the mere presence of his advancing column on the beach might persuade the Alexandrians to surrender, but they hadn't experienced European
firepower yet. The Mameluke cavalry was cocky and bold.
This caste of slave warriors, whose name meant "bought
men," had been organized by the famed Saladin as a personal

bodyguard in the time of the Crusades. So powerful were these warriors from the Caucasus that they conquered Egypt for the Ottoman Turks. It was the Egyptian Mamelukes who had first defeated the Mongol hordes of Genghis Khan, gaining undying renown as soldiers, and they had held Egypt in the ensuing centuries, neither marrying into its population nor even deigning to learn the Egyptian language. They were a warrior elite, treating their own citizens as vassals in the ruthless way that only an ex-slave, exposed to cruelty himself, can exhibit. They galloped into battle on Arabian steeds superior to any horses the French had, hurling themselves at enemies with musket, lance, scimitar, and a sash crammed with pistols. By reputation, their courage was matched only by their arrogance.

Slavery was different in the East than the hopeless tyranny I'd seen in New Orleans and the Caribbean. To the Ottomans, slaves were the most reliable allies, given that they were stripped from their past and not part of Turkish feuding families. Some became princes, meaning the most oppressed could rise the highest. And indeed, the Mameluke slaves had become masters of Egypt. Unfortunately, their greatest enemy was their own treachery—no Mameluke sultan ever died in bed because of their endless conspiracies for power—and their weaponry was as primitive as their steeds were beautiful, for they wielded antiques. Moreover, while slaves could become masters, free men were often treated like serfs. The Egyptian population had little love for their leaders. The French saw themselves as liberators, not conquerors.

While the invasion had taken the enemy by surprise, by morning the few hundred Mamelukes of Alexandria had assembled a ragged force of their own cavalry, Bedouin raiders, and Egyptian peasants coerced into forming a human shield. Behind, on the walls of the city's old Arab quarter, garrison musketeers and artillerymen had anxiously assembled on the ramparts. As the first French ranks approached, the enemy cannon were inexpertly fired, the shot pattering the sand well short of the European columns. The French stopped while Napoleon prepared to offer surrender terms.

No such opportunity presented itself, however, because the Mamelukes apparently took this pause as hesitation and started to drive a mass of crudely armed peasants toward us. Bonaparte, realizing the Arabs meant battle, signaled with flags for naval support. Shallow-draft corvettes and luggers began working in toward shore to bring their cannon to bear. The few light guns brought ashore in the longboats were also run forward on the sand.

I was thirsty, tired, sticky from salt and sand, and finally comprehending that I'd put myself in the middle of a war, thanks to the clumsy necklace. I was now bound to this French army for survival. Still, I felt oddly safe near Bonaparte. As he had implied, he carried an aura, not so much of invincibility as luck. Fortunately, our march had accumulated a skirt of curious Egyptian opportunists and beggars. Battles attract spectators like boys to a schoolyard fight. Shortly before dawn I'd spied a youth selling oranges, bought a bag for a silver franc, and earned favor with the general by sharing it. We stood on the beach sucking the sweet pulp, watching the mob-like Egyptian army shamble toward us. Behind the peasants the Mameluke knights galloped back and forth, bright as birds in their silk robes. They waved shiny swords and shouted defiance.

"I've heard that you Americans boast of your accuracy with your hunting rifles," Napoleon suddenly said, as if an idea for amusement had just occurred to him. "Do you care to demonstrate?"

Officers turned to look, even as the suggestion took me by surprise. My rifle was my pride, the maple oiled, my powder horn scraped thin to the point of translucence so I could see the fine black grains of French powder inside, and my brass polished, an affectation I'd never dare in the forests of North America where a gleam could give you away to animal or enemy. The voyageurs had rubbed theirs with green hazelnut to obscure any shine. As beautiful as my rifle was, however, some of these soldiers considered its long barrel an affectation. "I don't feel those men are my enemy," I said.

"They became your enemy when you stepped on this beach, monsieur."

True enough. I began to load my gun. I should have done it some time before, given the impending battle, but I'd been striding down the beach as if on holiday, all military bands, martial camaraderie, and distant gunshots. Now I'd have to earn my place by contributing to the fight. So are we seduced and then enlisted. I measured extra powder for long range and used the ramrod to push down the linen-wrapped ball.

As the Alexandrians came on and I primed the pan, attention suddenly swung from me to a dashing Bedouin who was riding up from the ranks behind us, his black horse spraying sand, black robes rippling in the wind. Clinging behind was a French cavalry lieutenant, weaponless and looking sick. Reining up near Bonaparte's cluster of staff, the Arab waved in salute and hurled a cloth at our feet. It opened as it fell, scattering a harvest of bloody hands and ears.

"These are men who will harass you no more, effendi," the Bedouin said in French, his face masked by the cowl of his turban. His eyes waited for approval.

Bonaparte made a quick mental tally of the butchered appendages. "You have done well, my friend. Your master was right to recommend you."

"I am a servant of France, effendi." Then his eyes fastened on me and widened, as if in recognition. I was disturbed. I knew no nomads. And why did this one speak our language?

Meanwhile the lieutenant slid off the Arab's horse and stood stricken and awkward to one side, as if not sure what to do next.

"This one I rescued from some bandits whom he chased too far in the dark," the Arab said. This was a trophy too, we sensed, and a lesson.

"I applaud your help." Bonaparte turned to the freed captive. "Find a weapon and rejoin your unit, soldier. You're luckier than you deserve."

The man's eyes were wild. "Please, sir, I need rest. I am bleeding . . ."

"He's not as lucky as you think," the Arab said.

"No? He looks alive to me."

"The Bedouin habit is to beat captive women . . . and rape captive men. Repeatedly." There was crude laughter among the officers and a slap to the back of the unfortunate soldier, who staggered. Some of the jocularity was sympathetic, some cruel.

The general pursed his lips. "I am to pity you?"

The young man began to sob. "Please, I am so ashamed . . ."

"The shame was in your surrender, not your torture. Take your place in the ranks to destroy the enemy who humiliated you. That's the way to erase embarrassment. As for the rest of you, tell this story to the rest of the army. There is no sympathy for this man! His lesson is simple: Don't be captured at all." He turned back to the battle.

"My pay, effendi?" The Arab waited.

"When I take the city."

Still the Arab didn't move.

"Don't worry, your purse is growing heavier, Black Prince. There will be even bigger rewards when we reach Cairo."

"If we reach it, effendi. I and my men have done all the fighting so far."

Our general was unperturbed by this observation, accepting insolence from this desert bandit he never would from his officers. "My American ally was just about to correct that by demonstrating the accuracy of the Pennsylvania longrifle. Weren't you, Monsieur Gage? Tell us its advantages."

All eyes were again on me. I could hear the tramp of the Egyptian army coming closer. Feeling the reputation of my country was at stake, I held up my gun. "We all know that the problem with any firearm is that you only get one shot and then must take anywhere from twenty seconds to a full minute to reload," I lectured. "In the forests of America, a miss means your quarry will be long gone, or an Indian will be on you with his tomahawk. So to us, the time it takes to load a longrifle is more than compensated by a fighting chance to hit something with that first shot, unlike a musket where the path of the bullet can't be predicted." I put the weapon to my shoulder. "Now, the long barrel is of soft iron, and that and the gun's weight helps to dampen a discharge's whip when the bullet leaves the muzzle. Also, unlike a musket, the inside of a rifle's barrel is grooved, putting a spin on the bullet to improve its accuracy. The length of the barrel adds velocity, and it allows the rear sight to be set well forward, so that you can keep both it and its target in focus with the human eye." I squinted. One Mameluke was riding ahead of his fellows, just to the rear of the peasant mob shambling in front of him. Allowing for the wind off the ocean and the bullet's drop, I aimed high at his right shoulder. No firearm is perfect—even a rifle gripped in a vise won't put each bullet atop each other—but my gun's "triangle of error" was only two inches at a hundred paces. I squeezed the set trigger, its click releasing the first trigger so that the second was at hair touch, minimizing any jerk. Then I kept squeezing and fired, figuring the bullet would hit the man square in the torso. The rifle kicked, there was a haze of smoke, and then I watched the devil buck backward off his stallion. There was a murmur of appreciation, and if you don't think there's satisfaction in such a shot, then you don't understand what drives men to war. Well, I was in it now. I put the stock down butt first on the sand, ripped open a paper cartridge, and began to reload.

"A good shot," Bonaparte complimented. Musket fire was so inaccurate that if soldiers didn't aim for the enemy's feet, the kick of the gun could send a volley over their heads. The only way for armies to hit each other was to line up tightly and blast away from close distances.

"American?" the Arab queried. "So far from home?" The Bedouin wheeled his horse, preparing to leave. "To study our mysteries, perhaps?"

Now I remembered where I'd heard his voice! It was the same as the lantern bearer in Paris, the man who had led the gendarmes to me when I had discovered the body of Minette! "Wait! I know you!"

"I am Achmed bin Sadr, American, and you know nothing."

And before I could say anything more, he galloped off.

* * *

Under shouted orders the French troops rapidly assembled into what would be their favorite formation against Mameluke cavalry, a hollow square of men. The squares were several ranks thick, each of the four sides of men facing outward so that there was no flank to turn, their bayonets forming a four-sided hedge of steel. To crisp the ranks, some officers drew lines in the sand with their sabers. Meanwhile the Egyptian army, or more accurately, its rabble, began to stream toward us with ululating cries under a hammer of drums and blare of horns.

"Menou, form another square next to the dunes," Napoleon ordered. "Kleber, tell the rest of them to hurry." Many of the French troops were still coming up the beach.

Now the Egyptians were running straight at us, a tide of peasants armed with staves and sickles, pushed by a line of brilliantly dressed horsemen. The commoners looked terrified. When they got within fifty meters, the first French rank fired.

The crash of gunfire made me jump, and the result was as if a giant scythe had swept a rank of wheat. The front line of peasants was shredded, scores falling dead and wounded, the rest simply collapsing in fright from a disciplined volley unlike any they'd seen before. A huge sheet of white smoke lashed out, obscuring the French square. The Mameluke cavalry stopped in confusion, the horses wary of stepping on the carpet of cowering bodies before them, and their masters cursed the underlings they'd been driving to slaughter. As the overlords slowly forced their mounts forward over their cringing subjects, the second French rank fired, and this time some of the Mameluke warriors toppled from their horses. Then a third French rank let loose, even as the first was finishing reloading, and horses screamed, plunging and writhing. After this hurricane of bullets the surviving peasantry rose as if on command and fled, pushing the horsemen back with them and making a fiasco of the first Egyptian attack. The warriors slashed at their subjects with the flat of their swords but it did nothing to stem the flight. Some peasants pounded on the gates of the city, demanding refuge, and others ran inland, disappearing into the dunes. Meanwhile the French coastal ships started firing at Alexandria, the shots exploding against the city walls like a hammering fist. The ancient ramparts began crumbling like sand.

"War is essentially engineering," Napoleon remarked. "It is order imposed on disorder." He stood with hands clasped behind his back and head swiveling, absorbing details like an eagle. He was unusual in being able to hold in his mind's eye a picture of the entire battlefield and to know where concentration would turn the outcome, and this is what gave him his edge. "It is discipline triumphing over irresolution. It is organization applied against chaos. Do you know, Gage, it would be remarkable if even one percent of the bullets fired actually hit their target? That's why line, column, and square are so important."

As much as I was taken aback by the brutality of his militarism, his coolness impressed me. Here was a modern man of scientific calculation, bloody accounting, and emotionless reasoning. In a moment of directed violence, I saw the grim engineers who would rule the future. Morality would be trumped by arithmetic. Passion would be harnessed by ideology.

"Fire!"

More and more French troops were arriving near the city walls, and a third square formed to the seaward of the first, its left side ankle-deep in seawater when the waves surged in. Between the squares some light artillery pieces were placed and loaded with grapeshot, which would sweep enemy cavalry with small iron balls.

The Mamelukes, now unencumbered by their own peasantry, attacked again. Their cavalry charged at full tilt, thundering down the beach in a spray of sand and water, the men shouting war cries, silken robes billowing like sails, feathers and plumes bobbing on fantastic turbans. Their speed made no difference. The French fired again and the Mameluke front rank went down, horses screaming and hooves churning. Some of the horsemen just behind collided with their stricken comrades and somersaulted as well; others managed to dodge or jump them. Yet no sooner would their cavalry form a newly coherent front than the French would fire again, a ripple of flame, bits of wadding spitting out like confetti. This advance too would be torn. The bravest of the survivors came on anyway, hurtling the corpses of their comrades, only to be met with swathes of grapeshot or balls from the field cannon. It was simple slaughter, as mechanical as Bonaparte implied, and even though I'd been in scrapes during my fur-trapping days, the ferocity of this massed violence shocked me. The sound was cacophonous, the fired metal shrieking through the air, and the human body contained more blood than I'd thought possible. Great plumes of it sometimes geysered when a body was severed with round shot. A few horsemen stumbled all the way to the French lines, probing with lance or raising their swords, but they couldn't get their mounts to close with the hedge of bayonets. Then the command would ring out in French, another volley would be fired, and they'd go down too, riddled with balls.

What was left of the ruling caste finally broke and galloped for the desert.

"Now!" Napoleon roared. "To the wall, before their leaders regroup!" Bugles sounded and, with a cheer, a thousand troops formed column and trotted forward. They had no ladders or siege artillery but had little need for them. Under the naval bombardment the walls of the old city were coming apart like rotted cheese. Some of the houses beyond were already in flames. The French approached within musket range and a brisk fire broke out on both sides, the defenders showing more courage in the face of this furious onslaught than I'd have expected. Bullets whined like hornets and a few of the Europeans at last fell over, barely balancing the carnage left in their wake.

Napoleon followed, I by his side, the pair of us stepping past still or groaning bodies of the enemy, great dark stains in the sand beneath. I was surprised to see that many of the Mameluke slain had much fairer skin than their subjects, their bared heads revealing red or even blond hair.

"White slaves from the Caucasus," the gigantic Dumas

growled. "They'll couple with the Egyptians, it is said, but won't have pups by them. They also lay with each other, and prefer their own sex and race to any kind of contamination. Fresh boys eight years old are bought every year from their home mountains, creamy pink, to continue the caste. Rape is their initiation, and cruelty their school. By the time they're full-grown they're grim as wolves and contemptuous of anyone who's not a Mameluke. Their only loyalty is to their bey, or chief. They also recruit the occasional exceptional black or Arab, but most view darkness with contempt."

I looked at the general's own racially mixed skin. "I suspect you'll not allow Egypt to sustain that prejudice, General."

He kicked at a dead body. "*Oui*. It's the color of the heart that matters."

We stayed just out of range at the base of a mammoth solitary pillar that jutted up outside the city walls. It was seventy-five feet high, thick as a man is tall, and named for the old Roman general, Pompey. We were on the rubble of several civilizations, I saw: an old Egyptian obelisk overthrown to help make the pillar's base. The column's pink granite was pitted and warm to the touch. Bonaparte, hoarse from shouting orders, stood on the rubble in the pillar's meager shade. "This is hot work." Indeed, the sun had climbed surprisingly high. How much time had gone by?

"Here, take a fruit."

He glanced at me with appreciation and I thought perhaps this small gesture seeded friendship. Only later was I to learn that Napoleon valued anyone who could do him a service, was indifferent to those of no use, and implacable toward his enemies. But now he sucked greedily like a child, seemingly enjoying my company while showing his command of the tableau before us. "No, no, not that way," he'd occasionally call. "Yes, that gate over there, that's the one to force!"

It was Generals Kleber and Jacques François Menou who were at the forefront of the attack. The officers fought like madmen, as if they believed themselves invulnerable to bullets. I was equally impressed by the suicidal courage of the defenders, who knew they had no chance. But Bonaparte was the grand choreographer, directing his dance as if the soldiers were toys. His mind was already beyond the immediate fight. He glanced up at the pillar, crowned by a Corinthian capital that supported nothing. "Great glory has always been acquired in the Orient," he murmured.

The Arab fire was slackening. The French had reached the foot of the shattered walls and were boosting each other up. One gate was opened from within; another collapsed after being battered by axes and musket butts. A tricolor appeared on a tower top, and others were carried inside the city walls. The battle was almost over, and soon came the curious incident that changed my life.

It had been a savage scuffle. The Arabs had grown so desperate when they ran out of powder that they'd hurled rocks. General Menou, hit by stones seven times, came away so dazed and battered that it took him several days to recover. Kleber received a grazing bullet wound over one eye and stormed about with his forehead wrapped in a bloody bandage. Yet suddenly, as if instantaneously communicating to each other the hopelessness of their cause, the Egyptians broke like a ruptured dam and Europeans flooded in.

Some of the inhabitants hunkered down in abject fear, wondering what barbarities this tide of Christians would perform. Others crowded into mosques. Many streamed out of the city to the east and south, most returning within two days when they realized they had no food or water and nowhere to go. A handful of the most defiant barricaded themselves in the city's tower and citadel, but their shooting soon slackened from lack of gunpowder. French reprisal was swift and brutal. There were several small massacres.

Napoleon entered the city in early afternoon, as emotionally impervious to the wails of the wounded as he'd been to the thunder of the guns. "A small battle, hardly worth a bulletin," he remarked to Menou, bending over the litter that carried the bruised general. "Although I will inflate it for consumption in Paris. Tell your friend Talma to sharpen his quill, Gage." He winked. Bonaparte had adopted the certain wry cynicism all the French officers exhibited since the Terror. They took pride in being hard.

As a city, Alexandria was disappointing. The glories of the East were contradicted by unpaved streets, scurrying sheep and chickens, naked children, fly-spotted markets, and murderous sun. Much of it was old ruins, and even without the battle it would have seemed half-empty, a shell around former glory. There were even half-sunken buildings at the harbor's edge, as if the city was slowly settling into the sea. Only when we glimpsed the shadowy interiors of fine houses through smashed doorways did we get a sense of a second, cooler, more opulent, and more secretive world. There we spied splashing fountains, shaded porticoes, Moorish carving, and silks and linens gently billowing in currents of dry desert air.

Random gunfire still echoed across the city as Napoleon and a cluster of aides made their way cautiously down the main avenue for the harbor, where the first French masts were now appearing. We were passing a fine section of merchant homes, with fitted stonework and wood-grilled windows, when there was a whine like an insect and a section of plaster exploded in a little geyser of dust just past Bonaparte's shoulder. I started, since the shot had barely missed me. The grazing had made the cloth fiber of our general's uniform suddenly stand erect like a file of his troops. Looking up, we saw a puff of white gun smoke at a screened window being wafted away by the hot wind. A marksman, firing from the shadowy shelter of a bedroom, had almost hit the expedition's commander.

"General! Are you all right?" a colonel cried.

As if in reply, a second shot rang out, and then a third, so close to the first that there were either two marksmen or the former was having his hands steadily filled with reloaded muskets. A sergeant standing a few paces ahead of Napoleon grunted and sat down, a bullet in his thigh, and another patch of plaster exploded behind the general's boot.

"I'll be more right behind a post," Bonaparte muttered, pulling our group under a portico and making the sign of the cross. "Shoot back, for God's sake." Two soldiers finally did so. "And bring up an artillery piece. Let's not give them all day to hit me."

A lively fight broke out. Several grenadiers began blasting away at the house that had become a doughty little fortress, and others ran back for a field gun. I took aim with my rifle, but the sniper was well screened: I missed like everyone else. It was a long ten minutes before a six-pounder appeared, and by this time several dozen shots had been exchanged, one of them wounding a young captain in the arm. Napoleon himself had borrowed a musket and fired a shot, to no better effect than the others.

It was the artillery piece that excited our commander. This was the arm he'd trained in. At Valence his regiment was exposed to the best cannon training in the army, and at Auxonne he had worked with the legendary Professor Jean Louis Lombard, who had translated the English *Principles of Artillery* into French. Napoleon's fellow officers had told me on *L'Orient* that he'd had no social life in these early posts as a second lieutenant, instead working and studying from four in the morning until ten at night. Now he aimed the cannon, even as bullets continued to peck around him.

"It's exactly as he did at the battle of Lodi," the wounded captain murmured in appreciation. "He lay some guns himself, and the men began calling him *le petit caporal*—the little corporal."

Napoleon applied the match. The gun barked, bucking against its carriage, and the round shot screamed and hit just below the offending window, buckling the stone and blowing apart the wooden grill.

"Again."

The gun was hastily reloaded and the general trained it at the house door. Another report and the entry blew inward in a shower of splinters. Smoke fogged the street.

"Forward!" This was the same Napoleon who had charged Arcola Bridge. The French advanced, me with them, their general with his sword out. We burst through the entry, firing at the stairs. A servant, young and black, came rolling down. Leaping over his body, the assault team surged upward. On the third floor we came to the place that the cannonball had struck. The ragged hole looked out on the rooftops of Alexandria and the chamber was strewn with rubble. An old man with a musket was half-buried with broken stone, obviously dead. Another musket had been hurled against a wall, its stock broken. Several more were scattered like matchsticks. A second figure, perhaps his loader, had been pitched into a corner by the concussion of the cannon shot, and moved feebly under a shroud of debris.

No one else was in the house.

"Quite a fusillade from an army of two," Napoleon commented. "If all Alexandrians fought like this, I'd still be outside the walls."

I went to the dazed fighter in the corner, wondering who the pair might be. The old man we'd killed didn't look entirely Arab, and there was something strange about his assistant, too. I lifted a section of shattered sash.

"Careful, Monsieur Gage, he might have a weapon," Bonaparte warned. "Let Georges here finish him with the bayonet."

I'd seen quite enough bayoneting for one day and ignored them. I knelt and lifted the dazed assailant's head to my lap. The figure groaned and blinked, eyes unfocused. A plea came out as a croak. "Water."

I started at the tone and fine features. The injured fighter was actually a woman, I realized, smudged by powder residue but otherwise recognizable as young, unwounded, and quite fine-looking.

And the request had been stated in English.

A search of the house revealed some water in jars on the ground floor. I gave the woman a cup, as curious as the French what her story might be. This gesture, and my own voice in English, seemed to earn some small measure of trust. "What's your name, lady?"

She swallowed and blinked, staring at the ceiling. "Astiza."

"Why are you fighting us?"

Now she focused on me, her eyes widening in surprise as if I were a ghost. "I was loading the guns."

"For your father?"

"My master." She struggled up. "Is he dead?"

"Yes."

Her expression was inscrutable. Clearly she was a slave or a servant; was she sad that her owner had been killed or relieved at her liberation? She seemed to be considering her new position with shock. I noticed an oddly shaped amulet hanging from her neck. It was gold, incongruous for a slave, and shaped like an almond eye, black onyx forming its pupil. A brow curled above, and there was an extension below in another graceful curve. The entire effect was quite arresting. Meanwhile, she kept glancing from her master's body to me.

"What's she saying?" Bonaparte demanded in French.

"I think she's a slave. She was loading muskets for her master, that man there."

"How does an Egyptian slave know English? Are these British spies?"

I put his first question to her.

"Master Omar had an Egyptian mother and an English father," she replied. "He had merchant ties with England. To perfect his fluency, we used the language in this house. I speak Arabic and Greek as well."

"Greek?"

"My mother was sold from Macedonia to Cairo. I was raised there. I am a Greek Egyptian, and impudent." She said it with pride.

I turned to the general. "She could be an interpreter," I said in French. "She speaks Arabic, Greek, and English."

"An interpreter for you, not me. I should treat her as a partisan." He was grumpy from being shot at.

"She was following the instruction of her master. She has Macedonian blood."

Now he became interested. "Macedonia? Alexander the Great was Macedonian; he founded this city, and conquered the East before us."

I have a soft spot for women, and Napoleon's fascination with the old Greek empire builder gave me an idea. "Don't you think that Astiza's survival after your cannon shot is a portent of fate? How many Macedonians can there be in this city? And here we encounter one who speaks my native tongue. She may be more useful alive than dead. She can help explain Egypt to us."

"What would a slave know?"

I regarded her. She was watching our conversation without understanding but her eyes were wide, bright, and intelligent. "She's had learning of some kind."

Well, talk of fate always intrigued him. "Her luck, then, and my own, that you're the one to find her. Tell her that I have killed her master in battle and thus have become her new master. And that I, Napoleon, award her care to my American ally—you."

CHAPTER SEVEN

Victory is sometimes more untidy than battle. An assault can be simplicity itself; administration an entangling nightmare. So it was in Alexandria. Bonaparte quickly accepted the surrender of ruling sultan Mohammed el-Koraim and swiftly unloaded the rest of his troops, artillery, and horses. The soldiers and scientists rejoiced for five minutes upon reaching dry land, and then immediately began grumbling about the lack of shelter, shortage of good water, and confusion of supply. The heat was palpable, a weight one pushed against, and dust covered everything with fine powder. There were three hundred French casualties and more than a thousand Alexandrian dead and wounded, with no adequate hospital for either group. The wounded Europeans were tucked into mosques or confiscated palaces, the comfort of their regal surroundings marred by pain, heat, and buzzing flies. The Egyptian injured were left to take care of themselves. Many died.

Meanwhile, the transports were sent back to France and the battleships placed in defensive anchorage at nearby Abukir Bay. The invaders still feared the reappearance of Nelson's fleet.

Most debarking soldiers found themselves either camping in the city's squares or in the dunes outside. Officers were luckier, appropriating the finer homes. Talma and I shared, with several officers, the home I'd helped capture from Astiza's master. Once the slave woman had recovered her senses she seemed to accept her new situation with odd equanimity, studying me out of the corner of her eye as if trying to decide if I was entirely a calamity or perhaps some new opportunity. It was she who took some coins, bartered with neighbors, and found us food, even while murmuring about our ignorance of Egyptian ways and barbaric habits. As if acquiescing to destiny, she adopted us as we'd adopted her. She was dutiful but wary, obedient but resigned, watchful but skittish. I was intrigued by her, as I am by too many women. Franklin had the same weakness and so, indeed, did the entire army: there were hundreds of wives, mistresses, and enterprising prostitutes. Once on land, the French women discarded their male disguises for dresses that displayed more of their charms, much to the horror of the Egyptians. The females also turned out to be at least as tough as their men, enduring the primitive conditions with less complaint than the soldiers. The Arab men regarded them with fear and fascination.

To keep his troops occupied, Napoleon sent some marching southeast toward the Nile by land, a seemingly simple sojourn of sixty miles. Yet this first step toward the capital at Cairo proved cruel, because what had been promised to be rich delta farmland was stunted at this end of the dry season, just before the Nile flood. Some wells were dry. Others had been poisoned or filled with stone. Villages were mud brick and thatch, and farmers tried to hoard their few scrawny goats or chickens. The troops initially thought the peasants exceedingly ignorant because they'd disdain French money and yet reluctantly trade food and water for the soldiers' buttons. Only later did we learn that the peasants expected their ruling Mamelukes to win, and that while a French coin would signal collaboration with the Christians, a button would be assumed to have been cut from European dead.

Their stifling march could be tracked by its pillar of dust. The heat exceeded one hundred degrees and some soldiers, depressed and crazed by thirst, committed suicide.

Things were not quite so grim for those of us back in Alexandria. Thousands of bottles of wine were unloaded alongside the tack of infantry rations, and bright dress uniforms filled the streets like an aviary of tropical birds, rainbow plumage highlighted by epaulettes, braid, frogging, and stripes. The dragoons and fusiliers were in green coats, the officers were wrapped at the waist with brilliant red sashes, the chasseurs had upright tricolor cockades, and the carabiniers boasted plumes of scarlet. I began to learn something about armies. Some branches took their name from their weapons, such as the light musket called a fusil that had originally equipped the fusiliers, the grenades apportioned to the heavy infantry called grenadiers, and the short carbines distributed to the blue-clad carabiniers. The chasseurs, or chasers, were light troops equipped for rapid action. The red-jacketed hussars were light cavalry or scouts, who took their name from cousin units in central Europe. The dragoons were heavy cavalry who wore helmets to ward off saber strokes.

The general plan of battle was for light infantry to disrupt and confuse the enemy as artillery pounded, until a line or column of heavy infantry with massed firepower could deliver the decisive blow to break the opposing formation. Cavalry would then swoop in to finish the destruction. In practice, the tasks of these units sometimes blurred together, and in Egypt the French army's task was simplified by the Mameluke reliance on cavalry and the French shortage of same.

Added to the French force was the Legion of Malta, recruited when that island was taken, and Arab mercenaries like Achmed bin Sadr. Napoleon already had plans to enlist a company of Mamelukes, once he had defeated them, and to organize a camel corps of Egyptian Christians.

The land force totaled thirty-four thousand, of which twenty-eight thousand were infantry and three thousand each were cavalry and artillery. There was an acute shortage of horses that would be remedied in Egypt only slowly and with difficulty. Bonaparte did unload 171 cannon, ranging from twenty-four-pounder siege guns to light field pieces capable of getting off up to three shots per minute, but again, the lack of horses limited how many he could immediately bring along. Rank-and-file infantry were even more ill equipped, suffering in the heat from heavy 1777 muskets, leather backpacks, blue Alpine wool uniforms, and bicorne hats. The dragoons boiled in their brass helmets, and military collars became stiff with salt. We savants were not as rigidly dressed—our jackets could come off—but we were equally dazed by the heat, gasping like landed fish. Except when traveling, I went without the garment that had given me the nickname "green coat" (as well as "the Franklin man") from the soldiers. One of Bonaparte's first orders was to secure enough cotton for new uniforms, but they wouldn't be ready for months and, when they were, proved too cold for winter.

The city itself was a disappointment, as I've said. It seemed half-empty, and half-ruined. There was no treasure, little shade, and no Ottoman temptresses. The richest and most beautiful Arab women were cloistered out of sight or had escaped to Cairo. Those few who did appear were usually shrouded head to foot like Inquisition priests, peering at the world over the brim of veils or through tiny slit-holes in their hoods. In contrast, peasant women were immodestly dressed—some of the poor showed their breasts as casually as their feet—but looked scrawny, dusty, and diseased. Talma's promise of lush harems and exotic dancing girls seemed a cruel joke.

Nor had my companion found any miracle cures yet. He announced he was succumbing to new fevers within hours of debarking, and disappeared into the souk seeking drugs. What he returned with were quack remedies. A man who gagged at red meat gamely tried such ancient Egyptian medicines as worm's blood, ass's dung, pounded garlic, mother's milk, hog's tooth, tortoise brain, and snake venom.

"Talma, all you're getting is a case of the runs," I lectured.

"It's purging my system. My druggist told me of Egyptian priests a thousand years old. He looks venerable himself."

"I asked and he's forty. The heat and his poisons have wrinkled him like a raisin."

"I'm sure he was joking. He told me that when the cramps go away, I'll have the vigor of a sixteen-year-old."

"And the sense, apparently."

Talma was newly flush with money. Though a civilian, his role as journalist made him essentially an adjunct of the army, and he'd written an account of our assault so flattering that I scarcely recognized it. Bonaparte's chief of staff, Berthier, had accordingly quietly slipped him some extra pay as reward. But I saw little in Alexandria's markets worth buying. The souk was hot, shadowy, swarming with flies, and poorly stocked after our capture of the city. Even so, through shrewd bargaining, the wily merchants fleeced our bored soldiers more thoroughly than their own city had been pillaged. They learned clumsy French with astonishing rapidity. "Come, look my stall, monsieur! Here is what you want! Not you want? Then I know you need!"

Astiza was a happy exception to our disillusion. Picked out of the rubble and given a chance to clean herself, she wrought a wondrous transformation. Neither as fair as the fierce Mamelukes nor as dark as common Egyptians, her features, bearing, and complexion were simply Mediterranean: skin of sun-polished olive, hair jet but streaked with strands of copper, lavish in its thickness, eyes almond shaped and liquid, her gaze demure, her hands and ankles fine, her breasts high, waist thin, hips transfixing. An enchantress, in other words, a Cleopatra, and I relished my luck until she made clear she viewed her rescue as dubious, and me with distrust.

"You're a plague of barbarians," she announced. "You're the kind of men who belong nowhere, and thus go everywhere, disrupting the lives of sensible people."

"We're here to help you."

"Did I ask for your help, at the point of a gun? Did Egypt ask to be invaded, to be investigated, to be saved?"

"It's oppressed," I argued. "It invited rescue by being backward."

"Backward to whom? My people were in palaces when yours were in huts. What about your own home?"

"I have no home, really."

"No parents?"

"Deceased."

"No wife?"

"Unattached." I grinned, fetchingly.

"I shouldn't wonder. No country?"

"I've always liked travel and had a chance to visit France when I was still a youth. I finished growing up there with a famous man named Benjamin Franklin. I like America, my native land, but I have wanderlust. Besides, wives want to nest."

She looked at me with pity. "It's not natural, how you spend your life."

"It is if you like adventure." I decided to change the subject. "What's that interesting necklace you wear?"

"An eye of Horus, homeless one."

"Eye of who?"

"Horus is the hawk god who lost his eye battling the evil Seth." Now I remembered! Something to do with resurrection, brother-and-sister sex, and this Horus as the incestuous result. Scandalous stuff. "As Egypt battles your Napoleon, so did Horus battle darkness. The amulet is good luck."

I smiled. "Does that mean it's lucky you now belong to me?"

"Or lucky that I live long enough to see you all go away."

She cooked us dishes I couldn't name—lamb with chickpeas and lentils, it tasted like—serving it with such grim duty that I was tempted to adopt one of the stray dogs to test each meal for poison. Yet the food was surprisingly good and she refused to take any pay. "If I'm caught with your coins I'll be beheaded, once the Mamelukes kill you all."

Nor did her services extend into the evenings, even though coastal Egyptian nights can be as cool as the days are hot.

"In New England we bundle together to ward off the chill," I informed her that first evening. "You're welcome to come closer if you'd like."

"If not for the invasion of our house by all your officers, we wouldn't even be in the same room."

"Because of the teachings of the Prophet?"

"My teachings come from an Egyptian goddess, not the Mameluke women-haters who rule my country. And you're not my husband, you're my captor. Besides, all of you smell of pig."

I sniffed, somewhat discouraged. "So you're not Muslim?"

"No."

"Nor Jewish or Coptic Christian or Greek Catholic?"

"No."

"And who is this goddess?"

"One you've never heard of."

"Tell me. I'm here to learn."

"Then understand what a blind man could see. Egyptians have lived on this land for ten thousand years, not asking, or needing, anything new. We've had a dozen conquerors, and not one has brought us as much contentment as we originally had. Hundreds of generations of restless men like you have only made things worse, not better." She'd say little more, since she considered me too ignorant to comprehend her faith and too kind to beat anything out of her. Instead she complied with my orders while carrying herself like a duchess. "Egypt is the only ancient land in which women had rights equal to men," she claimed, meanwhile remaining impervious to wit and charm.

It baffled me, frankly.

Bonaparte was having equal trouble winning over the population. He issued a proclamation of some length. I can give a sense of its tone, and his political instincts, by quoting its start:

> In the name of God, the clement and the merciful. There is no divinity save Allah, He has no son and shares His power with no one.
>
> In the name of the French Republic, founded on liberty and equality, the commander-in-chief Bonaparte lets it be known that the beys who govern Egypt have insulted the French nation and oppressed French merchants long enough: the hour of their punishment has come.
>
> For too many years the Mameluke gang of slaves, purchased in Georgia and the Caucasus, has tyrannized the

most beautiful region of the world. But Almighty God, who rules the Universe, has decreed that their reign shall come to an end.

People of Egypt, you will be told that I have come to destroy your religion. Do not believe it! Answer back to those imposters that I have come to restore to you your rights and to punish the usurpers; that I worship God more than the Mamelukes do and that I respect His Prophet Muhammad and the admirable Koran . . .

"Quite a religious beginning," I remarked as Dolomieu read this with mocking drama.

"Especially for a man who believes completely in the utility of religion and not at all about the reality of God," the geologist replied. "If the Egyptians swallow this load of stable dung, they deserve to be conquered."

A later clause in the proclamation got more to the point: "All villages that take up arms against the army will be burned to the ground."

Napoleon's religious entreaties soon came to naught. Word reached Alexandria that the mullahs of Cairo had declared all of us to be infidels. So much for revolutionary liberalism and the unity of religion! A contract for three hundred horses and five hundred camels that had been negotiated with local sheikhs immediately evaporated, and sniping and harassment increased. The seduction of Egypt was going to prove more difficult than Bonaparte had hoped. Most of his cavalry would march the early stages of his advance on Cairo carrying their saddles on their heads, and he would learn much in this campaign about the importance of logistics and supply.

Meanwhile, the people of Alexandria were disarmed and ordered to wear the tricolor cockade. The few who complied looked ridiculous. Talma, however, wrote that the population was joyful at their liberation from their Mameluke masters.

"How can you mail such rubbish back to France?" I said. "Half the population has fled, the city is pockmarked with cannonball holes, and its economy has collapsed."

"I'm talking about the spirit, not the body. Their hearts are uplifted."

"Who says so?"

"Bonaparte. Our benefactor, and our only source of orders to get back home."

It was on my third night in Alexandria that I realized I hadn't left my pursuers behind at the Toulon coach.

It had been hard enough to get to sleep. Word was starting to filter back of atrocities committed by the Bedouin on any soldier caught alone from his unit. These desert tribesmen roamed the Arabian and Libyan Deserts like pirates roam the sea, preying indiscriminately on merchants, pilgrims, and army stragglers. Mounted on camels and able to retreat back into the waste, they were beyond the reach of our army. They would kill or capture the unwary. Men were raped, burned, castrated, or staked out to die in the desert. I've always been cursed with a vivid imagination for such things and I could envision all too clearly how throats might be cut while troops slept. Scorpions were slipped into boots and backpacks. Snakes were concealed between jars of food. Carcasses were thrown into tempting wells. Supply was a tangle, the scientists were restless and grumpy, and Astiza remained as reserved as a nun in a barracks. Moving in the heat was like dragging a heavy sled. What madness had I enlisted in? I'd made no progress in deciphering what the medallion might mean, seeing nothing like it in Alexandria. So I brooded, troubled and dissatisfied, until I was finally exhausted enough to drift off.

I came awake with a jolt. Someone or something had landed on top of me! I was groping for a weapon when I recognized the scent of cloves and jasmine. Astiza? Had she changed her mind? She was straddling me, a silken thigh locked on either side of my chest, and even in my sleepy stupor my first thought was, Ah, this is more like it. The warm squeeze of her legs began to awaken all parts of me, and her tumble of hair and enchanting torso were delectably silhouetted in the dark. Then the moon moved from a cloud and enough light sifted in our grilled window to see that her arms were high over her head, holding something bright and sharp.

It was my tomahawk.

She swung.

I twisted in terror but she had me pinned. The blade whistled by my ear and there was a sharp thunk as it bit the wooden floor, joined by a hiss. Something warm and alive slapped the top of my head. She freed the tomahawk and chopped again, and again, the blade thunking next to my ear. I stayed paralyzed as something leathery kept writhing against my crown. Finally it was still.

"Serpent," she whispered. She glanced at the window. "Bedouin."

She climbed off and I shakily stood. Some kind of viper had been chopped into several portions, I saw, its blood spattered on my pillow. It was as thick as a child's arm, fangs jutting from its mouth. "Someone put this here?"

"Dropped through the window. I heard the villain scuttling like a roach, too cowardly to face us. You should give me a gun so I can properly protect you."

"Protect me from what?"

"You know nothing, American. Why is Achmed bin Sadr asking about you?"

"Bin Sadr!" He was the one who delivered severed hands and ears, and whose voice had sounded like the lantern bearer in Paris, as nonsensical as that seemed. "I didn't know he was."

"Every person in Alexandria knows you have made him your enemy. He's not an enemy you want to have. He roams the world, has a gang of assassins, and is a follower of Apophis."

"Who the devil is Apophis?"

"The serpent god of the underworld who each night must be defeated by Ra, the sun god, before dawn can return. He has legions of minions, like the demon god Ras al-Ghul."

By Washington's dentures, here was more pagan nonsense. Had I acquired a lunatic? "Sounds like a lot of trouble for your sun god," I quipped shakily. "Why doesn't he just chop him up like you did and be done with it?"

"Because while Apophis can be defeated, he can never be destroyed. This is how the world works. All things are eternally dual, water and land, earth and sky, good and evil, life and death."

I kicked aside the serpent. "So this is the work of some kind of snake cult?"

She shook her head. "How could you get in so much trouble so quickly?"

"But I've done nothing to Bin Sadr. He's our ally!"

"He's no one's ally but his own. You have something he wants."

I looked at the chunks of reptile. "What?" But of course I knew, feeling the medallion's weight on its chain. Bin Sadr was the lantern bearer with his snake-headed staff who somehow had a dual identity as a desert pirate. He must have been working for Count Silano the night I'd won the medallion. How had he gotten from Paris to Alexandria? Why was he some kind of henchman for Napoleon? Why did he care about the medallion? Wasn't he on our side? I was half tempted to give the thing to the next assailant who came along and be done with it. But what annoyed me is that no one ever asked politely. They shoved pistols in my face, stole boots, and threw snakes at my bed.

"Let me sleep in your corner, away from the window," I asked my protectress. "I'm going to load my rifle."

To my surprise she assented. But instead of lying with me, she squatted at the brazier, fanning its coals and sifting some leaves into it. A pungent smoke arose. She was making a small human figure out of wax, I saw. I watched her push a sliver of wood into the figure's cheek. I had seen the same thing in the Sugar Isles. Had the magic originated in Egypt? She began to make curious marks on a sheet of papyrus.

"What are you doing?"

"Go to sleep. I'm casting a spell."

Since I was anxious to get out of Alexandria before another serpent landed on my head, I was more than happy when the scientists gave me an early opportunity to move on toward Cairo without having to cross the hot delta of land. Monge and Berthollet were going to make the journey by boat. The savants would sail east to the mouth of the Nile and then ascend the river to the capital.

"Come along, Gage," Monge offered. "Better to ride than walk. Bring the scribe Talma, too. Your girl can help cook for all of us."

We would use a *chebek,* a shallow-draft sailing craft named *Le Cerf,* armed with four eight-pounders and skippered by Captain Jacques Perree of the French navy. It would be the flagship of a little flotilla of gunboats and supply craft that would follow the army upriver.

By first light we were underway, and by midday we were skirting Abukir Bay, a day's march east of Alexandria. There the French fleet had anchored in line of battle, in defense against any reappearance of Nelson's ships. It was an awesome sight, a dozen ships of the line and four frigates moored in an unbroken wall, five hundred guns pointed at the sea. We could hear the bosun whistles and cries of the sailors float over the water as we passed. Then on we went toward the great river, sailing into the brown plume that curled into the Mediterranean and bouncing over the standing waves at the river bar.

As the day's heat rose I learned more about the genesis of the expedition. Egypt, Berthollet informed me, had been the object of French fascination for decades. Sealed from the outside world by the Arab conquest of A.D. 640, its ancient glories were unseen by most Europeans, its fabled pyramids known more by fantastic story than fact. A nation the size of France was largely unknown.

"No country in the world has history as deep as Egypt," the chemist told me. "When the Greek historian Herodotus came to record its glories, the pyramids were already older to him than Jesus is to us. The Egyptians themselves built a great empire, and then a dozen conquerors made their mark here: Greeks, Romans, Assyrians, Libyans, Nubians, Persians. This country's beginning is so old no one remembers it. No one can read hieroglyphics, so we don't know what any of the inscriptions say. Today's Egyptians say the ruins were built by giants or wizards."

So Egypt slumbered, he related, until in recent years the handful of French merchants in Alexandria and Cairo had come under harassment from the arrogant Mamelukes. The Ottoman overseers in Constantinople who had governed Egypt since 1517 had shown little desire to intervene. Nor did France wish to offend the Ottomans, its useful ally against Russia. So the situation simmered until Bonaparte, with his youthful dreams of Oriental glory, encountered Talleyrand, with his grasp of global geopolitics. Between them the pair had seized upon the scheme of "liberating" Egypt from the Mameluke caste as a "favor" to the sultan in Constantinople. They would reform a backward corner of the Arab world and create a springboard to contest British advances in India. "The European power that controls Egypt," Napoleon had written to the Directory, "will, in the long run, control India." There was hope of recreating the ancient canal that had once linked the Mediterranean and Red Seas. The ultimate goal was to link up with an Indian pasha named Tippoo Sahib, a Francophile who had visited Paris and went by the title "Citizen Tippoo," and whose palace entertainment included a mechanical tiger that devoured puppet Englishmen. Tippoo was fighting a British general named Wellesley in southern India, and France had already sent him arms and advisers.

"The war in Italy more than paid for itself," Berthollet said, "and thanks to Malta, this one is guaranteed to do so as well. The Corsican has made himself popular with the Directory because his battles turn a profit."

"You still think of Bonaparte as Italian?"

"His mother's child. He told us a story once of how she disapproved of his rudeness to guests. He was too big to paddle, so she waited until he was undressing, unclothed enough to be embarrassed and defenseless, and pounced on him to twist his ear. Patience and revenge are the lessons of a Corsican! A Frenchman enjoys life, but an Italian like Bonaparte plots it. Like the ancient Romans or the bandits of Sicily, his kind believes in clan, avarice, and revenge. He's a brilliant soldier, but remembers so many slights and humiliations that he sometimes doesn't know when to stop making war. That, I suspect, is his weakness."

"So what are you doing here, Doctor Berthollet? You, and the rest of the scholars? Not military glory, surely. Nor treasure."

"Do you know anything at all about Egypt, Monsieur Gage?"

"It has sand, camels, and sun. Beyond that, very little."

"You're honest. None of us know much about this cradle of civilization. Stories come back of vast ruins, strange idols, and indecipherable writing, but who in Europe has really seen these things? Men want to learn. What is Maltese gold compared to being the first to see the glories of ancient Egypt? I came for the kind of discovery that makes men truly immortal."

"Through renown?"

"Through knowledge that will live forever."

"Or through knowledge of ancient magic," amended Talma. "That is why Ethan and I were invited along, is it not?"

"If your friend's medallion is truly magical," the chemist replied. "There's a difference between history and fable, of course."

"And a difference between mere desire for a piece of jewelry and the ruthlessness to kill to possess it," the scribe countered. "Our American here has been in danger since winning it in Paris. Why? Not because it's the key to academic glory. It's the key to something else. If not the secret to real immortality, then perhaps lost treasure."

"Which only proves that treasure can be more trouble than it's worth."

"Discovery is better than gold, Berthollet?" I asked, trying to feign nonchalance at all this dire talk.

"What is gold but a means to an end? Here we have that end. The best things in life cost nothing: Knowledge, integrity, love, natural beauty. Look at you here, entering the mouth of the Nile with an exquisite woman. You are another

Antony, with another Cleopatra! What is more satisfying than that?" He lay back to nap.

I glanced at Astiza, who was beginning to pick up French but seemed content to ignore our chatter and watch the low brown houses of Rosetta as we sailed by. A beautiful woman, yes. But one who seemed as locked and remote as the secrets of Egypt.

"Tell me about your ancestor," I suddenly asked her in English.

"What?" She looked at me in alarm, never anxious for casual conversation.

"Alexander. He was Macedonian like you, no?"

She seemed embarrassed to be addressed by a man in public but slowly nodded, as if to concede she was in the grasp of rustics and had to accede to our clumsy ways. "And Egyptian by choice, once he saw this great land. No man has ever matched him."

"And he conquered Persia?"

"He marched from Macedonia to India, and before he was done people thought he was a god. He conquered Egypt long before this French upstart of yours, and traversed the pitiless sands of our desert to attend the Spring of the Sun at the oasis at Siwah. There he was given tools of magic power, and the oracle proclaimed him a god, son of Zeus and Amon, and predicted he would rule the entire world."

"Must have been a convenient endorsement to have."

"It was his delight with this prophecy that convinced him to found the great city of Alexandria. He marked out its limits with peeled barley, in the Greek custom. When birds flocked to eat the barley, alarming Alexander's followers, his seers said this meant that newcomers would migrate to the new city and it would feed many lands. They were right. But the Macedonian general needed no prophets."

"No?"

"He was a master of destiny. Yet he died or was murdered before he could finish his task, and his sacred symbols from Siwah disappeared. So did Alexander. Some say his body was taken back to Macedonia, some say to Alexandria, but others say Ptolemy took him to a secret, final resting place in the desert sands. Like your Jesus ascending to Heaven, he seems to have disappeared from Earth. So perhaps he was a god, as the Oracle said. Like Osiris, taking his place in the heavens."

This was no mere slave or serving girl. How the devil had Astiza learned all this? "I've heard of Osiris," I said. "Reassembled by his sister Isis."

For the first time she looked at me with something resembling true enthusiasm. "You know Isis?"

"A mother goddess, right?"

"Isis and the Virgin Mary are reflections of each other."

"Christians wouldn't care to hear that."

"No? All kinds of Christian beliefs and symbols come from Egyptian gods. Resurrection, the afterlife, impregnation by a god, triads and trinities, the idea a man could be both human and divine, sacrifice, even the wings of angels and the hooves and forked tail of devils: all this predates your Jesus by thousands of years. The code of your Ten Commandments is a simpler version of the negative confession Egyptians made to profess their innocence when they died: 'I did not kill.' Religion is like a tree. Egypt is the trunk, and all others are branches."

"That's not what the Bible says. There were false idols, and the true Hebrew god."

"How ignorant you are of your own beliefs! I've heard you French say your cross is a Roman symbol of execution, but what kind of symbol is that for a religion of hope? The truth is that the cross combined your savior's instrument of death with our instrument of life, the ankh, our ancient key of life everlasting. And why not? Egypt was the most Christian of all countries before the Arabs came."

By the ghost of Cotton Mather, I could have paddled her for blasphemy if I hadn't been so dumbfounded. It wasn't just what she was claiming, but the casual confidence with which she claimed it. "No Biblical ideas possibly came from Egypt," I sputtered.

"I thought the Hebrews escaped from Egypt? And that the infant Jesus resided here? Besides, what does it matter—I thought your general assured us yours is not an army of Christians anyway? Godless men of science, are you not?"

"Well, Bonaparte puts on and takes off faiths like men do a coat."

"Or faiths and sciences have more unity than Franks care to admit. Isis is a goddess of knowledge, love, and tolerance."

"And Isis is *your* goddess."

"Isis belongs to no one. I am her servant."

"You truly worship an old idol?" My Philadelphia pastor would be apoplectic by now.

"She is newer than your last breath, American, as eternal as the cycle of birth. But I don't expect you to understand. I had to flee my Cairo master because he finally didn't either, and dared corrupt the old mysteries."

"What mysteries?"

"Of the world around you. Of the sacred triangle, the square of four directions, the pentagram of free will and the hexagram of harmony. Have you not read Pythagoras?"

"He studied in Egypt, right?"

"For twenty-two years, before being taken by the Persian conqueror Cambyses to Babylon and then finally founding his school in Italy. He taught the unity of all religions and peoples, that suffering was to be endured bravely, and that a wife was a husband's equal."

"He sounds like he saw things your way."

"He saw things the gods' way! In geometry and space is the gods' message. The geometric point represents God, the line represents man and woman, and the triangle the perfect number representing spirit, soul, and body."

"And the square?"

"The four directions, as I said. The pentagon was strife, the hexagram the six directions of space, and the double square was universal harmony."

"Believe it or not, I've heard some of this from a group called the Freemasons. It claims to teach as Pythagoras did, and says the ruler represents precision, the square rectitude, and the mallet will."

She nodded. "Precisely. The gods make everything clear, and yet men remain blind! Seek truth, and the world becomes yours."

Well, this scrap of the world, anyway. We were well into the Nile, that wondrous waterway where the wind often blows south and the current flows north, allowing river traffic both ways.

"You said you fled Cairo. You're an escaped slave?"

"It's more complicated than that. Egyptian." She pointed. "Understand our land before you try to understand our mind."

The pancake plainness of the country outside Alexandria had changed to the lush, more biblical picture I had expected from stories of Moses among the reeds. Brilliantly green fields of rice, wheat, corn, sugar, and cotton formed rectangles between ranks of stately date palms, as straight as pillars and heavy with their orange and scarlet fruit. Banana and sycamore groves rustled in the wind. Water buffalo pulled plows or lifted their horns from the river where they bathed, grunting at the fringe of papyrus beds. The frequency of chocolate-colored mud-brick villages increased, often topped by the needle of a minaret. We passed lateen-rigged felucca boats moored on the brown water. Measuring twenty to thirty feet long and steered by a long oar, these sailing craft were omnipresent on the river. There were smaller paddle skiffs, barely big enough to float an individual, from which fishermen tossed string nets. Harnessed and blindfolded donkeys drudged in a circle to lift water into canals in a scene unchanged for five thousand years. The smell of Nile water filled the river breeze. Our flotilla of gunboats and supply craft paraded past, French tricolor flapping, without leaving any discernible impression. Many peasants hardly bothered to look up.

What a strange place I'd come to. Alexander, Cleopatra, Arabs, Mamelukes, ancient pharaohs, Moses, and now Bonaparte. The entire country was a rubbish heap of history, including the odd medallion around my neck. Now I wondered about Astiza, who seemed to have a more complicated past than I'd suspected. Might she recognize something in the medallion that I would not?

"What spell did you cast back in Alexandria?"

It took a moment before she reluctantly replied. "One for your safety, as a warning to another. A second for the beginning of your wisdom."

"You can make me smart?"

"That may be impossible. Perhaps I can make you see."

I laughed, and she finally allowed a slight smile. By listening to her, I was getting her to let me inside a little. She wanted respect, not just for her but for her nation.

That languid night, as we lay at anchor and slept on the deck of the *chebek* under a desert haze of stars, I crept close to where she was sleeping. I could hear the lap of water, the creak of rigging, and the murmur of sailors on watch.

"Keep away from me," she whispered when she woke, squeezing herself against the wood.

"I want to show you something."

"Here? Now?" She had the same tone of suspicion Madame Durrell used when we discussed payment of my rent.

"You're the historian of plain truths. Look at this." I passed the medallion to her. In the glow of a deck lantern it was just discernible.

She felt with her fingers and sucked in her breath. "Where did you get this?" Her eyes widened, her lips slightly parted.

"I won it in a card game in Paris."

"Won it from whom?"

"A French soldier. It's supposed to come from Egypt. Cleopatra, he claimed."

"Perhaps you *stole* it from this soldier." Why would she say that?

"No, just outplayed him at cards. You're the religious expert. Tell me if you know what it is."

She turned it in her hand, extending the arms to make a V, and rubbed the disc between thumb and forefinger to feel its inscriptions. "I'm not sure."

That was disappointing. "Is it Egyptian?"

She held it up to see in the dim light. "Very early, if it is. It seems primitive, fundamental . . . so *this* is what the Arab lusts for."

"See all those holes? What do you think they are?"

Astiza regarded it for a moment and then rolled on her back, holding it up toward the sky. "Look at the way the light shines through. Clearly, they are supposed to be stars."

"Stars?"

"Life's purpose is written on the sky, American. Look!" She pointed south toward the brightest star, just rising on the horizon.

"That's Sirius. What about it?"

"It's the star of Isis, star of the new year. She waits for us."

CHAPTER EIGHT

W hen the well runs dry we know the worth of water," old Ben Franklin had written. Indeed, the French army's march to the Nile had been an ill-planned fiasco. Companies trampled each other at every good well and then drank it dry before the next regiment arrived. Men quarreled, collapsed, became delirious, and shot themselves. They were tantalized and tormented by a new phenomenon the savants dubbed a "mirage," in which distant desert looked like shimmering lakes of water. Cavalry would gallop toward it at full charge, only to find dry sand and the "lake" once more on the horizon, as elusive as the end of a rainbow. It was as if the desert was mocking the Europeans. When troops reached the Nile they stampeded like cattle, plunging into the river to drink until they vomited, even as other men tried to drink around them. Their mysterious destination, fabled Egypt, seemed as cruel as the mirage. The shortage of canteens and the failure to secure wells was a criminal oversight the other generals blamed Napoleon for, and he was not a man to readily shoulder blame. "The French complain of everything, always," he muttered. Yet the criticism stung because he knew it was just. In his campaign in fertile Italy, food and water was readily obtained on the march and army clothing fit the climate. Here he was learning to bring everything with him, but the lessons were painful. Tempers frayed in the heat.

The French army began marching up the Nile toward

Cairo, Egyptian peasants fleeing and reforming behind it like displaced fog. As a column approached each village, the women and children would drive livestock into the desert and hide amid the dunes, peeping over the lip like animals from burrows. The men would linger a little longer, trying to hide food and their meager implements from the locustlike invaders. As the tricolor entered the village boundary they would finally run for the river, straddling bundles of papyrus reed and paddling out into the water, bobbing offshore in the Nile like wary ducks. Division after division would tramp past their homes, a long caterpillar of dusty blue, red, white, and green uniforms. Doors would be kicked in, stables explored, and anything of use taken. Then the army would march on and the peasants would come back to take up their lives again, scouring our track for useful pieces of military litter.

Our little fleet paralleled the land force, bearing supplies and scouting the opposite bank. Each evening we'd land near Napoleon's headquarters company so that Monge, Berthollet, and Talma could make notes about the country we were traversing. It was dangerous to roam away from the soldiers' protection, so they would interview officers on what they'd seen and add to lists of animals, birds, and villages. Their reception was sometimes grumpy because we were envied our place in the boats. The heat was enervating, and the flies a torment. Each time we landed the tension between the army's officers seemed worse, since many supplies were still back on the ships or docks at Alexandria and no division had all it needed. Constant sniping from the Bedouin marauders and lurid stories of capture and torture kept the troops uneasy.

The tension finally boiled over when a particularly insolent group of enemy warriors managed to penetrate near Napoleon's tent one evening, whooping and firing from their splendid Arabians, their colorful robes like a taunting cape. When the furious general dispatched some dragoons and a young aide named Croisier to destroy them, the masterful Egyptian horsemen toyed with the troop and then escaped without losing a man. The small desert horses seemed able to run twice as far on half the water as the heavy European mounts, which were still recovering from the long sea voyage. Our commander went into a rage, humiliating the poor aide so badly that Croisier vowed to die bravely in battle to make up for his shame, a promise he would keep within a year. But Bonaparte was not to be mollified.

"Get me a real warrior!" he cried. "I want Bin Sadr!"

This enraged Dumas, who felt the honor of his cavalry was being impugned. It didn't help that the shortage of horses meant that many of his troopers remained without mounts. "You honor that cutthroat and insult my men?"

"I want flankers to keep the Bedouin away from my headquarters, not aristocratic dandies who can't catch a bandit!" The grim march and jealous seniors were wearing on him.

Dumas was not cowed. "Then wait for good horses instead of rushing into the desert without water! It is your incompetence, not Croisier's!"

"You dare to challenge me? I will have you shot!"

"I will break you in half before you do, little man . . ."

The argument was cut short by the galloping arrival of Bin Sadr and half a dozen of his turbaned henchmen, reining up between the quarreling generals. Kleber took the opportunity to drag the hotheaded Dumas backward while Napoleon fought to get himself under control. The Mamelukes were making fools of us.

"What is it, effendi?" Once more, the Arab's lower face was masked.

"I pay you to keep the Bedouin and Mamelukes off my flanks," Bonaparte snapped. "Why aren't you doing so?"

"Maybe because *you* aren't paying as you promised. I have a jar of fresh ears, and no fresh gold to show for it. My men are bought men, effendi, and they'll go to the Mamelukes if the enemy promises quicker coin."

"Bah. You're afraid of the enemy."

"I envy them! They have generals who pay when they promise!"

Bonaparte scowled and turned to Berthier, his chief of staff. "Why isn't he paid?"

"Men have two ears and two hands," Berthier said quietly. "There's been disagreement over how many he's really killed."

"You question my honesty?" the Arab shouted. "I will bring you tongues and penises!"

"For God's sake," Dumas groaned. "Why are we dealing with barbarians?"

Napoleon and Berthier began muttering with each other over money.

Bin Sadr scanned the rest of us with an impatient eye and suddenly his gaze fell on me. I could swear the devil was looking for the chain around my neck. I scowled back, suspicious that it was he who'd dropped a snake in my bed. His eye also strayed to Astiza, his look deepening to hatred. She remained impassive. Could this really be the lantern bearer who had tried to betray me in Paris? Or was I succumbing to fear and fantasy like the common foot soldiers? I hadn't really taken a good look at the man in France.

"All right," our commander finally said. "We pay you for the hands to date. There's double for all your men once we conquer Cairo. Just keep the Bedouin away."

The Arab bowed. "You'll not be bothered by those jackals again, effendi. I pluck out their eyes and force them to swallow their own sight. I geld them like cattle. I tie their intestines to their horse's tail and whip the animal across the desert."

"Good, good. Let word of that spread." He turned away, done with the Arab, his frustration spent. He looked embarrassed at his outburst, and I could see him mentally chastising himself for not maintaining control. Bonaparte made many mistakes, but seldom more than once.

But Bin Sadr was not done. "Our horses are swift but our guns are old, effendi. Might we have some new ones as well?" He gestured toward the short-barreled carbines that Dumas's cavalry carried.

"The hell you will," the cavalryman growled.

"New?" Bonaparte repeated. "No, we have none to spare."

"How about that man with his longrifle?" Now he pointed

at me. "I remember him and his shot at the walls of Alexandria. Give him to me, and together we'll send the devils who harass you to hell."

"The American?"

"He can shoot the ones who flee."

The idea intrigued Napoleon, who was looking for a distraction. "How about it, Gage? Do you want to ride with a desert sheikh?"

My attempted assassin, I thought, but didn't say that. I wasn't about to get near Bin Sadr except to strangle him, after I'd questioned him first. "I was invited as a scholar, not a sniper, general. My place is on the boat."

"Out of danger?" Bin Sadr mocked.

"But not out of range. Come down to the riverbank sometime and see how close I can come to hitting you, lantern bearer."

"Lantern bearer?" Bonaparte asked.

"The American has had too much sun," the Arab said. "Go, stay on your boat, thinking yourself out of danger, and maybe soon there will be some new use for your rifle. You may wish you had come with Achmed bin Sadr." And with that, taking a sack of coins from Berthier, he turned to gallop off.

As he did so the fabric that covered his lower face slipped briefly, and I got a glimpse of his cheek. There was an angry boil, covered by a poultice, at the same point that Astiza had lanced her wax figurine.

W e were already halfway to Cairo when word came that a Mameluke ruler named Murad Bey had assembled a force to oppose our passage. Bonaparte decided to seize the initiative. Orders were issued and troops departed on the evening of July 12 for a surprise night march to Shubra Khit, the next major town on the Nile. At dawn the French approach surprised a still-organizing Egyptian army of some ten thousand men, a thousand of them splendid Mameluke cavalry and the rest an unformed rabble of *fellahin*—peasants armed with little more than cudgels. They milled in uncertainty as the French formed battle ranks, and for a moment

I thought the whole mass of them might retreat without a fight. Then some encouragement seemed to stiffen them—we could see their chiefs pointing up the Nile—and they braced for battle as well.

I had a fine grandstand seat on board the anchored *Cerf.* As a golden sun rose to the east, we watched from the water as a French army band struck up the "Marseillaise," its notes floating out across the Nile. It was a tune that made troops shiver, and under its inspiration the French would come near to conquering the world. There was a throat-catching efficiency to the way the soldiers assembled into their hedgehog squares again, regimental standards tugged by the morning breeze. It is not an easy formation to master, and even harder to hold during an enemy charge, when every man is facing outward and relying on men behind him to hold. There's a natural tendency to want to back, threatening to collapse the formation, or for shirkers to drop their weapons to drag back the wounded. Sergeants and the toughest veterans man the rear ranks to keep those in front from quailing. Yet a square that is firm is virtually impregnable. The Mameluke cavalry circled to find a weak point and couldn't, the French formations clearly baffling the enemy. It appeared this battle would be another lopsided demonstration of European firepower against medieval Arab courage. We waited, sipping Egyptian mint tea, as the morning turned from pink to blue.

Then there were warning shouts and sails appeared from a bend upriver. Cries of triumph came from the Mamelukes on shore. We stood on our deck uneasily. The Nile was carrying an armada of Egyptian river craft from Cairo, their lateen triangles filling the river like a yard of laundry. Mameluke and Islamic banners flew from every masthead, and from hulls crowded with soldiers and cannon came a great clamor of trumpets, drums, and horns. Was this the use of my rifle that Bin Sadr had slyly warned me about? How had he known? The enemy strategy was obvious. They wanted to destroy our little fleet and take Bonaparte's army by flank from the river.

I emptied my tea over the side and checked the load of my

rifle, feeling trapped and exposed on the water. I wasn't to be a spectator after all.

Captain Perree began snapping orders to raise anchor as the French sailors in his little fleet sprang to their cannon. Talma got out his notebook, looking pale. Monge and Berthollet grasped the rigging and boosted themselves up on the gunwale to watch, as if at a regatta. For some minutes the two fleets slowly closed with stately grace, great swans gliding. Then there was a thud, a blossom of smoke from the prow of the Mameluke flagship, and something sizzled past us in the air, throwing up a geyser of green water off our stern.

"Don't we get to parley first?" I asked lightly, my voice more unsteady than I would have preferred.

As if in reply, the front rank of the entire Egyptian flotilla thundered as its bow cannon fired. The river seemed to heave and splashes erupted all around us, wetting us with warm mist. One ball landed directly on a gunboat to our right, kicking up a rain of splinters. Screams echoed across the water. There was that strange thrumming sound made by passing round shot, and holes opened in our sail like expressions of surprise.

"I think negotiations have ended," Talma said tightly, squatting by the wheel and scribbling notes with one of Conte's new pencils. "This will make an exciting bulletin." His fingers betrayed his tremble.

"Their sailors seem considerably more accurate than their comrades at Alexandria," Monge remarked admiringly, jumping down from the rigging. He was as imperturbable as if viewing a cannon demonstration at a foundry.

"The Ottoman sailors are Greek!" Astiza exclaimed, recognizing her countrymen from their costume. "They serve the bey in Cairo. Now you shall have a fight!"

Perree's men began firing back, but it was hard to swing against the river current to make a proper broadside, and we were clearly outgunned. While we luffed our sails to keep from closing with the enemy too quickly, the rival fleets were inevitably converging. I glanced ashore. The start of this naval cannonade had apparently been the signal for the land-based Mamelukes. They waved their lances and charged toward the picket of French bayonets, galloping straight into hissing sheets of French fire. Horses dashed against the squares like surf against a rocky shore.

Suddenly there was an enormous bang and Astiza and I were thrown from our feet, landing in an ungainly tangle. Given more ordinary circumstances I might have enjoyed this moment of unexpected intimacy, but it had been caused by a cannonball slamming into our hull. When we rolled apart I was sickened. The round had skipped along the main deck, clipping to pieces two of our gunners and spraying the forward half of the vessel with gore. Splinters had wounded several more men, including Perree, and our fire slackened even as that of the Arabs seemed to be increasing.

"Journalist!" the captain shouted at Talma, "Stop scribbling and take the wheel!"

Talma blanched. "Me?"

"I need to bind my arm and serve the cannon!"

Our scribe sprang to obey, excited and scared. "Which way?"

"Toward the enemy."

"Come, Claude-Louis!" Monge shouted to Berthollet as the mathematician clambered forward to take over another unmanned gun. "It's time to put our science to use! Gage, start using your rifle, if you want to live!" My God, the scientist was past fifty and seemed determined to win the battle himself! He and Berthollet ran to the forward cannon. Meanwhile I finally fired, and an enemy sailor tumbled out of his rigging. A fog of cannon haze rolled down on us, Arab boats gauzy in its murk. How long before we were boarded and cut to ribbons by scimitars? I noticed dimly that Astiza had crawled forward to help the scientists haul on the gun tackle. Her admiration of Greek marksmanship had apparently been overcome by her instinct for self-preservation. Berthollet himself had rammed home a charge and now Monge aimed the gun.

"Fire!"

The cannon belched a sheet of flame. Monge sprang up on the bowsprit and stood on his tiptoes to judge his aim, then leaped back disappointed. The shot had missed. "We need bearings to accurately calculate distance, Claude-Louis," he muttered, "or we're wasting powder and shot." He snapped at Astiza. "Sponge and reload!"

I aimed my rifle again, squeezing carefully. This time a Mameluke captain pitched out of sight. Bullets pattered around me in return. Sweating, I reloaded.

"Talma, hold a steady course, damn you!" Monge shouted back.

The scribe was clutching the wheel with pale determination. The Ottoman fleet was drawing steadily closer, and enemy sailors bunched at their prows, ready to board.

The scientists, I saw, were taking bearings on points ashore and sketching intersecting lines to get an accurate estimate of distance to the enemy flagship. Water was blasting into fountains all around us. Chips of debris buzzed through the air.

I primed my pan, shot a Greek Ottoman gunner through the brain, and ran to the bow. "Why don't you fire?"

"Silence!" Berthollet cried. "Give us time to check our arithmetic!" The two scientists were elevating the gun, aiming it as precisely as a surveying instrument.

"One more degree," Monge muttered. "Now!"

The cannon barked once more, its ball screamed, I could follow the shadow of its passage, and then—wonder of wonders—it actually struck the Mameluke flagship perfectly amidships, punching a hole into the vessel's bowels. By Thor, the two savants had actually figured the thing.

"Hooray for mathematics!"

A moment passed, and then the entire enemy boat blew up. Apparently the scientists had made a direct hit on the magazine. There was a concussive roar that radiated out a cloud of shattered wood, broken cannon, and human body parts, arcing outward and then sluicing into the opaque surface of the Nile. The clap of air sent us sprawling, and smoke roiled into the blue Egyptian sky in a vast mushroom. And then there was just disturbed water where the enemy flagship had been, as if it had vanished by magic. The Muslim fire immediately went silent in stunned consternation, and then a wail went up from the enemy flotilla as its smaller boats tacked to flee upriver. At the same moment the Mameluke cavalry, forming for a second charge after their first failed, suddenly broke and retreated southward at this seeming sign of French omnipotence. In minutes, what had been a swirling land-and-sea battle turned into a rout. With that single well-placed shot, the battle of Shubra Khit was won, and the wounded Perree was promoted to rear admiral.

And I, by association, was a hero.

When Perree went ashore to receive Bonaparte's congratulations he generously invited the two scientists, Talma, and me, giving us full credit for the decisive shot. Monge's precision was something of a marvel. Despite the Greek expertise, the new admiral later calculated that the two fleets had exchanged fifteen hundred cannon shots in half an hour and his flotilla had come away with just six dead and twenty wounded. Such was the state of Egyptian artillery, or ordnance in general, at the close of the eighteenth century. Cannon and musket fire was so inaccurate that a brave man could put himself at the forefront of a charge and actually have a decent chance of survival and glory. Men fired too soon. They fired blind in the smoke. They loaded in panic and forgot to discharge, ramming one bullet atop another without shooting at all, until their musket burst. They shot off the ears and hands of their comrades in the rank ahead of them, broke eardrums, and jabbed each other when fitting bayonets. Bonaparte told me that at least one out of ten battle casualties came from one's own comrades, which is why uniforms are so bright, to prevent friends from killing each other.

Expensive rifles like mine will someday change all this, I suppose, and warfare shall devolve into men groping in the mud for cover. What glory in murder? Indeed, I wondered what war would be like if savants did all the aiming and every bomb and bullet hit. But this, of course, is a fanciful notion that will forever be impossible.

While Monge and Berthollet were the ones who had laid the key gun, I was applauded for having fought with fervor for the French side. "You have the spirit of Yorktown!" Napoleon congratulated, clapping me on the back. Again, the presence of Astiza enhanced my reputation. Like any good French soldier I'd attached myself to an attractive woman, and a woman moreover with the spirit to haul on cannon tackle. I'd become one of them, while she used her skill or magic—in Egypt, the two seemed to be the same—to help bind the wounded. We males joined Napoleon for dinner in his tent.

Our general was in a good mood from the outcome of the brisk fight, which had settled both him and his army. Egypt might be alien, but France could become its master. Now Bonaparte's mind was full of plans for the future, even though we were still more than a hundred river miles from Cairo.

"My campaign is not one of conquest but of marriage," he proclaimed as we dined on poultry that his aides had liberated from Shubra Khit, roasting them on the ramrods of their muskets. "France has a destiny in the East, just as your young nation, Gage, has a destiny in the West. While your United States civilizes the red savage, we'll reform the Muslim with Western ideas. We'll bring windmills, canals, factories, dams, roads, and carriages to somnolent Egypt. You and I are revolutionaries, yes, but I'm a builder as well. I want to create, not destroy."

I think he truly believed this, just as he believed a thousand other things about himself, many of them contradictory. He had the intellect and ambition of a dozen men, and was a chameleon who tried to fit them all.

"These people are Muslim," I pointed out. "They won't change. They've been fighting Christians for centuries."

"I'm Muslim too, Gage, if there is only one God and every religion is just an aspect of central truth. That's what we must explain to these people, that we are all brothers under Allah or Jehovah or Yahweh or whomever. France and Egypt will unite once the mullahs see we are their brothers. Religion? It's a tool, like medals or bonus pay. Nothing inspires like unproven faith."

Monge laughed. "Unproven? I'm a scientist, general, and

yet God seemed quite proven once those cannon balls began whizzing by."

"Proven or wished, like a child wishes for his mother? Who knows? Life is brief, and none of our deepest questions are ever answered. So I live for posterity: death is nothing, but to live without glory is to die every day. I'm reminded of the story of an Italian duelist who fought fourteen times to defend his claim that the poet Aristo was finer than the poet Tasio. On his deathbed, the man confessed he'd read neither one." Bonaparte laughed. "Now *that* is living!"

"No, General," the balloonist Conte replied, tapping his wine cup. "*This* is living."

"Ah, I appreciate a good cup, or a fine horse, or a beautiful woman. Look at our American friend here, who rescues this pretty Macedonian, finds himself in the commander's tent, and is about to share in the riches of Cairo. He's an opportunist like me. Don't think I don't miss my own wife, who is a greedy little witch with one of the prettiest pussies I've ever seen, a woman so seductive that I went at her one time without even noticing that her little dog was biting me on the ass!" He roared at the memory. "Pleasure is exquisite! But it is history that is lasting, and no place has more history than Egypt. You'll record it for me, eh, Talma?"

"Writers thrive with their subjects, General."

"I will give authors a subject worthy of their talents."

Talma lifted his cup. "Heroes sell books."

"And books make heroes."

We all drank, to what, exactly, I cannot say.

"You have great ambition, General," I remarked.

"Success is a matter of will. The first step to greatness is to decide to be great. Then men will follow."

"Follow you where, General?" Kleber asked genially.

"All the way." He looked to each of us in turn, his gaze intense. "All the way."

After dinner I paused to say a good-bye to Monge and Berthollet. I'd had quite enough of river boats, having seen one of them explode, and Talma and Astiza wanted to be ashore as well. So we gave temporary farewells to the two scientists, under a desert sky ablaze with countless stars.

"Bonaparte is cynical but seductive," I remarked. "You can't listen to his dreams without being infected by them."

Monge nodded. "He's a comet, that one. If he's not killed, he'll leave his mark on the world. And on us."

"Always admire but never trust him," Berthollet cautioned. "We're all hanging onto the tiger's tail, Monsieur Gage, hoping we won't be eaten."

"Surely he won't eat his own kind, my chemist friend."

"But what are his own kind? If he doesn't quite believe in God, neither does he quite believe in us: that we are real. No one is real to Napoleon but Napoleon."

"That seems too cynical."

"No? In Italy he ordered a group of his soldiers to a sharp skirmish with the Austrians that left several men dead."

"That's war, is it not?" I remembered Bonaparte's comments on the beach.

"Not when there was no military need for the skirmish, or the deaths. A pretty Mademoiselle Thurreau was visiting from Paris and Bonaparte was anxious to bed her by demonstrating his power. He ordered the fight solely to impress her." Berthollet put his hand on my arm. "I'm glad you've joined us, Gage, you are proving brave and congenial. March with our young general and you'll march far, as he promised. But never forget that Napoleon's interests are Napoleon's, not your own."

I'd hoped that the remainder of our journey to Cairo would be a stroll down avenues of date palms and through the irrigated greenery of melon fields. Instead, to avoid the bends in the river and the narrow lanes of frequent villages, the French army left the Nile a few miles to the east and hiked through desert and dry farmland once more, crossing sun-baked mud and empty, axle-breaking irrigation canals. The alluvial valley, which the Nile flooded each wet season, sent up a cloud of dry, clinging powder that turned us into a horde of dust men, marching south on blistered feet. The heat in the middle of July routinely exceeded one hundred degrees, and when a hot wind blew the brilliantly azure sky turned milk on the horizon. Sand hissed over the top of sculpted dunes like an undulating sheet. Men began to suffer ophthalmia, temporary blindness from the ceaseless glare. So fierce was the sun that we needed to wrap our hands to pick up a rock or touch a cannon barrel.

It didn't help that Bonaparte, still fearing a British strike in his rear or more organized resistance to his front, scolded his officers for every pause and delay. While they focused on the march of the moment his mind was always on the greater picture, ticking off the calendar and strategically roaming from the mysterious whereabouts of the British fleet to ally Tippoo, in distant India. He tried to hold all of Egypt in his eye. The genial host we'd seen after the river fight had once more reverted to anxious tyrant, galloping from point to point to urge more speed. "The faster the pace, the less the blood!" he lectured. As a result, all the generals were sweating, dirty, and frequently cursing each other. The soldiers were depressed by the bickering and by the bleakness of the land they'd come to conquer. Many cast off equipment rather than carry it. Several more committed suicide. Astiza and I passed two of their bodies, left by our path because everyone was too hurried to bury them. Only the trailing Bedouin discouraged more men from desertion.

Our torrent of men, horses, donkeys, guns, wagons, camels, camp followers, and beggars flowed toward Cairo in an arrow of dust. When we halted to rest in the farmlands, muddy from sweat, our only amusement was to throw rocks at the innumerable rats. In the desert fringe the men shot at snakes and played with the scorpions, tormenting them into contests against each other. They learned that the scorpion bite was not as deadly as initially feared, and that crushing the insect against the sting released a goo that worked as a salve to help soothe the pain and hasten the healing.

There was no rain, ever, and rarely a cloud. At night we did not so much camp as sprawl, everyone collapsing in the sequence with which we'd marched, the lot of us immediately assaulted by fleas and midges. We ate cold food as often as hot because there was little wood for fuel. The night would cool toward dawn and we'd wake wet with dew, only half recovered. Then the cloudless sun would rise, remorse-

less as a clock, and soon we'd all be baking. Astiza, I noticed, lay steadily closer to me as the march went on, but we
were both so swaddled, filthy, and exposed in this horde that
there was nothing romantic in her decision. We simply
sought each other's warmth at night, and then bemoaned the
sun and flies by noon.

At Wardan the army was finally allowed to rest for two
days. The men washed, slept, foraged, and bartered for food.
Once again Astiza proved her value in being able to con-
verse with the villagers and trade for sustenance. So successful was she that I was able to supply some of the officers
at Napoleon's headquarters with bread and fruit.

"You're sustaining the invaders like the Hebrews were
sustained by manna from heaven," I tried to joke with her.

"I'm not going to starve ordinary soldiers because of the
delusions of their commander," she retorted. "Besides, fed
or starving, you'll all be gone shortly."

"You don't think the French can beat the Mamelukes?"

"I don't think they can beat the desert. Look at all of you,
with your heavy uniforms and hot boots and pink skin. Is
there anyone but your mad general who doesn't regret coming
here? These soldiers will leave on their own soon enough."

Her predictions were beginning to annoy me. She was a
captive, after all, spoiled by my kindness, and it was high
time I reprimanded her. "Astiza, we could have killed you as
an assassin in Alexandria. Instead, I saved you. Can't we
become not master and servant, or invader and Egyptian,
but friends?"

"A friend of whom? A man foreign to his own army? In
alliance with a military opportunist? An American who
seems neither true scientist nor soldier?"

"You saw my medallion. It's a key to something I'm to
figure out."

"But you want this key without understanding. You want
knowledge without study. Coins without work."

"I view this as damned hard work."

"You're a parasite looting another culture. I want a friend
who believes in something. Himself, first. And things greater
than himself."

Well, that was presumptuous! "I'm an American who believes in all kinds of things! You should read our Declaration of Independence! And I don't control the world. I just try to make my way in it."

"No. What individuals do *does* control the world. War has put us together, Monsieur Ethan Gage, and you are not an entirely unlikable man. But companionship is not true friendship. First you have to decide why you are in Egypt, what you mean to do with this medallion of yours, what you really stand for, and *then* we will be friends."

Well. Quite insolent for a merchant's slave, I thought! "And we will be *friends* when you acknowledge me as master and accept your new fate!"

"What task haven't I done for you? Where haven't I accompanied you?"

Women! I had no answer. This time we slept an arm's length away and my mind kept me from sleep until well past midnight. Which was just as well, because I narrowly escaped having a wandering donkey step on my head.

One day after the Egyptian new year, on July 20 at the village of Omm-Dinar, Napoleon finally received word of the Mameluke disposition for the defense of Cairo, now just eighteen miles ahead. The defenders had foolishly split their forces. Murad Bey led the bulk of the Mameluke army on our own western side of the river, but a jealous Ibrahim Bey had kept a sizable share on the east. It was the opportunity our general had been waiting for. The order to march came two hours after midnight, the shouts and kicks of officers and sergeants brooking no delay. Like a great beast rousing itself in its cave, the French expeditionary force stirred, rose, and marched south in the dark with a sudden anticipation that called to mind that prickly feeling I get from demonstrating Franklin's electricity. This would be the great battle, and the coming day would see either the destruction of the main Mameluke army or the rout of our own. Despite Astiza's lofty lecture about controlling the world, I felt no more in charge of my fate than a leaf on a current.

Dawn came red, with mist on the reeds of the Nile. Bonaparte urged us on, anxious to crush the Mamelukes before they joined forces or, worse, dispersed into the desert. I caught sight of him exhibiting a scowling intensity greater than any I'd yet observed, not just keen on a fight but obsessed with it. A captain made some mild objection and Napoleon snapped back with the bark of a cannon. His mood made the soldiers apprehensive. Was our commander worried about the coming battle? If so, all of us would worry too. None had gotten enough sleep. We could see another great pall of dust on the horizon where the Mamelukes and their foot soldiers were massing.

It was during a brief stop at a muddy village well that I learned the reason for the general's darkness. It was by chance that one of the general's aides, a recklessly brave young soldier named Jean-Andoche Junot, got down from his horse to drink while I did.

"The general seems awfully impatient for battle," I remarked. "I knew this fight must come, and that speed in war is paramount, but to rise in the middle of the night seems uncivilized, somehow."

"Stay away from him," the lieutenant warned quietly. "He's dangerous after last night."

"You were drinking? Gambling? What?"

"He'd asked me weeks before to make some discreet inquiries because of persistent rumors. Recently, I received some pilfered letters that prove Josephine is having an affair, a secret to none but our general. Last evening, shortly after word came of the Mameluke dispositions, he abruptly demanded what I'd learned."

"She's betrayed him?"

"She's in love with a fop named Hippolyte Charles, an aide to General Leclerc back in France. The woman has been cheating on Bonaparte since they were married, but he's been blind to her infidelities since he loves her like a madman. His jealousy is unbelievable, and his fury last night was volcanic. I was afraid he was going to shoot *me*. He looked insane, striking his head with his fists. Do you know what it's like to be betrayed by the one you love most hopelessly? He told me his emotions were spent, his ideal-ism over, and that nothing remained for him but ambition."

"All that over an affair? A Frenchman?"

"He loves her desperately, and hates himself for that love. He's the most independent and friendless of men, meaning he's captive to that trollop he married. He ordered this march immediately, and swore repeatedly that his own happiness was over and that before the sun sets, he would destroy the Egyptian armies to the last man. I tell you, Monsieur Gage, we're being led into battle by a general who is insane with rage."

This didn't sound good at all. If there's one thing a person hopes for in a commander, it's a cool head. I swallowed. "Your timing wasn't the best, Junot."

The lieutenant swung up onto his horse. "I had no choice, and my report should have come as no surprise. I know his mind, and he'll put the distraction aside when battle comes. You'll see." He nodded, as if to reassure himself. "I'm just glad I'm not on the other side."

CHAPTER NINE

It was 2 P.M., the hottest time of the day, when the French army began forming squares for the Battle of the Pyramids. It was more correctly the Battle of Imbaba, the closest town, but the pyramids on the horizon gave it a more romantic name in Talma's dispatches. Imbaba's melon fields were quickly overrun by soldiers seeking to quench their thirst before the coming combat. One of my memories is the bib of juice stain on their uniforms as the regiments and brigades formed ranks.

The pyramids were still a hazy fifteen miles away, but arresting in their perfect geometry. From that distance, they looked like the caps of colossal prisms, buried to their neck in the sands. We stirred at the sight of them, so fabled and so towering, the tallest structures that had ever been built. Vivant Denon was sketching furiously, trying to fit a panorama on a notepad and to catch the shimmer of the vault of air.

Imagine the magnificent panoply of the scene. On our left flank ran the Nile, shrunken before the floods that would soon start but nonetheless a majestic blue that reflected the brilliant sky. Beside was the lush green of the irrigated fields and date palms that bordered it, a ribbon of Eden. To our right were the rolling dunes, like the frozen waves of an ocean. And finally in the distance were the pyramids, those mystical structures that seemed to belong to a different world, assembled by a civilization we could scarcely imagine, rising to their perfect peaks. The pyramids! I'd seen Masonic pictures of them, angular and steep, topped with a glowing, all-seeing eye. Now they were real, squatter than I had imagined, wavering like a mirage.

Add to this the tens of thousands of uniformed men in crisp formations, the milling Mameluke cavalry, the lumbering camels, the braying donkeys, and the galloping French officers—already hoarse from shouting orders—and I was trapped in an environment so exotic that it seemed like I'd been transported to a dream. Talma was flying through sheets of paper as he wrote furiously, trying to record it all. Denon was muttering to himself that we all must pose before battle could be joined. "Wait. Wait!"

Arrayed against Bonaparte's army was a glittering host that seemed two to three times our twenty-five thousand men, topped by a thunderhead of dust. Were the Mamelukes better generals, it is possible we'd have been overwhelmed. But the Arab army was foolishly divided by the mighty river. Their infantry, this time Ottoman foot soldiers from Albania, was placed too far back to be of immediate use. A fatal weakness of the Mamelukes was not only that they did not trust each other; they trusted no Ottoman branch but their own. Their artillery was ill situated on our far left flank. Because of such incompetence, the French soldiers were confident of the outcome. "Look how foolish they are!" the veterans reassured their comrades. "They don't understand war!"

On the far bank, shimmering on the horizon, was Cairo itself, a city of a quarter-million people, spiked by its impossibly slim minarets. Would we all find fortune there? My mouth was dry, my mind dazed by sensation.

Once again the Arab army's heart was the Mamelukes, mounted cavalry now ten thousand strong. Their horses were superb Arabians and richly harnessed, their riders a kaleidoscope of robes and silks, their turbans topped with egret and peacock feathers, and their helmets gilded with gold. They were armed with a museum's worth of beautiful and dated weapons. Old muskets were inlaid with jewels and mother-of-pearl. Scimitars, lances, spears, battle axes, maces, and daggers all glinted in the sun. More muskets and pistols were holstered on their saddles or thrust in their sashes, and each Mameluke was trailed by two or three servants on foot carrying additional firearms and ammunition. These slaves would sprint forward to relay weapons so the Mamelukes wouldn't have to pause to reload. The warriors' horses pranced and snorted like circus steeds, heads rearing in impatience for the coming charge. No army had withstood them for five hundred years.

Prowling the outskirts of the Egyptian formations were the white-robed Bedouin on their camels, masked like bandits and circling like wolves. These waited to descend on our ranks to kill and plunder when we broke under the penultimate Mameluke charge. Our own wolf, Bin Sadr, was hunting them even as they hunted us. Dressed in black, his cutthroats lurked on the lip of the dunes and hoped not only to ambush Bedouin, but to strip dead Mamelukes of booty before French soldiers could get to them.

The Egyptians had strapped small cannon on the backs of camels. The animals brayed and snorted and trotted this way and that under the shouted commands of their anxious trainers, so unsteady that the aim would prove worthless. The river was once more thronged with the lateen-rigged feluccas of the Muslim fleet, crammed with hooting sailors. Again we heard the clamor of drums, horns, bugles, and tambourines, and a forest of flags, banners, and pennants fluttered above their assembly like a vast carnival. The French bands struck up as well, as the European infantry filed into position with stolid efficiency from long-practiced drill, priming their weapons and fixing bayonets. The sun sparkled on every deadly point. Regimental banners bore streamers of past victories. Drums thundered to communicate commands.

The air was an oven, heating our lungs. Water seemed to evaporate before it could travel from lips to throat. A hot wind was coming up out of the desert to the west, and the sky was an ominous brown in that direction.

By this time most of the scientists and engineers had caught up with the army—even Monge and Berthollet had come ashore—but our role in the coming showdown had not been specified. Now General Dumas, looking even more gigantic on a huge brown charger, came galloping by to roar a fresh command.

"Donkeys, scholars, and women to the squares! Take your place inside, you useless asses!"

I have seldom heard more comforting words.

Astiza, Talma, and I followed a herd of scientists, French women, and livestock into an infantry square commanded by General Louis-Antoine Desaix. He was perhaps the army's ablest soldier, the same age as Napoleon at twenty-nine, and one inch shorter, even, than our little corporal. Unlike the other generals, he was as devoted to his commander as a loyal hound. Homely, disfigured by a saber cut, and shy of women, he seemed happiest when sleeping between the wheels of a field piece. Now he formed his troops in such a robust square, ten soldiers deep facing in four directions, that entering was like taking refuge in a small fort made up entirely of human beings. I loaded my rifle again and looked out at Egypt from behind this formidable barrier of broad shoulders, high cockaded hats, and ready muskets. Mounted officers, dismounted scientists, and chattering women milled in the interior space, all of us nervous and hot. Field cannon were placed at each of the square's outside corners, the artillerymen relying on infantry support to keep from being overrun.

"By Moses and Jupiter, I've never seen such splendor," I muttered. "No wonder Bonaparte likes war."

"Imagine if Egypt was *your* home and you were looking at these French divisions," Astiza replied quietly. "Imagine facing invasion."

"It will bring better times, I hope." Impulsively, I took and squeezed her hand. "Egypt is desperately poor, Astiza."

Surprisingly, she did not pull away. "Yes, it is."

Once more the army musicians struck up the "Marseillaise," the music helping steady everyone's nerves. Then Napoleon rode by our square with his immediate staff, his steed black, his hat plumed, and his gray eyes like chips of ice. I climbed on a caisson—a two-wheeled ammunition wagon—to hear him. Word of his wife's infidelities had left no obvious mark, save furious concentration. Now he pointed dramatically at the pyramids, their geometric purity wavering in the heat as if seen through water. "Soldiers of France!" he cried. "Forty centuries look down upon you!"

The cheer was eruptive. As much as the common foot soldier complained about Bonaparte between battles, they welded to him like lovers in a fight. He knew them, knew how they thought and bellyached and breathed, and knew how to ask them the impossible for a bit of ribbon, a mention in a dispatch, or a promotion to an elite unit.

Then the general leaned closer to Desaix with quieter words that some of us could hear but which were not meant as an address to the army. "No mercy."

I felt a sudden chill.

Murad Bey, once more the commander of the Arab army in our front, saw that Napoleon intended to march his squares forward to bludgeon through the Arab center, splitting the Mameluke forces so they could be destroyed piecemeal. While the Egyptian ruler had no grasp of European tactics, he had the common sense to try to forestall whatever the French intended by attacking first. He raised his lance, and with their eerie, ululating cry, the Mameluke cavalry once again charged. These slave warriors had been invincible for centuries, and the ruling caste simply could not believe that technology was bringing its reign to an end. This was a much larger attack than any we had yet faced, and so many horses thundered forward that I literally could feel the quaking of the ground beneath the caisson I had mounted.

The infantry waited with nervous confidence, knowing by now that the Mamelukes had neither the artillery nor the musket discipline to prevail against the French formations. Still, the enemy's approach was furious as an avalanche. All of us tensed. The ground shook, sand and dust erupted at the breast of their line like oncoming surf, and lances, spears, and rifle muzzles were brandished like fields of shaking wheat. I felt a little reckless and giddy up on my perch, looking over the heads of the ranks before me, Astiza and Talma looking up at me as if I were crazy, but I hadn't seen a Mameluke weapon yet that I felt had much chance of hitting me at any range. I raised my own rifle and waited, watching the enemy banners ripple.

Nearer and nearer they came, the rumbling growing in volume, the Mamelukes sounding their high, wavering cry, the French whispering not a word. The open ground between us was being swallowed. Were we ever going to fire? I swear I could pick out the bright colors of the enemy's unexpected Caucasian eyes, the grimace of their teeth, the veins of their hands, and I became impatient. Finally, without conscious decision, I squeezed my trigger, my gun kicked, and one of the enemy warriors pitched backward, disappearing in the stampede.

It was as if my shot were the signal to commence. Desaix cried out and the front of the French erupted in the familiar sheet of flame. In an instant I was deaf and the attacking cavalry went down in a crashing wave of torn bodies, screaming horses, and thrashing hooves. Smoke and dust rolled over us. Then another volley from the rank behind, and another, and then another. Somewhere the field guns boomed and scythes of grapeshot whickered out. It was a storm of lead and iron. Even those Mamelukes not hit were colliding and catapulting over the mounts of their comrades. A furious charge had been churned into havoc in an instant, just yards from the first French bayonets. So close were the fallen enemy that some were hit by the burning wadding from the European muzzles. Tiny fires started on the clothes of the dead and wounded. I loaded and fired again too, to what effect I couldn't tell. We were wreathed in smoke.

The survivors wheeled away to regroup while Napoleon's soldiers swiftly and mechanically reloaded, every motion practiced hundreds of times. A few of the French had fallen from Mameluke fire and these were dragged backward into the middle of our square as the rank awkwardly reformed, sergeants beating at slackers to force them to duty. It was like a sea creature growing another arm, impervious to fatal damage.

The Mamelukes charged again, this time trying to penetrate the side and rear ranks of our infantry square.

The result was the same as before. The horses came in at

an angle and a few got closer, but even those steeds not hit pulled up at the hedge of bayonets, sometimes throwing their yelling riders. Fine silks and linens bloomed with red blossoms as the Arabs were hit with the thick lead balls, this time from two squares firing into each flank as the Mamelukes galloped between them. Once again the assault was thrown into confusion. The attackers were beginning to seem increasingly desperate. Some stood off and fired at us with musket and pistol, but the shots were too sporadic and inaccurate to seriously dent the French ranks. A few of our infantry grunted or cried and went down. Then another European volley would boom out, and these assailants too would be knocked from their horses. We were soon surrounded by a ring of the dead and dying, a heap of the military aristocracy of Egypt. It dwarfed the slaughter of the earlier battles.

Even though Arab bullets regularly whined overhead, I felt curiously immune to the havoc. There was a sense of unreality to the entire scene: the colossal pyramids in the far distance, the glassy air, the oppressive heat, the palms waving in the desert wind even as random shot clipped fronds from their tops. The fragments of green floated down like feathers. There were great rolling clouds of dust against the white sky as the enemy galloped this way and that to no apparent purpose, looking for a weakness in Bonaparte's squares and not finding it. The Egyptian infantry seemed rooted irresolutely in the rear, as if fatalistically awaiting their doom. The Mamelukes, fearing revolt, had let the lesser arms of their nation atrophy into paralyzed incompetence.

I looked to the west. The entire sky there was growing dark, the sun becoming an orange orb. Rain? No, I realized, these were other kinds of clouds—clouds of sand. The horizon had been blotted out with an approaching tempest.

No one else seemed to take notice of the weather. With undeniable courage, the Mamelukes reformed, took fresh rifles and pistols from their servants, and charged yet again. This time they seemed determined to concentrate all their fury on our own square alone. We fired, their front ranks went down as before, but their column was so thick that those to the rear survived to ride over their fallen comrades before we could reload. With desperate energy they drove their horses onto the French bayonets.

It was as if we'd been rammed by a ship. The square bent from the onslaught, horses dying even as they crushed Bonaparte's infantry beneath their weight. Some men fell back in panic. Other French rushed from the square's inner sides to reinforce the front before it buckled. There was a sudden desperate brawl of Mameluke sword, lance, and pistol against French bayonet and point-blank musket. Still perched on my caisson, I shot into a tossing sea. I had no idea who or what I was hitting.

Suddenly, as if fired from a cannon, a horse and gigantic warrior broke through, hurdling the entangled warriors. The Arabian mount was streaked with blood and its turbaned Mameluke spattered with gore, yet he fought with unstoppable frenzy. Infantry rushed to intercept him and his scimitar sliced through their musket barrels as if they were straw. The crazed animal was kicking and trampling, whirling in a circle like a dervish, its rider impregnable to bullets. The scientists scattered before the hooves, men toppling and shouting. Most disquieting of all, the attacker seemed to have his eye fixed on me, balanced as I was on the artillery supply wagon in my distinctive, unmilitary coat.

I took aim but before I could fire, the steed crashed into my caisson and catapulted me into the air. I came down hard, the wind knocked out, and the wild-eyed stallion danced toward me, eyes rolling, hooves thrashing. Its master seemed intent on me to the exclusion of all the hundreds around him, as if he'd decided to pick a personal enemy.

Then there was a cry and the horse reared and went down. Talma, I saw, had grabbed a lance and stabbed the animal's hindquarter. The rider slid off and landed as hard as I had, momentarily stunned. Before he could scramble up, Astiza gave a ferocious yell and with Talma's help pushed the caisson at him. Its wheels lodged against the crippled horse, pinning the fanatic rider between his saddle and the iron rims. The Mameluke had shoulders like an ox; he thrashed like an animal but was suddenly helpless. I crawled over and threw myself over the horse and onto him, my tomahawk at his throat. Astiza piled on as well, shouting in Arabic, and either her words or her gender seemed to freeze him. Then exhaustion overcame his frenzy and he slumped, looking dazed.

"Tell him to surrender!" I cried to Astiza.

She shouted something and the Mameluke nodded in defeat, his head falling backward against the sand. I'd won my first prisoner! It was an unexpectedly heady feeling, even more satisfying than a particularly lucky hand of whist. By Jove, I was beginning to understand the soldiers' enthusiasms. Living, after a whiff of death, is a heady thing.

Swiftly disarming the Arab, I borrowed an officer's pistol to finish the suffering horse. Other horsemen had also broken through, I saw, but each was eventually clubbed and hacked to earth by the French infantry. The exception was one bold chap who cut down two men, took a ball himself, and then jumped his horse back over the chaotic front rank to gallop away, warbling in desperate, wounded triumph. That was the kind of courage these devils had, and it led Napoleon to remark that with a handful of them, he'd whip the world. He would eventually recruit Mameluke survivors into his personal bodyguard.

Still, the escape of that warrior was a rare occurrence, and most of the enemy simply couldn't break through our hedge of men. Their horses were gutted on the rows of bayonets. Finally the survivors broke in despair, French grapeshot chasing their retreat and cutting still more from their saddles. Despite Egyptian bravery, it had been a massacre. The Europeans had dozens of casualties but the Mamelukes had thousands. The sand was clotted with their dead.

"Search his clothing," Astiza said as we sat on our captive. "They carry their wealth into battle, to be lost if they are lost."

Indeed, my prisoner proved a treasure chest. His turban was cashmere, and I knocked it aside to reveal a skullcap sewn with gold pieces like a yellow helmet. More gold was in a sash around his waist, his pistols were inlaid with mother-of-pearl and gems, and his scimitar had a black Damascus blade and a handle of rhinoceros horn inlaid with gold. In the span of a few seconds I'd become rich, but then so had much of the army. The French would later estimate that each Mameluke could be robbed, on average, of fifteen thousand francs. Men were capering over the dead.

"My God, who is he?" I said.

She gripped to turn his hand, looking at his rings, and stopped. "A son of Horus," she murmured. On his finger was the same symbol she wore as an amulet. It was not an Islamic sign.

He jerked his hand away. "That's not for you," he suddenly growled in English.

"You speak our language?" I asked, once more startled.

"I've had dealings with European merchants. And I've heard of you, the British in a green coat. What is a British doing with the Franks?"

"I'm American. Antoine is French, Astiza Egyptian and Greek."

He absorbed this. "And I a Mameluke." He was on his back, looking up at the sky. "So does war and destiny bring us together."

"What's your name?"

"I am Ashraf el-Din, a lieutenant of Murad Bey."

"And what's a son of Horus?" I asked Astiza.

"A follower of the ancients. This man is not the typical Mameluke from the Caucasus. He's of the old families here, aren't you?"

"The Nile runs in my veins. I'm a descendant of the Ptolomies. But I was sworn into Mameluke ranks by Murad Bey himself."

"The Ptolomies? You mean Cleopatra's clan?" I asked.

"And the generals of Alexander and Caesar," he said proudly.

"The Mamelukes despise the Egyptians they rule," Astiza explained, "but occasionally they've recruited from the great old families."

All this seemed a curious coincidence. I'm attacked by the rare Mameluke who swears by a pagan god and speaks English? "Can I trust you if we let you up?"

"I am your prisoner, taken in battle," Ashraf said. "I submit to your mercy."

I let him stand. He swayed a moment.

"Your name is a mouthful," I said. "I think I shall call you Ash."

"I will answer."

And all this good fortune would evaporate if I couldn't satisfy my colleagues by making sense of the medallion. Astiza with her Horus pendant had made a useful guess about it, and maybe this devil could too. With the division cheering and everyone's eyes on the battle, I took the medallion from my shirt and dangled it before him. Talma's eyes widened.

"I'm more than a warrior, son of Horus," I said. "I've come to Egypt to understand this. Do you recognize it?"

He blinked in wonder. "No. But another might."

"Who in Cairo knows what this means? Who knows the old Egyptian gods and your nation's history?"

He glanced at Astiza. She nodded at him and they jabbered together in Arabic. Finally she turned to me.

"More gods than you know are walking your shadow, Ethan Gage. You have captured a warrior who claims to know a man I've only heard of as rumor, who takes as his name that of one long lost."

"Who?"

"Enoch the wise, also known as Hermes Trismegistus, Hermes the trice-great, scribe of the gods, master of arts and sciences."

"My, my." Enoch was also the name of the Old Testament father of Methuselah. A long-lived bunch. My Masonic memories also recalled a supposed Book of Enoch, source of ancient wisdom. It had been lost several millennia ago. I peered at my bloody captive. "He knows this sage?"

She nodded as our prisoner blinked at my medallion in wonder. "Enoch," she said, "is his brother."

Suddenly we were advancing. The square reformed into columns and we marched toward the Egyptian fortifications at Imbaba, literally climbing up and over a windrow of the dead. I tied Ash's hands behind his back with a golden cord taken from his waist and left him bareheaded. His head was shaven except for the standard small tuft at the crown by which it was said that the Prophet Muhammad would, at their last breath, come and seize Mamelukes to raise them to paradise. His skullcap of coins was tucked into my own belt, and Astiza carried his fabulous sword. If I felt guilty about exposing my defeated enemy to the hot sky, the feeling was assuaged by the fact that the atmosphere was becoming more and more obscured by dust. While it was only about 4 P.M., the midsummer day was becoming dark.

As we moved across the wreckage of the battlefield, I got a better view of what had happened. While our square and that of Jean-Louis Raynier had borne the brunt of the Mameluke cavalry attacks, other divisions had moved forward. One broke through enemy lines near the shore of the Nile and began raking the rear of the Egyptian infantry with cannon fire. Two more assaulted Imbaba directly to put an end to Egyptian batteries there. The surviving Mameluke cavalry had been split, some seeking refuge in the fortified town and others pushed westward into the desert with Murad Bey. This latter group was now scattering. The battle was turning into a rout, and the rout to slaughter.

The French had carried the breastworks of Imbaba in their first emotional charge, the Albanian infantry disintegrating. Turning to flee, the Ottoman soldiers were shot down or forced into the Nile. Whenever there was any pause on the part of the French, they were ordered to keep firing by the commander-in-chief himself. Here was Napoleon's grim fury. At least a thousand Mamelukes were caught up in this panic and were pushed with their infantry into the river, swiftly sinking under the weight of their personal fortunes. Those who tried to stand their ground were killed. This was war at its most primeval. I saw some of the French emerge from the carnage so stained with blood that it looked as if they'd wallowed in a wine vat.

Our general galloped by, eyes shining. "Now! Crush them now, or we will pay more dearly later!"

We bypassed Imbaba and marched rapidly the last miles

until we were between the pyramids and Cairo, the city a fairyland of minarets and domes on the far side of the Nile. The half of the Mameluke army still safe there followed us on the opposite shore, screaming at our formations as if words would accomplish what bullets had not. We were out of range of each other. Then, when they came abreast of the fleet of feluccas moored at the quays of Cairo, the bravest of the Mamelukes embarked to set off across the river to try to attack us.

It was too late. Imbaba had become a charnel house. Murad Bey was already fleeing for the desert. The makeshift Mameluke armada of boats sailed toward a shore lined with French infantry, a watery charge even more hopeless than that of the Muslim cavalry. They sculled into a storm of bullets. Even worse, the entire battlefield was being swallowed by an oncoming wall of sand and dust, as if God, Allah, or Horus had decided on a final intervention. The boats were reaching into the teeth of the wind.

The storm was like a wall, blotting out the west. The light was growing dim as if from an eclipse of the sun. The western sky had grown black from the oncoming sandstorm, and the mighty pyramids, stupefying in their size and simplicity, were enveloped in brown fog. Toward this tempest rowed Ibrahim Bey and his bravest followers, their overloaded boats leaning farther and farther in the rising wind, the Nile frothy with whitecaps, and long lines of dusty French infantry drawn up on the bank with a storm of sand hammering their backs. The French fired again and again, in steady, disciplined volleys. Egyptians screamed, grunted, and toppled out of the boats.

The dust storm drew higher and higher, an infinite cliff, blotting out of the sky. Now I could see nothing of the fleeing Arabs on the western bank, or of the pyramids, or even of Napoleon and his staff. It was like the end of the world.

"Get down!" Ashraf cried. He, Astiza, Talma, and I crouched together, drawing up clothing to cover our mouths and noses.

The full power of the wind hit like a punch, shrieking, and then came sand like stinging bees. It was bad enough for the French, who crouched with their backs to the tempest, but the oncoming Mamelukes were face to it and caught on small, unstable boats. The arena went dark. The wind consumed all other noise. The battle stopped. The four of us held each other, trembling and praying to an assortment of gods, reminded at last that there are powers higher than our own. For several long minutes the sandstorm beat at us, seeming to rob our chests of air. Then, almost as quickly as it had come, it snuffed itself out and the noise died. Dust sifted down from the air above.

Slowly, shakily, thousands of French soldiers rose back up from their shallow graves of sand, seemingly resurrected but entirely brown. To a man they were speechless, overwhelmed, horrified. Overhead, the sky cleared. To the west, the sun was red as a ripped heart.

We looked out at Cairo and the river. The water was swept clean of boats. All the Mamelukes who had tried to attack us by water were drowned or shipwrecked on the eastern bank. Every boat had capsized. We could hear the wails of the survivors, and Astiza translated. "Now we are slaves of the French!" They fled into the city and through it, gathered wives and valuables, and disappeared into the growing dusk. The strange storm, supernatural in nature, had seemed to erase one group of conquerors and install another. The wind had extinguished the past and introduced a strange European future.

Flames flickered along the waterfront of the city as the few feluccas still moored there began to burn. Someone was hoping to delay the French crossing by firing the boats, a futile hope given the other craft available up and down the Nile. The feluccas flamed into the night, illuminating the city we were about to occupy like the lamps of a theater, the fantastic Moorish architecture flickering and dancing with the light of conflagration.

The French soldiers, having survived both battle and storm, were triumphant, exhausted, and filthy. They crowded into the Nile to wash and then sat in melon fields to eat and clean their muskets. Clumps of naked Arab dead were everywhere, stripped for booty. The French had suffered a few score dead and two hundred wounded; the Arabs countless thousands. Ordinary French soldiers were newly rich with loot. Napoleon's victory was complete, his hold on the army confirmed, his gamble rewarded.

He rode among his troops like a triumphant lion, receiving their accolades and bestowing congratulations in turn. All the disgruntlement and acrimony of the past weeks had disappeared in the joy of victory. Napoleon's intense fury appeared to have been sated by the day's intensity, and his wounded pride over his wife's betrayal had been assuaged by slaughter. It was as merciless a battle as I could imagine, and it had spent all emotion. Josephine would never know the carnage her games had unleashed.

The general found me sometime that evening. I don't know when—the shock of such a huge fight and storm had blurred my sense of time—or how. His aides had come looking specifically for me, however, and I knew with certain dread what it was he wanted. Bonaparte never gave himself leave to brood; he always thought ahead to the next step.

"So, Monsieur Gage," he said to me in the dark, "I understand you have captured yourself a Mameluke."

How did he know so much so quickly? "It seems so, General, by accident as much as intention."

"You have a knack for contributing to the action, it seems."

I shrugged with modesty. "Still, I remain a savant, not a soldier."

"Which is precisely why I've sought you out. I've liberated Egypt, Gage, and tomorrow I will occupy Cairo. The first step in my conquest of the East is completed. The second hinges on you."

"On me, General?"

"Now you will unravel the clues and discover whatever secrets these pyramids and temples hold. If there are mysteries, you will learn them. If there are powers, you will give them to me. And as a result, our armies will become invincible. We will march to unite with Tippoo, drive the British out of India, and seal the destruction of England. Our two revolutions, American and French, will remake the world."

It is difficult to exaggerate what the emotional effect of such a call can have on an ordinary human being. It's not that I cared a whit about England, France, Egypt, India, or making a new world. Rather that this short, charismatic man of emotional fire and blazing vision had enlisted me in partnership with something bigger than myself. I'd been waiting for the future to start, and here it was. In the day's carnage and supernatural augury of weather I'd seen proof, I thought, of future greatness: of a man who changed everything about him for better and worse, like a little god himself. Without thinking through the consequences, I was flattered. I bowed slightly, in salute.

Then, with my heart in my throat, I watched Bonaparte stalk away, remembering Sydney Smith's dark description of the French Revolution. I thought of the heaps of dead on the battlefield, the wailing of Egyptians, and the disgruntlement of homesick troops joking about their six acres of sand. I thought about the earnest investigations of the scholars, the European plans for reform, and Bonaparte's hope for an endless march to the borders of India, as Alexander had marched before him.

I thought of the medallion around my neck and how desire always seems to defeat simple happiness.

It was after Bonaparte had disappeared that Astiza leaned close.

"Now you will have to decide what you truly believe," she whispered.

CHAPTER TEN

T he home of Ashraf's oddly named brother was in one of Cairo's more reputable sections, which is to say it was in a neighborhood marginally less dusty, disease-ridden, rat-infested, stinking, and crowded than the city's norm. Just as in Alexandria, the glories of the East seemed to have eluded Egypt's capital, which had little provision for sanitation, garbage removal, street lighting, traffic management, or corralling the marauding dog packs that roamed its lanes. Of course I've said much the same of Paris. Still, if the Egyptians had marshaled their dogs instead of their cavalry, our conquest might not have been so easy. Scores of the mutts were shot or bayoneted each day by annoyed soldiers. The executions had no more impact on the canine population than swatting had on the incessant flies.

And yet, as in Alexandria or Paris, there was opulence amid the squalor. The Mamelukes were masters at squeezing taxes from the oppressed peasantry and spending it on monuments to themselves, their palaces exhibiting an Arabic grace missing from the heavier structures of Europe or America. While plain on the outside, the finer houses inside had shady courtyards of orange, palm, pomegranate, and fig, gracefully pointed Moorish arches, tiled fountains, and cool rooms rich with carpets, cushions, carved bookshelves, domed ceilings, and brass and copper tables. Some had intricate balconies and *mashrabiyya* screened windows that looked over the street, as carefully carved as a Swiss chalet

and as concealing as a veil. Bonaparte claimed for himself
the recently constructed marble-and-granite home of Mohammed Bey el-Elfi, which boasted baths on every floor, a
sauna, and glass windows. Napoleon's academics were housed
in the palace of another bey named Quassim who had fled to
Upper Egypt. His harem became the invention workshop for
the industrious Conte, and his gardens the seminar room for
the savants. The Muslim mosques were even more elegant,
their Moorish minarets and soaring domes matching in grace
and grandeur the finest Gothic churches in Europe. In the
markets the awnings were bright as rainbows, and the oriental
carpets draped on balustrades like a garden of flowers. The
contrasts of Egypt—heat and shade, wealth and poverty, dung
and incense, clay and color, mud brick and gleaming
limestone—were almost overwhelming.

The common soldiers found themselves in surroundings
considerably less luxurious than the officers: dark, medieval
homes with no conveniences. Many of them promptly proclaimed the city disappointing, its people hideous, the heat
enervating, and the food gut-wrenching. France had conquered a country, they wailed, that had no wine, no proper
bread, and no available women. Such opinion would moder-
ate as the summer cooled and some females began to form
liaisons with the new rulers. In time the troops even grump-
ily admitted that the *aish,* or baked flat bread, was actually
an agreeable substitute for their own. The dysentery that had
plagued the army since landing increased, however, and the
French army was beginning to suffer more casualties from
disease than bullets. The absence of alcohol had already
caused so much grumbling that Bonaparte ordered stills to
make a libation from dates, the most plentiful fruit. And
while officers were planning the planting of vineyards, their
troops quickly discovered the Muslim drug called hashish,
sometimes rolled into honeyed balls and spiced with opium.
Drinking its brew or smoking its seeds became commonplace, and throughout its occupation of Egypt, the army was
never able to get the drug under control.

The general entered his prize city through a main gate at
the head of a regiment, bands playing and flags flying. At

Ashraf's direction Astiza, Talma, and I entered a smaller gate and threaded through twisting lanes past bazaars that, two days after the great battle, were half-deserted, their flaws lit by the harsh sun of noon. Boys threw water to hold down the dust. Donkeys with baskets slung on either side forced us into entryways as they squeezed down alleys. Even in the heart of Cairo there were village sounds of barking dogs, snorting camels, crowing roosters, and the call of the muezzins to prayer, which to my ears sounded like cats mating. The shops looked like stables and the poorer houses like unlit caves, their men squatting impassively in their faded blue *galabiyyas* and smoking from *sheesha* water pipes. Their children, jaundiced and covered with sores, stared at us with saucer eyes. Their women hid. It was obvious that the majority of the nation lived in abject poverty.

"Maybe the finer neighborhoods are elsewhere," Talma said worriedly.

"No, this is what you have responsibility for," Ashraf said.

The notion of responsibility had been preying on my mind, and I told Ash that if his brother would receive us I'd grant the Mameluke his freedom. I really didn't want to support another dependent besides Astiza, and in fact the entire idea of servants and slaves had always made me uncomfortable. Franklin had a pair of Negroes once and was so discomfited by their presence that he'd set them free. Slaves were a poor investment, he'd concluded: costly to buy, expensive to maintain, and with no incentive to do good work.

Ashraf seemed less than pleased at my mercy. "How am I to eat if you cast me out like a foundling?"

"Ash, I am not a rich man. I have no means to pay you."

"But you do, from the gold you just captured from me!"

"I'm supposed to pay back what I just won in battle?"

"Is that not just? Here is what we will do. I will become your guide, Citizen Ash. I know all of Egypt. For this, you will pay me back what you stole. At the end, we will each have what we started with."

"That's a fortune that no guide or servant would ever earn!"

He considered. "This is true. So you will hire my brother as well with the money, to investigate your mystery. And pay to stay in his household, a thousand times better than the sties that we are passing. Yes, your victory and your generosity will buy you many friends in Cairo. The gods have smiled on all of us this day, my friend."

That would teach me to be generous. I tried to take solace in Franklin, who counseled that "he who multiplies riches multiplies cares." That certainly seemed true of my game winnings. Yet Ben was as obsessed with a dollar as any of us, and drove hard bargains, too. I never could get a raise out of him.

"No," I told Ash. "I will pay you a living wage, and your brother too. But only when we've discovered what the medallion means will I give you back the remainder."

"This is fair," said Astiza.

"And it shows you have the wisdom of the ancients!" Ashraf said. "Agreed! Allah, Jesus, and Horus be with you!"

I was pretty sure such inclusion was blasphemy in at least three religions, but never mind: he might do well as a Freemason. "Tell me about your brother."

"He is a very strange man, like you; you will like him. Enoch cares nothing for politics but everything for knowledge. He and I are nothing alike, because I am of this world and he is of another. But I love and respect him. He knows eight languages, including yours. He has more books than the sultan in Constantinople has wives."

"Is that a lot?"

"Oh yes."

And so we came to Enoch's house. Like all Cairo habitations the outside was plain, a three-story edifice with tiny, slitlike windows and a massive wooden door with a small iron grill. At first Ashraf's hammering brought no answer. Had Enoch fled with the Mameluke beys? But finally a peephole behind the grill was opened, Ash shouted imprecations in Arabic, and the door cracked open. A gigantic black butler named Mustafa ushered us inside.

The relief from the heat was immediate. We passed

through a small open atrium to a courtyard with murmuring fountain and shading orange trees. The home's architecture seemed to create a gentle breeze. An ornate wooden stair climbed one side of the court to screened rooms above. Beyond was the main living room, floored in intricate Moorish tile and covered at one end with oriental carpets and cushions, where guests could lounge. At the opposite end was a screened balcony where women could listen to the conversation of the men below. The beamed ceiling was ornate, the arches pleasingly peaked, and the sculpted bookcases crammed with volumes. Draperies billowed in puffs of desert air. Talma mopped his face. "It's what I dreamed."

We didn't stop here, however. Mustafa led us through a smaller courtyard beyond, bare except for an alabaster pedestal carved with mysterious signs. Above was a square of brilliantly blue sky at the top of towering white walls. The sun illuminated one side like snow and cast the opposite into shadow.

"It's a light well," Astiza murmured.

"A what?"

"Such wells at the pyramids were used for measuring time. At the summer solstice, the sun would be directly overhead, casting no shadow. That is how the priests could pinpoint the longest day of the year."

"Yes, that is right!" Ashraf confirmed. "It told the seasons and predicted the rising of the Nile."

"Why did they need to know that?"

"When the Nile rose, the farms flooded and labor was freed for other projects, like building pyramids," Astiza said. "The Nile's cycle was the cycle of Egypt. The measurement of time was the beginning of civilization. People had to be assigned to keep track of it, and became priests, and thought of all kinds of other useful things for people to do."

Beyond was a large room as dim as the courtyard was bright. It was crowded with dusty statuary, broken stone vessels, and chunks of wall with colorful Egyptian painting. Red-skinned men and yellow-skinned women posed in the stiff yet graceful poses I'd seen on the tablet in the hold of *L'Orient*. There were jackal-headed gods, the cat goddess

Bastet, stiffly serene pharaohs, black-polished falcons, and blocky wooden cases with life-sized paintings of humans on the outside. Talma had already described these elaborate coffins to me. They held mummies.

The scribe stopped before one in excitement. "Are these real?" he exclaimed. "A source like this could cure all my illnesses . . ."

I pulled. "Come on before you choke to death."

"These are cases from which the mummies have been removed," Ashraf told him. "Thieves would discard the coffins, but Enoch has let it be known he will pay to collect them. He thinks their decoration is another key to the past."

I saw that some were covered with hieroglyphics as well as drawings. "Why write on something that would be buried?" I asked.

"It may be to instruct the dead through the perils of the underworld, my brother says. For us the living, they are useful to store things in because most people are too superstitious to look inside. They fear a curse."

A narrow stone staircase at the rear of the room led down to a large vaulted cellar lit by lamps. At Ashraf's invitation, we descended to a large library. It was roofed with barrel vaults and floored with stone, dry and cool. Its wooden shelves were crammed floor to ceiling with books, journals, scrolls, and sheaves of parchment. Some bindings were sturdy leather, light glinting on gold lettering. Other tomes, often in strange languages, seemed held together by tendrils of old fabric, their smell as musty as the grave. At a central table, half the size of a barn door, sat the bent figure of a man.

"Greetings, my brother," Ashraf said in English.

Enoch looked up from his writing. He was older than Ashraf, bald, with a fringe of long gray locks and a heavy beard, looking as if Newton's gravity had tugged all his hair toward his sandals. Dressed in gray robes, he was hawk-nosed and bright-eyed and his skin was the color of the parchment he'd been bent over. He carried an air of serenity few people achieve, his eyes betraying a hint of mischief.

"So the French are occupying even my library?" The tone was wry.

"No, they come as friends, and the tall one is an American. His friend is a French scribe . . ."

"Who is interested in my dehydrated companion," Enoch said with amusement. Talma was staring, transfixed, at a mummy posed upright in an open coffin in one corner. This casket, too, was covered with fine, indecipherable writing. The mummy was stripped of bandages, some of the old linen in a tangle at its feet, and incisions had been made in its chest cavity. There was nothing reassuring about the body, a dark brownish gray looking starved from the drying, the eyes closed, the nose a snub, the mouth open in a rictus that showed small, white teeth. I found it disturbing.

Talma, however, was happy as sheep in clover. "Is this truly ancient?" he breathed. "An attempt at everlasting life?"

"Antoine, I think they failed," I observed dryly.

"Not necessarily," Enoch said. "To the Egyptians, the preservation of the dead physical body was a requirement for everlasting life. According to accounts that have come down to us, the ancients believed the individual consisted of three parts: his physical body, his *ba*—which we might call character—and his *ka,* or life force. These last two combined are equivalent to our modern soul. *Ba* and *ka* had to find each other and unite in a perilous underworld as the sun, Ra, journeyed each night through it, in order to form an immortal *akh* that would live amid the gods. The mummy was their daytime home until this task was completed. Instead of separating the material and the spiritual, Egyptian religion combined them."

"*Ba, ka,* and Ra? Sounds like a firm of solicitors." I was always uncomfortable with the spiritual.

Enoch ignored me. "I have decided the journey of this one should be completed by now. I've unwrapped and cut him to investigate ancient embalming techniques."

"There is talk these tissues could have medicinal qualities," Talma said.

"Which distorts what Egyptians believed," Enoch replied. "The body was a home to be animated, not the essence of life itself. Just as you are more than your ailments, scribe.

You know, your trade as scribe was that of the wise Thoth."

"I'm actually a journalist, come to record Egypt's liberation," Talma said.

"How artfully you put that." Enoch looked at Astiza. "And we have another guest, as well?"

"She is a . . ." Ashraf began.

"Servant," Enoch finished. He looked at her curiously. "So you have come back."

Blimey, did these two know each other as well?

"The gods appear to have willed it." She cast her eyes down. "My master is dead, killed by Napoleon himself, and my new master is the American."

"An intriguing twist of fate."

Ashraf moved forward to embrace his brother. "It is also by the grace of all the gods and the mercy of these three that I've seen you again, brother! I'd made my peace and prepared for paradise, but then I was captured!"

"You're now their slave?"

"The American has already set me free. He's hired me as his bodyguard and guide with the money he took from me. He wants to hire you as well. Soon I will have back all that I lost. Is this not fate as well?"

"Hire me for what?"

"He's come to Egypt with an ancient artifact. I told him you might recognize it."

"Ashraf is the bravest warrior I've ever seen," I spoke up. "He hurtled a French infantry square and it took all of us to bring him down."

"Bah. I was captured by a woman pushing a wagon wheel."

"He has always been brave," said Enoch. "Too much so. And vulnerable to women, as well."

"I am a man of this world, not the next, my brother. But these people seek your knowledge. They have an ancient medallion and want to know its purpose. When I saw it I knew I must bring them to you. Who knows more of the past than wise Enoch?"

"A medallion?"

"The American obtained it in Paris but thinks it Egyptian," Astiza said. "Men have tried to kill him to obtain it. The bandit Bin Sadr desires it. French savants are curious about it. Bonaparte favors him because of it."

"Bin Sadr the Snake? We'd heard he rides with the invaders."

"He rides with whoever pays him enough," Ashraf scoffed.

"And who truly pays him?" Enoch asked Astiza.

Again, she looked down. "Another scholar." Did she know more than she'd told me?

"He's a spy for this Bonaparte," Ashraf theorized, "and an agent, perhaps, for whoever wants this medallion most."

"Then the American should be most careful."

"Indeed."

"And the American threatens the peace of whatever home he comes into."

"As usual, you are quick with the truth, my brother."

"And yet you bring him to me."

"Because he may have what has long been rumored!"

I didn't like this talk at all. I'd just survived a major battle and yet was still in peril? "Just who *is* this Bin Sadr?" I asked.

"He was such a relentless grave robber that he became an outcast," Enoch said. "He had no sense of propriety or respect. Men of learning despised him, so he joined with Europeans investigating the dark arts. He became a mercenary and, by rumor, an assassin and began roaming the world in the company of powerful men. He disappeared for a time. Now he appears again, apparently working for Bonaparte."

Or for Count Alessandro Silano, I thought.

"Sounds like a splendidly interesting newspaper story," said Talma.

"He would kill you if you wrote it."

"But perhaps too complicated for my readers," the journalist amended.

Maybe I should just give the medallion to this Enoch, I thought. After all, like the booty I had seized from Ash, it had cost me nothing. Let him deal with snakes and highwaymen. But no, what if it led to real treasure? Berthollet might think the best things in life are free, but in my experience the people who say that are ones who already have money.

"So you're seeking answers?" Enoch asked.

"I'm seeking someone to trust. Someone to study it but not steal it."

"If your neckpiece is the kind of guidepost I think it is, I don't want it for myself. It is a burden, not a gift. But perhaps I can help understand it. Can I see it?"

I took it off and let it swing from its chain, everyone looking curiously. Then Enoch gave it the same inspection everyone else had, turning it, splaying the arms, and using a lamp to shine light through its perforations. "How did you get this?"

"I won it at cards from a soldier who claimed it once belonged to Cleopatra. He said it was carried by an alchemist named Cagliostro."

"Cagliostro!"

"You've heard of him?"

"He was in Egypt once." Enoch shook his head. "He sought secrets no man should learn, entered places no man should enter, and uttered names no man should say."

"Why shouldn't he say a name?"

"To learn a god's real name is to know how to call him to do your bidding," Ashraf said. "To say the name of the dead is to summon them. The old ones believed words, especially written words, were magic."

The old man looked from me to Astiza. "What is your role here, priestess?"

She bowed slightly. "I serve the goddess. She brought me to the American just as you have been brought, for her own purposes."

Priestess? What the devil did that mean?

"Which maybe is to hurl this necklace into the Nile," Enoch said.

"Indeed. And yet the ancients forged it so that it might be found, did they not, wise Hermes? And it has come to us in this unlikely way. Why? How much is chance, and how much is destiny?"

"A question I haven't answered in a life of learning." Enoch sighed, perplexed. "Now then." He studied the medallion anew, pointing to the perforations in the disc. "Do you recognize the pattern?"

"Stars," Astiza offered.

"Yes, but which ones?"

We all shook our heads.

"But it is easy! It is Draconis, or Draco. The dragon." He traced a line along the stars that looked like a writhing snake or a skinny dragon. "It is a star constellation, meant to guide the owner of this medallion, I suspect."

"Guide him how?" I asked.

"Who knows? The stars revolve in the night sky and shift position with the seasons. A constellation means little unless correlated with a calendar. So what good is this?"

We waited for an answer to what we hoped was a rhetorical question.

"I don't know," Enoch admitted. "Still, the ancients were obsessed with time. Some temples were built only to be illuminated on the winter solstice or the autumn equinox. The journey of the sun was like the journey of life. Did this come with no time piece?"

"No," I said. But I was reminded of the calendar that Monge had shown me in the hold of *L'Orient,* the one captured in the same fortress that had imprisoned Cagliostro. Maybe the old conjurer had carried the pair together. Could it be a clue?

"Without knowing when it should be used, this medallion may be worthless. Now, this line that bisects the circle, what does that mean?"

"I don't know," I said.

"These zigzag lines here are almost certainly the ancient symbol for water." I was surprised. I thought maybe they were mountains, but Enoch insisted they were the Egyptian symbol for waves. "But this little pyramid of scratches, it baffles me. And these arms . . . ah, but look here." He pointed and we bent closer. There was a notch or indentation halfway down each arm that I'd never really noticed, as if part of the arm had been filed away.

"Is it a ruler?" I tried. "That notch could mark a measurement."

"A possibility," Enoch said. "But it could also be a place to fit another piece onto this one. Perhaps the reason this medallion is so mysterious, American, is because it's not yet complete."

It was Astiza who suggested that I leave the medallion with the old man for study so that he could look for similar ornaments in his books. At first I was dubious. I'd gotten used to its weight and the security of knowing where it was at all times. Now I was going to give it up to a near-stranger?

"It's no good to any of us until we know what it is and what it's for," she reasoned. "Wear it and it can be taken from you in the streets of Cairo. Leave it in the cellar of a reclusive scholar and you've left it in a vault."

"Can I trust him?"

"What choice do you have? How many answers have you gotten in your weeks of possession? Give Enoch a day or two to make some progress."

"What I am supposed to do in the meantime?"

"Start asking questions of your own savants. Why would the constellation Draco be on this piece? A solution will come faster if we all work together."

"Ethan, it's too big a risk," Talma said, looking at Astiza with distrust.

Indeed, who was this woman who'd been called priestess? Yet my heart told me Talma's fears were exaggerated, that I'd been lonely in this quest and that now, unbidden, I had some allies to help unravel the mystery. The goddess's will indeed. "No, she's right," I said. "We need help or we're not going to make any progress. But if Enoch runs with my medallion, he'll have the entire French army after him."

"Run? He has invited us to stay in his house with him."

My bed chamber was the finest I'd enjoyed in years. It was cool and shadowy, the bed high off the floor and surrounded by gauze curtains. The tile was layered with carpets, and the washbasin and ewer were silver and brass. What a contrast to the grime and heat of campaigning! Yet

I felt myself being seduced into a story I didn't understand, and found myself going back over events. Wasn't it fortuitous that I'd met a Greek-Egyptian woman who spoke English? That the brother of this strange Enoch had charged straight at *me* after breaking into the middle of the square at the Battle of the Pyramids? That Bonaparte had not just permitted, but approved, this addition to my retinue? It was almost as if the medallion was working magic as a strange attractant, drawing people in.

Certainly it was time to put more questions to my supposed servant. After we'd bathed and rested I found Astiza in the main courtyard, now shadowy and cool. She was sitting by the fountain in expectation of my interrogation. Washed, changed, and combed, her hair shone like obsidian. Her breasts were cupped in folds of linen, their nubs distractingly draped, and her feet were slim and sandaled, her ankles crossed demurely. She wore bracelets, anklets, and an ankh at her throat, and was so breathtaking it was hard to think clearly. Nonetheless, I must.

"Why did he call you priestess?" I said without preamble, sitting next to her.

"Surely you didn't think my interests are limited to cooking and washing for you," she said quietly.

"I knew you were more than a serving girl. But priestess of what?"

Her eyes were wide, her gaze solemn. "Of faith that has run through every religion for ten thousand years: that there are worlds beyond the ones we see, Ethan, and mysteries beyond what we think we understand. Isis is a gate to those worlds."

"You're a bloody pagan."

"And what is a pagan? If you look at the origin of the word, it means country dweller, a person of nature who lives to the rhythm of seasons and the sun. If that is paganism, then I am a fervent believer."

"And a believer in what else, exactly?"

"That lives have purpose, that some knowledge is best left guarded, and some power sheathed and unused. Or, if released, that it be used for good."

"Did I lead you to this house or did you lead me?"

She smiled gently. "Do you think we met by accident?"

I snorted. "My recollection is by cannon fire."

"You took the shortest route to the harbor of Alexandria. We were told to watch for a civilian in a green coat coming that way, possibly accompanying Bonaparte."

"We?"

"My master and I. The one you killed."

"And your house just happened to be on our route?"

"No, but a house of a Mameluke who'd fled was. My master and I commandeered it and our acolytes brought us guns."

"You almost killed Napoleon!"

"Not really. The Guardian was aiming at you, not him."

"What!"

"My priesthood thought it best to simply kill you before you learned too much. But the gods apparently had other plans. The Guardian hit almost everyone *but* you. Then the room exploded and when I came to, there you were. I knew then that you had purpose, however blind you might be."

"What purpose?"

"I agree it's hard to imagine. But you are supposed to help, somehow, guard what should be guarded or use what should be used."

"Guard what? Use what?"

She shook her head. "We don't know."

By Franklin's lightning, this was the damnedest thing I'd ever heard. I was supposed to believe my captive had found me instead of the other way around? "What do you mean, the Guardian?"

"Simply one who keeps the old ways that made this land the world's richest and most beautiful, five thousand years ago. We too had heard rumors of the necklace—Cagliostro couldn't keep silent in his excitement at finding it—and of unscrupulous men on their way to dig and rob. But you! So ignorant! Why would Isis put it in your hands? Yet first they lead you to me. Then us to Ashraf, and from Ashraf to Enoch. Secrets that have slumbered for millennia are being awakened by the march of the French. The pyramids tremble. The gods are restless, and directing our hand."

I didn't know if she was daft as a lunatic or smart as a seer. "Toward what?"

"I don't know. All of us are half-blind, seeing some things but missing others. These French savants you boast of, they are wise men, are they not? Magi?"

"Magi?"

"Or as we in Egypt called them, magicians."

"I think men of science would draw a distinction between themselves and magicians, Astiza."

"In ancient Egypt, no such distinction existed. The wise knew magic, and performed many spells. Now, you and I must be a bridge between your savants and men like Enoch, and solve this puzzle before unscrupulous men do. We're in a race with the cult of the snake, the serpent god Apophis, and its Egyptian Rite. They want to learn the secret first and use it for their own dark designs."

"*What* designs?"

"We don't know, because none of us are entirely sure what it is we seek." She hesitated. "There are legends of great treasures and, more importantly, great powers, the kind of power that shakes empires. What, exactly, it is too early to say. Let Enoch study some more. Just be aware that many men have heard these stories throughout history and have wondered at the truth behind them.

"You mean Napoleon?"

"I suspect that he understands least of all, but hopes someone will find it so he can seize it for himself. Why, he isn't sure, but he's heard the legends of Alexander. All of us are in a fog of myth and legend, except perhaps Bin Sadr—and whoever Bin Sadr's true master is."

CHAPTER ELEVEN

I began with one of the expedition's astronomers, Nicholas-Antoine Nouet. While most of the French had cursed the desert for its enervating heat and scuttling vermin, Nouet had been delighted, saying the dry air made it unusually easy to chart the heavens. "It's an astronomer's paradise, Gage! A country without clouds!" I found him crouched at the new institute, coat off and sleeves rolled up, sorting through a stack of calibrated rods used to measure the position of the stars against the horizon.

"Nouet," I addressed, "is the sky constant?"

He looked up with irritation since I'd broken his chain of thought. "Constant?"

"I mean, do the stars move?"

"Well." He straightened, looking outside to the shaded garden that the scientists had expropriated. "The earth rotates, which is why the stars seem to rise and set like the sun. They make a wheel around our northern axis, the polestar."

"But the stars themselves don't move?"

"That is still under debate."

"So thousands of years ago," I pressed, "when the pyramids were built, the sky would have looked like it does now?"

"Ah, now I see what you're driving at. The answer is yes—and no. The constellations would basically be unchanged, but the earth's axis wobbles on a twenty-six-thousand-year cycle."

"Doctor Monge told me about that, on *L'Orient*. He said the position of the zodiac, relative to the rising sun on a particular date, changes. Would anything else?"

"One difference over many millennia would be the polestar. Because the earth's axis wobbles, it pointed to a different North Star thousands of years ago."

"Is there any chance that star might have been Draco?"

"Why, yes, I believe so. Why do you ask?"

"You've heard I have an artifact of the past. My preliminary investigations here in Cairo suggest it may represent the constellation of Draconis, the dragon. If Draco was the polestar . . ."

"It tells you to orient your artifact north, perhaps."

"Precisely. But why?"

"Monsieur, it is *your* fragment of antiquity, not mine."

"Monge showed me something else in the hold of *L'Orient*. It was a circular device with signs of the zodiac. He thought it was some kind of calendar, perhaps to predict future dates."

"That wouldn't be unusual among ancient cultures. Ancient priests exhibited great power if they could predict how the heavens would look in advance. They could forecast the rising of the Nile and optimum dates for sowing and reaping. The power of nations and the rise and fall of kings hinged on such knowledge. To them, religion and science were one. Do you have this device? Perhaps I could help decipher it."

"We left it aboard *L'Orient* with the Maltese treasure."

"Bah! So it could be melted down and spent by the next batch of rascals to seize control of the Directory? Why are such treasures on a warship that might go into battle? These are tools we need here in Egypt! Get Bonaparte to let you fetch it, Gage. These things are usually simple, once you puzzle them out."

I needed something more substantial before going to our general. Enoch was still ensconced with the medallion in his library when I learned, two days later, that the geographer Jomard whom I'd met in the hold of *L'Orient* was going to cross the Nile to Giza and make the first preliminary measurements of the pyramids. I volunteered my services and those of Ashraf as guide. Talma came too while Astiza, now subject to the customs of Cairo, stayed behind to help Enoch.

The four of us enjoyed the morning breeze as we ferried across. The river ran close to the mammoth structures, along a sand-and-limestone bluff that led up to the plateau where they were built. We beached and began climbing.

As remarkable as it had been to fight in sight of these famed structures, they'd been too distant from Imbaba to impress us with their size. It had been their geometric purity, set against the stark desert, which caught the eye. Now, as we labored up a trail from the great river, their immensity became apparent. The pyramids first peeked above the brow of the slope like perfect deltas, their design as harmonious as it was simple. The volume of their mass against the sky lifted the eye to their apex, beckoning us to heaven. Then, as they came into fuller view, their titanic dimensions were at last apparent, stone mountains ordained by mathematics. How had primitive Egypt built something so vast? And why? The very air seemed crystalline around them, and their majesty carried a strange aura, like the curious smell and prickling I sometimes feel when demonstrating electricity. It was very quiet here after the clamor of Cairo.

Adding to the pyramid's daunting effect was their famed guardian who stared due east. The gigantic stone head called the Sphinx, as remarkable as we'd imagined from written descriptions, guarded the slope a short distance below the pyramids. Its neck was a dune of sand, its leonine body buried beneath the desert. The statue's nose had been damaged years ago by Mameluke cannon practice, but its serene gaze, full African lips, and pharaoh's headdress created a visage so eternal as if to deny the toll of time. Its eroded and damaged features made it seem older than the pyramids beyond, and made me wonder if it had perhaps been built before them. Was there something sacred about this site? What kind of people had made such a colossus, and why? Was it a sentinel? A guardian? A god? Or mere vanity to one man, tyrant and master? I couldn't help but think of Napoleon. Would our republican revolutionary, liberator and common man, ever be tempted to commission a head like this?

Beyond were dunes strewn with scraps of rubble, broken walls, and the crumbled tips of smaller pyramids. The trio of major pyramids that dominated Giza made a diagonal line, northeast to southwest. The Great Pyramid of Khufu, called Cheops by the Greeks, was the closest to Cairo. A second, slightly smaller one beyond had been attributed by the Greeks to the pharaoh Khafre, or Khephren, and a third even smaller one to the southwest had been built by a Menkaure.

"One of the interesting things about the Great Pyramid is that it is aligned precisely with the cardinal directions and not just magnetic north," Jomard told us as we rested a moment. "It is so precise that its priests and engineers must have had a sophisticated knowledge of astronomy and surveying. Also, notice how you can judge the direction you face by the way the pyramids relate to each other. The pattern of shadow works as a kind of compass. You could use the relation of their apexes and shadows to orient a surveying tool."

"You think they are a kind of geodetic landmark?" I asked.

"That's one theory. The others depend on measurement. Come." He and Ashraf strode ahead, carrying reels of measuring tape. Talma and I, hot and winded from the climb, lagged a little behind.

"Not a scrap of green," Talma muttered. "A place of the dead, all right."

"But what tombs, eh, Antoine?" I looked back at the head of the Sphinx, the river below us, the pyramids above.

"Yes, and you without your magic key to get inside."

"I don't think I need the medallion for that. Jomard said they were opened centuries ago by Arab treasure hunters. I suppose we'll go in ourselves, eventually."

"Still, doesn't it bother you not to have the medallion?"

I shrugged. "It's cooler not to carry it, frankly."

He looked at the brown triangles above us, dissatisfied.

"Why do you trust the woman more than me?" The hurt in his voice surprised me.

"But I don't."

"When I've asked you where the necklace is, you've been coy. But she persuades you to give it to an old Egyptian we barely know."

"Loan it, for study. I didn't give it to her, I loaned it to him. I trust Enoch. He's a savant, like us."

"I don't trust her."

"Antoine, you're jealous."

"Yes, and why? Not just because she's a woman, and you run after females like a dog after a bone. No, because she's not telling us everything she knows. She has her own agenda, and it's not necessarily ours."

"How do you know that?"

"Because she's a woman."

"A priestess, she said, trying to help us."

"A witch."

"Trusting Egyptians is the only way we're going to solve the mystery, Antoine."

"Why? They haven't solved it in five thousand years. Then we come along with some trinket and suddenly we have more friends than we know what to do with? It's all too convenient for me."

"You're too suspicious."

"You're too naïve."

And with that we went on, neither satisfied.

As I trudged up the slippery sand toward the largest pyramid, sweating in the heat, I felt increasingly small. Even when I turned away the monument's bulk seemed omnipresent, looming over us. Everywhere around us was the sand-strewn wreckage of time. We threaded past rubble that must once have been the walls of causeways and courtyards. The great desert rolled beyond. Dark birds wheeled in the brassy air. At last we stopped before the highest and greatest of all structures on earth, dunes undulating along its base. The blocks it was built from looked like the bricks of giants, massive and heavy.

"And here, perhaps, is a map of the world," Jomard announced.

With his sharp features, the French savant reminded me of some of the carved stone falcons I had seen in Enoch's house: Horus. He was looking up at the triangular face of the pyramid with happy awe.

"A map of the world?" Talma asked skeptically.

"So said Diodorus and other ancient scholars. Or, rather, a map of its northern hemisphere."

The journalist, flushed and cranky from the heat, sat down on an upended block. "I thought the world was round."

"It is."

"I know you savants are cleverer than I, Jomard, but unless I'm hallucinating, I believe the structure before me comes to a rather noticeable point."

"An astute observation, Monsieur Talma. You have the makings of a savant yourself, perhaps. The idea is that the apex represents the Pole, the base the equator, and each side a quarter of the northern half-sphere. As if you had sliced an orange first in half, horizontally, and then into four vertical pieces."

"None of them flat triangles," Talma said, fanning himself. "Why not just build a mound, like a loaf, if you want to model half our planet?

"My maps of Egypt and the world are flat, and yet they represent something round," the savant replied. "Our question is, did the Egyptians, in an abstract way, design the pyramid with a precise angle and area to mathematically mirror our globe? The ancients tell us its dimensions correspond to a fraction of the 360 degrees in which we divide the earth. This is a sacred number that came from the Egyptians and Babylonians, based on the days of the year. So did they, in fact, choose proportions to demonstrate how to accurately translate a curved earth to a flat plane, like the face of a pyramid? Herodotus tells us that the area of the face of the pyramid is equal to the square of its height. It just so happens that such a proportion is an ideal way to calculate the surface area of a circle, like our planet, from a square, and translate the points of one to the other."

"Why would they do so?" the journalist asked.

"To boast, perhaps, that they knew how."

"But, Jomard," I objected, "People believed the world was flat until Columbus."

"Not so, my American friend. The moon is round. The sun is round. It occurred to the ancients that the earth, too, is round, and the Greeks used careful measurements to calculate the circumference. My idea is that the Egyptians preceded them."

"How could they know how big our planet is?"

"It is child's play if you understand basic geometry and astronomy, measuring fixed points against the shadow of the sun or the declination the stars."

"Ah, yes," said Talma. "As a babe I did it before my naps."

Jomard refused to be goaded. "Anyone who has seen the shadow the earth casts on the moon or watched a ship disappear below the horizon would suspect our planet is a sphere. We know the Greek Eratosthenes used the differing length of shadows cast by the noon sun at the summer solstice at two different points in Egypt to get within 320 kilometers of the correct answer in 250 B.C. This pyramid was nearly three thousand years old when he made his measurement. Yet what was to prevent its ancient builders from doing the same, or measuring relative star height at points north and south along the Nile to again calculate the angles and, by implication, the size of our planet? If you travel along the river the height of stars above the horizon changes by several degrees, and Egyptian mariners would surely have noticed that. Tycho Brahe did such star measurements with his naked eye to sufficient accuracy to calculate the size of the earth, so why not the ancients? We attribute the birth of knowledge to the Greeks, but they attributed it to the Egyptians."

I knew Jomard had read more of the ancient texts than any of us, so I regarded the great mass before me with new curiosity. Its outer sheathing of smooth limestone had been robbed centuries ago to build Muslim palaces and mosques in Cairo, so only the core blocks remained. Yet each piece of that was colossal, set in endless rows. I began to count the tiers of masonry and gave up after a hundred. "But the Egyptians had no ships to circle the globe, so why would they care what size the planet was?" I objected. "And build a mountain to contain a calculation? It makes no sense."

"As baffling as building St. Peter's to a being none but saints and lunatics can claim to see," Jomard retorted. "What makes no sense to one man is life's purpose to another. Can we even explain ourselves? For example, what is the point of your Freemasonry, Talma?"

"Well . . ." He had to think a moment. "To live harmoniously and rationally, instead of killing each other over religion and politics, I think."

"And here we are, a few miles from the offal of a battlefield produced by an army filled with Masons. Who is to say who is the lunatic? Who knows why the Egyptians would do such a thing?"

"I thought this was the tomb of the pharaoh," Talma said.

"A tomb with no occupant. When Arab treasure hunters broke in centuries ago and tunneled around granite plugs meant to seal the entrance forever, they found not a sign that any king, queen, or commoner had ever been laid to rest here. The sarcophagus was lidless and empty. There was no writing, and not a scrap of treasure or worldly goods to commemorate who it was built for. The greatest structure on the face of the earth, taller than the highest cathedrals, and empty as a peasant's cupboard! It is one thing to be a megalomaniac, harnessing tens of thousands of men to build your final resting place. It is quite another to do so and not rest there."

I looked at Ashraf, who had not followed our French. "What's the pyramid for?" I asked in English.

He shrugged, less in awe of the monument than we were. Of course, he'd lived in Cairo all his life. "To hold up the sky."

I sighed and turned back to Jomard. "So you think it's a map?"

"That is one hypothesis. Another is that its dimensions signify the divine. For thousands of years, architects and engineers have recognized that some proportions and shapes are more pleasing than others. They correspond to each other in interesting mathematical ways. Some feel such sublime relationships reveal fundamental and universal truths. When our own ancestors built the great Gothic cathedrals, they tried to use their dimensions and geometric proportions to express religious ideas and ideals, to in effect make the building itself holy by its very design. 'What is God?' Saint Bernard once asked. 'He is length, width, height, and depth.'"

I remembered Astiza's excitement over Pythagoras.

"So?" Talma challenged.

"So this pyramid may have been, to the ancients who built it, not a picture of the world, but a picture of God."

I stared uneasily at the vast structure, the hair prickling on my neck. It was utterly silent, and yet from nowhere I sensed a low, background hum, like the sound of a seashell pressed to the ear. Was God a number, a dimension? There was something godlike in the perfect simplicity before me.

"Unfortunately," Jomard went on, "all these ideas are difficult to verify until measurements are made to confirm whether height and perimeter match in scale the dimensions of our earth. That will be impossible to do until we excavate enough to find the pyramid's true base and corners. I'll need a small army of Arab workmen."

"I suppose we can go back then," Talma said hopefully.

"No," said Jomard. "We can at least begin to measure its height from the lowest course of stone we can see. Gage, you will help with the tape. Talma, you must take the utmost care to write down each stone height we give you."

My friend looked dubiously upward. "All that way?"

"The sun is declining. By the time we reach the top, it will be cooler."

Ashraf chose to remain below, clearly believing such a climb was something only sun-addled Europeans would do. And indeed, it wasn't easy. The pyramid seemed far steeper once we began to mount it.

"An optical illusion makes it appear squatter than it is, when viewed head on," Jomard explained.

"You didn't tell us that before we started up," Talma grumbled.

It took the three of us more than half an hour of careful ascent to get halfway. It was like climbing titanic children's blocks, a giant's staircase, with each step averaging two and a half feet in height. There was a real possibility of a nasty fall. We carefully measured each course of interior stone as we climbed, Talma keeping a running tally.

"Look at the size of these monsters," the journalist said. "They must weigh several tons. Why not build with smaller pieces?"

"Some engineering reason, perhaps?" I suggested.

"There's no architectural requirement for stones this big," Jomard said. "Yet the Egyptians cut these behemoths, floated them on the Nile, dragged them up that hill, and somehow hoisted them this high. Gage, you're our expert on electricity. Could they have used such a mysterious force to move these rocks?"

"If so, they had mastery of something we barely understand. I can devise a machine to give you a tingle, Jomard, but not to do any useful work." Once again I felt inadequate to the mission I'd given myself. I looked around for something tangible to contribute. "Here's something. Some of these stones have shells in them." I pointed.

The French savant followed my finger. "Indeed!" he said with surprise. He bent to inspect the limestone I'd pointed to. "Not shells, but the fossils of shells, as if these blocks originated from beneath the sea. It's a curiosity that has been noticed in mountain ranges in Europe, and has generated new debate about the age of the earth. Some say sea creatures were carried up there by the Great Flood, but others contend that our world is far older than biblical reckoning, and what today are mountains were once beneath the ocean."

"If that is true, the pyramids may be older than the Bible as well," I suggested.

"Yes. Changing the scale of time changes everything." He

was running his eye along the limestone, admiring the impressions of shells. "Look, there! We even have a nautilus!"

Talma and I peered over his shoulder. Imbedded in a pyramid block was the cross section of a spiral nautilus shell, one of the most beautiful shapes in nature. From its small corkscrew beginning its chambers grew larger, in pleasing and delicate proportion, as the sea creature grew in an elegant outward spiral. "And what does that make you think of?" Jomard asked.

"Seafood," Talma said. "I'm hungry."

Jomard ignored that, staring at the spiral in the rock, transfixed for a reason I didn't understand. Long minutes ticked by and I dared look out from our perch. A hawk was gliding by at our same elevation. It made me dizzy.

"Jomard?" Talma finally prompted. "You don't have to watch the fossil. It's not going to run away."

As if in reply, the savant suddenly took a rock hammer from his survey bag and tapped at the block's edges. There was already a crack near the fossil and he worked with this, succeeding in splitting the nautilus specimen loose and cupping it in his hand. "Could it be?" he murmured, turning the elegant creature to see its pattern in light and shadow. He seemed to have forgotten our mission, and us.

"We've still a way to go to the top," I warned, "and the day is getting late."

"Yes, yes." He blinked as if waking from a dream. "Let me think about this up there." He put the shell in his satchel. "Gage, hold the tape. Talma, ready your pencil!"

The summit took another half hour of careful climbing. It was more than 450 feet high, our measuring showed, but we could produce no more than a rough approximation. I looked down. The few French soldiers and Bedouins we could see looked like ants. Fortunately the pyramid's capstone was gone, so there was a space about the size of a bed on which to stand.

I did feel closer to heaven. There were no competing hills, just flat desert, the winding silver thread of the Nile, and the collar of green on each of its shores. Cairo across the river shimmered with a thousand minarets, and we could hear the

wail of the faithful being called to prayer. The battlefield of
Imbaba was a dusty arena, dotted with pits where the dead
were being tossed. Far to the north, the Mediterranean was
invisible over the horizon.

Jomard took out his stone nautilus again. "There is clarity
up here, don't you think? This temple focuses it." Plopping
down, he began to jot some figures.

"And not much else," Talma said, sitting himself in exaggerated resignation. "Did I mention that I'm hungry?"

But Jomard was lost again in some world of his own, so
finally we were quiet for a while, having become accus-
tomed to such meditation by the savants. I felt I could see
our planet's curve, and then scolded myself that it was illusion at this modest height. There did seem a kind of benign
focus at the structure's summit, however, and I actually enjoyed our quiet isolation. Had any other American been up
here?

Finally Jomard abruptly rose, picked up a limestone fragment as big as his fist, and hurled it as far as he could. We
watched the parabola of its fall, wondering if he could throw
far enough to clear the pyramid's base. He couldn't, and the
stone bounced off the pyramid's stone blocks below, shatter-
ing. Its pieces rattled down.

He looked down the slope for a moment, as if considering
his aim. Then he turned to us. "But of course! It's so obvious. And your eye, Gage, has been the key!"

I perked up. "It has?"

"What a marvel we are standing on! What a culmination
of thought, philosophy, and calculation! It was the nautilus
that let me see it!"

Talma was rolling his eyes.

"Let you see what?"

"Now, has either of you heard of the Fibonacci sequence
of numbers?"

Our silence was answer enough.

"It was brought to Europe about 1200 by Leonardo of
Pisa, also known as Fibonacci, after he had studied in Egypt.
Its real origin goes much further back than that, to times
unknown. Look." He showed us his paper. On it was written

a series of numbers: 1, 1, 2, 3, 5, 8, 13, 21, 34, 55. "Do you see the pattern?"

"I think I tried that one in the lottery," Talma said. "It lost."

"No, see how it works?" the savant insisted. "Each number is the sum of the two before it. The next in the sequence, adding 34 and the 55, would be 89."

"Fascinating," Talma said.

"Now the amazing thing about this series is that with geometry, you can represent this sequence not as numbers but as a geometric pattern. You do so by drawing squares." He drew two small squares side by side and put a number 1 inside each. "See, here we have the first two numbers of the sequence. Now we draw a third square alongside the first two, making it as long as they are combined, and label it number 2. Then a square with sides as long as a number 1 square and number 2 square combined, and label it 3. See?" He was sketching quickly. "The side of the new square is the sum of the two squares before it, just as the number in a Fibonacci sequence is the sum of the two numbers before. The squares rapidly get bigger in area."

Soon he had a picture like this:

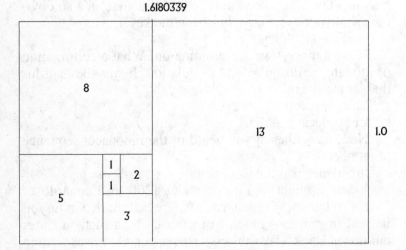

"What does that number at the top, the 1.6 something, mean?" I asked.

"It's the proportion of the length of the side of each of the squares to the smaller one before it," Jomard replied. "Notice that the lines of the square labeled 3 have a proportional length with the lines of the squares 2 as, say, the proportion between square 8 and square 13."

"I don't understand."

"See how the line at the top of square 3 is divided into two unequal lengths by its junction with squares 1 and 2?" Jomard said patiently. "That proportion between the length of the short line and the long line is repeated again and again, no matter how big you draw this diagram. The longer line is not 1.5 times the length of the shorter, but 1.618, or what the Greeks and Italians called the golden number, or golden section."

Both Talma and I straightened slightly. "You mean there's gold here?"

"No, you cretins." He shook his head in mock disgust. "Only that the proportions seem perfect when applied to architecture, or to monuments like this pyramid. There's something about that ratio which is instinctively pleasing to the eye. Cathedrals were built to reflect such divine numbers. Renaissance painters divided their canvases into rectangles and triangles echoing the golden section to achieve harmonious composition. Greek and Roman architects used it in temples and palaces. Now, we must confirm my guess with measurements more precise than those we've made today, but my hunch is that this pyramid is sloped precisely to represent this golden number, 1.618."

"What has the nautilus to do with anything?"

"I'm coming to that. First, imagine a line descending under our feet from the tip of this colossus to its base, straight down to the desert bedrock."

"I can confirm it is a long line, after that hard climb up," Talma said.

"More than four hundred and fifty feet," Jomard agreed. "Now imagine a line from the center of the pyramid to its outside edge."

"That would be half the width of its base," I ventured, feeling the same two steps behind that I'd always felt with Benjamin Franklin.

"Precisely!" Jomard cried. "You have an instinct for mathematics, Gage! Now, imagine a line running from that outside edge up the slope of the pyramid to where we are here, completing a right triangle. My theory is that if our line at the pyramid's base is set as one, such a line up to the peak here would be 1.618—the same harmonious proportion as shown by the squares I've drawn!" He looked triumphant.

We looked blank.

"Don't you see? This pyramid was built to conform to the Fibonacci numbers, the Fibonacci squares, the golden number that artists have always found harmonious. It doesn't just feel right to us, it *is* right!"

Talma looked across to the other two large pyramids that were our neighbors. "So are they all like that?"

Jomard shook his head. "No. This one is special, I suspect. It is a book, trying to tell us something. It is unique for a reason I don't yet understand."

"I'm sorry, Jomard," the journalist said. "I'm happy for you that you are excited, but the fact that imaginary lines equal 1.6, or whatever you said, seems an even sillier reason to build a pyramid than calling something pointed a hemisphere or building a tomb you won't be buried in. It seems perfectly possible to me that if any of this is true, your ancient Egyptians were at least as crazy as they were clever."

"Ah, but that is where you are wrong, my friend," the savant happily replied. "I don't blame your skepticism, however, because I didn't see what has been staring us in the face all day until sharp-eyed Gage here helped me find the fossil nautilus. You see, the Fibonacci sequence, translated into Fibonacci geometry, yields one of the most beautiful designs in all nature. Let's draw an arc through these squares, from one corner to another, and then connect the arcs." He flipped his drawing. "Then we get a picture like this:"

"There! What does that look like?"

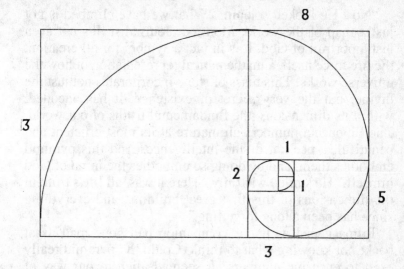

"The nautilus," I ventured. The man was damned clever, even though I still didn't get where he was heading.

"Precisely! Imagine if I expanded this picture by adding additional squares: 21, 34, and so on. This spiral would continue to grow, round and round, bigger and bigger, looking ever more like our nautilus. And this spiral pattern is something we see again and again. When you take the Fibonacci sequence and apply it to geometry, and then apply that geometry to nature, you see this sublime number pattern, this perfect spiral, being used by God himself. You will find the spiral in the seed head of a flower or the seeds of a pinecone. The petals on many flowers are Fibonacci numbers. A lily has 3, a buttercup 5, a delphinium 8, corn marigolds 13, some asters have 21, and some daisies 34. Not all plants follow the pattern, but many do because it is the most efficient way to push growing seeds or petals out from a common center. It is also very beautiful. So, *now* we see just how marvelous this pyramid is!" He nodded to himself, satisfied with his own explanation.

"It's a flower?" Talma ventured, relieving me of the burden of being dense.

"No." He looked solemn. "What we have climbed is not just a map of the world, Monsieur Journalist. It's not even just a portrait of God. It is in fact a symbol for all creation, the life force itself, a mathematical representation of how the universe works. This mass of stone incorporates not just the divine, but the very secret of existence. It has encoded, within its dimensions, the fundamental truths of our world. The Fibonacci numbers are nature at its most efficient and beautiful, a peek at divine intelligence. And this pyramid embodies them, and by doing so embodies the mind of God himself." He smiled wistfully. "Here it was, all life's truth in the dimensions of this first great building, and everything since has been a long forgetting."

Talma gaped as if our companion had gone mad. I sat back, not knowing what to think. Could the pyramid really exist to enshrine numbers? It seemed alien to our way of thinking, but perhaps the ancient Egyptians looked at the world differently. So was my medallion some kind of mathematical clue or symbol as well? Was it in any way connected to Jomard's strange theories? Or was the savant reading something into this heap of stone that its builders never intended?

Somewhere in that direction was *L'Orient,* with a calendar that might hold more keys to the puzzle, and that seemed the next thing I could examine. I went to touch the medallion hidden against my breast and suddenly felt disquiet that it wasn't there. Maybe Talma was right: I was too naïve. Was I right to trust Enoch? And with Jomard's right triangle in mind I imagined the medallion's arms as dowsing rods, pointing to something far below my feet.

I looked back down the dizzying way we'd come. Ashraf was walking to follow the line of the pyramid's shadow, his gaze toward the sand instead of up to the sky.

CHAPTER TWELVE

Napoleon was in a good mood when I asked for permission to return to the flagship, displaying the jocular confidence of a man who felt his schemes of Oriental glory were falling into place. While he'd been just one of many striving generals in the cockpit of Europe, here he was omnipotent, a new pharaoh. He delighted in the spoils of war, confiscating Mameluke treasure to add to his personal fortune. He even tried on the robes of an Ottoman potentate, but only once—his generals laughed at him.

While the black cloud that had enveloped Napoleon upon learning of Josephine's infidelities had not entirely lifted, he assuaged his pain by taking a concubine himself. Conforming to local custom, the French had reviewed a parade of Egyptian courtesans offered by the city's beys, but when the officers dismissed most of these alleged beauties as overweight and shopworn—Europeans liked their women young and skinny—Bonaparte consoled himself with the lissome sixteen-year-old daughter of Sheikh el-Bekri, a girl named Zenab. Her father offered her services in return for the general's help in a dispute with another noble over a young boy that both sheikhs had taken a fancy to. The father was granted the boy and Napoleon got Zenab.

This damsel, who submitted docilely to the arrangement, soon became known as the "General's Egyptian." Bonaparte was as eager to cheat on his wife as she was cheating on him, and Zenab seemed flattered that the "Sultan Kebir" had chosen her over more experienced women. Within months the general became bored with the girl and started an affair with the French beauty Pauline Foures, cuckolding her unfortunate husband by ordering the lieutenant on a dispatch mission to France. The British, who had heard gossip of the affair from captured letters, seized the lieutenant's ship and with a malicious sense of humor deposited him back in Egypt to complicate Napoleon's love life. So went a war in which gossip was a political weapon. We were in an age where passion was politics, and Bonaparte's all too human mix of global dreams and petty lusts fascinated all of us. He was Prometheus and Everyman, a tyrant and a republican, an idealist and a cynic.

At the same time, Bonaparte began to remake Egypt. Despite the jealousies of his fellow generals, it was clear to us savants that he was brighter than any of them. I for one judge intelligence not so much by what you know as by how much you want to know, and Napoleon wanted to know about everything. He devoured information the way a glutton devours food, and he had broader interests than any officer in the army, even Jomard. At the same time, he could lock his curiosity away, as if in a cabinet to be taken out later, while he concentrated furiously on the military task at hand. This combination is rare. Bonaparte dreamed of remaking Egypt as Alexander had remade the Persian Empire, and fired off memorandums to France requesting everything from seeds to surgeons. If the Macedonian had founded Alexandria, Napoleon was determined to found the richest French colony in history. Local beys were mustered into a divan council to help with administration and taxation, while the scientists and engineers were bombarded with queries about well digging, windmill construction, road improvements, and mineral prospecting. Cairo would be reformed. Superstition was to be succeeded by science. The Revolution had come to the Middle East!

So when I approached him for leave to return to the flagship, it was with an affable tone that he asked, "This ancient calendar will tell you what, exactly?"

"It may help make sense of my medallion and mission by telling us a key year or date. Just how is uncertain, but the calendar does no good in the hold of a ship."

"The hold *does* prevent it from being stolen."

"I intend to examine it, not sell it, General."

"Of course. And you'll not uncover secrets without sharing them with me, the man who shielded you from murder charges in France, will you, Monsieur Gage?"

"I am working in concert with your own savants right now."

"Good. You may be getting more help soon."

"Help?"

"You'll see. Meanwhile, I certainly hope you're not considering leaving our expedition by trying to take ship to America. You understand that if I give you leave to go back to *L'Orient* for this calendar device, your slave girl and Mameluke captive will stay here in Cairo, under my protection." His look was narrow.

"But of course." I recognized that he'd assigned an emotional importance to Astiza I'd yet to admit to myself. Did I care that she was hostage to my loyal conduct? Was she truly a guarantee that I'd return? I hadn't thought about her in those terms, and yet I was intrigued by her and I admired Napoleon's perception of my intrigue. He seemed to miss nothing. "I will hurry back to them. I do wish, however, to take my friend, the journalist Talma."

"The scribbler? I need him here, to record my administration."

But Talma was restless. He had asked to come along so he could visit Alexandria, and I enjoyed his wry company. "He's anxious to file his dispatches on the fastest ship. He also wants to see more of Egypt and interest France in the future of this country."

Napoleon considered. "Get him back here in a week."

"It will be ten days, at most."

"I'll give you dispatches to deliver to Admiral Brueys, and Monsieur Talma can carry some to Alexandria. You'll both give me your impressions upon your return."

* * *

Despite Talma's misgivings, I decided after careful consideration to leave the medallion with Enoch. I agreed with Astiza's reasoning that it was safer in the cellar of an old scholar than bandied about Egypt. It was a relief not to have the pendant around my own vulnerable neck and have it safe from robbery when I went back down the Nile. While leaving the pendant was clearly a risk after carrying it so carefully from Paris to Cairo, its possession was pointless if we didn't know what it was for, and I still had little clue. Enoch seemed my best bet for an answer—and I am, after all, a gambler. Given my admittedly soft spot for women, I gambled that Astiza felt some loyalty to my quest, and that Enoch was more interested in solving the puzzle than hawking the bauble for money. Let him keep thumbing through his books. Meanwhile, I would examine the calendar in the hold of *L'Orient* in hopes it could supply a hint to the medallion's purpose, and together perhaps we'd crack the mystery. I urged Astiza to stay safely inside, and told Ashraf to keep both of them guarded.

"Should I not guide you to the coast?"

"Bonaparte says your presence here ensures I'll want to return. And it will." I clapped him on the shoulder. "We are a partnership, all of us in this house, Citizen Ash. You will not betray me, will you?"

He drew himself straight. "Ashraf will guard this house with his life."

I didn't want to carry my heavy rifle for a brief trip in a conquered country, but neither did I want it toyed with. After reflection, I remembered Ash's remark about superstition and fear of curses and stored it and my tomahawk in one of Enoch's mummy sarcophagi. It should be safe there.

Uncharacteristically, Talma made no comment on my decision to entrust the medallion to the Egyptians, instead mildly asking Astiza if she had any message she wanted him to bring to Alexandria. She said no.

We hired a native felucca to take us back down the Nile. These able sailing craft, skimming up and down the broad and slow Nile under their triangular sails, were the taxis of the river in the way donkeys filled that role in the streets of Cairo. It took several minutes of tiresome bargaining, but at length we were aboard and headed for Abukir, steered by a helmsman who spoke no French or English. Sign language seemed sufficient and we enjoyed the ride. As we once more entered the fertile delta downriver from Cairo, I was struck again by the serene timelessness of the villages along the river's banks, as if the French had never passed this way. Trundling donkeys carried monumental heaps of straw. Small boys jumped and played in the shallows, indifferent to the crocodiles that lay like logs in quiet side channels. Clouds of white egrets rose flapping from islands of green reed. Silver fish darted between papyrus stalks. Clumps of vegetation bearing lilies and lotus flowers drifted down the Nile from the high reaches of Africa. Young girls in bright dresses sat on the flat roofs of houses, sorting red dates in the sun.

"I had no idea that conquering a country was so easy," Talma remarked as the current carried us downriver. "A few hundred dead and we're masters of the place where civilization started. How did Bonaparte know?"

"Easier to seize a country than to run it," I said.

"Exactly." He lay against a gunwale, lazily looking at the passing landscape. "Here we are, lords of heat, flies, dung, rabid dogs, and illiterate peasants. Rulers of straw, sand, and green water. I tell you, it's the stuff that legends are made of."

"Which is your specialty, as our journalist."

"Under my pen, Napoleon becomes a visionary. He let me come with you because I've agreed to write his biography. I have no objection. He told me hostile newspapers are more to be feared than a thousand bayonets, but that I can rise with him. This is not exactly news to me. The more heroic I make him seem, the sooner he fulfills his ambitions and we can all go home."

I smiled at the world-weary way that the French view life after so many centuries of wars, kings, and terrors. We Americans are more innocent, more earnest, more honest, and more easily disappointed.

"Yet it is a beautiful county, is it not?" I asked. "I'm surprised how rich the greens are. The Nile flood plain is a lush garden, and then you change to desert so abruptly that you could trace the boundary with a sword blade. Astiza told me the Egyptians call the fertile part the black land, for its soil, and the desert the red land, for its sand."

"And I call all of it the brown land, for mud brick, cantankerous camels, and noisy donkeys. Ashraf told me a story of a shipwrecked Egyptian who returns to his village years after being given up for dead. He's been absent as long as Odysseus. His faithful wife and children rush out to meet him. And his first words? 'Ah, there's my donkey!'"

I smiled. "How will you spend your hours in Alexandria?"

"We both remember what a paradise it is. I want to make some notes and ask some questions. There are books to be written here, more interesting ones than a simple hagiography of Bonaparte."

"I wonder if you could ask about Achmed bin Sadr."

"Are you sure it was him you saw in Paris?"

"I'm not sure. It was dark but the voice is the same. My guide had a staff, or lantern handle, carved like a snake. And then Astiza saved me from a snake in Alexandria. And he showed too much interest in me."

"Napoleon seems to rely on him."

"Yet what if this Bin Sadr truly works not for Bonaparte, but for the Egyptian Rite? What if he's a tool of Count Alessandro Silano, who wanted the medallion so badly? What if he had something to do with poor Minette's murder? Every time he's looked at me I've felt he's looking for the medallion. So who is he, really?"

"You want me to be your investigator?"

"A discreet inquiry. I'm tired of surprises."

"I go where truth leads. From top to bottom, and head to . . ."—he looked pointedly at my boots—"to feet."

His confession was instantly obvious. "It *was* you who took my shoes on *L'Orient!*"

"I didn't take them, Ethan, I borrowed them, for inspection."

"And pretended you hadn't."

"I kept a secret from you as you kept the medallion from me. I was worried you'd lost it during the attack on our coach but were too embarrassed to admit it. I sold your presence on this expedition to Berthollet partly on the strength of that medallion, but when we were reunited in Toulon you declined to show it to me. What was I to think? It was my responsibility to the savants to try to find out what game you were playing."

"There was no game. It was simply that every time I showed the medallion or talked about it, I seemed to find myself in trouble."

"Which I got you out of in Paris. You could have confided in me a little." He had risked his own life to help get me here, and I'd treated him as less than a full partner. No wonder he was jealous.

"You could have left my boots alone," I nonetheless rejoined.

"Keeping it hidden didn't protect you from having a snake dropped in your bed, did it? What's this business with snakes anyway? I hate snakes."

"Astiza said there's some serpent god," I said, agreeing to change the subject. "Its followers have a modern cult, I think, and perhaps our enemies are a part of it. You know, Bin Sadr's curious snake-headed staff reminds me of a Bible story. Moses threw his staff down before Pharaoh and it turned into a serpent."

"Now we're onto Moses?"

"I'm as confused as you, Antoine."

"Considerably more so. At least Moses had the sense to lead his people out of this crazy country."

"It's an odd story, isn't it?"

"What?"

"The ten plagues that Moses has to bring. Each time one of the disasters occurs, Pharaoh relents, and says he will let the Hebrews go. Then he changes his mind until Moses brings on the next plague. He must have really needed those slaves."

"Until the final plague, when the eldest sons died. Then Pharaoh *did* let them go."

"And yet even then he changed his mind and pursued Moses with his army. If he hadn't done that, he and his host would never have drowned in the closing of the Red Sea. Why didn't he give up? Why not let Moses just walk away?"

"Pharaoh was stubborn, like our own little general. Perhaps that's the lesson of the Bible, that sometimes you have to let things go. In any event, I'll ask about your snake friend, but I'm surprised you've not requested that I ask about another."

"Who?"

"Astiza, of course."

"She seems guarded. As gentlemen, we must respect a woman's privacy."

Talma snorted. "And now she has the medallion—the same medallion I wasn't allowed to see, and which the dreaded Bin Sadr has been unable to get his hands on!"

"You still don't trust her?"

"Trust a slave, a sniper, a beauty, a witch? No. And I even like her."

"She's no witch."

"She's a priestess who casts spells, you told me. Who is obviously casting a spell over you, and who has usurped what we came here with."

"She's a partner. An ally."

"I wish you'd bed her, as a master has every right to do, so you could clear your brain and see her for what she is."

"If I make her sleep with me it doesn't count."

He shook his head in pity. "Well, I'm going to ask about Astiza even if you're not, because I've already learned one thing you don't know."

"What?"

"That when she formerly lived in Cairo, she had some kind of relationship with a European scholar allegedly studying ancient secrets."

"What scholar?"

"An Italian-French nobleman named Alessandro Silano."

At Abukir Bay, the power of the French was manifest. Admiral François-Paul Brueys d'Aigalliers, who had viewed the disembarkation of Napoleon and his troops from his warships with the relief of a headmaster dismissing an unruly classroom, had created a defensive wall of wood and iron. His battleships were still moored in a long line, gun-ports open and five hundred muzzles pointed stoutly at the sea. A brisk northwesterly breeze was pushing swells against the ships, rocking them like majestic cradles.

Only when we sailed onto the leeward side behind the vessels did I realize that these were ships only half at war. The French had anchored a long mile and a half from the beach in the shallow bay, and the landward half of the hulls were under repair. Sailors had rigged scaffolding to paint. Longboats were tied to ferry supplies or sailors. Laundry and bedding dried in the sun. Cannon was moved aside for carpentry. Awnings had been rigged above the hot decks. Hundreds of sailors had gone ashore to dig wells and man-age trains of camels and donkeys bringing provisions from Alexandria. A fortress on one side was a market on the other.

Still, *L'Orient* was one of the largest warships in the world. It rose like a castle, and climbing its ladder was like climbing a giant. I called up to announce myself, and as the felucca pushed off to carry Talma to Alexandria, I was piped aboard. It was noon on the fourteenth day of Thermidor, Year Six, the sun blazing, the shore golden, the sea an empty, brilliant blue. In other words, August 1, 1798.

I was ushered to the admiral's great cabin, which he had reclaimed from Napoleon. Brueys was in a white cotton shirt, open at the neck, confronting a table of paperwork. He was still sweating despite the sea breeze, and looked unusu-ally pale. Physically, he was the general's opposite: middle-aged at forty-five, with long, pale hair, a wide, generous mouth, friendly eyes, and a tall build. If Bonaparte's appear-ance was energizing, Brueys was calming, a man more at ease with himself and his station. He took the dispatches from our general with a slight grimace, politely remarked on the past friendship between our two countries, and asked my purpose.

"The savants have begun their investigation of the ancient

ruins. I suspect that a calendar device with ties to Cagliostro might prove useful in understanding the mind of the Egyptians. Bonaparte has given me permission to examine it." I handed over an order.

"The mind of the Egyptians? What use is that?"

"The pyramids are so remarkable that we don't understand how they were built. This instrument is one of many clues."

He looked skeptical. "A clue if we wanted to build pyramids."

"My visit to your ship will be brief, Admiral. I have papers giving me permission to take the antiquity to Cairo."

He nodded wearily. "I apologize I am not more gracious, Monsieur Gage. It is not easy working with Bonaparte, and I've been plagued with dysentery since we came to this godforsaken country. My belly aches, my ships are beggared for supplies, and my undermanned crews are made up chiefly of those too invalid for the army."

The sickness explained his pallor. "Then I'll not be more of a burden than I must. If you could give me escort to the hold . . ."

"But of course." He sighed. "I'd have you to dinner if I could eat. What interruption are you when we sit here at anchor, waiting for Nelson to find us? It's madness to keep the fleet in Egypt, yet Napoleon clings to my ships like an infant to a blanket."

"Your ships are critical to all his plans."

"So he has flattered me. Well, let me give you the captain's son, he's a bright lad of promise. If you can keep up with him, you're fitter than I."

The midshipman Giocante, a boy of ten, was the son of ship's captain Luce Casabianca. A bright, dark-haired lad who had explored every cranny of *L'Orient,* he led me down to the treasury with the agility of a monkey. Our descent was brighter than the last time I'd gone this way with Monge, sunlight flooding through open gunports. There was a strong smell of turpentine and sawdust. I saw paint cans and oak lumber.

It didn't get dim until we descended to the orlop deck below the waterline. Now I could smell bilge water and the cheesy odor of stores going rancid in the climate. It was cooler down here, dark and secretive.

Giocante turned and gave a wink. "You'll not fill your pockets with gold pieces, now?" the boy teased me with the cheek of a captain's son.

"I wouldn't get away with you watching me, would I?" I lowered my voice to a conspiratorial whisper. "Unless you want to go in double, boy, and we'll both sneak ashore, rich as princes!"

"No need of that. My father says we'll capture a fat English prize one day."

"Ah. Your future is taken care of, then."

"My future is this ship. We are bigger than anything the English have, and when the time comes, we will teach them a lesson." He snapped orders at the marines who guarded the magazine and they began to unlock the treasury.

"You sound as confident as Bonaparte."

"I'm confident in my father."

"Still, it's a challenging life for a boy at sea, is it?" I asked.

"It's the best life because we have clear duty. That's what my father says. Things are easy if you know what you must do." And before I could consider or reply to this philosophy, he saluted and scampered up the ladder.

An admiral in the making, I thought.

The treasury had both a wooden door and an iron grill. Both were shut behind to lock me in. It took me some rooting in the dim lantern light amid boxes of coin and jewels to find the device that Monge and Jomard had shown me. Yes, there it was, tossed in one corner as the least valuable of all the treasures. It was, as I have described, the size of a dinner plate but empty in its center. The rim was made of three flat rings, covered in hieroglyphics, zodiac signs, and abstract designs, that rotated within each other. A clue, perhaps, but of what? I sat, enjoying the cool dampness, and worked them one way and another. Each twist aligned different symbols.

I studied the inner ring first, which was the plainest with

just four designs. There was an inscribed sphere hovering above a line, and on the opposite side of the circle another sphere below a line. At ninety degrees from each, dividing the calendar into quarters, there were half-spheres, like half-moons, one pointed up and the other down. The pattern reminded me of four cardinal markings on a compass or clock, but the Egyptians had neither, so far as I knew. I pondered. The one on top looked like a rising sun. So at length I guessed this innermost band must be a wheel of the year. The summer and winter solstice was represented by the sun being above and below the lines, or horizon. The half-suns were the March and September equinoxes, when day and night are roughly equal. Simple enough, if I was right.

And it told me absolutely nothing.

A wheel outside the first one turned a zodiac, I saw. I traced the twelve signs that were not so very different when this device was made than they are today. Then a third ring, the outermost, held strange symbols of animals, eyes, stars, sun rays, a pyramid, and the Horus symbol. In places, inscribed lines divided each wheel into sections.

My guess was that this calendar, if that's what it was, was a way to align the position of the constellations relative to the rising sun throughout the solar year. But what use was it to my medallion? What had Cagliostro seen in it, if indeed it had been his? Back and forth I played, trying combinations in hopes something would occur to me. Nothing did, of course—I've always hated puzzles, even though I've enjoyed figuring the odds at cards. Perhaps the astronomer, Nouet, could figure it out if I could bring it back with me.

Finally I decided to call the summer solstice, if that's what it was, the top, and then put the third ring's five-pointed star—not entirely unlike that on our American flag, or in Masonic symbolism—atop that. Like the polar star! Why not play with symbols I knew? And the zodiac ring I rotated until Taurus, the bull, was between the other two: The age, Monge had said, in which the pyramid had supposedly been built. There had been the age of the bull, the age of the ram, the age of the fish, Pisces, which we now occupied, and, ahead, the age of Aquarius. Now I examined the other signs. There seemed no particular pattern.

Except . . . I stared, my heart beating. When I arranged the rings so that summer, bull, and star were atop each other, the ends of the tilted inscribed lines connected to make two longer diagonal lines. They angled outward from the innermost circle like the splayed legs of the medallion— or the slope of the pyramid. It was enough of a resemblance that I felt like I was looking at an echo of what I'd left with Astiza and Enoch.

But what did it mean? I saw nothing at first. Crabs, lions, and Libra scales made senseless patterns. But wait! There was a pyramid on the outer ring, and this was now just below the sign for the fall equinox, directly adjacent to that sloping inscribed line. And there was a symbol for Aquarius on the second ring, and this, too, was adjacent to a time that, if I was reading the device correctly, occupied the four o'clock position on the ring, just below the three o'clock position that represented the autumn equinox, September 21.

The four o'clock position should correspond to one month later, or October 21.

If I'd guessed right, October 21, Aquarius, and the pyramid had some kind of link. Aquarius, Nouet had said, was a sign created by the Egyptians to celebrate the rising of the Nile, which would crest sometime in the fall.

Could October 21 be a holy day? The peak of the Nile flood? A time to visit the pyramid? The medallion had its wavelike symbol for water. Was there a connection? Did it reveal something on that particular day?

I sat back, uncertain. I was grasping at straws . . . and yet here was *something,* a date plucked out of nonsense. It was wild conjecture, but perhaps Enoch and Astiza could make sense of it. Tired of the puzzle, I found myself wondering about this strange woman who seemed to have secrets in layered depths I hadn't suspected. Priestess? What was her mission in all this? Were Talma's suspicions justified? Had she really known Silano? It seemed impossible, and yet the people I was meeting seemed oddly connected. But I didn't fear her—I missed her. I remembered a moment in Enoch's courtyard in the cool of early evening, the shadows blue, the sky a dome, the scent of spices and smoke from the house kitchen mingling with that of dust and fountain water. She sat on a bench without speaking, meditating, and I stood by a pillar not speaking. I simply gazed at her hair and cheek and she gave me leave and time to look. We were not master and servant then, nor Westerner and Egyptian, but man and woman. To touch her would have broken the spell.

So I simply watched, knowing this was a moment I'd carry with me the rest of my life.

Ship noise brought me back from my reverie. There were cries, running feet, and the rumble of drums. I glanced at the beams overhead. What now? Some drill for the fleet? I tried to concentrate, but the excitement only seemed to increase.

So I hammered to be let out. When the door opened, I spoke to the marine. "What's going on?"

His own head was tilted up, listening. "English!"

"Here? Now?"

He looked at me, his face somber in the dim lantern light. "Nelson."

CHAPTER THIRTEEN

I left the calendar and joined a tide of men climbing to the gun decks, sailors cursing the ship's lack of readiness. Our flagship was half warehouse, with no time now for careful stowage. Men were scrambling to reattach cannons to their proper tackle, hoist yards, and take down scaffolding.

I came up to the bright air of the main deck. "Get those awnings down!" Captain Casabianca was bawling. "Signal the men ashore to come back!" Then he turned to his son, Giocante. "Go organize the powder monkeys." The boy, who showed more anticipation than fear, disappeared below to supervise the transfer of ammunition to the hungry guns.

I went up to Admiral Brueys on the quarterdeck, who was studying the sea with his telescope. The horizon was white with sail, the wind swiftly blowing trouble our way. Nelson's squadron had every inch of canvas up and straining, and before long I could count fourteen ships of the line. The French had thirteen, plus four frigates—even enough odds—but we were anchored and half unready. Six were in line ahead of *L'Orient,* six behind. It was midafternoon, surely too late for battle, and perhaps Brueys could work out to sea during the night. Except that the British showed no sign of heaving to. Instead they were racing down on us like a pack of anxious hounds, spray flying from their bows. They meant to start a fight.

Brueys glanced aloft.

"Admiral?" I ventured.

"Hundreds of men ashore, our supplies unsecured, our yards and sails down, our crews half sick," he muttered to himself. "I warned of this. Now we must fight in place."

"Admiral?" I tried again, "I think my investigation is finished. Should I go ashore?"

He looked at me blankly for a moment, and then remembered my mission. "Ah, yes, Gage. It's too late, American. All our boats are engaged retrieving sailors."

I went to the leeward rail and looked. Sure enough, the fleet longboats were making for the beach to pick up men stranded there. To my eye, they didn't seem in any great hurry to get back.

"By the time the boats return, the English will be upon us," Brueys said. "You'll be our guest for the battle, I'm afraid."

I swallowed and looked again at the English ships, great leaning cloud castles of taut canvas, men inching along the yardarms like ants, every gun run out, their battle flags flapping red. Damned if they didn't look like an eager lot. "The sun's going down," I said uneasily. "Surely the British won't attack in the dark."

The admiral watched the approaching squadron with a mouth set in resignation. I decided now that he looked positively gaunt from his dysentery, and about as ready for a hard fight as a man who has just run twenty miles. "No sane man would," he replied. "But this is Nelson." He snapped the telescope shut. "I suggest you get back down to the treasury. It's below the waterline and safest there."

I didn't want to fight the English, but it seemed cowardly not to. "If you could spare a rifle . . ."

"No, don't get in the way. This is the navy's fight. You are a savant, and your mission is to return to Bonaparte with your information." He clapped my shoulder, turned, and began snapping more orders.

Too curious to scurry below yet, I moved to the rail, feeling perfectly useless and silently cursing the impatient Nelson. Any normal admiral would have shortened sail as the sky turned orange, maneuvered his fleet into a tidy line of battle, and given his men a warm meal and a good night's sleep before starting a tangle. But this was Nelson, who had famously boarded not just one French ship but the next one beyond, leaping from one to the other and capturing both. Once again, he showed no signs of slowing. The nearer he got, the more cries of consternation went up among the French sailors. This was madness! And yet it was increasingly obvious that the battle was going to begin at day's end.

The sailors on shore were still climbing into the longboats, trying to get back to their ships.

A few cannon thumped, to no effect. I could see the lead English vessels making for the western end of the French line near Abukir Island, where the French had sited a land battery. That end of the bay was thick with shoals, and Brueys had been confident that the English fleet couldn't negotiate it. Yet no one had told Nelson that, and two English battleships, aptly named *Zealous* and *Goliath,* were racing each other for the privilege of running aground. Insanity! The sun was on the horizon, blood red, and the French shore howitzers were firing, except they couldn't reach the English ships with their arcing shells. The *Goliath* pulled ahead in its little race, nicely silhouetted against the sinking orb, and instead of striking a rock it slipped neatly between *Le Guerrier* and the shore. Then it turned smartly and sailed up the French line on the leeward side, between Brueys and the beach! It luffed sails as it came abreast the second ship of the formation, *Le Conquerant,* neatly dropped anchor as if it had arrived in port, and promptly let loose a broadside at the unready side of the French ship. There was a clap of thunder, a huge gush of smoke roiling out to envelop both vessels. *Le Conquerant* heeled as if punched by a fist. I could see great sprays of splinters arcing skyward as the French ship was pounded. Then screams began to float down the line. Anchored as we were, the wind against us, we could do nothing but wait our turn.

The *Zealous* anchored opposite *Le Guerrier,* and the British ships *Orion, Audacious,* and *Theseus* followed into Abukir Bay, also taking the French on their unprotected flank. Brueys's formidable wall suddenly seemed hapless. Gunsmoke rose to form thunderheads, and what had at first been the distant thudding of guns drew closer and closer, climbing to a roar. The sun had gone down, the wind dying, the sky dusk. Now the rest of the English fleet slowed to a crawl and menacingly drifted down the seaward side, meaning each French ship at the head of Brueys's anchored line was being raked from both sides, outnumbered two to one. While the first six French ships were being pounded, the ships in the rear of the assembly had no means of getting into battle. They sat at anchor, their crews watching help-lessly. It was plain bloody murder. I could hear raw English cheering in the dusk, while the French cries were of horror and hatred at the growing butchery. Napoleon would be cursing if he could see it.

There is a horrible stateliness to a sea battle, a languid ballet that heightens the tension before each broadside. Boats materialize out of the smoke like looming giants. Cannons roar, and then long seconds tick by while batteries are reloaded, wounded dragged aside, and buckets thrown on smoldering fires. Here at the Nile, some of the ships hammered at each other from anchor. Smoke created a vast fog, barely penetrated by the light of a rising full moon. Those ships that remained mobile maneuvered half blinded. I saw an English ship emerge near our own—*Bellerophon,* it read—and heard English shouts of aim. It drifted as pon-derously as an iceberg.

"Get down!" Brueys shouted to me. On the deck below I could hear Captain Casabianca crying, "Fire! Fire!" I flat-tened myself on the quarterdeck and the world dissolved to a roar. *L'Orient* heeled, both from the discharge of her own guns and the weight of the answering English shot slam-ming home. The ship quaked beneath me and I could hear splintering sounds as our ship was gutted. Yet the French tactics of aiming for the rigging caused havoc on the other side as well. Like a fall of axed timber, *Bellerophon*'s masts came down in a huge creaking tangle, smothering its top deck with a terrifying crash. The British battleship began to float away. Now it was the turn of the French sailors to cheer. I shakily stood up, embarrassed that no one else had dropped to the deck. Yet at least a score were dead or wounded, and Brueys was bleeding from head and hand. He refused to be bandaged, dripping bright blood on the deck.

"I meant get down to the hold, Monsieur Gage," he amended.

"Maybe I'm good luck," I said shakily, watching *Bellerophon* disappear in the bank of gun smoke.

Yet I'd no sooner said so than one of the British guns stabbed orange in the dark and a cannon ball came whistling across to clear the rail and neatly clip the admiral in the thigh. His lower leg was plucked off like a tooth jerked by a string, flying away into the night in a fine mist of blood, tumbling and white. Brueys stood momentarily on one leg, looking at his absent member with disbelief, and then slowly toppled like a broken stool, hitting the deck with a thud. His officers cried out and gathered around him. Blood ran like spilled sauce.

"Get him to the infirmary!" Captain Casabianca roared.

"No," Brueys gasped. "I want to die where I can see."

Everything was chaotic. A sailor staggered by with half his scalp gone. A midshipman lay thrown against a gun like a piece of litter, a one-foot splinter through his chest. The main deck had become a perfect hell of flying splinters, falling rigging, evisceration, and gore. Men treaded on their companions' ruptured organs. Powder boys skidded on sheets of lubricating blood, gushing faster than the sand thrown across it could soak it up. Cannons barked, muskets cracked, shot screamed by, and the sheer concentration of havoc seemed far worse than a land battle. The night throbbed with the flashes of the guns, so that one saw the battle in flickering glimpses. I could barely hear anymore, and all I could smell and taste was smoke. Two more British ships had anchored near us, I realized, and were beginning to pound us with fresh broadsides. *L'Orient* was shuddering from the impact of round shot like a chastened dog, and our own barking was slower as French cannon were disabled.

"He's dead," Casabianca announced, standing. I looked down at the admiral. He seemed white and empty, as if deflated by the blood that had poured out of him, but newly serene. At least he wouldn't have to answer to Napoleon.

Then another British broadside and another explosion of splinters. This time Casabianca grunted and went down. Another officer's head had simply disappeared, dissolving at the shoulders into red rain, and a lieutenant caught a ball midbody and was hurled overboard as if catapulted. I was too terrified to move.

"Father!" The midshipman who had guided me before suddenly appeared and rushed to Casabianca's side, eyes wide with fright. In reply, the captain cursed and picked himself up. He was pattered with small splinter wounds, more angry than seriously hurt. "Get below like I told you," he growled.

"I'll not leave you!"

"You'll not leave your duty." He grasped his son's shoulder. "We are examples to our men and to France!"

"I'll take him," I said, grabbing the youth and pulling. Now I was anxious to get off this slaughter deck myself. "Come, Giocante, you're worth more fetching powder down there than dead up here."

"Let me go!"

"Do as you're ordered!" his father shouted.

The boy was torn. "I'm afraid you'll be killed."

"If I am, your responsibility is to help rally the men." Then he softened. "We'll be all right."

The boy and I descended into Hadean gloom. Each of the three gun decks were fogged with choking smoke and cacophonous with noise: the blast of guns, the crash of enemy shot, and the screams of the wounded. The concussions had left many of the gunners' ears bleeding. The midshipman spied some useful duty and darted off, while I, with nothing to offer, descended farther until I was below the waterline once more. If L'Orient went down, at least I could take the calendar off the ship with me. Here in the pit the surgeons were sawing at limbs to screaming made bearable only by my relative deafness, their lanterns swinging to each rumble of the guns. Sailors passed buckets of water to wash away the blood.

There was a chain of boys like a line of apes passing up sausagelike bagged cartridges from the magazine. I pushed past them to the treasure room, where the light had gone out.

"I need a lantern!" I shouted to the sentry.

"Not near the powder, you fool!"

Swearing, I groped in the dark for the calendar device. Here I was pawing over a king's ransom, and the only way to get any of it out was through a hurricane of fire. What if we sank? Millions of francs of treasure would go to the bottom. Could I stuff some in my boot? I could feel the roll of *L'Orient* as each British broadside shoved the warship this way and that. The timbers of the ribs and deck trembled. I hunched like a child, moaning as I searched. The cannonade was like a ram battering a door, sure to eventually stave us in.

And then I heard a sailor's most dreaded words: "Fire!"

I looked out. The magazine door had been slammed shut and the powder monkeys were scampering upward. That meant our own cannons would quickly go silent. Everything was orange overhead. "Open the cocks to flood the magazine!" someone shouted, and I began to hear the gush of water. I put my hand to the deck overhead and flinched. It was already uncomfortably hot. The wounded were screaming in terror.

A head appeared in the hatch above. "Get out of there, you crazy American! Don't you know the ship is on fire?"

There! The calendar! I felt its shape, grasped it, and mounted the ladder in fear, leaving a fortune behind. Flames were everywhere, spreading faster than I'd thought possible. Tar, hemp, paint, dry wood, and canvas: we were fighting on a heap of kindling.

A French marine loomed before me, bayonet fixed, eyes wild. "What's that?" He looked at the odd thing I carried.

"A calendar for Bonaparte."

"You stole from the treasury!"

"I've orders to save it."

"Show them!"

"They're with Brueys." Or, I thought, on fire.

"Thief! It's to the brig with you!"

He'd gone mad. I looked around in desperation. Men were leaping from the gun ports like fleeing rats.

I had only a second to decide. I could fight this lunatic for a ring of metal or trade it for my life. "Here!" I pitched the calendar to him. He let his musket barrel droop to awkwardly catch it and I used the moment to shove past him, scrambling up to the next deck.

"Come back, you!"

Here the fire and smoke were even worse. It was a charnel house of horror, a butcher's banquet of mangled bodies beginning to roast in the heat. Sightless eyes stared at me, fingers clutching for succor. Many of the dead were in flames, their tissues sizzling.

I kept climbing and finally gained the quarterdeck again, coughing and gasping. All the rigging was alight, a great pyramid of fire, and even as smoke roiled upward to obscure the moon, burning bits rained down like pitch from hell. The grit of ash crunched under my feet. Gun carriages were smashed, marines lay toppled like ninepins, and gratings were crushed. I staggered toward the stern. On either bulwark, dark forms were hurling themselves into the sea.

I literally stumbled on Captain Casabianca. He was lying down now, a great new sucking wound on his chest, his son once more next to him, the boy's leg twisted where it had broken. I'd tripped on a father who was a dead man, I knew, but there was still a chance for his son. I crouched next to them. "We've got to get you out of here, Giocante, the ship may be ready to blow." I coughed. "I'll help you swim."

He shook his head. "I won't leave my father."

"You can't help him now."

"I won't leave my ship."

There was a crash as a yardarm, flaming, hit and bounced on the deck. The British fired yet another salvo and the French flagship trembled, groaning and creaking.

"You don't have a ship anymore!"

"Leave us, *Américain*," the captain gasped.

"But your son . . ."

"It is over."

The boy touched my face in sad farewell. "Duty," he said.

"You've done your duty! You've a whole life ahead!"

"*This* is my life." There was a tremble to his voice but his face was as calm as an angel in a grotto of hell. So this is what deciding what to believe in is like, I thought. So this is duty. I felt horror, admiration, inferiority, fury. A wasted young life! Or *was* it wasted? Blind belief had been the cause of half of history's miseries. And yet wasn't it also what saints and heroes were made of? His eyes were as hard and dark as shale, and if I'd had time to look into them, perhaps I would have learned all the secrets of the world.

"Abandon ship! Abandon ship!" It was being shouted again and again by the few surviving officers.

"Damn it, I won't let you kill yourself." I grabbed him.

The boy pushed me so hard I sprawled. "You are not France! Leave!"

And then I heard another voice.

"You!"

It was the crazed marine, who had staggered to this top deck. His face was burned, his clothes smoking. Blood soaked half his coat. And yet he was aiming at me!

I ran to the stern rail, veiled by smoke, and took one look back. Father and son were obscured, their forms wavering in the heat. It was insane how wedded they were to their ship, their duty, their fate. It was glorious, monstrous, enviable. Did I care for anything half as much? And was I fortunate not to do so? I prayed they'd go quickly. The marine beyond was blinded by smoke and blood, swaying so pitifully he couldn't hold his aim, flames reaching to claim him.

So, unable to be anything but the man I am, I jumped.

It was a leap of faith into utter blackness; I couldn't see a thing but knew the water below would be choked with thrashing men and chunks of debris. Somehow I missed all of it and plunged into the Mediterranean, salt gushing into my nose. The water was a shock of cool relief, a balm for my blisters. I sank into a womb of blackness, and then kicked. When I came up I struck out away from the burning battleship as fast as I could, knowing it was a lethal powder keg if the magazine didn't flood in time. I could feel its heat on the crown of my head as I stroked. If I could ride some flotsam to shore . . .

And with that, *L'Orient* blew up.

None had ever heard such sound. It was a thunderclap in Alexandria some twenty-three miles distant, lighting the town as if by day. The concussion reached the Bedouin watching the contest from the beach and hurled them from their rearing horses. It slapped and deafened me. Masts shot up like rockets. Cannon were tossed like pebbles. There was am explosive penumbra of wood splinters and sea spray driven up and outward, a corona of debris, and then the bits of ship began to rain down for hundreds of yards in every direction, still hitting and killing men. Bent forks fell from the sky to stick into railings. Shoes banged down holding nothing but smoking feet. The very sea flexed, driving me away, and then the hulk below the waterline cracked and went under, sucking all of us back toward its swirling maw. I thrashed desperately and caught at a piece of wood before being yanked back down into darkness. I clung like a lover, feeling the pain in my ears as I spiraled deeper. Lord, it was like being gripped by a monster's paw! At least the suction saved me from the bombardment of debris that pattered the surface like nails. Looking up at the orange water above, I saw the surface shatter like a broken stained-glass window. What seemed likely to be my last sight had an eerie beauty.

How deep I was dragged I don't know. My head pounded, my lungs burned. Then, just when I thought I could hold my breath no more, the sinking ship seemed to release its grasp and the buoyant wood I'd clung to finally began to carry me upward. I burst to the surface with my last air, shrieking with pain and fear, rolling with my stump of yard that had saved my life. And because of my sting and ache, I knew I'd survived once more, for better or worse. I lay on my back, blinking at stars. The smoke was drifting away. Dimly I became aware of what was around me. The sea was carpeted with wood and broken bodies. There was a stunned silence except for a few faint calls for help. So stupendous was the explosion of *L'Orient* that all firing stopped.

The crew of one British ship tried a cheer, but it stuck in their throats.

I drifted. The calendar was gone. So was all the other treasure in *L'Orient*'s hold. The moon illuminated a tableau of smashed and burning ships. Most were hamstrung by missing masts. Surely it was over now. But no, the crews gradually awoke from their stunned horror, as if from a dream, and after a quarter hour the cannon started up again, thuds echoing across the water.

So the battle went on. How can I explain such madness? Savage broadsides echoed through the night like the hammering of the devil's foundry. Hour after hour I floated in a daze, growing colder, until the guns finally grumbled away in mutual exhaustion and the sea lightened some thousand years later. With dawn men slept, sprawled on their hot artillery.

Sunrise revealed the full extent of the French disaster. The frigate *La Sérieuse* had been the first to sink, settling in the shadows, but didn't strike her colors until five in the morning. *Le Spartiate* ceased firing at 11 P.M. *Franklin,* named for my mentor, surrendered to the British at 11:30. *Le Tonnant*'s mortally wounded captain blew his brains out before she surrendered. *L'Heureux* and *Le Mercure* were deliberately grounded to prevent their sinking. The frigate *L'Artemise* blew up after being fired by her captain, and *Le Timoleon* was driven aground to be burned by her crew the next day. *Aquilon, Le Guerrier, Le Conquerant,* and *Peuple Souverain* simply surrendered. For the French, the Battle of the Nile was not just a loss but an annihilation. Only two battleships and two frigates had gotten away. Three thousand Frenchmen were killed or wounded in the battle. In a single fight, Nelson had destroyed French naval power in the Mediterranean. Just one month after landing in Egypt, Napoleon was cut off from the outside world.

Hundreds of survivors, some burned and bleeding, began to be plucked from the sea by British longboats. I watched in numbed fascination, and then dimly realized that I could be rescued too. "Over here!" I finally shouted in English, waving.

They hauled me aboard like a played-out fish. "What ship you with, mate?" they asked me. "How the bloody hell did you get in the water?"

"*L'Orient,*" I replied.

They looked at me as if I were a ghost. "You a frog? Or a bloody traitor?"

"I'm an American." I was trying to blink the salt from my eyes as I held up the finger that held a unicorn ring. "And an agent for Sir Sidney Smith."

Imagine a pugilist after a hard-won boxing match, and you have my first impression of Horatio Nelson. The lion of England was bandaged and woozy from a nasty head wound above his blind eye, a blow that came within an inch of killing him. He spoke with difficulty because of a sore tooth and, at age forty, had white hair and a face lined with tension. That's what losing an arm and an eye in earlier fights, and chasing Bonaparte, will do for you. He was barely a shade taller than Napoleon and even slighter in build, his cheeks sunken and his voice nasal. Yet he relished the chance to dish out a thrashing as much as the French general did, and on this day he'd won a victory so decisive as to be unprecedented. He had not just beaten the enemy—he had obliterated them.

His one good eye burned as if lit by divine light, and indeed Nelson saw himself on a mission from God: a quest for glory, death, and immortality. Put his ambition and Bonaparte's in the same room and they'd spontaneously combust. Turn them with a crank and they'd throw off sparks. They were Leyden jars of electric charge, set among us mortal kegs of gunpowder.

Like Napoleon, the British admiral could leave a roomful of subordinates entranced by his very presence; but Nelson commanded not just with energy and drive, but with charm, even affection. He had more charisma than a royal courtesan, and some of his captains had the look of happy puppies. They were clustered around him now in his great cabin, regarding their admiral with unabashed worship, and me with deep suspicion.

"How the devil do you know Smith?" Nelson asked as I stood before him, damp and exhausted, my ears ringing.

Rum and fresh water had washed some of the salt from my throat. "After his escape from Temple Prison, Sir Sidney followed me because of rumors that I'd be accompanying Bonaparte to Egypt," I croaked. "He helped save my life in a skirmish on the highway to Toulon. He asked if I'd keep an eye on Napoleon. So I got myself back to the French fleet, figuring you'd find it sooner or later. Didn't know how things would turn out, but if you won . . ."

"He's lying," one of the captains said. Hardy, I think his name was.

Nelson smiled thinly. "We've not much use for Smith here, you know."

I looked at the unfriendly array of assembled captains. "I didn't know."

"The man's as vain as I am." There was dead silence. Then the admiral abruptly laughed, the others joining the joke. "Vain as me! We both live for glory!" They roared. They were exhausted but had that satiated look of men who'd come through a good scrape. Their ships were drifting wrecks, the sea was littered with carnage, and they'd just endured horrors enough for a lifetime of nightmares. But they were proud, too.

I did my best to smile.

"Good fighter though," Nelson amended, "if you don't have to be in the same room with him. His escape made him the talk of England."

"He did get back, then."

"Yes. And didn't mention you, as I recall."

"Our meeting was inconclusive," I admitted. "I didn't pledge to be his spy. But he anticipated your skepticism and left me this." I held up my right hand. "It's a signet ring, inscribed with his symbol. He said it would prove my story."

I took it off and passed it around, the officers grunting in recognition.

Nelson held it up to his good eye. "It's the bastard Smith, all right. Here's his horn, or should I say prick?" Again, they all laughed. "You enlisted with that devil Napoleon?"

"I'm a member of his team of savants who are studying Egypt. I apprenticed to Benjamin Franklin. I was trying to arrange some trade agreements, there were legal problems in Paris, an opportunity for adventure . . ."

"Yes, yes." He waved his hand. "What's the situation of Bonaparte's army?"

"It has defeated the Mamelukes and is in possession of Cairo."

There was a murmur of disappointment in the cabin.

"And yet he now has no fleet," Nelson said, to his officers as much as me. "Which means that while we can't get at Boney, quite yet, Boney can't get to India. There will be no linkup to Tippoo Sahib, and no threat to our army there. He's marooned."

I nodded. "It would seem so, Admiral."

"And the morale of his troops?"

I considered. "They grumble, like all soldiers. But they've also just conquered Egypt. I suppose they feel like sailors who have conquered Brueys."

Nelson nodded. "Quite. Land and sea. Sea and land. His numbers?"

I shrugged. "I'm not a soldier. I know his casualties have been light."

"Humph. And supplies?"

"He resupplies from Egypt herself."

He slammed his hand down. "Damn! It will be like prying out an oyster!" He looked at me with his one good eye. "Well, what do you want to do now?"

What indeed? It was dumb luck I hadn't already been killed. Bonaparte was expecting me to solve a mystery that still baffled me, my friend Talma was suspicious of my friend Astiza, an Arab cutthroat no doubt wanted to drop more snakes in my bed, and there was a baffling heap of pyramidal stone built to represent the world, or God, or who knows what. Here was my chance to cut and run.

But I wasn't done figuring out the medallion, was I? Maybe I could get a fist of treasure, or a share of mysterious power. Or keep it from the lunatics of the Egyptian Rite and the Apophis snake cult. And a woman was waiting, wasn't she?

"I'm no strategist, admiral, but perhaps this battle changes everything," I said. "We won't know how Bonaparte will react until news reaches him. Which I, perhaps, could bear. The French know nothing of my connection to Smith." Go back? Well, the battle and the dying boy had shaken me to the core. I had a duty too, and it was to get back to Astiza and the medallion. It was to finish, finally, something I'd started. "I'll explain the situation to Bonaparte and, if that doesn't move him, then learn what I can in coming months and report back to you." A plan had formulated in my mind. "A rendezvous off the coast near the end of October, per-haps. Just after the twenty-first."

"Smith is scheduled to be in the region then," Nelson noted.

"And your own self-interest in doing this?" Hardy asked me.

"I have scores of my own to settle in Cairo. Then I'd like passage to a neutral port. After *L'Orient,* I've had enough of war."

"Three months before you report back?" Nelson ob-jected.

"It may take that long for Bonaparte to react and form the new French plans."

"By God," objected Hardy, "this man served on the en-emy flagship and now he wants to be put ashore? I don't trust a word he says, ring or no ring."

"Not served. Observed. I didn't fire a shot."

Nelson thought, fingering my ring. Then he held it out. "Done. We've smashed enough ships that you hardly make a difference. Tell Boney exactly what you observed: I want him to know he's doomed. However, it will take months for us to assemble an army to get the Corsican out of Egypt. In the meantime, I want you to make a count of his strength and gauge the mood. If there is any chance of surrender, I want to hear about it immediately."

Napoleon is about as likely to give up as you are, Admiral, I thought, but I didn't say that. "If you can get me ashore . . ."

"We'll get an Egyptian to put you on the beach tomorrow to erase any suspicion you've been talking to us."

CHAPTER FOURTEEN

My first task, upon hearing this disturbing news, was to reunite with Talma, who likely assumed me dead once word of the explosion of *L'Orient* reached Alexandria. Silano here? Was that the "help" that Bonaparte had hinted at?

The battered British fleet did not attempt to force the repaired forts at Alexandria's harbor. Instead they began patrolling in blockade. As for me, an Arab lighter deposited me on the beach at Abukir Bay. No one took particular note of my landing, as dhows and feluccas were sweeping the water to salvage debris and rob the dead. French and British longboats were also retrieving bodies in a makeshift truce, and on shore, wounded men lay groaning under crude canvas shelters. I splashed up the beach looking as ragged as the rest, helped carry some wounded to the shade of a shell-pocked sail, and then joined a desultory procession of French sailors straggling toward Alexandria. They were sullen in defeat, quietly vowing revenge on the English, but also had the hopeless look of the stranded. It was a long, hot hike in a pillar of dust, and when I paused and looked back, I could see columns of smoke where some of the beached French ships were still burning. As we marched we passed the rubble of long-vanished civilizations. A sculpted head was toppled on its side. A royal foot as big as a table, with toes the size of pumpkins, peeked from debris. We were a

ruin trudging past ruins. I didn't reach the city until midnight.

Alexandria buzzed like a disturbed hive. It was by going
from lodging to lodging, asking for news of a short, bespec-
tacled Frenchman with an interest in miracle cures that I finally discovered that Talma had lodged in a dead Mameluke's
mansion that had been turned into an inn by an opportunis-
tic merchant.

"The sickly one?" the proprietor responded. "He's disappeared without taking his bag or his medicine."

This didn't sound good at all. "He left no word for me,
Ethan Gage?

"You're a friend of his?"

"Yes."

"He owes me one hundred francs."

I paid his debt and claimed Talma's luggage as my own,
hoping the journalist had rushed back to Cairo. Just to be
sure he hadn't sailed away, I checked the docks. "It's not like
my friend Talma to go off by himself," I told a French port
supervisor worriedly. "He's really not very adventurous."

"Then what is he doing in Egypt?"

"Seeking cures for his ailments."

"Fool. He should have taken the waters in Germany."

This supervisor confirmed that Count Silano had indeed arrived in Egypt, but not from France. Instead, he'd sailed
from the Syrian coastline. He reportedly had disembarked
with two enormous trunks of belongings, a monkey on a
golden chain, a blonde mistress, a cobra in a basket, a pig in
a cage, and a gigantic Negro bodyguard. If that were not
conspicuous enough, he had adopted an Arab's flowing
robes and added a yellow sash, Austrian cavalry boots, and
French rapier. "I am here to decipher the mysteries of
Egypt!" he'd proclaimed. With lingering gunfire still grumbling as the sun rose over the ruins of the French fleet, Silano had commissioned a caravan of camels and set off for
Cairo. Could Talma have gone with him? It seemed unlikely.
Or had Antoine trailed the count to spy?

I joined a cavalry patrol to Rosetta and then took a boat to
Cairo. From a distance the capital seemed curiously un-

changed after the apocalypse at Abukir, but I soon learned that news of the disaster had indeed preceded me.

"It's like we're clinging to a rope," said a sergeant who escorted me to Napoleon's headquarters. "There's the Nile, and this narrow band of green that follows it, and nothing but empty desert on either side. Fall into the sands and they kill you for your buttons. Garrison a village, and you might wake to a knife sawing your windpipe. Bed a woman, and you might find your drink poisoned or your balls gone. Pet a dog, and you risk rabies. We can march in only two dimensions, not three. Is the rope to hang us?"

"The French have advanced to the guillotine," I quipped inanely.

"And Nelson has already cut off our head. Here's the body, flopping in Cairo."

I didn't think Bonaparte would like that analogy, preferring that the British admiral had cut off our feet while he, the brains, remained defiant. When I reported back to him at headquarters, he alternated between casting all blame on Brueys—"Why didn't he sail for Corfu?"—to insisting the essential strategic situation was unchanged. France was still the master of Egypt and within striking distance of the Levant. If India now seemed more remote, Syria remained a tempting target. Soon Egypt's wealth and labor would be harnessed. Christian Copts and renegade Mamelukes were being recruited into French forces. A camel corps would turn the desert into a navigable sea. Conquest would continue, with Napoleon as the new Alexander.

Yet after repeating all this as if to convince himself, Bonaparte's dark brooding couldn't be hidden. "Did Brueys show courage?" he asked me.

"A cannonball took the admiral's leg off but he insisted on remaining at his post. He died a hero."

"Well. There's that, at least."

"So did Captain Casabianca and his young son. The deck was aflame and they refused to abandon ship. They died for France and for duty, general. The fight could have gone either way. But when *L'Orient* blew up . . ."

"The entire Maltese treasure was lost. Damn! And Admiral Villeneuve fled?"

"There was no way his ships could get into the fight. The wind was against them."

"And *you* lived, too." The observation seemed a bit sour.

"I'm a good swimmer."

"So it seems. So it seems. You're quite the survivor, aren't you, Gage?" He toyed with calipers and looked at me sideways. "I've a new arrival inquiring about you. A Count Silano, who says he knows you from Paris. He shares your interest in antiquities and has been doing his own research. I told him you were fetching something from the ship and he expressed interest in examining it as well."

I wasn't about to share information with Silano. "The calendar was lost in the battle, I'm afraid."

"*Mon dieu*. Has nothing good come of this?"

"I've also lost track of Antoine Talma, who disappeared in Alexandria. Have you seen him, General?"

"The journalist?"

"He's worked hard to emphasize your victories, you know."

"As I've worked hard to win them. I'm depending on him to write my biography for distribution in France. The people need to know what's really happening here. But no, I don't take personal roll of thirty-five thousand men. Your friend will turn up if he hasn't run." The idea that some of us would try to sneak away from the Egyptian expedition seemed to gnaw at Bonaparte. "Are you any closer to understanding the pyramids and this necklace of yours?"

"I examined the calendar. It may suggest auspicious dates."

"For what?"

"I don't know."

He snapped the calipers shut. "I'm beginning to wonder about your usefulness, American. And yet Silano tells me there could be significant lessons, military lessons, in what you're researching."

"Military lessons?"

"Ancient powers. Egypt remained preeminent for thousands of years, building masterworks while the rest of the world was in huts. How? Why?"

"That's just the question that we savants are beginning to address," I said. "I'm curious to find if there are any ancient references to the phenomena of electricity. Jomard has speculated they could have used it to move their mammoth building blocks. But we can't read their hieroglyphics, everything is half-buried in sand, and we've simply not had enough time at the pyramids yet."

"Which we're about to remedy. I'm going to investigate them myself. But first, you will come to my banquet tonight. It's time you conferred with Alessandro Silano."

I was surprised at the depth of my relief at seeing Astiza. Perhaps it was having survived another terrible battle, or my worry about Talma, or the French sergeant's gloomy assessment of our position in Egypt, or Silano's appearance in Cairo, or Bonaparte's impatience with my progress: in any event, I felt lonely. Who was I but an American exile, cast up with a foreign army in an even more foreign land? What I *did* have was this woman who—while withholding intimacies—had become my companion and, in a secret estimation I wouldn't risk sharing with her, a friend. Yet her past was so vague that I was forced to ask myself whether I knew her at all. I looked carefully for some sign of hidden feelings when she greeted me, but she simply seemed happy that I'd returned unscathed. She and Enoch were eager to hear my firsthand account, since Cairo was a hotbed of rumor. If I'd any doubts about her quickness, they were dispelled when I heard how rapidly her French had improved.

Enoch and Ashraf had no word from Talma, but plenty of stories about Silano. He'd arrived in Cairo with his retinue, made contact with some Freemasons in the French officer corps, and conferred with Egyptian mystics and magicians. Bonaparte had granted him fine quarters in the home of another Mameluke bey, and any number of characters had been seen slipping in and out during all hours of the day and night. He'd reportedly asked General Desaix about impending plans to send French troops up the Nile.

"He directs men greedy for the secrets of the past," Astiza added. "He has assembled his own bodyguard of Bedouin cutthroats, been visited by Bin Sadr, and parades his yellow-haired trollop in a fine carriage."

"And there is word he asked about you," Enoch added. "Everyone has wondered if you were trapped at Abukir. Did you bring the calendar?"

"I lost it, but not before I had a chance to examine it. I'm guessing, but when I aligned the rings in a way that reminded me of the medallion and the pyramids, I sensed it was pointing to a date one month after the fall equinox, or October 21. Is that day significant here in Egypt?"

Enoch thought. "Not really. The solstice, the equinox, or the New Year when the Nile begins to rise all have meaning, but I know of nothing to do with that date. Perhaps it was an ancient holy day, but if so the meaning has been lost. I will consult my books, however, and mention the date to some of the wiser imams."

"And what of the medallion?" I asked. I'd felt uneasy being so separated from it, yet at the same time was thankful I hadn't risked it at Abukir Bay.

Enoch brought it out, its gold gleam familiar and reassuring. "The more I study it, the older I think it is—older, I think, than most of Egypt. The symbols may date to the deep time when the pyramids were built. It is so old, no books survive from that period, but your mention of Cleopatra intrigued me. She was a Ptolemy who lived three thousand years after the pyramids, and Greek by blood as much as Egyptian. When she consorted with Caesar and Antony, she was the last great link between the Roman world and ancient Egypt. By legend there is a temple, its location lost, dedicated to Hathor and Isis, the goddesses of nurture, love, and wisdom. Cleopatra worshipped there."

He showed me pictures of the goddesses. Isis looked like a conventionally beautiful woman with high headdress, but Hathor was odd, her face elongated and her ears jutting out like those of a cow. Homely, but in a pleasant way.

"The temple was probably rebuilt in Ptolemaic times,"

Enoch said, "but its origin is far older than that, perhaps as old as the pyramids. Legend contends it was oriented to the star Draco when that star marked the north. If so, secrets might have been shared between the two sites. I've been looking for something that refers to a puzzle, or a sanctuary, or a door—something this medallion might point to—so I've been combing the Ptolemaic texts."

"And?" I could see he enjoyed working this puzzle.

"And I have an ancient Greek reference to a small temple of Isis favored by Cleopatra that reads, 'The staff of Min is the key to life.'"

"Staff of Min? Bin Sadr has a staff, a snake-headed one. Who's Min?"

Astiza smiled. "Min is a god who became the root word of "man," just as the goddess Ma'at or Mut became the root word for "mother." His staff is not like Bin Sadr's."

"Here's another picture." Enoch slid it across. On it was a drawing of a stiff-postured bald fellow with one particularly arresting feature: a rigid, upright male member of prodigious length.

"By the souls of Saratoga. They put this in their churches?"

"It's just nature," Astiza said.

"Well-endowed nature, I'd say." I was unable to keep envy from my voice.

Ashraf had a wicked grin. "Typical for Egyptians, my American friend."

I looked at him sharply and he laughed.

"You're all having fun with me," I grumbled.

"No, no, Min is a real god and this is a real representation," Enoch assured me, "though my brother is exaggerating our countrymen's anatomy. Ordinarily I would read 'The staff of Min is the key to life' as a mere sexual and mythical reference. In our creation stories, our first god swallows his own seed and spits and shits out the first children."

"The devil you say!"

"And it is the ankh, the predecessor to your Christian cross, which is usually referred to as a key to eternal life.

But why Min in a temple of Isis? Frequented by Cleopatra? Why 'key' as opposed to 'essence' or some other word? And why this after it: 'The crypt will lead to heaven'?"

"Why, indeed?"

"We don't know. But your medallion may be an uncompleted key. The pyramids point to heaven. What is in that crypt? We do know, as I said, that Silano has been making inquiries about going south, up the Nile, with Desaix."

"Into enemy territory?"

"Somewhere south is where the temple of Hathor and Isis lies."

I pondered. "Silano has been doing some studying of his own in ancient capitals. Perhaps he has the same clues you've found. But he still needs the medallion, I'm gambling. Keep it here, hidden. I'm going to see the sorcerer at a banquet tonight, and if the subject comes up I'll tell him I lost it at Abukir Bay. It might be our only advantage if we're in a race to this key of life."

"Don't go to the banquet," Astiza said. "The goddess tells me we must stay away from this man."

"And my little god, Bonaparte, tells me I must sup with him."

She looked uncomfortable. "Then tell him nothing."

"Of my investigations?" Here was the issue the journalist had raised. "Or you?"

A blush rose in her cheeks. "He has no interest in your servants."

"Doesn't he? Talma told me he'd heard that you knew Silano in Cairo. The reason Antoine went to Alexandria was to ask not about Bin Sadr, but about you. Just how much do you know about Alessandro Silano?"

She was quiet too long. Then, "I knew of him. He came to study the ancients, as I did. But he wanted to exploit the past, not protect it."

"Knew *of* him?" By Hades, I knew *of* Chinamen, but I'd never had a thing to do with them. That's not what Talma had implied. "Or knew him in ways you don't want to admit, and which you've kept from me all these days?"

"The problem with modern men," Enoch interrupted, "is

that they ask too much. They respect no mystery. It causes endless trouble."

"I want to know if she knew . . ."

"The ancients understood that some secrets are best undisturbed, and some histories best forgotten. Don't let your enemies make you lose your friends, Ethan."

I fumed as they watched me. "But surely it is no coincidence that he is here," I insisted.

"Of course not. *You* are here, Ethan Gage. And the medallion."

"I want to forget him," Astiza added. "And what I remember of him is that he is more dangerous than he seems."

I was flummoxed, but it was clear they weren't giving out intimate details. And maybe I was imagining more than had occurred. "Well, he can't do us any harm in the middle of the French army, can he?" I finally said, to say something.

"We aren't *in* the middle of the army anymore, we're in a side street of Cairo." She looked worried. "I was terrified for you when I heard news of the battle. Then came word of Count Silano."

It was an opportunity to respond in kind, but I was too confused. "And now I'm back, with rifle and tomahawk," I said, in order to say something. "I'm not afraid of Silano."

She sighed, her scent of jasmine intoxicating. Since the rigors of the march she had transformed herself with Enoch's help into an Egyptian beauty, her gowns of linen and silk, her limbs and neck adorned with gold jewelry of ancient design, her eyes large, luminous, and highlighted with kohl. Cleopatra eyes. Her figure recalled the curves of alabaster jars of unguents and perfume I'd seen in the marketplace. She reminded me how long it had been since I'd had a woman, and how much I'd like to have her now. Because I was a savant, I would have expected my mind would remain occupied with loftier things, but it didn't seem to work that way. Yet how much should I trust?

"Guns are no proof against magic," she said. "I think it best if I share your night chambers again, to help watch over you. Enoch understands. You need the goddesses' protection."

Now here was progress. "If you insist . . ."

"He has made me an extra bed."

My smile was as tight as my breeches. "How thought-ful."

"It's important that we focus on the mystery." She said it with sympathy, or was it with torturous intent? Perhaps they are the same in women.

I tried to be nonchalant. "Just make sure you're close enough to kill the next snake."

M y mind a muddle of hope and frustration—the usual peril for getting emotionally involved with a female— I went to Bonaparte's banquet. Its purpose was to remind the senior officers that their position in Egypt was still sound, and that they must communicate that soundness to their troops. It was also important to demonstrate to the Egyptians that despite the recent naval disaster, the French were behaving with equanimity, enjoying dinners as they had before. Plans were underway to impress the population by celebrating the Revolution's new year, the autumn equinox of September 21, one month ahead of my guessed-at calendar date. There would be band music, horse races, and a flight of one of Conte's gas balloons.

The banquet was as European as possible. Chairs had been assembled so nobody would have to sit on the floor in Muslim style. The china plates, the wine and water goblets, and the silverware had been packed and carried across the desert as carefully as cartridges and cannon. Despite the heat, the menu included the usual soup, meat, vegetables, and salad of home.

Silano, in contrast, was our Orientalist. He'd come in robes and a turban, openly wearing the Masonic symbol of compass and square with the letter G in the middle. Talma would have been fuming at this appropriation. Four of his fingers bore rings, a small hoop adorned one ear, and the scabbard of his rapier was a filigree of gold on red enamel. As I entered, he stood from the table and bowed.

"Monsieur Gage, the American! I was told that you were

in Egypt, and now it is confirmed! We last enjoyed each other's company over cards, if you remember."

"*I* enjoyed it, at least. I won, as I recall."

"But of course, someone must lose! And yet the pleasure is in the game itself, is it not? Certainly it was an amusement I could afford." He smiled. "And I understand the medallion you won has brought you to this expedition?"

"That, and an untimely death in Paris."

"A friend?"

"A whore."

I could not disconcert him. "Oh, dear. I won't pretend to understand that. But of course you are the savant, the expert in electricity and the pyramids, and I am mere historian."

I took my place at the table. "I've modest knowledge of both, I'm afraid. I'm honored to have been included in the expedition at all. And you are a magician as well, I'm told, master of the occult and Cagliostro's Egyptian Rite."

"You exaggerate my capabilities as I, perhaps, exaggerate yours. I am a mere student of the past who hopes it might provide answers for the future. What did Egyptian priests know that has been lost until now? Our liberation has opened the way to fuse the technology of the West with the wisdom of the East."

"Yet wisdom of what, Count?" rumbled General Dumas past a mouthful of food. He ate like he rode, at full gallop. "I don't see it in the streets of Cairo. And the scholars, be they scientists or sorcerers, haven't accomplished much. They eat, talk, and scribble."

The officers laughed. Academics were viewed with skepticism, and soldiers felt the savants were pursuing pointless aims, pinning the army in Egypt.

"That is unfair to our savants, General," Bonaparte corrected. "Monge and Berthollet aimed a crucial cannon shot in the river battle. Gage has proven his marksmanship with his longrifle. The scientists stood with the infantry in the squares. Plans are underway for windmills, canals, factories, and foundries. Conte plans to inflate one of his balloons! We soldiers begin liberation, but it is the scholars who fulfill it. We win a battle, but they conquer the mind."

"So leave them to it and let's go home." Dumas went back to a drumstick.

"The ancient priests were equally useful," Silano said mildly. "They were healers and lawgivers. The Egyptians had spells to heal the sick, win the heart of a lover, ward off evil, and acquire wealth. We of the Egyptian Rite have seen spells influence weather, provide invulnerability to harm, and cure the dying. Even more may be learned, I hope, now that we control the cradle of civilization."

"You're promoting witchcraft," Dumas warned. "Be careful with your soul."

"Learning is not witchcraft. It puts tools in soldiers' hands."

"Saber and pistol have served well enough up to now."

"And where did gunpowder come from, but from experiments with alchemy?"

Dumas belched in reply. The general was huge, slightly drunk, and a hothead. Maybe he would get rid of Silano for me.

"I am promoting the tapping of unseen powers, like electricity," Silano went on smoothly, nodding at me. "What is this mysterious force we can observe simply by rubbing amber? Are there energies that animate the world? Can we transform base elements to more valuable ones? Mentors like Cagliostro, Kolmer, and Saint-Germain led the way. Monsieur Gage can apply the insights of the great Franklin . . ."

"Ha!" Dumas interrupted. "Cagliostro was exposed as a fraud in half a dozen countries. Invulnerable to harm?" He put his hand on his heavy cavalry saber and began to pull. "Try a spell against *this*."

Yet before he could draw there was a blur of motion and Silano had the point of his rapier against the general's fist. It was like the flicker of a hummingbird wing, and the air hummed from the swift arc of his drawn sword. "I don't need magic to win a mere duel," the count said with quiet warning.

The room had gone silent, stunned by his speed.

"Put your swords away, both of you," Napoleon finally ordered.

"Of course." Silano sheathed his slim blade almost as quickly as he'd drawn it.

Dumas scowled but let his saber drop back into its scabbard. "So you rely on steel like the rest of us," he muttered.

"Are you challenging my other powers as well?"

"I'd like to see them."

"The soul of science is skeptical test," the chemist Berthollet agreed. "It is one thing to claim magic and another to perform it, Count Silano. I admire your spirit of inquiry, but extraordinary claims demand extraordinary proof."

"Perhaps I should levitate the pyramids."

"That would impress all of us, I'm sure."

"And yet scientific discovery is a gradual process of experimentation and evidence," Silano went on. "So it is with magic and ancient powers. I do hope to levitate pyramids, become invulnerable to bullets, or achieve immortality, but at the moment I am a mere investigator, like you savants. That is why I have made the long journey to Egypt after inquiries in Rome, Constantinople, and Jerusalem. The American there has a medallion that may prove useful to my research, if he will let me study it."

Heads swung to me. I shook my head. "It is archeology, not magic, and not for alchemical experiment."

"For study, I said."

"Which real savants are providing. Their methods are credible. The Egyptian Rite is not."

The count had the look of a teacher disappointed in a pupil. "Are you calling me a liar, monsieur?"

"No, I am," Dumas interrupted again, throwing down his bone. "A fraud, a hypocrite, and a charlatan. I have no use for magicians, alchemists, savants, gypsies, or priests. You come here in robe and turban like a Marseille clown and talk of magic, but I see you sawing your meat like the rest of us. Flick that little needle of yours all you want, but let's test it in real battle against real sabers. I respect men who fight or build, not those who talk and fantasize."

Now Silano's eyes flickered with a dangerous annoyance.

"You have impugned my honor and dignity, General. Perhaps I should challenge *you*."

The room stirred with anticipation. Silano had a reputation as a deadly duelist, having slain at least two foes in Paris. Yet Dumas was a Goliath.

"And perhaps I should accept your challenge," the general growled.

"Dueling is forbidden," Napoleon snapped. "Both of you know that. If either tries it, I will have you both shot."

"So you are safe for now," Dumas said to the count. "But you'd better find your magic spells, because when we return to France . . ."

"Why wait?" Silano said. "May I suggest a different contest? Our esteemed chemist has called for skeptical test, so let me propose one. For dinner tomorrow, let me bring a small suckling pig I have shipped from France. As you know, the Muslims will have nothing to do with the animal; its only caretaker is me. You imply that I have no powers. Let me then, two hours before dinner, present you with the pig to prepare in any way you desire: roasted, boiled, baked, or fried. I will not come near it until it is served. You will cut the meal into four equal parts, and serve to me whichever quarter you prefer. You will eat another portion yourself."

"What is the point of this nonsense?" Dumas asked.

"The day after this dinner, one of four things will happen: either we will both be dead or neither of us will be dead; or I will be dead and you will not; or you will be dead and I will not. Of these four chances I will give you three and bet five thousand francs that, the day after the meal, you will be dead and I will be well."

There was silence at the table. Dumas looked flustered. "That is one of Cagliostro's old wagers."

"Which none of his enemies ever accepted. Here is your chance to be the first, General. Do you doubt my powers enough to dine with me tomorrow?"

"You'll try some kind of trickery or magic!"

"Which you said I can't perform. Prove it."

Dumas looked from one to the other of us. In a fight he was confident, but this?

"Dueling is prohibited, but this bet I would like to see," Bonaparte said. He was enjoying the torment of a general who'd challenged him on the march.

"He would poison me with sleight of hand, I know it."

Silano spread his arms wide, sensing victory. "You can search me from head to toe before we sit down to eat, General."

Dumas gave in. "Bah. I wouldn't dine with you if you were Jesus, the devil, or the last man on earth." He stood, shoving his chair back. "Coddle his investigations if you must," he addressed the room, "but I swear to you there's nothing in this damned desert but a bunch of old rock. You'll regret listening to these hangers-on, be it this charlatan or the American leech." And with that he stormed out of the room.

Silano turned to us. "He is wiser than his reputation, having turned down my challenge. It means he will live to have a son who will do great things, I predict. As for me, I only ask leave to make inquiries. I wish to hunt for temples when the army marches upriver. I give you brave soldiers all my respect and ask for some small portion in return." He looked at me. "I'd hoped we could work together as colleagues, but it appears we are rivals."

"I simply feel no need to share your goals, or my belongings," I replied.

"Then *sell* me the medallion, Gage. Name your price."

"The more you want it, the less inclined I am to let you have it."

"Damn you! You are an impediment to knowledge!" He shouted this last, his hand slapping the table, and it was as if a mask had slipped from his countenance. There was a rage behind it, rage and desperation, as he looked at me with eyes of implacable enmity. "Help me or prepare to endure the worst!"

Monge jumped up, the very picture of stern establishment admonition. "How dare you, monsieur! Your impertinence reflects on you poorly. I'm tempted to take you up on your wager myself!"

Now Napoleon stood, clearly annoyed that the discussion

was getting out of hand. "No one is eating poisoned pig. I want the animal bayoneted and thrown into the Nile this very night. Gage, you're here instead of the docket in Paris at my indulgence. I order you to help Count Silano in every way you can."

I stood too. "Then I must report what I was reluctant to admit. The medallion is gone, lost when I went overboard at the battle at Abukir."

Now the table broke into a buzz, everyone betting whether I was telling the truth. I rather enjoyed the notoriety, even though I knew it could only mean more trouble. Bonaparte scowled.

"You said nothing of this before," Silano said skeptically.

"I'm not proud of my mishap," I replied. "And I wanted the officers here to see the greedy loser that you are." I turned to the others. "This nobleman is not a serious scholar. He is nothing more than a frustrated gambler, trying to get by threat what he lost by cards. I'm a Freemason too, and his Egyptian Rite is a corruption of the precepts of our order."

"He's lying," Silano seethed. "He wouldn't have come back to Cairo if the medallion were not still his."

"Of course I would. I am a savant of this expedition, no less than Monge or Berthollet. The person who hasn't come back is my friend, the writer Talma, who disappeared in Alexandria the same time you arrived."

Silano turned to the others. "Magic, again."

They laughed.

"Do not make jokes, monsieur," I said. "Do you know where Antoine is?"

"If you find your medallion, perhaps I can help you find Talma."

"The medallion is lost, I told you!"

"And I said I don't believe you. My dear General Bonaparte, how do we know which side this American, this English-speaker, is even on?"

"That's outrageous!" I shouted, even while secretly wondering which side I *should* be on, even while firmly determined to stay on my own side—whatever that was. As Astiza had said, what did I truly believe? In bloody treasure,

beautiful women, and George Washington. "Duel with me!"
I challenged.

"There will be no duels!" Napoleon ordered once more.
"Enough! Everyone is acting like children! Gage, you have
permission to leave my table."

I stood and bowed. "Perhaps that would be best." I backed
through the door.

"You are about to see just how serious a scholar I am!"
Silano called after me. And I heard him speaking to Napoleon, "That American, you should not trust him. He's a man
who could make all our plans come to naught."

It was past noon the next day that Ash, Enoch, Astiza, and
I were resting by Enoch's fountain, discussing the dinner
and Silano's purpose. Enoch had armed his servants with
cudgels. For no obvious reason, we felt under siege. Why
had Silano come all this way? What was Bonaparte's interest? Did the general desire occult powers as well? Or were
we magnifying into a threat what was only idle curiosity?

Our answer came when there was a brief pounding at
Enoch's door and Mustafa went to answer it. He came back
not with a visitor, but with a jar. "Someone left this."

The clay-colored container was fat, two feet high, and
heavy enough that I could see the biceps flex in the servant's
arms as he carried it to a low table and put it down. "There
was no one there and the street was empty."

"What is it?" I asked.

"It's a jar for oil," Enoch said. "It's not the custom to deliver a gift this way." He looked wary, but stood to open it.

"Wait," I said. "What if it's a bomb?"

"A bomb?"

"Or a Trojan horse," said Astiza, who knew her Greek
legends as well as her Egyptian ones. "An enemy leaves this,
we carry it inside . . ."

"And out jump midget soldiers?" asked Ashraf, somewhat
amused.

"No. Snakes." She remembered the incident in Alexandria.

Now Enoch hesitated.

Ash stood. "Stand back and let me open it."

"Use a stick," his brother said.

"I'll use a sword, and be quick."

We stood a few steps back. Using the point of a scimitar, Ashraf broke a wax seal on the rim and loosened the lid. No sound came from inside. So, using the tip of his weapon, Ash slowly raised and flipped the covering off. Again, nothing. He leaned forward cautiously, probing with his sword . . . and jumped back. "Snake!" he confirmed.

Damn. I'd had enough of reptiles.

"But it can't be," the Mameluke said. "The jar is full of oil. I can smell it." He cautiously came back again, probing. "No . . . wait. The snake is dead." His face looked troubled. "May the gods have mercy."

"What the devil?"

Grimacing, the Mameluke plunged his hand into the jar and lifted. Out came a snakelike fistful of oily hair entangled with the scales of a reptile. As he hoisted his arm, we saw a round object wrapped in the coils of a dead serpent. Oil sluiced off a human head.

I groaned. It was Talma, eyes wide and sightless.

CHAPTER FIFTEEN

T hey killed him as a message to me," I said.
"But why would they kill your friend for something
you said you didn't have? Why didn't they kill *you?*"
Ashraf asked.

I was wondering the same thing. Poor Talma's head had
been temporarily dipped back into the jar, his hair like river
weed. I didn't want to guess where the body might be.

"Because they don't believe him," Astiza reasoned. "Only
Ethan knows for sure if the medallion still exists and what it
might mean. They want to coerce him, not kill him."

"This is a damned poor way to do it," I said grimly.

"And who is they?" Enoch asked.

"The Bedouin, Achmed bin Sadr."

"He's a tool, not a master."

"Then it must be Silano. He warned me to take him seriously. He arrives, and Antoine dies. All this is my fault. I
asked Talma to investigate Bin Sadr in Alexandria. Talma
was kidnapped, or followed Silano to spy on him. He was
caught and wouldn't talk. What did he even know? And his
death is supposed to frighten me."

Ash clapped my shoulder. "Except that he doesn't know
what a warrior you are!"

Actually, I was human enough to have nightmares for a
month, but that's not what one confesses at times like this.
Besides, if there was one thing I was certain of, Silano
would never, ever get my medallion.

"It's my fault," Astiza said. "You said he went to Alexandria to investigate me."

"That was his idea, not mine or yours. Don't blame yourself."

"Why didn't he just ask me his questions directly?"

Because you never fully answer them, I thought. Because you enjoy being an enigma. But I said nothing. We sat in gloomy silence for a while, wrestling with self-recrimination. Sometimes the more innocent we are, the more we blame ourselves.

"Your friend will not be the last to perish if Silano gets his way," Enoch finally said heavily.

It sounded as if the old man knew more than he'd let on. "What do you mean?"

"There is more at stake here than you may realize, or have been told. The more I study, the more I fear, and the more I am convinced."

"Of what?"

"Your medallion may be some kind of clue or key to open a sacred door to a long-hidden vault. The pendant has been sought and fought over for millennia, and then, its purpose undeciphered, probably lay forgotten on Malta until Cagliostro learned of it in his studies here and sought it out. It curses the unworthy and drives them mad. It taunts the brilliant. It has become a riddle. It is a key with no lock, a map to no destination. None remember what it relates to. It has baffled even me."

"So perhaps it is useless," I said with a mixture of hope and regret.

"Or, its time has at last come. Silano wouldn't have followed you here after his own studies if he didn't have real expectation."

"To find treasure?"

"If only it were that. There is treasure, and then there is power. I don't know which truly motivates this mysterious European and his so-called Egyptian Rite, but were Silano to ever find what so many have sought, he would have not only immortal life and wealth unimaginable, but access to secrets that could undo the very warp and weave of the world. The right man might build with them. The wrong . . ."

"*What* secrets? What the devil are all you people really after?"

Enoch sighed, considering what to say. Finally he spoke. "The Book of Thoth."

"The book of what?"

"Thoth is the Egyptian god of wisdom and knowledge," Astiza said. "Your English word 'thought' comes from his name. He is the thrice great, the one the Greeks called Hermes. When Egypt began, Thoth was there."

"The origins of our nation are mysterious," Enoch said. "No history exists. But Egypt came before all. Instead of legends of a gradual awakening, our civilization seems to have sprung from the sand wholly formed. There is no precedent, and then suddenly kingdoms emerge with all the necessary arts. Where did knowledge come from? We attribute this sudden birth to the wisdom of Thoth."

"It was he who invented writing, drawing, surveying, mathematics, astronomy, and medicine," Astiza explained. "From whence he came we don't know, but he started all that has come since. To us he is like Prometheus, who brought fire, or Adam and Eve, who ate from the apple of knowledge. Yes, your Bible story suggests a similar great awakening, but recalls it with dread. We believe men were wiser in those days, and knew magical things. The world was cleaner and happier." She pointed to a painting on the wall of Enoch's library. It was of a man with the head of a bird.

"That's Thoth?" There's something disturbing about people with the heads of animals. "Why a bird? They're dumber than donkeys."

"It's an ibis, and we Egyptians find the unity of humans and animals quite beautiful." There was a certain frost in her tone. "He's also portrayed as a baboon. Egyptians believed there were no sharp differences between humans and animals, man and god, life and death, creator and created. All are part of one. It is Thoth who presides when our hearts are weighed against a feather before a jury of the forty-two gods. We must proclaim the evil we did not commit, lest our soul be devoured by a crocodile."

"I see," I said, even though I didn't.

"Sometimes he would roam the world to observe and would disguise his wisdom as he learned still more. Men called him 'the Fool.'"

"The Fool?"

"The jester, the wit, the truth teller," Enoch said. "He emerges again and again. The saying is that the fool shall seek the Fool."

Now I was really disturbed. Wasn't that what the gypsy Sarylla had said in the French forest when she dealt the tarot cards? Had what I dismissed as vague nonsense actually been real prophecy? She had called me the fool, as well. "But why all the excitement about one more book?"

"This is not another book, but the first book," said Enoch. "And surely you agree that books can drive the world, be it the Bible, the Koran, the works of Isaac Newton, or the songs of the Iliad that inspired Alexander. At their best, they are a distillation of thought, wisdom, hope, and desire. The Book of Thoth is reputed to be forty-two papyrus scrolls, a mere sampling of the 36,535 scrolls—one hundred for each day of the solar year—on which Thoth inscribed his secret knowledge and hid around the earth, to be found only by the worthy when the time was right. On these scrolls is a summary of the deepest power of the masters who built the pyramids: Might. Love. Immortality. Joy. Revenge. Levitation. Invisibility. The ability to see the world as it truly is, rather than the dreamlike illusion we live in. There is some pattern that underlies our world, some invisible structure, which legend says can be manipulated to magical effect. The ancient Egyptians knew how to do so. We have forgotten."

"That's why everyone is so desperate for this medallion?"

"Yes. It may be a clue for a quest as old as history. What if people didn't have to die, or could be revived if they did? For an individual, time alone would eventually allow the accumulation of knowledge that would make him master of all other men. For armies, it would mean indestructibility. What would an army be like that knew no fear? What would a tyrant be like who had no end? What if what we call magic was nothing more than ancient science, directed by a book brought by a being, or beings, so ancient and wise that we've lost all memory of who they were and why they came?"

"Surely Bonaparte doesn't expect . . ."

"I don't think the French know exactly what they seek or what it could do for them, or else they'd already be taking our nation apart. There are stories, and that is enough. What do they have to lose by seeking? Bonaparte is a manipulator. He has put you to work on the problem, and savants like Jomard, as well. Now Silano. But Silano is different, I suspect. He pretends to work for the French government, but really he uses their support to work for himself. He's following Cagliostro's footsteps, trying to see if the legends are real."

"But they aren't," I objected. "I mean, this is crazy. If this book exists, why don't we see some sign of it? People have always died, even in ancient Egypt. They must, for society to renew, for young people to succeed the old. If they didn't, people would go crazy with impatience. Natural death would be supplanted by murder."

"You have wisdom beyond your years!" Enoch cried. "And you have begun to understand why such powerful secrets were rarely used and must continue to sleep. The book exists, but remains dangerous. No mere mortal man can handle godlike power. Thoth knew his knowledge must be safeguarded until our moral and emotional advancement balanced our cleverness and ambition, so he hid his books somewhere. Yet the dream runs through all of history, and perhaps fragments of the writings have been learned. Alexander the Great came to Egypt, visited the oracle, and went on to conquer the world. Caesar and his family triumphed after he studied with Cleopatra here. The Arabs became the world's most powerful civilization after overrunning Egypt. In the Middle Ages, the Christians came to the Holy Land. For the Crusades? Or for deeper, more secret reasons? Later, other Europeans began to roam the ancient places. Why? Some contended it was for Christian artifacts. Some cite the legend of the Holy Grail. But what if the grail is a metaphor for this book, a metaphor of ultimate wisdom itself? What if it stands for the most dangerous kind of Promethean fire? Have any of the battles you've witnessed so far convinced you we are ready for such knowledge? We're barely more than animals. So our old order slowly wakened from its lethargy, fearing that graves long buried were about to be reopened, that a book of secrets long lost might be rediscovered. Yet we know not ourselves what, precisely, it is we are guarding! Now the godless magi have come with your Bonaparte."

"You mean the savants."

"And this conjurer, Silano."

"Do you want to destroy the medallion, then, so the book can't be found?"

"No," said Ashraf. "It has been rediscovered for a reason. Your coming is a sign in itself, Ethan Gage. But these secrets are for Egypt, not for France."

"We have our own spies," Astiza went on. "Word came that an American was arriving with something that could be a key to the past, an artifact that had been lost for centuries and was a clue to powers lost for millennia. They warned it would be best just to kill you. But in Alexandria you killed my master instead, and I saw that Isis had another plan."

"Word came from whom?"

She hesitated. "Gypsies."

"Gypsies!"

"A band sent warning from France."

I sat back, rocked by this new revelation. By Jupiter and Jehovah, had I been betrayed by the Rom as well? Had Stefan and Sarylla been distracting me while word was sent ahead of my coming? What kind of string puppet was I? And were these people around me now, these people I liked and trusted, true informants who could lead me to a treasured book—or a nest of lunatics?

"Who *are* you?"

"The last priests of the old gods, who were earthly manifestations of a time and race with far more wisdom than ours," Enoch said. "Their origins and purpose are lost in the fog of the past. We are our own kind of Masonry, if you will, the heirs of the beginning and the watchmen of the end. We are guardians not entirely certain of what it is we are guarding, but entrusted to keep this book out of the wrong hands. The old religions never completely die; they are simply absorbed into the new. Our task is to discover the door before unprincipled opportunists do—and then shut it again forever."

"What door?"

"That is what we don't know."

"And you want to shut it only after taking a peek."

"We cannot decide what best to do with the book until we find it. We should see if it offers hope or peril, redemption or damnation. But until we do find it, we live with the fear that someone else far less scrupulous could find it first."

I shook my head. "Between bungling my assassination in Alexandria and not having much more of a clue than I do, you're not much of a priesthood," I grouched.

"The goddess does things in her own good time," Astiza said serenely.

"And Silano does his in his." I looked grimly at our little gathering. "Isis didn't help poor Talma, and she won't protect us. I don't think we're safe here."

"My house is guarded . . . ," Enoch began.

"And known. Your address is no longer a secret, that oil jar tells us. You must move, now. You think he won't come knocking if he's desperate enough?"

"Move! I will not run from evil. I will not leave the books and artifacts I've spent a lifetime accumulating. My servants can protect me. And besides, trying to move my library would give any new hiding place away. My job is to keep researching, and yours to keep working with the savants, until we learn where this door is and secure it before Silano can enter. We are in a race for rediscovery. Let's not lose it by fleeing now." Enoch was glowering. Trying to send him into hiding would be like budging a barnacle.

"Then at least we need a safe place for both Astiza and

the medallion," I argued. "It's madness to keep it here now. And if I'm assaulted or killed, it's imperative they not find the medallion on me. In fact, if I'm kidnapped, its absence might be the only thing to keep me alive. Astiza could be used as a hostage. Even Napoleon has noticed my, er, interest in her." I kept my eyes averted while I said it. "Meanwhile, Bonaparte is about to lead a group of savants to the pyramids. Maybe in combination we'll learn something to head Silano off."

"One cannot send a beautiful young woman off by herself," said Enoch.

"So where *does* one put a woman, in Egypt?"

"A harem," Ashraf suggested.

I'll confess that some erotic fantasies concerning that mysterious institution flickered through my mind. I had a vision of shallow bathing pools, fanning slaves, and half-draped, sex-starved women. Could I visit? But then, if Astiza went into a harem, could she get back out?

"I'm not going to be locked in a seraglio," Astiza said. "I belong to no man."

Well, you belong to me, I thought, but it didn't seem the time to push the issue.

"In a harem, no man except the master can enter, or even learn what goes on," insisted Ashraf. "I know a nobleman who did not flee the French, Yusuf al-Beni, who has retained possession of his house and his household. He has a harem for his women and could give the priestess refuge. Not as a harem girl, but as a guest."

"Can Yusuf be trusted?"

"He can be bought, I think."

"I don't want to sit blinded from events, sewing with a bunch of silly women," Astiza said. Damnation, she was independent. It was one of the things I liked about her.

"Nor do you want to be dead or worse," I replied. "Ashraf's idea is excellent. Hide there as a guest, with the medallion, while I go to the pyramids and Enoch and I solve this thing. Don't go out. Don't give the neckpiece any significance, should anyone in the harem see it. Our best hope is that Silano's scheming may be his undoing. Bonaparte will see through it and realize the count wants these powers for himself, not for France."

"It's just as risky to leave me alone," Astiza said.

"You won't *be* alone, you'll be with a bunch of silly women, as you said. Stay hidden and wait. I'll find this Book of Thoth and come get you."

CHAPTER SIXTEEN

N apoleon's visit to the pyramids was a grander excursion than the visit I'd made earlier with Talma and Jomard. More than a hundred officers, escorting soldiers, guides, servants, and scientists crossed the Nile and hiked up to the Giza plateau. It was like a holiday outing, a train of donkeys bearing French wives, mistresses, and a cornucopia of fruits, sweets, meats, and wine. Parasols were held in the sun. Carpets were spread on the sand. We would dine next to eternity.

Conspicuous by his absence was Silano, who I was told was conducting his own investigations in Cairo. I was glad I'd tucked Astiza safely out of the way.

As we trudged up the slope I reported Talma's hideous death to Bonaparte, to gauge his reaction and plant doubt in his mind about my rival. Unfortunately, my news seemed to annoy our commander more than shock him. "The journalist had barely started my biography! He shouldn't have wandered off before the country is pacified."

"My friend disappeared when Silano arrived, General. Is that coincidence? I fear the count may be involved. Or Bin Sadr, that Bedouin marauder."

"That marauder is our ally, Monsieur Gage. As is the count, an agent of Talleyrand himself. He assures me he knows nothing about Talma, and in any event he has no motive. Does he?"

"He said he wanted the medallion."

"Which you said you lost. In a nation of a million restive natives, why do you suspect only the people who are on our side?"

"But *are* they on our side?"

"They are on *my* side! As you will be, when you begin to solve the mysteries we brought you here for! First you lose your medallion and calendar, and now you make accusations against our colleagues! Talma died! Men do in war!"

"They don't have their heads delivered in a jar."

"I have seen parts worse than that delivered. Listen. You saw the defeat of our fleet. Our success is imperiled. We are cut off from France. Rebel Mamelukes are gathering in the south. The population is not yet resigned to its new situation. Insurgents commit atrocities precisely to sow the kind of terror and confusion you're exhibiting. Stand fast, Gage! You were brought to solve mysteries, not create them."

"General, I'm doing my best, but Talma's head was clearly a message . . ."

"A message that time is of the essence. I cannot afford sympathy, because sympathy is weakness, and any weakness on my part invites our destruction. Gage, I tolerated an American's presence because I was told you might be useful in investigating the ancient Egyptians. Can you make sense of the pyramids or not?"

"I am trying, General."

"Succeed. Because the moment you are of no use to me, I can have you jailed." He looked past me, the admonition given. "Ah. They are big, aren't they?"

The same awe that I'd felt on my initial visit was experienced by others as they came within view of the Sphinx and the pyramids behind. Customary chatter went silent as we clustered on the sand like ants, the depth of time palpable. Their shadows on the sand were as distinct as the pyramids themselves. It was not the ghosts of the long-vanished workmen and pharaohs I experienced, but rather the serene spirit of the structures themselves.

Napoleon, however, scrutinized the monuments like a quartermaster. "As simple as a child might build, but they certainly have size. Look at that volume of stone, Monge!

Building this big one here would be like marshalling an army. What are the dimensions, Jomard?"

"We're still digging, trying to find the base and the corners," the officer replied. "The Great Pyramid is at least seven hundred and fifty feet on each side and more than four hundred and fifty feet high. The base covers thirteen acres, and while the building stones are huge, I calculate there are at least two and a half million of them. The volume is large enough to easily contain any of the cathedrals in Europe. It is the largest structure in the world."

"So much stone," Napoleon murmured. He asked the dimensions of the other two pyramids as well and, using a Conte pencil, began jotting calculations of his own. He played with mathematics in the way other men might doodle. "Where do you think they got the stone, Dolomieu?" he asked as he worked.

"Somewhere nearby," the geologist replied. "Those blocks are limestone, the same as the bedrock of the plateau. That's why they appear eroded. Limestone isn't very hard, and wears easily from water. In fact, formations of limestone are frequently perforated with caves. We might expect caves here, but I must assume this plateau is solid, given the aridity. Reportedly there is also granite inside the pyramid, and that must have come from many miles away. I suspect the facing limestone also came from a separate quarry of finer rock."

Napoleon displayed his calculations. "Look, it is absurd. With the stone in these pyramids you could build a wall two meters high and one meter thick around all of France."

"I hope you don't expect us to do so, General," Monge joked. "It would weigh millions of tons to take home."

"Indeed." He laughed. "At last I have found a ruler who eclipses my own ambition! Khufu, you dwarf me! Yet why not simply tunnel into a mountain? Is it true the Arab tomb robbers didn't find a corpse inside?"

"There is no evidence anyone was ever buried here," Jomard said. "The main passage was blocked by enormous granite plugs that seem to have guarded . . . nothing."

"So we are presented with another mystery."

"Perhaps. Or perhaps the pyramids serve some other purposes, which is my own theory. For example, the pyramid's
placement, near the thirtieth parallel, is intriguing. It is almost exactly one-third of the way from the equator to the
North Pole. As I was explaining to Gage here, the ancients
hint that the Egyptians might have understood the nature
and size of our planet."

"If so, they are ahead of half the officers in my army,"
Bonaparte said.

"Equally striking, the Great Pyramid and its companions
are oriented in the cardinal directions of north, south, east,
and west more precisely than modern surveyors typically
achieve. If you draw a line from the pyramid's center to the
Mediterranean, it exactly bisects the Nile Delta. If you draw
diagonal lines from one pyramid corner to the opposite and
extend those, one going northeastward and one northwest-
ward, they form a triangle that perfectly encloses the delta.
This location was no accident, General."

"Intriguing. A symbolic location to tie upper and lower
Egypt together, perhaps. The pyramid is a political state-
ment, do you think?"

Jomard was encouraged by this attention to his theories,
which other officers had jeered at. "It is also interesting to
consider the pyramid's apothem," he said enthusiastically.

"What's an apothem?" I interrupted.

"If you drew a line down the middle of one face of the
pyramid," the mathematician Monge explained, "from point
to base, so that you divide its triangle in two, that line is the
apothem."

"Ah."

"The apothem," Jomard went on, "appears to be exactly
six hundred feet, or the length of the Greek stadia. That's a
common measurement found throughout the ancient world.
Could the pyramid be a standard of measurement, or be
built to a standard that long predates the Greeks?"

"Possibly," Bonaparte said. "Yet using this as a measuring stick seems an even more absurd excuse for such a monument than a tomb."

"As you know, General, there are sixty minutes in each

degree of latitude or longitude. That apothem also happens to be one-tenth of one minute of one degree. Is this mere coincidence? Even odder, the perimeter of the pyramid's base equals half a minute, and two circuits a full minute. Moreover, the perimeter of the pyramid's base appears to be equal to the circumference of a circle whose radius is the pyramid's height. It's as if the pyramid was sized to encode the dimensions of our planet."

"But dividing the earth into three hundred sixty degrees is a modern convention, is it not?"

"On the contrary, that number can be traced to Babylon and Egypt. The ancients picked three hundred sixty because it signifies the days of the year."

"But the year is three hundred sixty-five," I objected. "And a quarter."

"The Egyptians added five holy days when that became apparent," Jomard said, "just as we revolutionaries have added holidays to our thirty-six ten-day weeks. My theory is that the people who built this structure knew the size and shape of the earth and incorporated those dimensions into this structure so they'd not be lost, should learning decline in the future. They anticipated, perhaps, the Dark Ages."

Napoleon looked impatient. "But why?"

Jomard shrugged. "Perhaps to reeducate mankind. Perhaps simply to prove that they knew. We build monuments to God and military victory. Perhaps they built monuments to mathematics and science."

It seemed improbable to me that people so long ago could know so much, and yet again there was something fundamentally *right* about the pyramid, as if it were trying to convey eternal truths. Franklin had mentioned a similar rightness to the dimensions of Greek temples, and I remember that Jomard had tied everything to that strange Fibonacci number sequence. Again I wondered if these games of arithmetic had anything to do with the secret of my medallion. Mathematics made my mind fog.

Bonaparte turned to me. "And what does our American friend think? What is the view from the New World?"

"Americans believe things should be done for a purpose,"

I said, trying to sound wiser than I was. "We're practical, as you said. So what is the practical use of this monument? Perhaps Jomard has a point that this is more than a tomb."

Napoleon was not fooled by my rambling. "Well, the pyramid has a point, at least." We dutifully laughed. "Come. I want to look inside."

While most of our party was content to picnic, a handful of us entered the dark hole on the pyramid's north face. There was a limestone portal marking the pyramid's original entrance that had been constructed by the ancient Egyptians. This entry, Jomard explained, was only revealed when Muslims stripped off the pyramid's casing for stone to build Cairo; in ancient times it had been disguised by a cleverly hidden hinged door of stone. No one had known precisely where it lay. So before it was revealed, medieval Arabs made an attempt to plunder the pyramid by simply starting their own entry. In 820, Caliph Abdullah al-Mamun, knowing that historians recorded a northern entrance, had a band of engineers and stone masons chew their own tunnel into the pyramid in hopes of striking the structure's corridors and shafts. As luck would have it, he began below the earlier door. It was this excavation we entered.

While their guess of the entry's placement was off, the tunneling Arabs soon struck a narrow shaft inside the pyramid that had been built by the Egyptians. Just under four feet high, this shaft descended from the original entrance at an angle that Jomard had calculated was twenty-three degrees. Crawling upward, the Arabs found the original entrance to the outside and a second shaft ascending into the pyramid at the same slope the first descended. Such an upward shaft had never been mentioned in ancient chronicles, and it was blocked with granite plugs too hard to chisel through. Sensing he had found a secret pathway to treasure, Al Mamun ordered his men to tunnel around the plugs through the softer surrounding limestone blocks. It was hot, dirty, noxious work. The first granite plug was succeeded by another, and then a third. After great effort they rejoined the upward shaft, but found it was now plugged with limestone.

Determined, they excavated even that. Finally, they broke through, and found . . .

"Nothing," Jomard said. "And yet something, which you will see today."

Under the geographer's direction, we reconnoitered this architectural confusion of entrances and junctions, and then stoop-walked to peer down the descending shaft that the Arabs had first encountered. The blackness at its end was total.

"Why a slope and not steps?" Napoleon wondered.

"To slide things, perhaps," Jomard said. "Or maybe this is not an entry at all but serves some other function, such as a pipe, or a telescope pointed at a particular star."

"The biggest monument in the world," Bonaparte said, "and it makes no sense. There's something here we are missing."

With the help of torches carried by local guides we cautiously made our way downward about one hundred meters, stepping sideways for purchase. Carved blocks gave way to a smooth shaft through limestone bedrock, and then the shaft ended in a cavelike room with a pit and an uneven floor. It seemed unfinished.

"As you can see, this shaft seems to lead nowhere," Jomard said. "We've found nothing of interest."

"Then what are we doing here?" Bonaparte asked.

"The lack of obvious purpose is what is intriguing, don't you think? Why did they dig down here? And wait, it gets better. Let's go up again."

We did so, panting, and sweaty. Dust and bat guano stained our clothes. The air in the pyramid was warm, moist, and musty.

Back at the junction of tunnel and shafts, we now ascended above our original entry point and entered the ascending shaft so laboriously excavated by al-Mamun's men. This one rose at the same angle the initial one descended, and again, it was too low to stand upright. There were no steps and it was awkward to climb. After sixty meters, hot and panting, we emerged at another junction. Ahead, running level, was a low passage that led to a largely featureless room with gabled roof that the Arabs had dubbed the Queen's Chamber, even though our guides told us there was no evidence any queen had ever been buried there. We crawled to it and stood up. There was an alcove at one end, possibly for a statue or upright coffin, but it was empty. The room was remarkable only in its plainness. Its granite blocks were absolutely featureless, each weighing many tons and so finely jointed that I couldn't slip a piece of paper between them.

"The gabled roof might deflect some of the pyramid's weight to the chamber walls," Jomard said.

Napoleon, impatient at the dirty indignities we were enduring, curtly ordered us back out to the junction where the shaft continued to ascend. He wanted to see the King's Chamber above.

Now the cramped, dwarflike passageway changed to one for giants. The ascending passage broadened and rose, forming an inclined gallery that climaxed in a corbelled roof almost thirty feet above our heads. Again there were no steps; it was like climbing a slide. Fortunately, guides had fixed a rope. Once more, the stonework was as perfect as it was plain. This section's height seemed as inexplicable as the dwarf-sized passage before.

Had humans really built this?

An Arab guide held his torch high and pointed at the ceiling. I could see dark clots up there, marring the perfect symmetries, but I didn't know what they were.

"Bats," Jomard whispered.

Wings twitched and rustled in the shadows.

"Let's hurry up," Napoleon commanded. "I'm hot and half suffocated." The torch smoke stung.

The gallery was forty-seven meters long, Jomard announced after unreeling a tape, and again had no obvious purpose. Then the climb ended and we had to stoop to advance horizontally again. Finally we entered the pyramid's biggest room, built a third of the way up the structure's mass.

This King's Chamber was a featureless rectangle built of colossal red granite blocks. Again, the simplicity was odd.

The roof was flat and the floor and walls barren. There was no sacred book or bird-headed god. The only object was a lidless black granite sarcophagus set at the far end, as empty as the room itself. At about seven feet long, three and a half feet wide, and three feet high, it was too big to have fit through the tight entry we'd just crawled through, and must have been put in place as the pyramid was built. But Napoleon for the first time seemed intrigued, inspecting the rock casket closely.

"How could they have hollowed this out?" he asked.

"The room's dimensions are also interesting, General," Jomard said. "I measure thirty-four feet long, seventeen wide. The chamber floor represents a double square."

"Imagine that," I said, more mocking than I meant.

"He means its length is twice its width," Monge explained. "Pythagoras and the Greeks were interested in the harmony of such perfect rectangles."

"The chamber's height is half the length of the room's diagonal," Jomard added, "or nineteen feet. Gage, help me here and I'll show you something else. Hold this end of my tape in that corner."

I did so. Jomard extended his tape diagonally to the opposite wall, exactly halfway along its length. Then, as I held the tape in my corner, he walked his end across the room until what had been a diagonal now lay alongside the wall I occupied. "Voilà!" he cried, his voice echoing in the rock room.

Once more I did not display the anticipated excitement.

"Don't you recognize it? It's what we talked about at the pyramid's summit! The golden number, or golden mean!"

Now I saw it. If you divided this rectangular room into two squares, measured the diagonal of one of those squares, and laid that line on the long side of the chamber, the ratio between that length and what was left was the supposedly magical 1.618.

"You're saying this room incorporates Fibonacci numbers in the same way the pyramid itself does," I said, trying to sound casual.

Monge's eyebrows raised. "Fibonacci numbers? Gage,

you're more of a mathematician than I would have guessed."

"Oh, I've just been picking it up here and there."

"So what's the practical use of these dimensions?" Napoleon asked.

"It represents nature," I ventured.

"And it encodes the Egyptian kingdom's basic units of measurement," Jomard said. "In its length and proportions, I think it lays out a system of cubits, just as we might design the metric system into the proportions of a museum."

"Interesting," the general said. "Still, to build so much—it's a puzzle. Or a lens, perhaps, like a lens to focus light."

"That's what I feel," Jomard said. "Any thought you think, any prayer you make, seems amplified by the dimensions of this pyramid. Listen to this." He began a low hum, then a thrumming chant. The sound echoed weirdly, seeming to vibrate through our bodies. It was like striking a note of music that lingered in the air.

Our general shook his head. "Except that this focuses—what? Electricity?" He turned to me.

If I'd grandly said yes, he probably would have given me a reward. Instead, I looked vacant as an idiot.

"The granite coffer is also interesting," Jomard said, to fill the awkward silence. "Its interior volume is exactly half its exterior volume. While it seems sized for a man or a casket, I suspect its precise dimensions are no accident."

"Boxes within boxes," Monge said. "First this chamber, then the outside of the sarcophagus, then the inside . . . for what? We have a host of theories, but no one answer I feel is conclusive."

I looked up. It felt like millions of tons were pressing down toward us, threatening at any moment to obliterate our existence. For a moment I had the illusion the ceiling was descending! But no, I blinked, and the chamber was as before.

"Leave me," Bonaparte suddenly commanded.

"What?"

"Jomard is right. I feel power here. Don't you feel it?"

"It feels oppressive and yet alive," I offered. "Like a grave, and yet you feel light, insubstantial."

"I want to spend some time in here alone," the general told us. "I want to see if I can feel the spirit of this dead pharaoh. Perhaps his body is gone but his soul remains. Perhaps Silano and his magic are real. Perhaps I can feel Gage's electricity. Leave me with an unlit torch in the dark. I'll come down when I'm ready."

Monge looked concerned. "Perhaps if one of us remained as guard . . ."

"No." He climbed over the lip of the black sarcophagus and lay down, staring at the ceiling. We looked down at him and he smiled slightly. "It's more comfortable than you might think. The stone is neither too cold nor hot. Nor am I too tall, are you surprised?" He smiled at his little joke. "Not that I plan to remain here forever."

Jomard looked troubled. "There are accounts of panic . . ."

"Never question my courage."

He bowed. "To the contrary, I salute you, my general."

So we dutifully filed out, each torch in turn disappearing through the low entryway until our commander was left alone in the dark. We worked our way down the Grand Gallery, letting ourselves down by the rope. A bat took flight and flapped down toward us, but an Arab waved a torch and the blind creature veered away from the heat, settling again on the ceiling. By the time we got down to the smaller shaft that led down to the pyramid entrance, I was soaked with sweat.

"I'll wait for him here," Jomard said. "The rest of you file outside."

I needed no encouragement. The day seemed lit with a thousand suns when we finally emerged on the outside of the pyramid's sand-and-rubble slope, clouds of dust puffing off our now-filthy clothes. My throat was parched, my head aching. We found shade on the east side of the structure and sat to wait, sipping water. The party members who had remained outside had scattered over the ruins. Some were circuiting the other two pyramids. Some had erected little awnings and were having lunch. A few had climbed partway up the structure above us, and others competed to see how high up the pyramid's side they could hurl a rock.

I mopped my brow, acutely conscious that I seemed no closer to solving the medallion's mystery. "All this great pile for three little rooms?"

"It doesn't make sense, does it?" agreed Monge.

"I feel like there's something obvious we're not seeing."

"I'm guessing we're to see numbers, as Jomard said. It may be a puzzle meant to occupy humankind for centuries." The mathematician took out paper and began his own calculations.

Bonaparte was absent for a full hour. Finally there was a shout and we went back to meet him. Like us he emerged dirty and blinking, skidding down the rubble to the sand below. But when we ran up I saw he was also unusually pale, his eyes having the unfocused, haunted look of a man emerging from a vivid dream.

"What took you so long?" Monge asked.

"Was it long?"

"An hour, at least."

"Really? Time disappeared."

"And?"

"I crossed my arms in the sarcophagus, like those mummies we've seen."

"*Mon dieu,* General."

"I heard and saw . . ." He shook his head as if to clear it. "Or did I?" He swayed.

The mathematician grasped his arm to hold him up. "Heard and saw what?"

He blinked. "I had a picture of my life, or I think it was my life. I'm not even sure if it was the future or the past." He looked around, whether to be evasive or to tease us, I know not.

"What kind of picture?"

"I . . . it was very strange. I won't speak of this, I think. I won't . . ." Then his eyes fell on me. "Where's the medallion?" he abruptly demanded.

He took me by surprise. "It's lost, remember?"

"No. You're mistaken." His gray eyes were intent.

"It went down with *L'Orient,* General."

"No." He said it with such conviction that we looked at each other uneasily.

"Would you have some water?" Monge asked worriedly.

Napoleon shook his head as if to clear it. "I will not go in there again."

"But, General, what did you see?" the mathematician pressed.

"We will not speak of this again."

All of us were uncomfortable. I realized how much the expedition relied on Bonaparte's precision and energy, now that I'd seen him dazed. He was imperfect as a man and a leader, but so commanding, so dominant in purpose and intellect, that all of us had unconsciously surrendered to him. He was the expedition's spark and its compass. Without him, none of this would be happening.

The pyramid seemed to be looking down on us mockingly, the perfect peak.

"I must rest," Napoleon said. "Wine, not water." He snapped his finger and an aide ran to fetch a flask. Then he turned to me. "What are you doing here?"

Had he lost all his senses? "What?" I was confused by his confusion.

"You came with a medallion and a promise to make sense of this. You've claimed to have lost the one and haven't fulfilled the other. What is it I felt in there? Is it electricity?"

"Possibly, General, but I have no instrument to tell. I'm as baffled as anyone."

"And I am baffled by you, a suspected murderer and an American, who comes on our expedition and seems to be of no use and yet is everywhere! I'm beginning to not trust you, Gage, and it is not comfortable being a man I don't trust."

"General Bonaparte, I have been working to earn your trust, on the battlefield and here! It does no good to make wild guesses. Give me time to work on these theories. Jomard's ideas are intriguing, but I've had no time to evaluate them."

"Then you will sit here in the sand until you do." He took the flask and drank.

"What? No! I have studies in Cairo!"

"You're not to return to Cairo until you can come back and tell me something useful about this pyramid. Not old stories, but what it is for and how it can be harnessed. There's power here, and I want to know how to tap it."

"I want nothing less! But how am I to do that?"

"You are a savant, supposedly. Discover it. Use the medallion you pretend to have lost." Then he stalked away.

Our little group watched him in stupefaction.

"What the devil happened to him in there?" Jomard said.

"I think he hallucinated in the dark," Monge said. "Lord knows I wouldn't stay in there alone. Our Corsican has guts."

"Why did he focus on me?" His antagonism had shaken me.

"Because you were at Abukir," the mathematician said. "I think the defeat is gnawing on him more than he will admit. Our strategic future is not good."

"And I'm to camp out here staring at this structure until it is?"

"He'll forget about you in a day or two."

"Not that his curiosity isn't warranted," Jomard said. "I need to read the ancient sources again. The more I learn of this structure, the more fascinating it seems."

"And pointless," I grumbled.

"Is it, Gage?" asked Monge. "There's far too much precision for pointlessness, I think. Not only too much labor, but too much thought. In doing more calculations just now, another correlation occurred to me. This pyramid is indeed a mathematical plaything."

"What do you mean?"

"I will need to check my guess against Jomard's figures, but if we extrapolate the pyramid's slope to its original peak, a bit higher than it is now, and compare its height to the length of two of its sides, I believe we arrive at one of the most fundamental numbers in all mathematics: pi."

"Pi?"

"The ratio of a circle's diameter to its circumference, Gage, is considered by many cultures to be sacred. It's about twenty-two parts to seven, or 3.1415 . . . the number has never been completely computed. Still, every culture has tried to come as close as they can. The ancient Egyptians came up with 3.160. The pyramid's ratio of height to two of its sides appears to come very close to that number."

"The pyramid stands for pi?"

"It was built, perhaps, to conform to the Egyptian value of that number."

"But again, why?"

"Once more we butt up against ancient mysteries. But it's interesting, is it not, that your medallion included a diameter inside a circle? Too bad you lost it. Or did you?"

Interesting? It was a revelation. For weeks I'd been journeying blindly. Now I felt like I knew definitely what the medallion was pointing to: the pyramid behind me.

CHAPTER SEVENTEEN

I reluctantly stayed as ordered to help Jomard and Monge make more measurements of the pyramids, sharing the tent they'd staked a short distance from the Sphinx. After having promised a quick return, I was uneasy being such a distance from Astiza and the medallion, especially with Silano in Cairo. But if I ignored Napoleon's very public command I risked being arrested. Besides, I felt I was getting closer to the secret. Perhaps the medallion was a map to another passageway in the big heap of stone. Then there was October 21, a date I'd plucked off the lost ancient calendar that might or might not have any accuracy or significance, and was still two months away. I didn't know how any of this fit together, but maybe the savants would turn up another clue. So I sent a message to Enoch's house, explaining my predicament and asking that he get word to Yusuf's harem of my delay. At least I knew what I should be looking at, I added. I simply lacked clear understanding of what I should be looking for.

My temporary exile from the city was not entirely bad. Enoch's house was confining and Cairo noisy, while the empty silence of the desert was a respite. A company of soldiers bivouacked in the sand to protect us against roaming Bedouin and Mamelukes, and I told myself that staying here a couple nights might actually be the safest thing for Astiza and Enoch, since my absence should deflect attention from them. Silano had hopefully accepted my story that the medallion was at the bottom of Abukir Bay. I'd not forgotten poor Talma, but proof of his killer, and revenge, would have to wait. In short I pretended, as humans are wont to do, that the worst was for the best.

As I've said, there are three large pyramids at Giza, and all three have small passageways and chambers that are empty. Kephren's pyramid is still covered at its top by the kind of limestone casing that at one time gave all three structures a perfectly smooth, polished white surface. How they must have glistened, like prisms of salt! Using surveying instruments, we calculated that the Great Pyramid, when it came to a precise point, had a height of 480 feet, more than a hundred feet higher than the pinnacle of the cathedral of Amiens, the tallest in France. The Egyptians used only 203 tiers of masonry to reach this prodigious altitude. We measured the slope of its side at fifty-one degrees, precisely that needed to make height and half its circumference equal to both pi and Jomard's Fibonacci sequence.

Despite this eerie coincidence, the pyramids' purpose still eluded me. As art they were sublime. For utility, they seemed nonsensical. Here were buildings so smooth when built that no one could stand on them, housing corridors awkward for humans to negotiate, leading to chambers that seemed never to have been occupied, and codifying mathematics that seemed obscure to all but a specialist.

Monge said the whole business probably had something to do with religion. "Five thousand years from now, will people understand the motive behind Notre Dame?"

"You'd better not let the priests hear you say that."

"Priests are obsolete; science is the new religion. To the ancient Egyptians, religion was their science, and magic an attempt to manipulate what couldn't be understood. Mankind then advanced from a past in which every tribe and nation had its own groups of gods to one in which many nations worship one god. Still, there are many faiths, each calling the others heretics. Now we have science, based not on faith, but reason and experiment, and centered not on one nation, or pope, or king, but universal law. It doesn't matter if you are Chinese or German, or speak Arabic or Spanish:

science is the same. That's why it will triumph, and why the Church instinctively feared Galileo. But this structure behind us was built by a particular people with particular beliefs, and we might never rediscover their reasoning because it was based on religious mysticism we can't comprehend. It would help if we could someday decipher hieroglyphics."

I couldn't disagree with this prediction—I was a Franklin man, after all—and yet I had to wonder why science, if so universal, hadn't swept all before it already. Why were people still religious? Science was clever but cold, explanatory and yet silent on the biggest questions. It answered how but not why, and thus left people yearning. I suspected people of the future *would* understand Notre Dame, just as we understand a Roman temple. And, perhaps, worship and fear in much the same way. The revolutionaries in their rationalist fervor were missing something, I thought, and what was missing was heart, or soul. Did science have room for that, or hopes of an afterlife?

I said none of this, however, simply replying, "What if it's simpler than that, Doctor Monge? What if the pyramid is simply a tomb?"

"I've been thinking about that and it presents a fascinating paradox, Gage. Suppose it was supposed to be, at least principally, a tomb. Its very size creates its own problem, does it not? The more elaborately you build a pyramid to safeguard a mummy, the more you call attention to the mummy's location. It must have been a dilemma for pharaohs seeking to preserve their remains for all eternity."

"I've thought of another dilemma as well," I replied. "The pharaoh hopes to be undisturbed for eternity. Yet the perfect crime is one that no one realizes has occurred. If you wanted to rob the tomb of your master, what better way than to do it just before it is sealed up, because once it is, no one can discover the theft! If this is a tomb, it relied on the faithfulness of those closing it. Who could the pharaoh trust?"

"Unproven belief again!" Monge laughed.

Mentally, I reviewed what I knew about the medallion. A bisected circle: a symbol, perhaps, for pi. A map of the constellation containing the ancient polar star in its upper half.

A symbol for water below. Hash marks arranged in a delta like a pyramid. Perhaps the water was the Nile, and the marks represented the Great Pyramid, but why not etch a simple triangle? Enoch had said that the emblem seemed incomplete, but where to find the rest? The shaft of Min, in some long-lost temple? It seemed a joke. I tried to think like Franklin, but I was not his match. He could toy with thunderbolts one day and found a new nation the next. Could the pyramids have attracted lightning and converted it into power? Was the entire pyramid some kind of Leyden jar? I hadn't heard a roll of thunder or seen a drop of rain since we'd arrived in Egypt.

Monge left to join Bonaparte for the official christening of the new Institute of Egypt. There the savants were at work on everything from devising ways to ferment alcohol or bake bread (with sunflower stalks, since Egypt lacked adequate wood) to cataloguing Egypt's wildlife. Conte had set up a workshop to replace equipment, such as printing presses, that had been lost with the destruction of the fleet at Abukir. He was the kind of tinkerer who could make anything from anything. Jomard and I lingered in the pinks and gold of the desert, laboriously unreeling tapes, pitching aside rubble, and measuring angles with surveying staffs. Three days and nights we spent, watching the stars wheel around the tips of the pyramids and debating what the monuments might be for.

By morning of the fourth day, bored with the meticulous work and inconclusive speculation, I wandered to a viewpoint overlooking Cairo across the river. There I saw a curious sight. Conte had apparently manufactured enough hydrogen to inflate a balloon. The coated silk bag looked to be about forty feet in diameter, its top half covered with a net from which ropes extended downward to hold a wicker basket. It hovered on its tether a hundred feet off the ground, drawing a small crowd. I studied it through Jomard's telescope. All those watching appeared to be Europeans.

So far the Arabs had displayed little wonder about Western technology. They seemed to regard us as a temporary intrusion of clever infidels, obsessed with mechanical tricks and careless with our souls. I'd earlier enlisted Conte's help to make a cranked friction generator for a store of electricity in what Franklin had called a battery, and was invited by the savants to give a mild shock to some of Cairo's mullahs. The Egyptians gamely joined hands, I jolted the first with a charge from my Leyden jar, and they all jumped in turn as the current passed through them, provoking great consternation and laughter. But after their initial surprise they seemed more amused than awed. Electricity was cheap magic, good for nothing but parlor games.

It was while watching the balloon that I noticed a long column of French soldiers issue from Cairo's southern gate. Their regularity was a marked contrast to the mobs of merchants and camel drovers who clustered around the city's entrances. The soldiers tramped in a line of blue and white, regimental banners limp in the hot air. On and on the ranks came, a glittering file undulating like a millipede, until it seemed a full division. Some of the force was mounted, and more horses pulled two small field guns.

I called to Jomard and he joined me, focusing the spyglass. "It is General Desaix, off to chase the elusive Murad Bey," he said. "His troops are going to explore and conquer an upper Egypt that few Europeans have ever seen."

"So the war isn't over."

He laughed. "We're talking about Bonaparte! War will never be over for him." He continued to study the column, dust drifting ahead of the soldiers as if to announce their coming. I could imagine them good-naturedly cursing it, their mouths full of grit. "I think I see your old friend as well."

"Old friend?"

"Here, look for yourself."

Near the column's head was a man in turban and robes with half a dozen Bedouin riding as bodyguard. One of his henchmen held a parasol above his head. I could see the slim rapier bouncing on his hip and the fine black stallion he'd purchased in Cairo: Silano. Someone smaller rode by his side, swathed in robes. A personal servant, perhaps.

"Good riddance."

"I envy him," Jomard said. "What discoveries they'll make!"

Had Silano given up his quest for the medallion? Or gone to look for its missing piece in Enoch's southern temple? I picked out Bin Sadr as well. He was leading the Bedouin bodyguard, rocking easily on the back of a camel while holding his staff.

Had I avoided them? Or were they escaping me?

I looked again at the smaller, shrouded figure and felt disquiet. Had I been too obedient, lingering at the pyramids too long? Who was that riding at Silano's side?

I knew of him, she had confirmed.

And she had never explained what, precisely, that meant.

I snapped the telescope shut. "I have to get back to Cairo."

"You can't go, by Bonaparte's orders. We need a compelling hypothesis first."

But something disastrous had happened in my absence, I feared, and I realized that by staying out so long, I'd unconsciously been putting off the task of tackling the medallion and avenging Talma. My procrastination may have been fatal. "I'm an American savant, not a French private. To hell with his orders."

"He could have you shot!"

But I was already running down the slope, past the Sphinx, toward Cairo.

The city seemed more ominous on my return. Even as Desaix's division had emptied some houses of French troops, thousands of inhabitants who'd fled after the Battle of the Pyramids were returning. Cairo was emerging from postinvasion shock into being the center of Egypt again. As the city grew more crowded, the inhabitants regained their urban confidence. They carried themselves as if the city still belonged to them, not us, and their numbers dwarfed ours. While French soldiers could still cause pedestrians to scatter as they rode racing donkeys or marched on patrol, there was less scuttling out of the way of lone foreigners such as myself. As I hurried through the narrow lanes I was bumped and jostled for the first time. Again I was reminded of the oddities of electricity, that strange prickling in the air after the parlor experiments that women found so erotic. Now Cairo seemed electric with tension. News of the defeat at Abukir Bay had reached everyone, and no longer did the Franks seem invincible. Yes, we were dangling on a rope all right, and I could see it beginning to fray.

Compared to the bustle of adjacent lanes, the street at Enoch's house seemed far too quiet. Where was everyone? The home's façade looked much as I'd left it, its face as unreadable as that of the Egyptians. Yet when I got near I sensed something was amiss. The door wasn't tight against its frame, and I spied the bright yellow of splintered wood. I glanced around. Eyes watched me, I sensed, but I could see no one.

When I pounded on the entry it gave slightly. "*Salaam*." My greeting's echo was answered by the buzzing of flies. I pushed, as if shoving against someone holding the door on the other side, and finally it yielded enough that I could squeeze in. It was then I saw the obstruction. Enoch's gigantic Negro servant, Mustafa, was lying dead against the door, his face shattered by a pistol shot. The house had the sickeningly sweet scent of recent death.

I looked at a window. Its wooden screen had been shattered by intruders.

I went on, room by room. Where were the other servants? There were spatters and streaks of blood everywhere, as if bodies had been dragged after battle and butchery. Tables had been toppled, tapestries ripped down, cushions overthrown and cut. The invaders had been looking for something, and I knew what it was. My absence had saved no one. Why hadn't I insisted that Enoch hide, instead of staying with his books? Why had I thought my absence and that of the medallion would protect him? At length I came to the antiquities room, some of its statuary broken and its caskets overthrown, and then the stairs to the musty library. Its door had been staved in. Beyond was dark, but the library stank of fire. Heartsick, I found a candle and descended.

The cellar was a smoky shambles. Shelves had been toppled. Books and scrolls lay heaped like piles of autumn leaves, their half-burned contents still smoldering. At first I thought this room was empty of life too, but then someone groaned. Paper rustled and a hand came up from the litter, fingers painfully curled, like an avalanche victim reaching from snow. I grasped it, only to elicit a howl of pain. I dropped the swollen digits and shoveled blackened papers aside. There was poor Enoch, sprawled on a pile of smoldering books. He was badly scorched, his clothes half-gone, and his chest and arms roasted. He'd thrown himself onto a bonfire of literature.

"Thoth," he was groaning. "Thoth."

"Enoch, what happened?"

He couldn't hear me in his delirium. I went upstairs to his fountain and used an ancient bowl to get some water, even though the fountain ran pink from spilled blood. I dripped some on his face and then gave him a sip. He sputtered, and then sucked like a baby. Finally his eyes focused.

"They tried to burn it all." It was a groaning whisper.

"Who did?"

"I broke free to run into the blaze and they didn't dare follow." He coughed.

"My God, Enoch, you threw yourself on the fire?"

"These books are my life."

"Was it the French?"

"Bin Sadr's Arabs. They kept asking where it was, without saying what they meant. I pretended not to know. They wanted the woman, and I said she'd gone with you. They didn't believe me. If I hadn't run into the fire they would have forced me to tell far more. I hope the household didn't talk."

"Where is everybody?"

"The servants were herded into storerooms. I heard screams."

I felt utterly futile: foolish gambler, dilettante soldier, and pretend savant. "I've brought all this on you."

"You brought nothing the gods did not wish." He groaned. "My time is over. Men are becoming greedier. They want science and magic for power. Who wants to live in a time like that? But knowing and wisdom are not the same things." He clutched me. "You must stop them."

"Stop them from what?"

"It was in my books after all."

"What? What are they after?"

"It's a key. You must insert it." He was fading.

I leaned closer. "Enoch, please: Astiza. Is she safe?"

"I don't know."

"Where's Ashraf?"

"I don't know."

"Did you learn anything about the twenty-first of October?"

He grasped my arm. "You need to believe in something, American. Believe in her."

Then he died.

I sat back, hollowed. First Talma, now this. I was too late to save him, and too late to learn what he'd learned. I used my fingers to close his eyes, shaking with rage and impotence. I'd lost my best link to the mysteries. Was there anything left in this library to explain the medallion? Amid the ashes, how could I know?

Cradled to Enoch's breast was a particularly thick volume, bound in leather and blackened at the edges. Its writing was Arabic. Had it been of particular importance in deciphering our quest? I pried it loose and looked in ignorance at its ornate script. Well, perhaps Astiza could make sense of it.

If she was still in Cairo. I had a grim idea who the small, shrouded figure was who'd been riding next to Silano as Desaix's troops marched south.

Anxious and lost in my own worries, I trudged back up the stairs and into the antiquities room without caution. It almost cost me my life.

There was a high, anguished cry and then a lance thrust out from behind a statue of Anubis the jackal like a bolt of lightning. It crashed into my chest, knocking me backward, and I collided with a stone sarcophagus, my wind gone. As I slid down, dazed, I looked at the shaft. Its spear point had pierced Enoch's book, only the last pages stopping it from thrusting into my heart.

Ashraf was at the end of the spear. His eyes widened. "You!"

I tried to speak but could only gasp.

"What are you doing here? I was told you were held by the French at the pyramids! I thought you were one of the assassins, looking for secrets!"

I finally found enough air to speak. "I spied Silano leaving the city with General Desaix, riding south. I didn't know what that meant, so I hurried back."

"I almost killed you!"

"This book saved me." I pushed it, and the spear point, aside. "Can't even read it, but Enoch was cradling it. What's it about, Ash?"

Using his boot to hold the book while he wrenched the lance free, the Mameluke stooped and opened it. Fragments puffed out like spores. He read a moment. "Poetry." He threw it aside.

Ah. What we choose to die with.

"I need help, Ashraf."

"Help? You're the conqueror, remember? You who are bringing science and civilization to poor Egypt! And this is what you've brought to my brother's house: butchery! Everyone who knows you dies!"

"It was Arabs, not French, who did this."

"It was France, not Egypt, which upset the order of things."

There was no answer to that, and no denying that I'd become a part of it. We choose for the most expedient of reasons, and upend the world.

I took a labored breath. "I have to find Astiza. Help me, Ash. Not as prisoner, not as master and slave, not as employee. As a friend. As a fellow warrior. Astiza has the medallion. They'll kill her for it as brutally as they killed Talma, and I don't trust asking the army for help. Napoleon wants the secret too. He'll take the medallion for himself."

"And be cursed like everyone who touches it."

"Or discover the power to enslave the world."

Ashraf's reply was silence, letting me realize what I'd just blurted about the general I'd been following. Was Bonaparte a Republican savior? Or a potential tyrant? I'd seen hints of both in his character. How did one tell the difference between the two? Both required charm. Both required ambition. And maybe a feather on the scales of Thoth would tip a leader's heart one way or the other. But of course it didn't matter, did it? I had to decide for myself what I believed. Now Enoch had given me an anchor: believe in *her*.

"My brother gave you help and look where it got him," Ashraf said bitterly. "You are no friend. I was wrong to have led you into Cairo. I should have died at Imbaba."

I was desperate. "Then if you won't help as a friend, I order you to help me as my captive and servant. I paid you!"

"You dare lay claim to me after this?" He took out a purse and hurled it at me. Coins exploded, rolling away on the stone floor. "I spit on your money! Go! Find your woman yourself! I must prepare the funeral of my brother!"

So I was alone. At least I had the integrity to leave his money where it had scattered, despite knowing how few coins I had of my own. I took what I had cached in an empty coffin: my longrifle and my Algonquin tomahawk. Then I stepped again over Mustafa's body and went back into Cairo's streets.

I wouldn't be coming back.

The house of Yusuf al-Beni, where Astiza had been secreted in a harem, was more imposing than Enoch's, a turreted fortress that shadowed its narrow street with brooding overhangs. Its windows were high on its face, where sun shone and swallows glided, but its door was shadowed by a heavy arch as thick as the entrance to a medieval castle. I stood before it in disguise. I'd wrapped my weapons in a cheap, hastily purchased carpet and dressed myself in Egyptian clothes in case the French might be looking to return me to Jomard at the pyramid. The loose-fitting riding trousers and galabiyya were infinitely lighter, more anonymous, and more sensible than European garb, and the head scarf provided welcome shelter from the sun.

Was I once more too late?

I pounded on Yusuf's door and a doorman the size of Mustafa confronted me. Shaved, huge, and as pale as Enoch's servant had been dark, he filled the entry like a bale of Egyptian cotton. Did every rich house have a human troll?

"What do you want, rug merchant?" I could understand the Arabic by now.

"I'm no merchant. I need to see your master," I replied in French.

"You're a Frank?" he asked in the same tongue.

"American."

He grunted. "Not here." He began to close the door.

I tried to bluff. "The sultan Bonaparte is looking for him." Now cotton bale paused. It was enough to make me believe Yusuf was somewhere in the house. "The general has business with the woman who is a guest here, the lady called Astiza."

"The general wants a slave?" The tone was disbelief.

"She's no slave, she's a savant. The sultan needs her expertise. If Yusuf is gone, then you must fetch the woman for the general."

"She is gone too."

It was an answer I didn't want to believe. "Do I have to bring a platoon of soldiers? The sultan Bonaparte is not a man who wants to be left waiting."

The doorman shook his head in dismissal. "Go away, American. She is sold."

"Sold!"

"To a Bedouin slave trader." He went to slam the door in my face, so I jammed the end of the carpet in it to stop him.

"You can't sell her, she's mine!"

He grasped the end of my carpet with a hand that had the span of a frying pan. "Take your rug from my door or you will leave it here," he warned. "You have no business with us anymore."

I rotated the carpet to aim at his midriff and slipped my hand up the other end of the roll, grasping my rifle. The click of its hammer being pulled back was clearly audible, and that checked his arrogance. "I want to know who bought her."

We studied each other, wondering if either was quick enough to overcome the other. Finally he grunted. "Wait."

He disappeared, leaving me feeling like a fool or a penitent. How dare the Egyptian sell Astiza? "Yusuf, come out here, you bastard!" My cry echoed in the house. I stood for long minutes, wondering if they would simply ignore me. If they did, I'd go in shooting.

Finally I heard the heavy tread of the doorman returning. He filled the doorway. "It's a message from the woman's buyer, and is simple to relate. He says you know what is needed to buy her back." Then the door slammed shut.

That meant Silano and Bin Sadr had her. And it meant they didn't have the medallion, and must not know I didn't either.

Yet wouldn't they keep her alive in hopes I'd bring it? She was a hostage, a kidnap victim.

I stepped back from the entryway, trying to think what to do. Where was the medallion? And with that something tiny fell past my ear, landing with a soft splat in the dust. I looked up. A grilled opening in an ornate screen far above was being closed by a feminine hand. I picked up what had been dropped.

It was a packet of paper. When I unrolled it I found Astiza's golden eye of Horus and a message, this time in English in Astiza's writing. My heart soared:

"The south wall at midnight. Bring a rope."

CHAPTER EIGHTEEN

There was no wider gulf between the invading French army and the Egyptians than the subject of women. To the Muslims, the arrogant Franks were dominated by crass European females who combined vulgar display with imperious demands to make a fool of every man who came into contact with them. The French, in turn, thought that Islam locked its greatest source of pleasure away in opulent but shadowy prisons, foregoing the titillating wit of female company. If the Muslims thought the French slaves to their women, the French thought the Muslims frightened of theirs. The situation was made even tenser by the decision of some Egyptian females to form liaisons with the conquerors and to be displayed, without veil, arms and necks bare, in officers' carriages. These new mistresses, giddy at the freedoms the French had granted them, would call up gaily to the screened windows their carriages trotted past, shouting, "Look at our freedom!" The imams thought we were corrupting, the savants thought the Egyptians medieval, and the soldiers simply wanted the pleasures of the bed. While under strict orders not to molest Muslim women, there was no such prohibition against paying for them, and some were more than willing to be bought. Other Egyptian damsels defended their virtue like vestal virgins, withholding favors unless an officer promised marriage and life in Europe. The result was a great deal of friction and misunderstanding.

The grain-sack draping of Muslim women, designed to control male lust, instead made every passing female, her age and form unknown, a subject of intense speculation among the French soldiers. I was not immune to such discussion, and in my imagination the glories of Yusuf's female household were fueled by stories of Scheherazade and the Arabian Nights. Who had not heard of the famed seraglio of the sultan in Constantinople? Or of the skilled concubines and castrated eunuchs of this strange society, in which the son of a slave could grow up to be a master? It was a world I struggled to understand. Slavery had become a way for the Ottomans to inject fresh blood and loyalty into a stultified and treacherous society. Polygamy had become a reward for political loyalty. Religion had become a substitute for material self-improvement. The remoteness of Islamic women made them all the more desired.

Was the medallion still inside the harem's walls, even if Astiza was not? This was my hope. She had persuaded her captors that I still held it, and then left a message for me behind. Clever woman. I found an alley alcove to temporarily hide my rifle, covering it with my rug, and set off to buy a rope and provisions. If Astiza was a prisoner of Silano, I wanted her back. We had no proper relationship, yet I felt a mix of jealousy, protectiveness, and loneliness that surprised me. She was the closest thing I had left to a true friend. I'd already lost Talma, Enoch, and Ashraf. I'd be damned if I lost her too.

My European complexion under Arab dress drew only casual glances, given that the Ottoman Empire was a rainbow of colors. I entered the dim warren of corridors in the Khan al-Khalili bazaar, the air redolent with charcoal and hashish, piled spices making brilliant pyramids of green, yellow, and orange. After buying food, a rope, and a blanket for the desert nights, I carried these supplies to my depository and set off again to bargain for a horse or camel with the last of my money. I'd never ridden the latter, but knew they had more endurance for a long chase. My mind was boiling with questions. Did Bonaparte know that Silano had taken Astiza? Was the count after the same clues I was? If the medallion was a key, where was the lock? In my haste and preoccupation, I stumbled onto a French patrol before remembering to squeeze into shadow.

The sweating soldiers had nearly filed past when their lieutenant suddenly pulled out a paper tucked in his belt, glanced at me, and cried a halt. "Ethan Gage?"

I pretended not to understand.

Half a dozen musket barrels came up, needing no translation. "Gage? I know it's you. Don't try to run, or we'll shoot you down."

So I stood straight, slipped off my head covering, and tried to bluff. "Please don't give away my identity, Lieutenant. I'm on a mission for Bonaparte."

"On the contrary, you are under arrest."

"Surely you're mistaken."

He looked at the picture on his paper. "Denon did a quick sketch of you and it's quite a good likeness. The man has talent."

"I am just about to return to my studies at the pyramid . . ."

"You are wanted for investigation in the murder of the scholar and imam Qelab Almani, who also goes by the name Enoch, or Hermes Trismegistus. You were spotted hurrying from his house with gun and hatchet."

"Enoch? Are you mad? I'm trying to *solve* his murder."

He read from his poster. "You are also under arrest for being absent from the pyramids without leave, insubordination, and being out of uniform."

"I'm a savant! I don't *have* a uniform!"

"Hands *up!*" He shook his head. "Your crimes have caught up with you, American."

I was taken to a Mameluke barracks that had been turned into a makeshift prison. Here French authorities tried to sort out the insurgents, petty criminals, deserters, profiteers, and prisoners of war the invasion had swept up. Despite my protests I was thrown in a cell that was a polyglot mix of thieves, charlatans, and rogues. I felt as if I were back in a gambling salon in Paris.

"I demand to know the charges against me!" I cried.

"Uselessness," growled the sergeant who locked the door.

The absurdity of jailing me for Enoch's death was exceeded only by the calamity of missing my midnight rendezvous at the south wall of Yusuf's house. Whoever had dropped the eye of Horus probably didn't have many opportunities to help a male stranger gain access to the harem. What if they gave up, and the medallion was sold or lost? Meanwhile, if Astiza was in the hands of Silano and being taken south by Desaix's expedition to upper Egypt, she was drawing farther away by the hour. At the one time in my life when I didn't have a moment to waste, I was immobilized. It was maddening.

At last a lieutenant appeared to enter my name in the prison record books.

"At least get me an interview with Bonaparte," I pleaded.

"You're wiser to stay out of his sight, unless you want to be shot immediately. You are suspected of murder here because of earlier reports of the death of a courtesan in Paris. Something about unpaid debts, as well . . ." he studied his papers. "A landlady named Madame Durrell?"

I groaned inwardly. "I didn't kill Enoch! I discovered the body!"

"And you promptly reported it?" His tone was as cynical as my creditors.

"Listen, the entire expedition may be in jeopardy if I can't complete my work. Count Silano is trying to monopolize important secrets."

"Don't try to slander Silano. It was he who provided affidavits about your character from Madame Durrell and a lantern bearer. He predicted your predilection for deviant behavior." He read again. "Characteristics of a de Sade."

So. While I held a measuring tape at the pyramids, Silano had been busy in Cairo enhancing my reputation.

"I have the right to legal representation, do I not?"

"An army solicitor should get to you within a week."

Was I cursed? How convenient for my enemies that I was locked up, unable to follow the count, contest the charges, or make my midnight rendezvous at Yusuf's harem! The sun was slanting low through the tiny cell window, and supper looked like a wretched pea-and-lentil mash. Our beverage was stale barrel water, our privy a bucket.

"I need a hearing now!"

"It's possible you'll be returned to Paris to face charges there."

"This is insane!"

"Better the guillotine there than a firing squad here, no?" He shrugged and left.

"Better *how*?" I shouted after him, slumping to the floor.

"Have some mash," said a private, a would-be entrepreneur caught trying to sell a cannon for scrap metal. "Breakfast is worse."

I turned away.

Well, I'd gambled and lost, hadn't I? If I couldn't lose in Paris, I couldn't get a single lucky card here. Of course if I'd followed Franklin's homilies, I'd have an honest profession, but his 'early to bed, early to rise' advice seemed so counter to basic nature. One of the things I liked about him was that he didn't always follow his own advice. Even when nearly eighty, he'd party if a pretty lady was in the offing.

Soon it was dark. With every moment, Astiza was farther away.

It was while I was digging deeper into the pit of despair, with a side shaft of self-pity and a veritable mine of regret—all the time trying to ignore the stink of my cellmates—that I heard a hiss from the cell's window. "Ethan!"

What now?

"Ethan?" The voice was low and anxious. "The American? Is he there?"

I pushed through my fellows and put my face to the small opening. "Who's there?"

"It is Ashraf."

"Ash! I thought you'd abandoned me!"

"I thought better of it. My brother would want me to help you, I know. You and the priestess are the only hope to safeguard the secrets he lived to protect. And then I hear you've been arrested! How did you get in so much trouble so quickly?"

"It's a talent."

"Now I must get you out of there."

"But how?"

"Move as far away from the window as you can, please. And cover your ears."

"What?"

"It might be a good idea to crouch, too." He disappeared.

Well, that was ominous. Mamelukes had a head-on way of doing things. I pushed my way to the opposite corner of the cell and addressed the others in the dimness. "I think something dramatic is about to happen. Please move to this side of our apartment."

No one moved.

So I tried again. "I have some hashish, if you'll all just gather around."

They formed a nice shield just before there was a loud boom. The outer cell wall below the window blew inward with a spray of stone, a cannonball sailing on to hit the wood-and-iron cell door. The entry flexed, shuddered, and fell neatly away from its frame, hitting the corridor outside with a clang. The cannonball was imbedded in the wood like a berry in a muffin. We'd all sprawled in a heap, me at the bottom, my ears ringing and the air full of dust. Yet I knew opportunity when I saw it. "Now! Rush the bailiff!" I cried.

As the others struggled up and stormed into the corridor, I crawled the opposite way outside, through the hole in the jail wall that Ash had just created. He was crouched in the shadows, waiting. He had a musket slung on one shoulder, two pistols stuffed in his shaft, and a sword at his waist. I recognized the weapons I'd confiscated from him when he was captured. Well, so much for my trophies.

"Where the devil did you get a cannon?"

"It was sitting in the yard back here, impounded as evidence."

"Evidence?" Ah, yes, the soldier who'd tried to hock it. "They left it loaded?"

"To use against the prisoners, if they tried to escape."

There were musket shots, and we ran.

* * *

We flitted through the dark streets like thieves, retrieving my weapons, rope, and provisions where I'd hid them. Then we watched the march of the moon, waiting for the appointed hour. When we crept to the south wall of Yusuf's house I wasn't sure what to expect. The heavy door that marked the separate women's entrance at the rear was thick wood with a large iron lock. There was no entry that way. So all I could do was wait silently below a south wall window, hoping that the French patrols scouring the city didn't stumble upon us.

"Now I've made you a fugitive too," I whispered.

"The gods would not let you avenge my brother's murder by yourself."

The night was lengthening, and I heard nothing and saw nothing from the screened windows above. Was I too late for the rendezvous? Had my informant been found out? Impulsive and impatient, I finally took the golden eye of Horus from my pocket and lofted it upward at the opening. To my surprise, it didn't fall back.

Instead, the charm weighted a silken thread that slithered down. I tied my rope to the thread and watched as it was hauled skyward. I gave a moment for it to be tied off, pulled to test, and planted my feet on the wall. "Wait here," I told Ashraf.

"You think my eyes aren't as curious as yours?"

"I'm the expert on women. You hold the rifle."

The harem window was fifty feet overhead, the shutter in its screen just big enough to get my head and shoulders inside. Panting from anticipation and exertion, I heaved my way in, my tomahawk on my belt. Given the trying events of the day, I was more than ready to use it.

Fortunately, lithe young arms helped drag me into the room, putting me in a better mood. My anonymous assistant, I saw, was young, pretty, disappointingly clothed, and even veiled. But then her almond eyes alone were enough to make a man fall in love: maybe there was method to Muslim madness. Her finger went to where her lips would be, signaling quiet. She handed me a second piece of paper and whispered, "Astiza."

"*Fayn?*" I asked. Where?

She shook her head and pointed at the paper. I opened it. "It is hidden to be seen," it said in English, in Astiza's hand.

So she *had* left the medallion behind! I looked about and suddenly noticed half a dozen pair of eyes staring at me, like animals from a forest. Several of the women in the harem were silently awake, but like my young guide they were dressed for the street, and timid as deer. All put fingers to veiled lips. Clear enough.

Whatever fantasies I had about limpid pools, serenading damsels, and diaphanous garments were disappointed. The harem quarters looked plainer and more cramped than the public rooms I'd seen, and no one seemed to be preening herself for Yusuf's next nocturnal visit. It was, I realized, simply a segregated wing from which the women could cook, sew, and gossip without intruding on male territory.

They watched me in fear and fascination.

I began moving around their dim quarters looking for the medallion. Hidden to be seen? Did she mean by a window? All were shielded with *mashrabiyya* screens. The harem had one large central room and a warren of small ones, each with a rumpled bed, chest, and pegs hung with clothes, some revealing and others concealing. It was a world turned upside down, all color turned inward, all thought confined, all pleasure locked.

Where had I hidden it? In a shoe, a cannon, a chamber pot. None of those were "hidden to be seen," it seemed to me. I bent to lift up a bed covering, but the young woman who was my guide stayed my hand. They were waiting for me to spot it, I realized, to prove that I knew what I was looking for. And then of course the obviousness of my task became clear to me. I straightened, looking around more boldly. Hidden in plain sight, she'd meant. Round a neck, on a table, on . . .

A jewelry rack.

If there is one thing universal in human culture, it's the love of gold. What these women would never display on the street they would drape on their skin for Yusuf and each other: rings, coins, bracelets and bangles, earrings and anklets, tiaras and waist chains. On a dressing table was a waterfall of gold, a yellow delta, a treasure like a small echo of *L'Orient*'s. And there in the midst of it all, thrown as casually as a copper in a tavern, was the medallion, its shape obscured by the necklaces atop it. Bin Sadr and Silano never got in here, of course, and no one else had bothered to look.

I untangled it. As I did so, a heavy bangle of an earring came off the table and dropped to the floor like a gong.

I froze. Suddenly other heads came up from beds, these faces older. One started at the sight of me and leaped out, pulling street robes around her.

She spoke sharply. The young one replied impatiently. A hissing conversation broke out in rapid Arabic. I began easing toward the window. The older one gestured at me to put the medallion down, but instead I slid it over my neck and inside my shirt. Isn't this what they'd expected? Apparently not. The older one gave a shout, and several of the women began to wail and scream. Now I heard a eunuch's cry from outside the door, and male shouts from below. Was that the scrape of drawn steel? It was time to go.

As I made for the window the older woman tried to block me, arms flailing, sleeves wide, like a huge black bat. I shoved past, even as her fingers scrabbled creepily at my neck. She fell away, yelling. A bell began clanging, and there was a gunshot of alarm. They'd rouse the whole city! I grabbed the frame and kicked, busting out half the wooden screen. Pieces rattled down into the alley below. I rolled out the window and started slithering down the rope. Below, I saw the rear door burst open and servants, armed with clubs and staves, stream out. Other men burst into the harem behind me. Even as I descended, someone began trying to haul the rope back up.

"Jump!" Ashraf shouted. "I will catch you!"

Did he know what I weighed? And I didn't want to simply let go because I figured we might use the line I'd bought just that afternoon. I grabbed the tomahawk from my belt and chopped at the rope above my head. It snapped and I fell the last thirty feet, landing with a whump in something soft and stinking. It was in an alley cart that Ash had wheeled to catch my fall. I heaved myself over the side, clutching the remains of the rope, and braced to fight.

There was a bang, the sound of Ashraf's musket, and one of the servants charging from the rear door pitched backward. My rifle was shoved into my hands and I shot a second man, then whooped like an Indian and cracked the head of a third with the tomahawk. The others fell back in confusion. Ashraf and I dashed the other way, vaulting a low wall and sprinting down twisting lanes.

Yusuf's men came in a mob after us, but were shooting blind. I paused to reload my own rifle. Ash had his sword out. Now we had only to escape the city . . .

"There they are!"

It was a French military patrol. We cursed, wheeled, and fled back the way we had come. I heard the French commands to aim and fire, so I grabbed Ash to pitch both of us down to the dirt of the street. There was a roar, and several bullets sizzled overhead. Then cries and screams ahead. They'd hit Yusuf's men.

We crawled into a side street, using the smoke as cover. Now we could hear shouts of alarm and wild shots in all directions.

"What was that excrescence I fell into?" I panted to Ash.

"Donkey dung. You have fallen into what the Franks call *merde,* my friend."

Another bullet wanged off a stone post. "I can't disagree."

At length we rose to a crouch and rounded a corner. Then we trotted until we entered a wider avenue leading more or less to the southern gate. We seemed to have lost immediate pursuit.

"We've also lost my provisions. Damn that old woman!"

"Moses found manna in the desert."

"And King George will find crumpets at his tea table, but I'm not him, am I?"

"You're becoming surly."

"It's about time."

We were almost to Cairo's wall when a squadron of French cavalry turned onto our street. They were on routine patrol, not yet spotting us, but they blocked our path.

"Let's hide in that alcove," Ashraf suggested.

"No. Don't we need horses? Tie our rope to that pillar, as high as the shoulder of a mounted officer." I took the other end and did the same on the opposite side of the street. "When I shoot, get ready to steal a horse."

I strode to the middle of the street, facing the approaching cavalry, and casually waved my rifle to let them see me in the dark.

"Who goes there?" an officer called. "Identify yourself!"

I fired, plucking off his cap.

They charged.

I darted toward a pool of shadow, slung my rifle, jumped to catch a pole, and swung myself up to an awning and sill. The cavalry patrol hit the rope at a dead run. The lead troopers were plucked from their saddles like puppets, colliding with the rank just behind. Horses reared, men toppled. I leaped, knocking a rider loose from his plunging mount. Ashraf had wrestled his way onto another horse. Pistols went off in the dark but the bullets whined harmlessly. We lashed our way out of the tangle.

"The French are going to begin wondering whose side you're on," Ash gasped as we began our gallop, looking back at the shouting troopers.

"So am I."

We rode for the wall and the gate. "Open wide! Couriers for Bonaparte!" I cried in French. They saw the cavalry horses and tack before they spied us, lying low in our Arab robes. By then it was too late. We burst through the sentries toward the desert beyond, shots buzzing overhead as we galloped into the night.

I was out, the medallion mine, free to rescue Astiza, find the Book of Thoth, and become master of the world—or at least its savior!

And I was now prey for every Bedouin, Mameluke, and French cavalryman in Egypt.

CHAPTER NINETEEN

The Egyptian desert west of the Nile is a trackless ocean of sand and rock, interrupted by only a few oasis islands. The desert east of the Nile and south of Cairo—a sterile plateau separated from the Red Sea by moonlike mountains—is emptier yet, a roasting pan seemingly unchanged from the birth of the world. The blue sky bleaches to a dull haze on the shimmering horizon, and dryness threatens to mummify an intruder each pitiless afternoon. There is no water, no shade, no birdcall, no plant, no insect, and seemingly no end. For millennia, monks and magi retreated here to find God. When I fled I felt I'd left him far behind, in the waters of the Nile and the great green forests of home.

Ashraf and I rode in that direction because no sane man would. We passed first through Cairo's City of the Dead, the Muslim beehive tombs as white as ghosts in the night. Then we trotted quickly through a ribbon of green farmland that followed the Nile, dogs barking as we passed. Long before sunrise we were dots on an arid plain. The sun rose, blinding as we angled east, and arced so slowly that it became a pitiless clock. The saddles of our captured mounts had canteens that we made last until noon, and then thirst became the central fact of existence. It was so hot that it hurt to breathe, and my eyes squinted against desert whiteness bright as snow. Powdery dust caked lips, ears, clothes, and horses, and the sky was a weight we carried on our shoulders and the crowns of our heads. The chain of the medallion burned into my neck. A mirage of a lake, the cruel illusion all too familiar by now, wavered just out of reach.

So this is Hades, I thought. So this is what happens to men without proper direction, who drink, fornicate, and gamble for their daily bread. I longed to find a scrap of shade to crawl into and sleep forever.

"We must go faster," Ashraf said. "The French are pursuing."

I looked back. A long plume of white dust had been caught by the wind and spun into a lazy funnel. Somewhere under it was a platoon of hussars, following our hoof prints.

"How can we? Our horses have no water."

"Then we must find them some." He gestured ahead at undulating humps of hills that looked like cracked loaves.

"In a bed of coals?"

"Even in a bed of coals a diamond can hide. We'll lose the French in the canyons and wadis. Then we'll find a place to drink."

Kicking our tired horses and tightening our cloaks against the dust, we pressed on. We entered the uplands, following a maze of sandy wadis like a snarl of string. The only vegetation was dry camel thorn. Ashraf was looking for something, however, and soon found it: a shelf of bare, sun-blasted rock to our left that led to a choice of three canyons. "Here we can break our tracks." We turned off, hooves clacking, and picked our way across the stone table. We took the middle limestone canyon because it looked narrowest and least hospitable: perhaps the French would think we went another way. It was so hot that it was like riding into an oven. Soon we could hear the frustrated shouts of our pursuers in the dry desert air, arguing about which way we'd gone.

I lost all sense of direction and docilely followed the Mameluke. Higher and higher the crests reached, and I could begin to see the jagged lines of real mountains, the rock black and red against the sky. Here was the range that separated the valley of the Nile from the Red Sea. Nowhere was there a spot of green or glisten of water. The silence was unnerving, broken only by our own clop and creak of leather. Was this desert—the fact that ancient Egyptians could walk from the fertile Nile to absolute nothingness—the reason they seemed so preoccupied with death? Was the contrast between their fields and the ever-encroaching sand the origin of the idea of an expulsion from Eden? Was the waste a reminder of the brevity of life and a spur to dreams of immortality? Certainly the dry heat would mummify corpses naturally, long before the Egyptians did it as religious practice. I imagined someone finding my husk centuries from now, my frozen expression one of vast regret.

Finally the shadows seemed to be growing longer, the sounds of pursuit fainter. The French must be as thirsty as we were. I was dizzy, my body sore, my tongue thick.

We stopped at what looked like a rock trap. High cliffs rose all around us, the only exit being the narrow canyon we'd just ridden through. The towering walls were finally so high, and the sun so advanced, that they cast welcome shadow.

"Now what?"

Ashraf stiffly got down. "Now you must help me dig." He knelt on the sand at the base of a cliff, at a cleft where a waterfall might have pooled if such an absurdity could exist here. But perhaps it did: the rock above was stained dark as if water occasionally flowed down. He began burrowing into the sand with his hands.

"Dig?" Had the sun driven him mad?

"Come, if you don't want to die! It rains a torrent once a year, or perhaps once a decade. Like that diamond in coals, some water remains."

I joined in. At first the exercise seemed pointless, the hot grit burning my hands. Yet gradually the sand grew gratefully cool and then, astonishingly, damp. Smelling water, I began throwing sand away like a terrier. At last we reached true moisture. Water oozed, so thick with sediment it was like coagulating blood.

"I can't drink mud!" I reached to dig again.

Ashraf grabbed my arm and rocked us back on our heels. "The desert asks patience. This water may have come from a century ago. We can wait moments more."

As I watched impatiently, sweet liquid began to pool in the depression we'd dug. The horses snorted and whinnied.

"Not yet, my companions, not yet," Ash soothed.

It was the shallowest bowl I'd ever seen, and as welcome as a river. After an eternity we bent to kiss our puddle, like Muslims bowing to Mecca. As I lapped and swallowed the dirty leakage it gave me a shiver and a glow. What bags of water we are, so helpless if not constantly replenished! We slurped until we'd drained it back to mud, sat back, regarded each other, and laughed. Our drinking had made a circle of clean wetness around our lips, while the rest of our face was painted with dust. We looked like clowns. There was an impatient wait for our meager well to refill and then we cupped some for the horses, guarding that they didn't drink too much too soon. As dusk settled this became our job, carrying water in a saddlebag to the thirsty mounts, sipping ourselves, and slowly mopping the rest of the grit from our heads and hands. I began to feel faintly human again. The first stars popped out, and I realized I hadn't heard any sounds of French pursuit for some time. Then the full panoply of the heavens blossomed, and the rocks glowed silver.

"Welcome to the desert," Ashraf said.

"I'm hungry."

He grinned. "That means you're alive."

It grew cold but even if we'd had wood, we dared not light a fire. Instead we huddled and talked, giving each other small comfort by sharing our grief about Talma and Enoch, and small hope as we talked about vague futures: with Astiza for me, and with Egypt as a whole for Ash.

"The Mamelukes are exploitive, it is true," he admitted. "We could learn things from your French savants, just as they learn from us. But Egypt must be ruled by the people who live here, Ethan, not pink-skinned Franks."

"Can't there be a collaboration of both?"

"I don't think so. Would Paris want an Arab on its town council, even if the imam had the wisdom of Thoth? No. This is not human nature. Suppose a god came down from the sky with answers to all questions. Would we listen, or nail him to a cross?"

"We all know the answer to that one. So each man to his place, Ash?"

"And wisdom to its place. I think this is what Enoch was trying to do, to keep Egypt's wisdom locked away where it belongs, as the ancients decided."

"Even if they could levitate rocks or make people live forever?"

"Things lose value if they're done too easily. If any nation or man could make a pyramid with magic, then it becomes no more remarkable than a hill. And live forever? Anyone with eyes can see that this goes against all nature. Imagine a world full of the old, a world with few children, a world in which there was no hope of advancement because every office was filled with patriarchs who had gotten there centuries ahead of you. This would not be a paradise, it would be a hell of caution and conservatism, of stale ideas and shopworn sayings, of old grudges and remembered slights. Do we fear death? Of course. But it is death that makes room for birth, and the cycle of life is as natural as the rise and fall of the Nile. Death is our last and greatest duty."

We waited a day to make sure the French weren't waiting for us. Then, assuming a lack of water had driven them back to Cairo, we started south, traveling at night to avoid the worst of the heat. We paralleled the Nile but stayed many miles to the east to avoid detection, even though it was a struggle to negotiate the serpentine hills. Our plan was to catch up with Desaix's main column of troops, where Silano and Astiza rode. I would pursue the count as the French pursued the Mameluke insurgents up the river. Eventually I would rescue Astiza, and Ashraf would have revenge on whoever had killed poor Enoch. We would find the staff of Min, unscramble the way into the Great Pyramid, and find the long-lost Book of Thoth, protecting it from the occult Egyptian Rite. And then . . . would we secrete it, destroy it, or keep it for ourselves? I would cross that bridge when I came to it, as old Ben would say.

Along our way, we found nests of life in the desert after all. A Coptic monastery of brown domed buildings sprouted like mushrooms in a forest of rock, a garden of palms promising the presence of a well. The Mameluke habit of carrying their wealth into battle now displayed a practical purpose: Ashraf had retrieved the purse he'd thrown at me and had enough coins to purchase food. We drank our fill, bought larger water bags, and found more wells as we continued south, spaced like inns on an invisible highway. The dried fruit and unleavened bread was simple but sustaining, and my companion showed how to coat my cracked lips with mutton fat to keep them from blistering. I was beginning to become more comfortable in the desert. The sand became a bed, and my loose robes—washed of donkey stink—caught every cooling breeze. Where before I had seen desolation, now I began to see beauty: there were a thousand subtle colors in the sinuous rocks, a play of light and shadow against crumbled white limestone, and a magnificent emptiness that seemed to fill the soul. The simplicity and serenity reminded me of the pyramids.

Occasionally we would zigzag closer to the Nile, and Ashraf would descend to a village at night to barter as a Mameluke for food and water. I'd stay up in the barren hills, overlooking the serene green belt of farmland and blue river. Sometimes the wind would bring the sound of camel or donkey bray, the laughter of children, or the call to prayer. I would sit on the edge, an alien peeking in. Toward dawn he would rejoin me, we'd make a few miles, and then as the sun rose over the cliffs we'd shovel away sand at places he knew and creep into old caves cut into the bluffs.

"These are tombs of the ancients," Ash would explain, as we risked a small fire to cook whatever he had bartered for, using purchased charcoal and washing our meal down with tea. "These caves were hollowed out thousands of years ago." They were half-filled with drifting sand, but still magnificent. Columns carved like bundles of papyrus held up the stone roof. Bright murals decorated the walls. Unlike the barren granite of the Great Pyramid, here was a representation of life in a place of death, painted in a hundred colors. Boys wrestled. Girls danced and played. Nets drew in swarms of fish. Old kings were enveloped in trees of life, each leaf representing a year. Animals roamed in imagined forests. Boats floated on painted rivers where hippos reared and crocodiles swam. Birds filled the air. There were no skulls or morbid ravens as in Europe or America, but instead paintings that evoked a lush, wild, happier Egypt than the one I was traversing now.

"It looks like a paradise in those days," I said. "Green, uncrowded, rich, and predictable. You don't sense a fear of invasion, or a dread of tyrants. It's as Astiza said, better then than at any time afterward."

"In the best times the whole land was united upriver as far as the third or fourth cataract," Ashraf agreed. "Egyptian ships sailed from the Mediterranean to Aswan, and caravans brought riches from Nubia and lands like Punt and Sheba. Mountains yielded gold and gems. Black monarchs brought ivory and spices. Kings hunted lion in the desert fringe. And each year the Nile would rise to water and renew the valley with silt, just as it is doing now. It will peak about the time you said your calendar indicated, on October 21. Each year the priests watched the stars and zodiac to keep track of the optimal times for sowing and reaping and measured the level of the Nile." He pointed to some of the pictures. "Here the people, even the noblest, bring offerings to the temple to ensure the cycle continues. There were beautiful temples up and down the Nile."

"And the priests took those offerings."

"Yes."

"For a flooding that occurred every year anyway."

He smiled. "Yes."

"That's the profession for me. Predict that the seasons will turn, the sun will come up, and rake in the common people's gratitude."

"Except it was not predictable. Some years there was no flood, and famine followed. You probably didn't want to be a priest then."

"I'm betting they had some good excuse for the drought and asked people to double the tribute." I have an eye for easy work and could just imagine their tidy system. I looked around. "And what's this writing?" I asked of graffiti atop some pictures. "I don't recognize the language. Is it Greek?"

"Coptic," Ashraf said. "Legend has it that early Christians hid in these caves from the persecution of the Romans. We are the latest in a long chain of fugitives."

Another wall took my eye. It seemed to be a tally of something, a series of hash marks in the old language none of us could read. Some seemed plain enough: one mark to designate 1, three for 3, and so on. There was something familiar about those marks and I mused about it as we lay on sand that had sifted through the entrance, half filling the cave. Then it came to me. I took out the medallion.

"Ash, look at this. This little triangle of notches on my medallion—they look like the marks on that wall!"

He glanced from one to the other. "Indeed. What of it?"

What of it? This might change everything. If I was right, the bottom of the medallion was not meant to represent a pyramid, it represented numbers! I was carrying something that bore some kind of sum! The savants might be lunatics for mathematics, but my weeks enduring them was paying off—I'd seen a pattern I otherwise might have missed. True, I couldn't make much sense of the numbers—they seemed a random grouping of 1s, 2s, and 3s.

But I was getting closer to the mystery.

After many days and miles, we came to the crest of a steep limestone bluff near Nag Hammadi, the Nile curling around its edge and green fields on the far shore. There, across the river, we saw our quarry. Desaix's division of French soldiers, three thousand men and two guns, formed a column more than a mile long, marching slowly beside the Nile. From our vantage point they were insects on a timeless canvas, crawling blind on a sheen of oils. It was at this moment that I realized the impossibility of the task the French had set for themselves. I grasped finally the vast sprawl not just of Egypt, but of Africa beyond, an endless rolling vista that made the French division seem as insignificant as a flea on an elephant. How could this little puddle of men truly subdue this empire of desert, studded with ruins and swarming with horse-mounted tribesmen? It was as audacious as

Cortez in Mexico, but Cortez had the heart of an empire to aim for, while poor Desaix had already captured the heart, and now was pursuing the thrashing but defiant arms, in a wilderness of sand. His difficulty was not conquering the enemy, but finding him.

My problem was not finding my enemy, who must be somewhere in that column of soldiers, but coming to grips with him now that I was a French outlaw. Astiza was down there too, I hoped, but how could I get a message to her? My only ally was a Mameluke; my only clothes my Arab robes. I didn't even know where to start, now that we had the division in view. Should I swim the river and gallop in, demanding justice? Or try to assassinate Silano from behind a rock? And what proof did I have that he was really my enemy at all? If I succeeded, I'd be hanged.

"Ash, it occurs to me that I'm like a dog after an ox cart, not at all certain how to handle my prize should I catch it."

"So don't be a dog," the Mameluke said. "What is it you're really after?"

"The solution to my puzzle, a woman, revenge. Yet I have no proof yet that Silano is responsible for anything. Nor do I know exactly what to do with him. I'm not afraid to face the count. I'm just uncertain what he deserves. It's been simpler riding through the desert. It's empty. Uncomplicated."

"And yet in the end a man can no more be one with the desert than a boat can be of the sea—both pass on its surface. The desert is a passage, not a destination, friend."

"And now we near the end of the voyage. Will Silano have the army's protection? Will I be regarded as a fugitive? And where will Achmed bin Sadr be lurking?"

"Yes, Bin Sadr. I do not see his band down there with the soldiers."

As if in answer, there was a ping off a nearby rock and the delayed echo of a gun's report. A chip of rock flew up in the air and then plopped into the dirt.

"See how the gods answer all?" Ashraf pointed.

I twisted in my saddle. To the north behind us, from the hills where we'd come, were a dozen men. They were in Arab dress, riding camels, rocking as they trotted fast, their image wavering in the heat. Their leader was carrying something too long to be a musket—a wooden staff, I surmised.

"Bin Sadr, the devil himself," I muttered. "He keeps raiders off the back of the French. Now he's spotted us."

Ashraf grinned. "He comes to me so easily, having killed my brother?"

"The cavalry must have asked him to track us."

"His misfortune, then." The Mameluke looked ready to charge.

"Ash, stop! Think! We can't attack a dozen at once!"

He looked at me with scorn. "Are you afraid of a few bullets?"

More smoke puffed from the oncoming Arabs, and more spouts of dust twanged up around us. "Yes!"

My companion slowly raised a sleeve of his robe, displaying fabric neatly holed in a near-miss. He grinned. "I felt the wind of that one. Then I suggest we flee."

We kicked and sped off, angling down the back side of the ridge and away from the Nile in a desperate effort to get distance and cover. Our horses could outrun a camel in a sprint, but the dromedaries had more endurance. They could go a week without water, and then drink a volume that would kill any other animal. The French cavalry we'd lost easily. These desert warriors might be more persistent.

We skidded into a side valley, our horses fighting to maintain balance as pebbles flew, and then on flatter ground leaned into a dead run, trying to ignore the excited warble and random gunshots of our pursuers behind. They came after us hard, a trail of their dust hanging in their wake, frozen by the still and heavy air.

For an hour we kept them at a healthy distance, but with the heat and lack of water our mounts began to tire. We'd been days with no grazing and little to drink, and our animals were wearing out. We'd skitter up one sun-baked ridge and then drop down its other side, hoping somehow to confuse the chase, but our own dust marked us like a beacon.

"Can you slow them down?" Ash finally asked.

"I certainly outrange them. But at the speed they're coming I only have one good shot. It takes almost a minute to reload." We stopped at a high point and I took off the long-rifle I carried across my back. Its strap had bit into my shoulder for three hundred miles, but I was never tempted to leave its reassuring weight behind. It was uncomplaining and deadly. So now I sighted across my saddle, aiming for Bin Sadr, knowing that to kill him might end the pursuit. He was a good four hundred paces off. There was no wind, dry air, a target charging head-on . . . and enough heat to ripple his image like a flapping flag. Damn, where exactly was he? I aimed high, allowing for the bullet drop, squeezed, and fired, my horse starting at the report.

There was a long moment for the bullet to arrive. Then his camel tumbled.

Had I got him? The pursuing Bedouins had all reined in an anxious circle, shouting in consternation and loosing a few shots even though we were far out of musket range. I leaped on my horse and we galloped on as best we could, hoping we'd at least bought ourselves time. Ash looked back.

"Your friend has shoved one of his companions off his camel and is mounting it himself. The other warrior is doubling with another. They'll come more cautiously now."

"But he survived." We stopped and I reloaded, but that lost us most of the little ground we'd gained. I didn't want to be pinned down in a firefight because they'd overrun us while we loaded. "And they are still coming."

"It would seem so."

"Ash, we cannot fight them all."

"It would seem not."

"What will they do if they catch us?"

"Before, just rape and kill us. But now that you have shot his camel, I suspect they will rape us, strip us, stake us to the desert, and use scorpions to torment us while we die of thirst and sun. If we're lucky, a cobra will find us first."

"You didn't tell me that before I fired."

"You didn't tell me you were going to hit the camel, not the man."

We rode into a twisting canyon, hoping it wouldn't dead-end like the one where we'd dug for water. A dry wash or wadi gave it a sandy floor, and it twisted like a snake. Yet our trail was obvious, and our horse flanks were streaked with foam. They'd give out soon.

"I'm not going to give him the medallion, you know. Not after Talma and Enoch. I'll bury it, eat it, or throw it down a hole."

"I wouldn't ride with you if I thought you would."

The canyon ended in a steep rubble slope that led to its rim. We dismounted and dragged at the reins, pulling our exhausted horses upward. Unwillingly they advanced a few yards, heads thrashing, and then in frustration reared and kicked. We were as tired and unbalanced as they were. We slid on the slope, the reins jerking in our hands. No matter how hard we hauled, they were dragging us backward.

"We have to go another way!" I shouted.

"It's too late. If we turn back we ride into Bin Sadr. Let them go." The reins flew out of our hands and our mounts skittered back down into the canyon, fleeing in the direction of the oncoming Arabs.

To be dismounted in the desert was tantamount to death.

"We're doomed, Ashraf."

"Didn't the gods give you two legs and the wits to use them? Come, fate hasn't brought us this far to be done with us now." He began climbing the slope on foot, even as the Arabs came round a bend to spot us, warbled in triumph, and began firing more shots. Bits of rock exploded behind us where each bullet hit, giving me energy I didn't know I had. Fortunately, our pursuers had to pause to reload as we scrambled upward, and the steep slope would be challenging for camels as well. We climbed over the lip of the latest hill, panting, and looked about. It was a landscape of desolation, not a living thing in sight. I trotted to the rim of the next ravine . . .

And stopped short in amazement.

There, in a shallow depression, was a huddled mass of people.

Hunched, the whites of their eyes like a field of agates, were at least fifty blacks—or they would have been black if they were not covered by the same powdery Egyptian dust that coated us. They were naked, dotted with sores and flies, and laced together with chains, men and women alike. Their wide eyes stared at me as if from masks of stage makeup, as shocked to see us as we to see them. With them were half a dozen Arabs with guns and whips. Slavers!

The slave drivers were crouched with their victims, no doubt puzzled by the echoing gunfire. Ashraf shouted something in Arabic and they answered back, an excited chatter. After a moment, he nodded.

"They were coming down the Nile and saw the French. Bonaparte has been confiscating the caravans and freeing slaves. So they came up here to wait until Desaix and his army passes. Then they heard shots. They are confused."

"What should we do?"

In reply, Ash brought up his musket and calmly fired, hitting the slave caravan's leader full in the chest. The slaver pitched backward without a word, eyes wide with shock, and before he'd even hit the ground the Mameluke had two pistols out and fired both, hitting one drover in the face and another in the shoulder.

"Fight!" my companion cried.

A fourth slaver was pulling his own pistol when I killed him before I could think. Meanwhile Ash had drawn his sword and was charging. In seconds the wounded man and a fifth were dead and the sixth was running for his life back the way he'd come.

The suddenness of my friend's ferocity left me stunned.

The Mameluke strode to the leader, wiped his sword on the dead man's robes, and searched his body. He straightened with a ring of keys. "These slavers are vermin," he said. "They don't capture their slaves in battle, they buy them with trinkets and grow rich off misery. They deserved to die. Reload our guns while I unshackle these others."

The blacks cried and jostled with so much excitement that they tangled their own chains. Ash found a couple who spoke Arabic and gave sharp orders. They nodded and shouted to their fellows in their own language. The group stilled enough to let us free them, and then at Ash's direction they obediently picked up the Arab weapons, which I reloaded, and rocks.

Ashraf smiled at me. "Now we have our own little army. I told you the gods have their ways." Gesturing, he led our new allies back up to the crest of the ridge. Our posse of pursuing Arabs must have paused at the sounds of the fighting on the other side of the hill, but now they were coming up after us, pulling at their reluctant camels. Ash and I stepped up within view and Bin Sadr's henchmen shouted as triumphantly as if they'd spotted a wounded stag. We must have looked lonely on the pale blue skyline.

"Surrender the medallion and I promise you no harm!" Bin Sadr called in French.

"Now there's a promise I'd believe," I muttered.

"Ask for mercy yourself or I will burn you like you burned my brother!" Ashraf shouted back.

And then fifty newly freed blacks emerged on the ridge crest to form a line to either side of us. The Arabs halted, stunned, not understanding that they had walked into a trap. Ash called out a sharp command and the blacks gave a great cry. The air filled with stones and pieces of hurled chain. Meanwhile, the two of us fired, and Bin Sadr and another man went down. The blacks passed us the dead slavers' arms to shoot as well. Bedouin and camels, pelted with rocks and metal, went sprawling, screaming, and bawling in outrage and terror. Our pursuers tumbled down the steep slope in a small avalanche of rubble, their own aim spoiled by their precarious position. Hurled stones followed them, a meteor shower of released frustration. We killed or injured several in their pell-mell retreat, and when the survivors gathered in a little cluster at the base of the canyon, they peered up at us like chastened dogs.

Bin Sadr was holding one arm.

"The snake has Satan's luck," I growled. "I only wounded him."

"We can only pray it will fester," Ashraf said.

"Gage!" Bin Sadr yelled in French. "Give me the medallion! You don't even know what it's for!"

"Tell Silano to go to hell!" I shouted back. Our words echoed in the canyon.

"We'll give you the woman!"

"Tell Silano I'm coming to take her!"

The echoes faded away. The Arabs still had more guns than we did, and I was leery of leading the freed slaves down into a pitched battle. Bin Sadr was no doubt weighing the odds as well. He considered, then painfully mounted. His followers did so too.

He started to ride slowly away, then turned his camel and looked up at me. "I want you to know," he called, "that your friend Talma screamed before he died!" The word *died* reverberated in the wilderness, bouncing again and again and again.

He was out of range now, but not out of sight. I fired in frustration, the bullet kicking up dust a hundred paces short of him. He laughed, the sound amplified in the canyon, and then with the companions who were left, turned and trotted back the way he'd come.

"So will you," I muttered. "So will you."

Our horses gone, we took two of the slavers' camels and gave the four others to the freed blacks. There were enough provisions to get the party started on the long trek back to their homeland, and we gave them the captured guns to hunt for game and fend off slavers who would no doubt try to recapture them. We showed them how to load and fire, a task they learned with alacrity. Then they clutched at our knees to give thanks so fervently that we finally had to pry them off. We'd rescued them, it was true, but they'd also rescued us. Ashraf sketched a path for them through the desert hills that would keep them away from the Nile until they were above the first cataract. Then we went our separate way.

It was my first time on a camel, a noisy, grumpy, and somewhat ugly beast with its own community of fleas and midges. Yet it was well-trained and reasonably docile, dressed in rich and colorful harness. At Ash's direction I took my perch as it sat, then held on as it lurched upward. A few cries of "Hut, hut!" and it began moving, following the lead of Ash's beast. There was a rocking rhythm it took some time to get used to, but it was not altogether unpleasant. It felt like a boat in a seaway. Certainly it would do until I found a horse again, and I needed to reach the French expeditionary force before Bin Sadr did. We followed the ridge crest to a point above a Nile ferry and then descended to cross to Desaix's side of the river.

On the far bank we crossed the trampled wake of the army, rode through a banana grove, and at length struck desert again to the west and aimed for low hills, circling around to the army's flank. It was late afternoon when we spied the column again, camping along the dark course of the Nile. Shadows of date palms combed the ground.

"If we go on now we can enter their lines before sunset," I said.

"A good plan. I leave you to it, friend."

"What?" I was startled.

"I have done what I needed to, freeing you from jail and getting you here, yes?"

"More than you needed to. I am in your debt."

"As I am in yours giving me my freedom, trust, and companionship. It was wrong to blame you for the death of my brother. Evil comes, and who knows why? There are dual forces in the world, forever in tension. Good must fight bad, it is a constant. And so we will, but each in our own way, for now I must go to my people."

"Your people?"

"Bin Sadr has too many men to take on alone. I am still Mameluke, Ethan Gage, and somewhere in the desert is the fugitive army of Murad Bey. My brother Enoch was alive until the French came, and I fear many more will die until this foreign presence is driven from my country."

"But Ashraf, I'm part of that army!"

"No. You're no more a Frank than a Mameluke. You are something strange and out of place, American, sent here for the gods' purpose. I'm not certain what role you've been chosen to play, but I do feel that I'm to leave you to play it, and that Egypt's future relies on your courage. So go to your woman and do what her gods ask you to do."

"No! We aren't just allies, we've become friends! Haven't

we? And I've lost too many friends already! I need your help, Ashraf. Avenge Enoch with me!"

"Revenge will come at the god's chosen time. If not, Bin Sadr would have died today, because you seldom miss. I suspect he has a different fate, perhaps more terrible. Meanwhile, what you need is to get what this Count Silano has come here to find, and fulfill your destiny. Whatever happens on future battlefields can't alter the bond we've made over these many days. Peace be upon you, friend, until you find what it is you're looking for."

And with that he and his camel disappeared toward the setting sun and I started, more alone than ever, to find Astiza.

CHAPTER TWENTY

I knew that the notion of galloping into Desaix's division of French soldiers, shouting for Silano, was unlikely to produce anything other than my own arrest. But what I lacked in power I made up for in possession: I had the medallion, and my rival did not. It would be far easier, I realized, to have Silano come to me.

It was near dusk when I approached a squad of camped sentries, my arms raised. Several ran out with muskets, having learned to view any approaching Egyptian with suspicion. Too many unwary Frenchmen had died in a war that was becoming crueler.

I gambled that news of my escape from Cairo had not reached these pickets. "Don't shoot! I'm an American recruited to Berthollet's company of scholars! I've been sent by Bonaparte to continue my investigation of the ancients!"

They looked at me suspiciously. "Why are you dressed like a native?"

"Without escort, do you think I'd still be alive if I were not?"

"You came alone from Cairo? Are you mad?"

"The boat I was riding hit a rock and has to be repaired. I was impatient to come ahead. I hope there are ruins here."

"I recognize him," one said. "The Franklin man." He spat.

"Surely you appreciate the opportunity to study the magnificent past," I said lightly.

"While Murad Bey taunts us, always a few miles ahead. We beat him. And then we beat him again. And then again. Each time he runs, and each time he comes back. And each time a few more of us will never return to France. And now we wait at ruins while he escapes deeper into this cursed country, as out of reach as a mirage."

"If you can even see the mirage," joined another. "A thousand troops have sore eyes in this dust and sun, and a hundred are hobbling blind. It's like a jest out of a play. Ready to fight? Yes, here is our rank of blind musketeers!"

"Blindness! That's the least of it," added a third. "We've shit twice our weight between here and Cairo. Sores don't heal. Blisters become boils. There are even cases of plague. Who hasn't lost half a dozen kilos of flesh on this march alone?"

"Or been so horny they're ready to mate with rats and donkeys?"

All soldiers like to grumble, but clearly, disillusionment with Egypt was growing. "Perhaps Murad is on the brink of defeat," I said.

"Then let's defeat him."

I patted my rifle. "My muzzle has been as warm as yours at times, friends."

Now their interest brightened. "Is that the American long-rifle? I hear it can kill a Red Indian at a thousand paces."

"Not quite, but if you only have one shot, this is the gun you want. I recently hit a camel at four hundred." No need to tell them what I'd been aiming at.

They crowded around. Men find unity in admiring good tools and it was, as I've said, a beautiful piece, a jewel amid the dross of their regulation muskets.

"Today my gun stays cold because I have a different task, no less important. I'm to confer with Count Alessandro Silano. Do you know where I could find him?"

"The temple, I suppose," a sergeant said. "I think he wants to live there."

"Temple?"

"Away from the river, beyond a village called Dendara. We've stopped so Denon can scribble more pictures, Malraux can measure more stone, and Silano can mutter more spells. What a circus of lunatics. At least *he* brought a woman."

"A woman?" I tried not to betray any particular interest.

"Ah, that one," a private agreed. "I sleep with her in my dreams." He jerked his fist up and down and grinned.

I restrained the inclination to club him with my rifle. "Which way to this temple?"

"You intend to go dressed like a bandit?"

I straightened. "I look, I believe, like a sheikh."

That drew a laugh. They pointed and offered escort, but I declined. "I need to confer with the count alone. If he's not already at the ruins and you see him, give him this message. Tell him he can find what he's looking for at midnight."

Silano wouldn't arrest me, I gambled. He'd want me to first find what we both were looking for, and then surrender it for Astiza.

T he temple glowed under stars and moon, an immense pillared sanctuary with a flat stone roof. It and its sub-sidiary temples were enclosed by a mud-brick wall a square kilometer in circumference, eroded and half buried. The wall's primary gateway jutted out of the sand as if half drowned, with clearance just high enough to walk under. It was carved with Egyptian gods, hieroglyphs, and a winged sun flanked by cobras. Beyond, the courtyard was filled with dunes like ocean swells. A waning moon gave pale il-lumination to sand as smooth as the skin of an Egyptian woman, sensuous and sculpted. Yes, there was a thigh, be-yond it a hip, and then a buried obelisk like a nipple on a breast . . .

I'd been away from Astiza too long, hadn't I?

The main building had a flat façade, with six immense pillars rearing from the sand to hold up the stone roof. Each column was topped by the eroded visage of a broad-faced goddess. Or rather four faces: on each pillar she looked in the four cardinal directions, her Egyptian headdress coming down behind cowlike ears. With her wide-lipped smile and huge, friendly eyes, Hathor had a bovine serenity. The head-dress was colored with faded paint, I noted, evidence that the structure had once been brilliantly colored. The temple's long abandonment was apparent from the dunes that rolled inside. Its front looked like a dock being consumed by a rising tide.

I looked about, but saw no one. I had my rifle, my tomahawk, and no certain plan except that this might be the temple that would house the staff of Min, that Silano might meet me here, and that I might spot him before he spied me.

I slogged up the dune and passed through the central entry. Because of the heaping sand, I wasn't far from the ceiling as I passed inside. When I lit a candle I had taken from the soldiers, it revealed a roof painted blue and covered with yellow five-pointed stars. They looked like starfish or, I thought, the head, arms, and legs of men who had taken their place in the night sky. There was also a rank of vultures and winged suns decorated in reds, gold, and blues. We seldom look up and yet the entire ceiling was as intricately decorated as the Sistine Chapel. As I went deeper into the temple's first and grandest hall the sand receded and I descended from the ceiling, beginning to get a sense of just how high the pillars really were. The interior felt like a grove of massive trees, painstakingly carved and painted with symbols. I wandered amid the eighteen gigantic columns in awe, each crowned with the placid faces of the goddess. The pillars banded as they rose. Here was a row of ankhs, the sacred key of life. Then stiff Egyptian figures, giving offerings to the gods. There were the indecipherable hieroglyphs, many enclosed in ovals the French had dubbed *cartouches,* or cartridges. There were carvings of birds, cobras, fronds, and striding animals.

At either end of this room the ceiling was even more elaborate, decorated with the signs of the zodiac. A huge nude woman, stretched like rubber, curled around them: a sky goddess, I guessed. Yet the sum was bewildering and overwhelming, a crust of gods and signs so thick that it was like walking inside an ancient newspaper. I was a deaf man at an opera.

I studied the sand for tracks. No sign of Silano.

At the rear of this great hall there was an entry to a second, smaller hall, equally high but more intimate. Rooms opened off it, each decorated on walls and ceiling but empty of furniture for millennia, their purpose unclear. Then a step up to another entry, and beyond it another, each room lower and smaller than the one before. Unlike a Christian cathedral, which broadened as one advanced, Egyptian temples seemed to shrink the farther one penetrated. The holier the enclosure, the more it was lightless and exclusive, rays of light reaching it only on rare days of the year.

Could that be the meaning of my October date?

So wondrous were the decorations that for a brief time I forgot my mission. I had flickering glimpses of snakes and lotus flowers, boats that floated in the sky, and fierce and terrible lions. There were baboons and hippos, crocodiles and long-necked birds. Men marched in gloriously decorated processions, carrying offerings. Women offered their breasts like life itself. Deities as regal and patient as emperors stood in sideways poses. It seemed crude and idolatrous, this mix of animals and animal-headed gods, and yet for the first time I recognized how much closer the Egyptians were to their gods than we are to ours. Ours are sky gods, distant, unworldly, while the Egyptians could see Thoth each time an ibis stepped across a pond. They could sense Horus with each flight of a falcon. They could report having talked to a burning bush, and their neighbors would accept the story calmly.

There was still no sign of Silano or Astiza. Had the soldiers led me astray—or was I walking into a trap? Once I thought I heard a footstep, but when I listened there was nothing. I found some stairs and mounted them, ascending in a twisting pattern like the climb of a hawk. Carved on the walls was an upward procession of men carrying offerings. There must have been ceremonies up here. I emerged on the temple's roof, surrounded by a low parapet. Still not sure what I was looking for, I wandered amid small sanctuaries set on its terrace. In one, small pillars topped by Hathor made a gazebo-like enclosure reminiscent of a Paris park. In the northwest corner was a door leading to a small, two-roomed sanctum. The inner chamber had bas reliefs showing a pharaoh or god rising from the dead in more ways than one: his phallus was erect and triumphant. It reminded me of the tumescent god Min. Was this the legend of Isis and Osiris I'd been told when we sailed toward Egypt? A falcon floated above the being about to be resurrected. Again, my poor brain could detect no useful clue.

The outer room, however, gave me a tingle of excitement. On the ceiling, two nude women flanked a spectacular circular relief crammed with figures. After studying it for a while, I decided the carving must be a representation of the sacred sky. Upheld by four goddesses and eight representations of the hawk-headed Horus—did they represent the twelve months?—was a circular disc of the symbolic heavens, painted with faded colors of blue and yellow. I spied signs of the zodiac again, not too dissimilar from what had come down to us in modern times: the bull, the lion, the crab, the twin fish. At the circumference was a procession of thirty-six figures, both human and animal. Could these represent the Egyptian and French ten-day weeks?

I craned my neck, trying to make sense of it. At the northern axis of the temple was a figure of Horus, the hawk, who seemed to anchor all the rest. Toward the east was Taurus, the bull, signifying the age in which the pyramids had been built. To the south was a half-fish, half-goat creature, and near it a man pouring water from two jars—Aquarius! This was the sign of the future age, centuries hence, and the symbol for the vital rising of the Nile. Aquarius, like the water symbol on the medallion around my neck, and Aquarius, like the sign on the lost calendar of *L'Orient* that I'd guessed pointed to October 21.

The ceiling's circle reminded me of a compass. Aquarius was oriented to the southwest.

I stepped outside, trying to get my bearings. A stone stairway led up to the parapet at the rear edge of the temple, so I climbed to look. To the southwest was another smaller temple, more decayed than the one I was in. Enoch had said there would be a small temple of Isis, and within it, perhaps, the mysterious staff of Min. Beyond it the dunes swept over the compound's periphery wall, and distant hills glowed silver under cold stars.

I felt the medallion against my chest. Could I find its completion?

A second flight of stairs took me back to the ground floor. Its straightness was like the dive of a hawk that had spiraled upward on the other side. Now men with offerings were marching downward. Once again I was in the main temple, but a door to one side led again to the sands of the compound. I looked up. The main temple wall loomed above me, lion heads jutting like gargoyles.

My rifle ready, I walked to the rear, toward the smaller temple I'd seen. To my right, palms grew from the ruins of the sacred lake. I tried to imagine this place in ancient times, the dunes at bay, the causeways paved and shining, the gardens tended, and the lake shimmering as priests bathed. What an oasis it must have been! Now, ruins. At the temple's rear I turned the corner and stopped short. Gigantic figures were carved on the wall, thirty feet high. A king and queen, I guessed from their headdress, were offering goods to a full-breasted goddess, perhaps Hathor or Isis. The queen was a slim and stylish woman with a towering crown, her arms bare, her legs long and slim. Her wig was braided, and a cobra like a golden tiara was poised above her forehead.

"Cleopatra," I breathed. It had to be her, if Enoch was right! She was opposite her little temple of Isis, which sat about twenty meters to the south of the main building.

I glanced about. Still the compound seemed lifeless, except for me. I had the sense that it was poised, waiting. For what?

The Isis temple was built on a raised terrace, a drift of sand between it and the Cleopatra carving on the main building. Half the small temple was a walled sanctuary like the larger temple I'd just come from. The other half was open and ruined, a shadowy mass of pillars and beams, open to the sky. I climbed up broken blocks to the door of the walled section. "Silano?" My query echoed back at me.

Hesitantly, I stepped inside. It was very dark, the only light coming from the door and two high openings barely big enough to fit pigeons. The room was taller than it was long or wide, and claustrophobic, its smell acrid. I took another step.

Suddenly there was a whir of wings and I instinctively ducked. Warm wind thrashed at me, extinguishing my light. Bats flew by, squeaking, scraping my scalp with leathery wings. Then they funneled outside. I relit my candle with shaking hand.

Again, the walls were thick with carvings and traces of old paint. A woman I assumed was Isis dominated. I saw no sign of Min and his staff, or anything else. Was I on a wild goose chase? Always I felt like I was groping blind, with clues no reasonable man could understand. What was I supposed to see?

I noticed, finally, that this room was considerably smaller than the enclosed temple's perimeter. There had to be a second chamber. I stepped back on the stone porch and realized there was a second door and high room, even narrower than the first, and just as baffling. This one, however, had a stone table, like an altar. The pedestal was the size of a small writing desk, perched in the room's center. It was plain, unremarkable, and I might have passed it by except for a peculiar occurrence. As I bent over the altar the chain round my neck came loose and snagged the pedestal. The medallion broke free and struck the stone floor with an audible clink. This had never happened before. I swore, but when I bent to retrieve it, what I saw arrested me.

Carved onto a floor slab were two faint Vs, overlapping like compass and square. In the Egyptian style they were geometric, and yet the resemblance was clear.

"By the Great Architect," I muttered. "Can it be?" I remembered Enoch's script: *The crypt will lead to heaven.*

I refastened the medallion and stamped on the floor slab. It shifted. Something hollow was under there.

Kneeling in excitement now, my rifle set to one side, I pried with the blade of my tomahawk until I could grasp the slab. It lifted like a heavy trapdoor and released a rush of stale air, an announcement that it hadn't been opened in a long time. Holding my candle, I leaned over. The light glimmered on a floor below. Could there be treasure? Leaving my gun for a moment and sliding feet first, I dropped, falling ten feet and landing like a cat. My heart was hammering. I looked up. Easy enough for Silano to slide the lid back in place if he was watching me. Or was he waiting to see what I might find?

Passages led in two directions.

Again there was a riot of carving. The ceiling bore a field of the five-pointed stars. The walls were thick with gods, goddesses, hawks, vultures, and rearing snakes, a motif repeated again and again. The first passage dead-ended within twenty feet at a mound of clay amphoras—dull, dusty jars that seemed unlikely to hold anything of value. Just to be sure, however, I used my tomahawk to crack one open. When it split apart, I raised my candle.

And jumped. Looking back at me was the hideous face of a mummified baboon, flesh desiccated, eye sockets huge, jaws full of teeth. What the devil?

I broke another jar and found another baboon inside. Another symbol, I remembered, for the god Thoth. So this was a kind of catacomb, full of bizarre animal mummies. Were they offerings? I put my candle near the ceiling so the light would reach farther in the gloom. The clay jars were heaped as far back as the light would reach. Little things moved in the shadows—some kind of insect.

I turned and went the other way, down the other passage. I desperately wanted out of this crypt, yet if Enoch's clue made any sense there must be something down here. My candle stub was getting low. And then there was more movement, something slithering away on the floor.

I looked with my meager light. There were tracks on the sand and dust of a damned snake, and a crack into which it had probably crawled. I was sweating. Was Bin Sadr down here too? Why had I left my rifle?

And then something glittered.

The other tunnel ended too, but now there were no jars, but instead a relief carving of the now-familiar priapic figure of Min, probably a figure of some fascination to the sensual Cleopatra. He was stiff as a board, his member erect and startlingly bright.

Min was decorated not with paint, but with gold. His manhood was outlined with twin sticks of gold connected with a hinge at one end, half obscenity, half tool of life. Without knowing about the riddle of the medallion, one would assume the golden shafts were solely sacred decoration.

But I think Cleopatra had another idea. Maybe she left this piece in Egypt if she really took the other medallion to Rome, to ensure its secret stayed in her native country. I pried the gold member loose until it popped into my hand, and worked the hinge. Now the golden shafts formed a V. I took out the medallion, splayed its arms, and laid this new V across them. When I formed the now-familiar Freemason symbol, a compass crossed with a square, the notches on the medallion's arms locked. The result was a diamond of overlapping arms, swinging below the medallion's inscribed disc but without, of course, the European letter *G,* which the Masons used to denote God or gnosis, knowledge.

Splendid. I had completed the medallion, and perhaps found a root symbol of my own fraternity.

And still had no clue what it meant.

"Ethan."

The sound was faint, almost like a whisper of wind or trick of the ear, but it was Astiza's voice, I knew, coming faintly from somewhere outside. The call was as electrifying as a bolt of lightning. I dropped the newly complex medallion around my neck, rushed down the passageway, saw to my relief the slab was still askew, and swiftly wiggled my way up and out the crypt shaft. My gun lay where I had left it, untouched. I picked it up and crouched. All was silent. Had her call been my imagination? I moved quietly to the entrance, peering cautiously outside. I could see Cleopatra on the main temple wall opposite, her carved form picked out by moonlight.

"Ethan?" It was a near sob, coming from the open pillars adjacent to the enclosure I was in.

I stepped out on the temple's porch and advanced as silently as an Indian, rifle ready. On this half of the temple platform, the columns rose to horizontal beams that held up nothing, framing squares of sky. I could see the stars between them. A different face, this of the serene Isis, was carved into the pillars' design.

"Astiza?" My voice echoed among the columns.

"Do you have it?"

I stepped around a pillar and there she was. I stopped, confused.

She was stripped to my fantasy of a harem girl, her linen translucent, her legs visible through her gown, her jewelry heavy, and her eyes lined. She'd been dressed for seduction. Her arms were lifted because her wrists were chained to shackles that led to a stone beam above. The posture lifted her breasts, twisting her waist and hips, and the effect was an erotic helplessness, a tableau of a princess in peril. I stopped, stupefied by this apparition from a fairy tale. Her own look was pained.

"Is it complete?" she asked in a small voice.

"Why are you dressed like that?" It was the most mundane of a hundred questions ricocheting like billiard balls in my mind, but I felt I was in a hallucinatory dream.

The answer was the press of a sword point in the small of my back. "Because she is distracting," Count Silano murmured. "Drop your rifle, monsieur." The sword pressed more painfully.

I tried to think. My weapon thumped to the stone.

"Now, the medallion."

"It's yours," I tried, "if you unchain her and let us flee."

"Unchain her? But why, when she can simply lower her arms?"

And Astiza did so, her slim wrists slipping from loose shackles, her look apologetic. The chains swung gently, an empty prop. The gossamer veils draped her body like a classical statue, her undergarments only calling attention to the places they concealed. She looked embarrassed at her fraudulence.

Once more, I felt the fool.

"Haven't you realized that she's with me, now?" Silano said. "But then you're American, aren't you, too direct, too trusting, too idealistic, too naïve. Did you come all this way

fantasizing about rescuing her? Not only did you never understand the medallion; you never understood her."

"That's a lie." I stared up at her as I said it, hoping for
confirmation. She stood trembling, rubbing her wrists.

"Is it?" Silano said behind me. "Let's review the truth.
Talma went to Alexandria to ask questions about her not just
because he was your friend, but because he was an agent for
Napoleon."

"That's a lie too. He was a journalist."

"Who cut a deal with the Corsican and his scientists, promising to keep an eye on you in return for access to the highest
councils of the expedition. Bonaparte wants the secret found,
but doesn't trust anyone. So Talma could come if he spied
on you. Meanwhile, the journalist suspected Astiza from the
beginning. Who was she? Why did she come with you like
an obedient dog, trudging with an army, acquiescing to a
harem? Because of infatuation with your clumsy charm? Or
because she's always been in alliance with me?"

He certainly enjoyed boasting. Astiza was looking up at
the ruined beams.

"My dear Gage, have you understood a single thing that's
happened to you? The journalist learned a disturbing thing
about our Alexandrian witch: not that word of your coming
was sent by gypsies, as she told you, but by *me*. Yes, we
were in communication. Yet instead of helping kill you, as
I recommended, she seemed to be using you to discover the
secret. What was her game? When I landed in Alexandria,
Talma thought he could spy on me as well, but Bin Sadr
caught him. I told the fool he could join me against you and
we could sell whatever treasure we found to the highest-
bidding king or general—Bonaparte too!—but we couldn't
reason with him. He threatened to go to Bonaparte and have
the general interrogate us all. Nor was he a bargaining chip
once you insisted on the fiction that the medallion was lost.
His last chance was to steal it from whoever had it and deliver it to me, but he refused. In the end, the little hypochon-
driac was more loyal than you deserved, and a French patriot
to boot."

"And you are not." My voice was cold.

"The Revolution cost my family everything it had. Do you think I consort with rabble because I care about liberty? Their liberty took everything from me, and now I'm going to use them to get it all back. I do not work for Bonaparte, Ethan Gage. Bonaparte, unwittingly, works for me."

"So you sent Talma to me in a jar." I was so rigid, fists clenched, that my knuckles were white. The sky seemed to be wheeling, the chains a pendulum like some trick of Mesmer. I had just one chance.

"A casualty of war," Silano replied. "If he'd listened to me, he'd have been richer than Croesus."

"But I don't understand. Why didn't your lantern bearer, Bin Sadr in disguise, just take the medallion that first evening in Paris, the moment I stepped into the street?"

"Because I thought you'd given it to the whore, and I didn't know where she lived. But she didn't confess to it even when the Arab gutted her. Nor did my men find it in your chambers. Frankly, I wasn't even sure of its importance, not until I asked more questions. I assumed I'd have the leisure to strip you of it in prison. But you ran, allied with Talma, and were on your way to Egypt as a savant—what amusement!—before I was even certain the trinket was what we'd all been looking for. I still don't know where you hid the medallion that first night."

"In my chamber pot."

He laughed. "Irony, irony! Key to the greatest treasure on earth, and you cover it with shit! Ah, what a clown. Yet what uncommon luck you've had, eluding an ambush on the Toulon highway and an Alexandrian street, dodging snakes, coming unscathed through major battles, and even finding your way here. You have the devil's luck! And yet in the end you come to me, bringing the medallion with you, all for a woman who won't let you touch her! The male mind! She told me that all we had to do was wait, provided Bin Sadr didn't get you first. Did he ever find you?"

"I shot him."

"Really? Pity. You've been a most troublesome man, Ethan Gage."

"He survived."

"But of course. He always does. You will not want to meet him again."

"Don't forget that I'm still in the company of savants, Silano. Do you want to answer to Monge and Berthollet for my murder? They have the ear of Bonaparte, and he has an army. You'll hang if you harm me."

"I believe it is called self-defense." He pushed slightly with his sword and I felt a faint sting through my robes, and a trickle of my own blood. "Or is it attempted capture of a fugitive from revolutionary justice? Or a man who lied about losing a magic medallion so he could keep it for himself? Any will suit. But I am a nobleman with my own code of honor, so let me offer you mercy. You're a hunted fugitive, without friends or allies and no threat to anyone, if you ever were. So, for the medallion I give you back . . . your life. *If* you promise to tell me what Enoch learned."

"What Enoch learned?" What was he talking about?

"Your enfeebled mentor threw himself on a bonfire to grasp a book before we could torture him. French troops were coming. So, what did the book contain?"

The villain was referring to the book of Arabic poetry that Enoch had clutched at. I was sweating. "I still want the woman, too."

"But she doesn't want you, does she? Did she tell you we were once lovers?"

I looked. Astiza had put her hands to one of the swaying manacles as if to hold herself up, looking at both of us with sorrow. "Ethan, it was the only way," she whispered.

I tasted the same ashes that Bonaparte must have bit when he learned of the betrayal of Josephine. I'd come so far—for this? To be held at sword point by an aristocratic braggart? To be humiliated by a woman? Robbed of all I'd struggled for? "All right." My hands went to my neck and I lifted the talisman clear, holding it out in front of me where it rocked like a pendulum. Even at night it shone coldly. I could hear both of them gasp slightly at its new shape. They had led me, and I had found the part to complete it.

"So it *is* the key," Silano breathed. "Now all we must do is understand the numbers. You will help me, priestess. Gage? Turn slowly now, and give it up."

I did so, moving back slightly from his rapier. I needed just a moment's distraction. "You're no closer to solving the mystery than I am," I warned.

"Aren't I? I solved more than you. My journey around the Mediterranean took me to many temples and libraries. I found evidence that the key would be in Dendara, at the temple of Cleopatra. That I was to look to Aquarius. And here to the south I found the temple of Cleopatra, who would of course worship the lovely and all-powerful Isis, not the cow-faced Hathor with her bovine ears and tits. Yet I couldn't figure where to look."

"There's a crypt with the phallic god Min. It had the missing piece."

"How scholarly of you to find it. Now, give me the trinket."

Slowly, leaning over the point of his rapier, I handed it to him. He snatched it with the greed of a child, his look triumphant. When he held it up it seemed to dance, this sign of the Freemasons. "Odd how sacred memory is passed down even by those who don't realize its origin, isn't it?" Silano said.

And it was then that I threw.

The tomahawk in the small of my back had rested just inches from his sword point, itching beneath my concealing robe. I needed just a moment to steal it out, once my back was turned and he was triumphantly hoisting the medallion. The test, however, would be whether Astiza cried out when she saw what I was doing.

She hadn't.

Which meant that perhaps she wasn't on Silano's side after all. That the man was indeed a liar. That I was not entirely a fool.

So I was quick, very quick. Yet Silano was quicker. He ducked as the hatchet whistled by his ear, spinning to land in the sands beyond the temple terrace. Still, the throw had put him off-balance, requiring an instant to recover. It was enough to seize my rifle! I brought it up . . .

And he leaned forward, lithe and sure, and rammed his rapier blade right into the mouth of the barrel. "*Touché,* Monsieur Gage. And now we are at an impasse, are we not?"

I suppose we looked ridiculous. I had frozen, my muzzle pointed at his breast, and he was a statue too, neatly balanced, his sword in my weapon's throat.

"Except that I," he went on, "have a pistol." He reached beneath his coat.

So I pulled the trigger.

My plugged rifle exploded, the shattered stock kicking back at me and the barrel and broken sword whirling over Silano's head. We both went sprawling, my ears ringing and my face cut by pieces of the ruptured gun.

Silano howled.

And then there was an ominous creak and rumble.

I looked up. A precariously balanced stone beam, already partly dislodged from its ancient perch from some long-ago earthquake, was rocking against the stars. The chain was wrapped around it, I now noticed, and Astiza was pulling with all her might.

"You moved the chains," Silano said to her stupidly, looking at Astiza in stunned confusion.

"Samson," she replied.

"You'll kill us all!"

The beam slid off the column and fell like a hammer, crashing against a leaning pillar and starting it falling, too. The worn columns were a house of cards. There was a grinding creak, a growing roar, and the whole overhead edifice began to give way. I winced and rolled as tons of heavy rock came smashing down, heaving the very ground. I heard a pop as Silano's pistol went off and bits of shattered rock flew like shrapnel, but its sound was dwarfed by groaning columns that rolled and tumbled. Then Astiza was jerking me upward, pushing me toward the edge of the temple platform amid the chaos. "Run, run! The noise will bring the French!" We leaped, a cloud of dust rolling out with us, and hit the sand just as a section of pillar bounced over us like a runaway barrel. It crashed against Cleopatra's feet. Back on the ruined terrace, Silano was screaming and cursing, his voice coming from the dust and wreckage of the toppled ruins.

She stooped and handed me the tomahawk I'd hurled. "We may need this."

I looked at her in amazement. "You brought the whole temple down."

"He forgot to sheer my hair. Or hold his prize." The medallion, wide and clumsy in its new assembly, swung from her fist like a cat's toy.

I hefted the tomahawk. "Let's go back inside and finish him."

But there were shouts of French from the front of the temple compound, and the signal shots of sentries. She shook her head. "There's no time."

So we ran, fleeing out a rear gate in the eastern wall and into the desert beyond, weaponless, horseless, without food, water, or sensible clothing. We heard more shouts, and shots, but no bullet buzzed near.

"Hurry," she said. "The Nile has almost peaked!"

What did that mean?

We had nothing except the tomahawk and the cursed medallion.

And each other.

But, who was this woman I had rescued, who had rescued me?

CHAPTER TWENTY-ONE

The Nile was high, brown, and powerful. It was October, the year's peak flood, and we were approaching the date the circular calendar seemed to suggest. We stole a small boat and set off down the river, headed back for the Great Pyramid that Monge had suggested must be the key to the riddle. I'd give it a last crack, and if we couldn't puzzle it out I'd just keep going to the Mediterranean. Whether the strange woman beside me would follow, I had no idea.

By the time the sun rose we were miles from Desaix's army, drifting with the current. I might have relaxed except that I saw a French courier galloping along the riverbank, spying us and then cutting inland on a shortcut while we took the river's looping bends. No doubt he was carrying word of our escape. I lowered the boom to set the lateen sail, giving us even more speed, the boat leaning with the wind and water hissing as I tacked. We passed a yawning crocodile, prehistoric and hideous. Water glistened on his scales, and yellow eyes looked at us with reptilian contemplation. After Silano, he seemed an improvement in company.

What a pair we made, I in Arab costume and Astiza in temptress regalia, sprawled on the muddy floorboards of a small felucca that stank of fish. She'd said little since we reunited, gazing over the Nile and fingering the medallion she'd draped around her own neck with an air of ownership. I hadn't asked for it back.

"I came a long way to find you," I finally said.

"You followed the star of Isis."

"But you weren't chained as you pretended."

"No. Nothing was as it seemed. I fooled him, and you."

"You knew Silano before?"

She sighed. "He was a master and lover who turned to darker arts. He believed Egypt's magic was as real as Berthollet's chemistry and that he, following in the footsteps of Cagliostro and Kolmer, could find occult secrets here. He cared nothing for the world, only for himself, because he was bitter over what he'd lost in the Revolution. When I realized how selfish he was, we had a falling-out. I fled to Alexandria and found sanctuary with a new master, the guardian. Silano's dreams were shallow. Alessandro wanted Egypt's secrets to make him powerful, even immortal, so I played a double game."

"Did he buy you from Yusuf?"

"Yes. It was a bribe to the old lecher."

"Lecher?"

"Yusuf's hospitality was not entirely selfless. I needed to get away from there." She saw my look. "Don't worry, he didn't touch me."

"So you went with your old lover."

"You hadn't come back from the pyramids. Silano told me he hadn't found you at Enoch's. Going with the count was the only way to make progress in solving the mystery. I knew nothing of Dendara, and neither did you. That place had been forgotten for centuries. I told Alessandro you had the medallion, and then left you a message of where to find it in the harem. We both knew you'd come after us. And then I rode freely, because the French would have asked too many questions if I'd been bound."

Alessandro! I didn't like the familiarity of a first name. "And then you brought a temple down on him."

"He believes in his own charm, like you."

As did she, toying with both of us as a means to her end. "You asked me what I believed in, Astiza. Who do *you* believe in?"

"What do you mean?"

"You helped Silano because you want the secret too."

"Of course. But to safeguard it, not ransom it to some greedy tyrant like Bonaparte. Can you imagine that man with an army of immortals? At its peak, Egypt was defended by an army of just twenty thousand men, and seemed impregnable. Then something seemed to happen, something was lost, and invasions began."

"Going with the men who murdered Talma . . ."

"Silano knew things I did not. I knew things he did not. Could you have found the temple of Dendara that we came from by yourself? We didn't know which temple Enoch's books referred to, but Silano did after his studies in Rome and Constantinople and Jerusalem. We would never have found the other arms of the medallion by ourselves, just as Silano could not complete the medallion without you and Enoch. You had some clues and the count had others. The gods brought us all together."

"The gods, or the Egyptian Rite? Gypsies didn't tell you I was coming to Egypt."

She looked away. "I couldn't tell you the truth because you'd misunderstand. Alessandro lied and sent word that you'd stolen the medallion from him. I pretended to help so I could use him. You survived our assassination attempt. Then Enoch persuaded Ashraf to try to find us in the battle—you, the man in a green coat, who conveniently stood up on an artillery caisson—so that he could see this medallion all were so curious about. Everything that happened was supposed to, except poor Talma's death."

My mind was whirling. Maybe I *was* naïve. "So we're all just tools for you—me for the medallion, Silano for his occult knowledge? No different, here to be used?"

"I did not fall in love with Silano."

"I didn't say you were in love with him, I said . . ." I stopped. She was looking away from me, rigid, trembling, her long fine hair blowing in the warm wind that kicked up little wavelets on the river. Not in love? With *him*. Did that mean that perhaps my pursuit had not gone unnoticed, my charm not entirely unappreciated, my good intentions not misunderstood? But then how much did I feel about her now? I wished to have her, yes, but to love her? I didn't even know her, it seemed. And love was truly dangerous ground for a man like me, a prospect more daunting than a Mameluke charge or a naval broadside. It meant believing in something, committing to more than a moment. What did I really feel toward this woman who'd seemed to betray me but perhaps had not?

"What I mean is, I haven't loved anyone else either," I stumbled. Not the most eloquent of replies. "That is, I'm not even sure love exists."

She was exasperated. "How do you know electricity exists, Ethan?"

"Well." That was actually a damned good question, since it seemed naturally invisible. "By sparks, I suppose. You can feel it. Or a lightning bolt."

"Exactly." Now she was looking at me, smiling like a sphinx, enigmatic, unapproachable, except that now the door had been opened and all I had to do was step through it. What had Berthollet surmised about my character? That I had not realized my potential? Now here was a chance to grow up, to commit not to an idea, but to a person.

"I don't even know what side you're on," I stalled.

"I'm on *our* side."

Which side was that? And then, before our conversation could get to some kind of agreeable conclusion, the crack of a gun echoed across the river.

We looked downstream. A felucca was sailing toward us, its rigging taut, deck thick with men. Even at a distance of three hundred meters, I could recognize the bandaged arm of Achmed bin Sadr. By all the tea in China, could I not get clear of this man? I hadn't felt so weary of someone's company since Franklin had John Adams to dinner and I had to hear his irascible opinions on half the politicians in the United States.

We had no weapons except my tomahawk, and no chance, so I put the rudder over and made for shore. Perhaps we could find a cliffside tomb to hide in. But no, now a squadron of red-and-blue-jacketed hussars was spilling down a hill to the bank to greet us. French cavalry! Had I even gotten twenty miles?

Well, better them than Bin Sadr. They'd take me to Bonaparte, while the Arab would do things to Astiza and me that I didn't even want to think about. When we met Napoleon, Astiza could simply claim I'd kidnapped her, and I'd confirm it. I considered grabbing the medallion from her pretty neck and hurling it into the Nile, but couldn't bring myself to do it. I'd invested too much. Besides, I was as curious about what it might lead to as anyone. It was our only map to the Book of Thoth.

"You'd best hide that," I told her.

She slipped it between her breasts.

We grounded on a sandbank and splashed ashore. Bin Sadr's felucca was still working its way against the current toward our position, the Arabs shouting and firing into the air. The dozen French horsemen had spread into a semicircle to close with us, preventing any chance of escape, and I raised my hands in surrender. Soon we were ringed with dusty horses.

"Ethan Gage?"

"At your service, lieutenant."

"Why are you dressed like a heathen?"

"It's cooler."

His eyes kept straying to Astiza, not daring to ask why she was dressed as a harlot. In 1798, there were still some manners left. "I am Lieutenant Henri d'Bonneville. You are under arrest for theft of state property and destruction of antiquities, for murder, trespass, and disorder in Cairo, and for escape, evasion, misrepresentation, spying, and treason."

"Not murder at Dendara? We did kill Silano, I hope."

He stiffened. "The count is recovering from his injuries and is organizing a party to join our pursuit."

"You did forget kidnapping." I nodded at Astiza.

"I did not forget. The woman, having been rescued, will cooperate in the prosecution or be interrogated herself."

"It's the charge of treason I take exception to," I said. "I'm

American. Wouldn't I have to be French to betray your country?"

"Sergeant, bind them both."

The pursuing felucca grounded and Bin Sadr and his remaining band of cutthroats stormed ashore, pushing past the French cavalry horses like traders at a camel bazaar. "This one is mine!" the Arab snarled, shaking his snake-headed staff. I saw with some satisfaction that his left arm was in a sling. Well, if I couldn't kill the rotten pair outright, then maybe I could peck away at them, like the French were doing to Nelson.

"I see you've become a sailor, Achmed," I greeted. "Fall off your camel?"

"He will come on my boat!"

"I'm afraid I must disagree, monsieur," Lieutenant d'Bonneville said. "The fugitive Gage surrendered to my cavalry and is wanted for questioning by French authorities. He is under army jurisdiction now."

"The American killed some of my men!"

"Which you can take up with him when we're done, if there's anything left to address."

Well, there was a cheery thought.

Bin Sadr scowled. Now he had a boil on his other cheek, and I wondered if he simply had a bad complexion or if Astiza had been up to more mischief. Any chance she could give the devil leprosy, or maybe the plague?

"Then we take the woman." His men nodded in wicked agreement.

"I think not, monsieur." The lieutenant gave a quick glance to his sergeant, who in turn flashed a look to his men. The carbines that had been aimed at me swung in the direction of Bin Sadr's gang. Their muskets in turn tilted toward the French cavalry. It was a considerable relief not to have everyone aiming at me, and I tried to think how I could take advantage of it.

"Do not make me your enemy, Frenchman," Bin Sadr growled.

"You are a paid mercenary with no authority," d'Bonneville crisply replied. "If you don't get back in your boat this instant, I will arrest you for insubordination and consider whether to hang you as well." He glanced about imperiously. "That is, if I can find a tree."

There was a long moment of awful silence, the sun so intense it seemed to make a background sizzle. Then one of the cavalrymen coughed, jerking, and as he sagged we heard the report of the distant shot that had killed him, echoing off the Nile hills. Then more gunshots sounded, and one of Bin Sadr's men grunted and went down.

Now all the guns swung to the ridge above the river. A line of men had crested and spilled down it, robes billowing, lances sparkling. It was a company of Mamelukes! We'd been caught by a unit of the elusive Murad Bey, and it looked like they outnumbered the lot of us, five to one.

"Dismount!" d'Bonneville cried. "Form a skirmish line!" He turned to the Arabs. "Form with us!"

But the Arabs were running for their felucca, clambering on board, and shoving off into the Nile.

"Bin Sadr, you damned coward!" d'Bonneville roared.

The Arab's gesture was obscene.

So now the Frenchmen turned alone to the Mameluke assault. "Fire!" The lieutenant's cry brought a ragged volley of cavalry carbines, but this was no disciplined salvo from a French infantry square. A few Mamelukes tumbled and then they overran us. I waited for the thrust of a lance, wondering what the gambling odds were to encounter three enemies on one patch of riverbank at one time: the ill-fortuned opposite of a face-card triplet in a high-stakes game of *brelan,* I supposed. Then the Mameluke I expected would kill me leaned from his saddle, arm outstretched, and plucked me off the ground like a grape. I yelped, but his arm was a vise round my chest. He hurtled on through the French ranks straight toward the Arab boat, warbling a war cry as I dangled, sword held high in his other hand while he steered his mount with his knees. "Now I avenge my brother! Stand and fight, viper!"

It was Ashraf!

We crashed into the shallows, water spraying, and Bin Sadr turned to meet us from the bow of his boat, one-armed as well. Ash swung and the snake-headed staff came up to meet him. There was a clang, like steel upon steel, and I realized the staff had some kind of metal core. The fury of the Mameluke's charge shoved the Arab backward with a grunt, but as he fell among his fellows the others fired and Ash was forced to swerve. The boat drifted into deeper water. Then we were galloping away, even as shouts, cries, and shots sounded from the battle behind. I was slung over the saddle like a bag of wheat, the wind knocked out of me, and I could barely see back through our dust. The officer who'd saved us was already down, I glimpsed, a Mameluke crouched over him with a knife. Another hussar was crawling with a lance jutting from his back, trying to slice an enemy's throat before dying himself. Capture was worse than death, and the soldiers were selling their lives as dearly as they could. Bin Sadr's Arabs were drifting farther out into the river, not even bothering to shoot in support.

We galloped up a long dune and stopped at its crest, overlooking the Nile. Ash released his grip and I dropped to my feet. As I staggered for balance, his grin had an edge of pain to it.

"Always I am having to rescue you, my friend. At some point my debt from the Battle of the Pyramids will be repaid."

"It has been more than paid already," I wheezed, watching as another horse galloped up and Astiza, slung like I was, her hair drooping down, was unceremoniously dropped by another warrior. I looked down at the river. The little skirmish had ended, the Frenchmen sprawled and still. Bin Sadr had raised sail and was making his way upriver toward Desaix and Dendara, probably to report my likely massacre. I had a hunch the bastard would claim my supposed killing for himself. Silano, however, would want to make sure.

"So you have joined the bey," I said.

"Murad is going to win, sooner or later."

"Those were good men just slain."

"As my good friends were slaughtered at the pyramids. War is where good men die."

"How did you find us?"

"I joined my people and trailed you, figuring Bin Sadr would as well. You do have a knack for trouble, American."

"And for getting out of it, thanks to you." Now I saw a stain of red on his robes. "You've been wounded!"

"Bah! Another scratch from a nest of snakes, enough to keep me from finishing the coward, yes, but not enough to kill me." Yet he was leaning now, clearly hurt. "Someday I will catch him alone, and then we'll see who is scratched. Or perhaps fate has another misery in store for him. I can hope."

"You need to get that dressed!"

"Let me look at it," Astiza said.

He stiffly dismounted, breathing shallowly and embarrassed as the woman sliced open the robe at his torso to inspect the damage.

"The ball passed through your side as if you were a ghost, but you're losing blood. Here, we'll use your turban to bind it. This is a serious wound, Ashraf. You're not going to be riding for a while, unless you're anxious to get to paradise."

"And leave you two fools alone?"

"Maybe that, too, the gods intended. Ethan and I must finish this."

"If I leave him for a moment he puts himself in peril!"

"I'll look after him, now."

Ashraf considered. "Yes, you will." Then he whistled. Two fine Arabian mounts came trotting over the rise, saddled and with manes and tails flouncing. They were better horses than I'd ever had. "Take these, then, and give a prayer for the men who recently rode them. Here is a sword from Murad Bey, Gage. If any Mamelukes try to take you, show it and they will leave you alone." He glanced at Astiza. "Are you going back to the pyramids?"

"That's where Egypt begins and ends," she said.

"Ride hard, for the French and their Arabs will be after you soon enough. Safeguard the magic you bear or destroy it, but don't let it fall into the hands of your enemies. Here, a robe against the sun." He gave her a cape, then turned to me. "Where's your famous rifle?"

"Silano stuck his sword in it."

He looked puzzled.

"It was the oddest thing. Jammed his rapier down the barrel, and I was so angry that I pulled the trigger and my oldest friend blew up. Served him right when Astiza pulled a roof down on him, but the bastard survived."

Ashraf shook his head. "He has the luck of the demon god Ras al-Ghul. And someday, friend, when the French are gone, you and I will sit and try to make sense of what you just said!" He painfully mounted and slowly rode down to meet the others, amid the wreckage and the bodies of war.

We galloped north as he instructed, following the river. It would be more than two hundred miles back to the pyramids. There were satchels of bread, dates, and water on the horses, but by sunset we were exhausted from travel and tension, having had no sleep the night before. We stopped at a small village by the Nile and were given shelter in the simple hospitality Egyptians habitually display, falling asleep before we could finish our dinner. The charity we were shown was astounding, given that these people were taxed unmercifully by the Mamelukes and looted by the French. Yet what little these poor peasants had they shared with us, and after we fell asleep they covered us with their own thin blankets, after dressing the cuts and scratches we'd received. As we'd instructed, we were roused two hours before first light and pushed north again.

The second night found us sore but somewhat more recovered, and we took our own private shelter in a riverside orchard of palms away from houses, humans, or dogs. We needed some time to ourselves. Since the attack of the Mamelukes we'd seen no forces from either side, just timeless villages in their timeless cycle. The inhabitants were working from reed rafts because the risen Nile had flooded their fields, bringing fresh silt from the mysterious center of Africa.

I used some flint and Ash's sword to make a fire. As the night deepened, the nearness of the rolling Nile seemed reassuring, a promise that life would go on. Both of us were in shock from the events of the past days and weeks, and we sensed this interlude of quiet wouldn't last long. Somewhere to the south, Bin Sadr and Silano were no doubt discovering that we weren't dead and starting their pursuit. So we were grateful for the quiet of the stars, the cushioning embrace of sand, and the lamb and fruit we'd been given by the last village.

Astiza had taken the medallion out again to wear, and I had to admit it looked better on her than me. I'd decided I trusted her, because she could have warned Silano of my tomahawk, or fled from me with the talisman after the pillars came down, or left me after the river fight. She hadn't, and I remembered what she'd said on the boat: that she hadn't loved *him*. I'd been turning the phrase over in my head ever since, but still wasn't sure what to do with it.

"You're not certain exactly what secret door we're looking for?" I asked her instead.

She smiled sadly. "I'm not even sure it should, or can, be found. And yet why would Isis allow us to come this far, if not for a reason?"

In my experience, God didn't care much about reasons, but I didn't say that. Instead, I gathered up my courage. "I've already found my secret," I said.

"What?"

"You."

Even by the light of the fire I could see her blush as she turned away. So I put my hand to her cheek and turned her back toward me.

"Listen, Astiza, I've had a lot of hard desert miles to think. The sun had the breath of a lion, and the sand burned through my boots. There were days when Ashraf and I lived on mud and fried locusts. Yet I didn't think of that. I thought of you. If this Book of Thoth is a book of wisdom, maybe it would simply say to find what you already have, and to enjoy this day instead of worrying about the next one."

"That doesn't sound like my restless wanderer."

"The truth of the matter is, I fell in love with you, too," I confessed. "Almost from the very beginning, when I pulled the wreckage off you and saw you were a woman. It was just hard to admit to myself." And I kissed her, foreigner though

I was, and damn if she didn't kiss back, more greedily than I expected. There's nothing like surviving a scrape or two to bring a man and woman together.

Isis, it turns out, is not as prudish a god as some of the more modern ones, and Astiza seemed to have as good an idea of what she wanted as I did. If the medallion looked fine on her tattered harem clothes, it looked positively glorious on her breast and belly, so we let the moon clothe us, made a little bed of our meager things, and lived for this night as if another might never come.

The trinket did prick when it got between us, so she took it off and left it for a time in the sand. Her skin was as perfect as the sculpted desert, her scent as sweet as the holy lotus. There is more sacred mystery in the soul and presence of a woman than in any dusty pyramid. I worshipped her like a shrine and explored her like a temple, and she whispered in my ear, "This, for one night, is immortality."

Later, lying on her back, she let the medallion's chain curl on her fingers and pointed to the sky and its crescent moon. "Look," she said. "The knife of Thoth."

CHAPTER TWENTY-TWO

Our ride back north toward Cairo was a journey through layers of time. Grassy mounds marked the remains of ancient cities, peasants told us. Rolling dunes sometimes revealed the tip of a buried temple or sanctuary. Near Minya we came across two colossal stone baboons, fat and polished, their serene gaze toward the rising sun. They were twice the height of a man, draped in what looked like feathered cloaks, as majestic as nobles and as timeless as the Sphinx. The gigantic apes were manifestations, of course, of the mysterious Thoth.

We skirted hundreds of mud-brick villages by riding on the desert fringe next to ranks of date palms, as if the green sward were a sea lapping at a beach. We passed a dozen pyramids I hadn't seen before, some crumbled into little more than hills and others still showing their original geometry. Fragments of temples littered the sand around them. Ruined causeways sloped down to the lush green bottomland of the Nile. Pillars jutted into the air, holding up nothing. Astiza and I moved in our own small bubble, aware of our mission and possible pursuit, yet oddly content. Our alliance was a refuge from anxiety and burden. Two had become one, ambiguity had been replaced with commitment, and aimlessness had found purpose. As Enoch had suggested, I'd found something to believe in. Not empires, not medallions, not magic, and not electricity, but partnership with the woman beside me. Everything else could start from that.

The trio of pyramids that were our goal finally rose from the rim of the desert like islands from the sea. We'd ridden hard to arrive on October 21, the date I'd guessed had some mysterious significance. The weather had cooled, the sky a perfect blue dome, the sun a dependable god's chariot drawing its daily transect of heaven. The high Nile was just visible through its belt of trees. For hours the monuments seemed to get no closer. Then, as the afternoon's shadows began to lengthen, they appeared to inflate like one of Conte's balloons, huge, beckoning, and forbidding. They reared out of the earth, as if their apex had erupted from the underworld.

That image gave me a thought.

"Let me see the medallion," I suddenly asked Astiza.

She took it off, the yellow metal on fire in the sun. I looked at the overlapping Vs of its arms, one pointed up, the other pointed down. "This looks like two pyramids, doesn't it? Their bases joined, and their summit pointed in opposite directions?"

"Or the reflection of a single one in a mirror or water."

"As if there was as much below the surface as above, like the roots of a tree."

"You think there's something under the pyramid?"

"There was under that temple of Isis. What if the medallion represents not the outside, but the inside? When we explored the interior with Bonaparte, the shafts inside sloped like the pyramid's sides. The angles were different, but an echo of them. Suppose this is not a symbol of the pyramids, but a map of pyramid shafts?"

"You mean the ascending and descending corridors?"

"Yes. There was a tablet on the ship I came to Egypt on." I'd suddenly remembered the silver-and-black tablet of Cardinal Bembo that Monge had showed me in *L'Orient*'s treasure hold. "It was filled with levels and figures as if it might be a map or diagram of some underground place with different levels."

"There are stories that the ancients had books to instruct the dead how to negotiate the perils and monsters of the underworld," she said. "Thoth would weigh their heart, and their book would guide them past cobras and crocodiles. If their book was correct they would emerge on the other side into paradise. What if there is some truth to this? What if somehow bodies interred in the pyramid actually took a physical journey through some cavernous gauntlet?"

"That could explain the absence of any mummies," I mused. "But when we explored the pyramid we confirmed that its descending corridor dead-ends. It doesn't rise again in the opposite direction like this medallion. There is no descending V."

"That is true of the corridors we know," Astiza said, suddenly excited. "But what side of the pyramid is the entrance on?"

"The north."

"And what constellation does the medallion display?"

"Alpha Draconis, the polestar when the pyramids were built. So?"

"Hold the medallion out as if the constellation were in the sky."

I did so. The circular disc was held against the northern sky, light shining through the tiny perforations and making the pattern of Draconis, the dragon. When I did so, the medallion's arms were perpendicular to north.

"If that medallion were a map, which sides of the pyramid would the shafts be on?" Astiza asked.

"East and west!"

"Meaning perhaps there are entrances not yet discovered on the east or west flanks of the pyramids," she reasoned.

"But why haven't they been found? People have climbed all over the pyramids."

Astiza frowned. "I don't know."

"And why the connections to Aquarius, the rising Nile, and this time of year?

"I don't know that, either."

And then we saw a scrap of white, like snow, in the desert.

It was a curious tableau. French officers, aides, savants, and servants were arranged in a semicircle for a picnic in the desert, their horses and donkeys picketed behind. The party faced the pyramids. Camp field tables had been put end to end and covered with white linen. Felucca sails had been rigged as canopies, with captured Mameluke lances as tent poles and French cavalry sabers thrust into the sand as pegs. French crystal and golden Egyptian goblets had been laid out with heavy European silver and china. Bottles of wine were open and half-empty. There were lavish heaps of fruit, bread, cheese and meat. Candles were ready for lighting. Seated on folding stools were Bonaparte and several of his generals and scientists, all of them chatting amiably. I also spotted my mathematician friend, Monge.

Dressed as we were in Arab robes, an aide-de-camp came to shoo us away like any other curious Bedouins. Then he noticed my complexion and Astiza's beauty, only partly covered under the tattered cloak that she'd drawn around her as best she could. He gaped more at her than me, of course, and while he was doing so, I addressed him in French.

"I'm Ethan Gage, the American savant. I'm here to report that my investigations are nearing completion."

"Investigations?"

"Of the secrets of the pyramid."

He went to murmur my message and Bonaparte stood, peering like a leopard. "It's Gage, popping up like the very devil," he muttered to the others. "And his woman."

He beckoned us forward and the soldiers looked greedily at Astiza, who kept her gaze over their heads and walked with as much decorum as our costumes would allow. The men restrained from rude comment because there was something different about us, I think, some subtle signs of partnership and propriety that signaled we were a couple, and that she was to be respected and left alone. So their gaze reluctantly turned from her to me.

"What are you doing in that dress-up?" Bonaparte demanded. "And didn't you desert my command?" He turned to Kleber. "I thought he deserted."

"Damned rascal broke out of jail and eluded a pursuing patrol, if I recall," the general said. "Disappeared into the desert."

Thankfully, word did not appear to have reached them of the events at Dendara. "To the contrary, I've been much at risk in your service," I said blithely. "My companion here was held for ransom by Silano and the Arab, Achmed bin Sadr: her life for the medallion we've discussed. It was her courage and my own determination that got us free to resume our studies. I've come looking for Doctor Monge to consult on a mathematical question that I hope will shed light on the pyramids."

Bonaparte looked at me with disbelief. "Do you think me an idiot? You said the medallion was lost."

"I said so only to keep it from Count Silano, who does not have your interests, or those of France, at heart."

"So you lied."

"I dissembled to protect the truth from those who would misuse it. Please listen, General. I'm not jailed, not captured, and not fleeing. *I* came looking for *you* because I think I'm near a major discovery. All I need now is the help of the other savants."

He looked from me to Astiza, half-angry and half-amused. Her presence gave me a curious immunity. "I don't know whether to reward you or shoot you, Ethan Gage. There's something baffling about you, something that goes beyond your crude American habits and rustic education."

"I just try the best I can, sir."

"The best you can!" He looked to the others, because I'd given him a subject to pontificate on. "It is never enough to *do* your best, you must *be* the best. Is this not true? I do what's necessary to exert my will!"

I bowed. "And I am a gambler, General. My will is irrelevant if the cards don't go my way. Whose fortune doesn't vary? Isn't it true you were a hero at Toulon, then imprisoned briefly after the fall of Robespierre, and then a hero again when your cannon saved the Directory?"

He scowled a moment, then shrugged as if to concede the point, and finally smiled. If Napoleon didn't suffer fools, he did enjoy the stimulation of argument. "True enough, American. True enough. Will *and* luck. In one day I went from a cheap Parisian hotel, in debt for my uniform, to having my own house, coach, and team. In one day of fortune!" He addressed the others. "Do you know what happened to Josephine? She was imprisoned too, destined for the guillotine. In the morning the jailer took her pillow away, saying she wouldn't need it because by nightfall she wouldn't have a head! Yet just hours later word came that Robespierre was dead, assassinated, that the Terror had ended, and that instead of being executed, she was free. Choice *and* destiny: What a game we play!"

"Destiny seems to have trapped us in Egypt," a half-drunken Kleber said. "And war is not a game."

"On the contrary, Kleber, it is the ultimate game, with death or glory the stakes. Refuse to play and you only guarantee defeat. Right, Gage?"

"Not every game must be played, General." How strange this man was, who mixed political clarity with emotional restlessness, and the grandest dreams with the meanest cynicism, daring us to call him on it. A game? Is that what he'd say to the dead?

"No? Life itself is war, and all of us are defeated in the end, by death. So we do what we can to make ourselves immortal. The pharaoh chose that pyramid. I choose . . . fame."

"And some men choose home and family," Astiza said quietly. "They live through their children."

"Yes, that's enough for them. But not for me, or the men who follow me. We want the immortality of history." Bonaparte took a swallow of wine. "What a philosopher you've made me at this meal! Consider your woman, there, Gage. Fortune is a woman. Grasp her today, or you will not have her tomorrow." He smiled dangerously, his gray eyes dancing. "A beautiful woman," he told his companions, "who tried to shoot me."

"It turns out, General, that she was trying to shoot *me*."

He laughed. "And now you're a pair! But of course! Fortune also turns enemies into allies, and strangers into confidants!" Then he abruptly sobered. "But I'll not have you running around the desert in Egyptian dress until this matter with Silano is sorted out. I don't understand what's going on between you and the count, but I don't like it. It's important we all stay on the same side. We're discussing the next stage of our invasion, the conquest of Syria."

"Syria? But Desaix is still pursuing Murad Bey in Upper Egypt."

"Mere skirmishing. We have the means to push north and east as well. The world awaits me, even if the Egyptians can't seem to grasp how I could remake their lives." His smile was tight, his disappointment obvious. His promise of Western technology and government had not won the population over. The reformer I'd seen in the great cabin of *L'Orient* was changing, his dreams of enlightenment dashed by the seeming obtuseness of the people he'd come to save. Napoleon's last innocence had evaporated in the desert heat. He waved aside a fly. "Meanwhile, I want this pyramid mystery resolved."

"Which I can best do without the count's interference, General."

"Which you *will* do with the count's cooperation. Right, Monge?"

The mathematician looked puzzled. "I suppose it depends on what Monsieur Gage thinks he has figured out."

And then there was a rumble, like distant thunder.

We turned toward Cairo, its minarets lacy across the Nile. Then another echo, and another. It was the report of cannon.

"What's that?" Napoleon asked no one in particular.

A column of smoke began rising into the clear sky. The gunfire went on, a low mutter, and then more smoke appeared. "Something's happening in the city," Kleber said.

"Obviously." Bonaparte turned to his aides. "Get this mess packed away. Where's my horse?"

"I think it may be an uprising," Kleber added uneasily. "There's been street rumor, and mullahs calling from their towers. We didn't take it seriously."

"No. The Egyptians have not taken *me* seriously."

The little party had lost all focus on me. Camels lurched

upright, horses whinnied in excitement, and men ran to their mounts. As sabers were pulled from the sand, the awnings began to droop. The Egyptians were rising in Cairo.

"What about him?" the aide-de-camp said, pointing at me.

"Leave him for now," Bonaparte said. "Monge! You and the savants take Gage and the girl with you. Get back to the institute, close the doors, and let no one in. I'll send a company of infantry to protect you. The rest of you, follow me!" And he set off on a gallop across the sands toward the boats that had transported them across the river.

As the soldiers and servants hurriedly packed away the last awnings and tables, Astiza quietly kept a candle. Then they scurried off too, following the trail of officers. In minutes we were left alone with Monge, except for the footprints of the vanished banquet. A whirlwind had passed, once more leaving us all breathless.

M y dear Ethan," Monge finally said as we watched the exodus toward the Nile, "you do have a way of arriving with trouble."

"I've been trying since Paris to stay out of it, Dr. Monge, with little success." The sound of revolt was an unmelodic rattle echoing across the river.

"Come, then. We scientists will keep our heads down during this latest emergency."

"I can't go back to Cairo with you, Gaspard. My business is with this pyramid. Look, I've got the medallion and am on the brink of understanding, I think." At my gesture, Astiza brought out the pendant. Monge started at the new design and its seeming Masonic symbolism.

"As you can see," I went on, "we've found another piece. This trinket is a kind of map, I think, to hidden places in the Great Pyramid, the one you said embodied pi. The key is this triangle of scratches on the central disc. In a tomb to the south I realized they must represent Egyptian numbers. I think they're a mathematical clue, but of what?"

"Scratches? Let me see it again." He took the piece from Astiza and studied it under a hand lens.

"Imagine each bunch of scratches as a digit," I said.

He counted silently as his lips moved, then looked surprised. "But of course! Why didn't I see this before? Now this *is* an odd pattern, but appropriate given where we are. Oh dear, what a disappointment." He looked at me with pity, and my heart began to sink. "Gage, have you ever heard of Pascal's triangle?"

"No, sir."

"Named for Blaise Pascal, who wrote a treatise on this particular progression of numbers just one hundred and fifty years ago. He said many wise things, not the least of which was the more he'd seen of men, the better he liked his dog. See, it's a pyramidal kind of progression." Borrowing a dragoon's saber, he began scratching in the sand and drew a number pattern that looked like this:

"There! You see the pattern?"

I must have looked like a goat trying to read Thucydides. Groaning inwardly, I remembered Jomard and his Fibonacci numbers.

"Except for the ones," Monge said patiently, "you'll notice that every number is the sum of the two numbers to each side above it. See that first 2? Above it are two 1s. And the 3 there: above it are a 1 and a 2. The 6? Above it are two 3s. That's Pascal's triangle. That's just the beginning of the patterns you can detect, but the point is that the triangle can be extended downward indefinitely. Now, look at the scratches on your medallion."

"It's the start of the same triangle!" I exclaimed. "But what does that mean?"

Monge passed the medallion back. "It means the pendant can't possibly be ancient Egyptian. I'm sorry, Ethan, but if this is Pascal's triangle, your entire quest has been futile."

"What?"

"No ancient mathematicians knew this pattern. It must undoubtedly be a modern fraud."

I felt as if I'd been hit by a blow to the stomach. A fraud? Was this one of the tricks of the old conjurer Cagliostro? Had this long journey—Talma's and Enoch's death—been for nothing? "But it looks like a pyramid!"

"Or a pyramid looks like a triangle. What better way to pass on a crude piece of old jewelry than by linking it to the pyramids of Egypt? Yet it was probably some scholar's toy or good-luck piece, with pi and the legs of a compass. Perhaps it was a joke. Who knows? I merely suspect, my friend, that you've been duped by some kind of charlatan. The soldier you won it from, perhaps." He put his hand on my shoulder. "There's no embarrassment. All of us know that you're not really a savant."

I was reeling. "I was sure we were so close . . ."

"I like you, Ethan, and don't want to see you come to any harm. So let me give you some advice. Don't go back to Cairo. God knows what's happening there." The sounds of firing kept getting louder. "Bonaparte suspects your uselessness, and frustration is making him impatient. Take a boat to Alexandria with Astiza and take ship for America. The British will let you through if you explain yourself, as you do so well. Go home, Ethan Gage." He shook my hand. "Go home."

I stood in shock, barely comprehending that all my exertions had been for nothing. I'd been certain the medallion pointed a way into the pyramid, and now the greatest mathematician in France had told me I'd been bilked! Monge smiled at me sadly. And then, gathering up his few belongings, he mounted the donkey that had borne him here and slowly began riding back to the capital and his institute, gunfire growling in the distance.

He turned. "I wish I could do the same!"

* * *

Astiza was looking after Monge in frustration, her face dark and contemptuous. When he was out of earshot she exploded. "That man is a fool!"

I was startled. "Astiza, he has one of the finest minds in all of France."

"Who apparently believes that learning begins and ends with his pompous opinions and his own European ancestors. Could he build this pyramid? Of course not. And yet he insists that the people who built it knew far less of numbers than him, or this Pascal."

"He didn't put it that way."

"Look at those patterns in the sand! Don't they look like the pyramid before you?"

"Yes."

"And yet they have nothing to do with why we are here? I don't believe it."

"But what's the connection?"

She looked from sand to pyramid, pyramid to sand. "It is obvious, I think. These numbers correspond to the blocks of the pyramid. A single one at the top, missing now. Then two on this face, then three, and so on. Row after row, block after block. If you follow this pattern, each block will have a number. This Monge is blind."

Could she be right? I felt a rising excitement. "Let's complete a few more rows."

The pattern soon became more apparent. Not only did the numbers grow rapidly bigger near the pyramid's apothem, the imaginary line that bisected the pyramid's face, but to either side of this center point they would pair outward. The next line, for example, read 1, 5, 10, 10, 5, 1. Then 1, 6, 15, 20, 15, 6, 1. And so on, each row getting broader and its numbers bigger. By the thirteenth row from the top, the center number was 924.

"What number are we looking for?" I asked.

"I don't know."

"Then what good is this?"

"It will make sense when we see it."

On we figured. As the sun sank toward the western horizon

the pyramid shadows lengthened. Astiza touched my arm and pointed to the south. There was a plume of dust that way, marking the approach of a sizable party. I felt uneasy. If Silano and Bin Sadr had survived, that was the direction they'd be coming from. To the northeast we could begin to see the glow of fires in Cairo and hear the now-steady roar of French artillery. A full-scale battle had broken out in the supposedly pacified capital. Napoleon's grip was more fragile than it seemed. I saw a round bag begin to lift into the air. It was Conte's balloon, no doubt being used by observers to direct the fight.

"We'd better hurry," I muttered.

I began sketching numbers faster, but each row added to the sequence was two numbers longer than the one before, and more complicated. What if we made a mistake? Astiza helped fill in the numbers with the necessary arithmetic, murmuring as she added in her quick mind. On and on our pyramid grew, number by number, block by block, as if we were duplicating its construction on the sand. Soon my back ached, my eyes began to blur. Numbers, numbers, numbers. Was it all a hoax, as Monge had implied? Had the ancient Egyptians known such puzzles? Why would they invent something so obscure and then leave a clue to find it? Finally, some one hundred and fifty rows of blocks from the top, we came to a stone that had the same digits as what the mathematician had told me was the Egyptian value for pi: 3160.

I stopped, stunned. Of course! The medallion was a map to a certain point on the pyramid! Face north. Imagine a shaft and door on the west or east faces. Remember pi. Look for a block valued pi under this ancient number game. Time it to Aquarius as the Egyptian used the sign, for the rising of the Nile, and . . . enter.

If I was right.

The western face of the pyramid glowed pink as we began to climb it. It was late in the afternoon, the sun low and fat, like Conte's balloon. Our horses were tied below, and the sounds of gunfire in Cairo were muffled by the bulk of the monument between us and the city. As before, our climb was an awkward scramble, the blocks high, steep, and eroded. I counted as we climbed, trying to find the row and block that corresponded to pi, the eternal number codified into the dimensions of the pyramid.

"What if the numbers refer to the facing stones, now gone?" I said.

"They would match these inner ones, I hope. Or close to it. This medallion would be directing us to a stone that led to the core."

We had just reached the fifty-third row, panting, when Astiza pointed. "Ethan, look!"

Rounding the corner of the adjacent pyramid was a party of galloping horsemen. One of them spied us, and they began to shout. Even in the dying light I had no trouble making out the bandaged figures of Bin Sadr and Silano, lashing at lathered horses. If this didn't work we were dead—or worse than dead, if Bin Sadr had his way.

"We'd better find that stone."

We counted. There were thousands of blocks on this western face, of course, and when we came to the supposed candidate, it looked no different than its brothers around it. Here was a rock eroded by millennia of time, weighing several tons, and firmly wedged by the colossal weight above it. I pushed, heaved, and kicked, to no effect.

A bullet pinged off the stonework.

"Stop! Think!" Astiza urged. "There has to be a special way or any fool could have stumbled upon this." She held up the medallion. "It must have something to do with this."

More shots pattered around us.

"We're like targets on a wall up here," I muttered.

She looked out. "No. He needs us alive to tell him what we've discovered. Bin Sadr will enjoy making us talk."

Indeed, Silano was shouting at those who had fired and shoving their muskets down, instead pushing them toward the base of the pyramid.

"Great." I fumbled with the medallion. Suddenly I realized the second pyramid was shadowing our own, its long triangle reaching across the sands and climbing the layers of stone to where we were standing, pointing at us. Its capstone was intact, its point more perfect, and its apex seemed to shadow a block a few to the right and several courses lower than where we were standing. Each day, as the sun marched along the horizon, the shadow would touch a different stone, and this was the date I'd surmised from the calendar. Was our count of the blocks off slightly? I bounded down to just above the shadow and held the medallion up to the sun. Light shone through the tiny perforated holes, making a star pattern of Draconis on the sandstone.

"There!" Astiza pointed. A faint tracery of holes, or rather chisel points, near the base of the stone, mimicking the constellation pattern on the medallion. And beneath it, the joint between our stone and the one below was slightly wider than the usual. I crouched and blew the dust away from this tiniest of cracks. There was the subtlest of Masonic signs chiseled into the stone as well.

I could hear Arabs shouting to each other as they started to climb. "Gage, give it up!" Silano called. "You're too late!"

I could feel a shallow breath of wind, air coming from some hollowness on the other side. "It's here," I whispered. I slammed the stone with my palm. "Move, damn you!"

Then I recalled what others had named the medallion since I'd won it. A key. I tried sliding the disc into the crack but it was slightly convex and its swell wouldn't fit.

I looked back down. Now Silano and Bin Sadr were climbing as well.

So I reversed the pendant, easing in the linked arms. They stuck, I jiggled, they moved in farther . . .

Suddenly there was a click. As if pulled by a string, the medallion arms jerked deeper into the stone, the disc breaking off and bouncing down the blocks toward Silano. There was the creak and groan of stone upon stone. The men below us were shouting.

The stone had suddenly become weightless, lifted a fraction of an inch off the rock below. I pushed, and now it rotated in and up as if it were made of down, revealing a dark shaft that sloped downward at the same precarious angle of the descending corridor I'd explored with Napoleon. A ten-thousand-pound block of stone had become a feather. The key had disappeared into the rock as if swallowed.

We'd found the secret. Where was Astiza?

"Ethan!"

I whirled. She'd climbed down the precipitous slope to nab the disc. Silano's hand had closed on her cloak. She wrenched free, leaving him holding cloth, and scrambled back upward. I pulled out Ash's sword and leaped down to help. Silano pulled out a new rapier of his own, eyes gleaming.

"Shoot him!" Bin Sadr shouted.

"No. This time he has no trick with his rifle. He's mine."

I decided to forego finesse for brute desperation. Even as his blade whickered through the air toward my torso, I yelled like a Viking and cleaved down as if I were chopping wood. I was a course higher than him, giving me a two-foot height advantage, and was so quick he was forced to parry instead of thrust. Steel rang on steel and his blade bent under my blow, not breaking but twisting against his wrist. It was still sore, I gambled, from when my rifle exploded. He turned to save his grip but the move cost him his balance. Cursing, he lurched and collided with some of the other brigands. The lot of them went spilling down, clutching at the rock to arrest their bumpy fall. I threw the sword like a spear, hoping to stick Bin Sadr, but he ducked and another villain took the point instead, howling as he tumbled.

Now Bin Sadr charged up at me, a deadly point jutting from the end of his snake-headed staff. He thrust. I dodged, but not quite quick enough. The blade, sharp as a razor, shallowly sliced my shoulder. Before he could twist to cut deeper, a stone hit him in the face. Astiza, her hair wild as a Medusa, was hurling down broken pieces of pyramid.

Bin Sadr was sore too, wielding the staff with one arm because of his bullet wound, and I sensed a chance to truly unsettle him. I grabbed the snake shaft, hauling upward, even as he desperately pulled it back, blinking against Astiza's bombardment of rocks. I relaxed my grip for a moment and he tilted dangerously backward, unbalanced. Then I jerked again and he lost the staff entirely and fell, bouncing down several courses of stones. His face was bloody, his precious staff mine. For the first time I saw a flicker of fear.

"Give it back!"

"It's firewood, bastard."

Astiza and I retreated to the hole we'd made, our only refuge, and crawled inside. Bracing ourselves against the walls of the shaft so we wouldn't slide, we reached up and pulled at the entrance stone. Bin Sadr was scrambling up toward us like a madman, howling with rage. The block came down as easily as it had risen, but as it swung it retrieved its own weight, gaining momentum, and it slammed shut in the villain's face with a boom like a great boulder. In an instant we were plunged into darkness.

We could hear faint howls of frustration as the Arabs pounded on the stone door from the outside. Then Silano called out, in rage and determination, "Gunpowder!"

We might not have much time.

It was black as a bowel until Astiza struck something on the sides of the shaft and I saw the glint of sparks. She lit the candle she'd taken from Napoleon's table. So dark was it that the shaft seemed to flare from this feeble light. I blinked, breathing hard, trying to collect myself for the next step. There was an alcove next to the entrance, I saw, and in it, jutting up to and connected by a hinged arm to the stone door we'd come through, was a shaft of glittering gold. The shaft was a stunning thing, at least two inches thick, the gold probably sheathing some base material from corrosion or rot. It seemed to be a mechanism to take up the weight of the stone door, moving up and down like a piston. There was a socket where it connected, and a long well that it descended through. I had no idea how it worked.

I tried tugging the door. It was wedged like a cork, once more impossibly heavy. Retreat seemed impossible. We were temporarily safe and permanently trapped. Then I noticed a detail I hadn't observed before. Ranked along the shaft wall, like a stand of arms, were dry brushwood torches, mummified by desiccation.

Someone wanted us to find our way to the bottom.

CHAPTER TWENTY-THREE

Once more the shaft seemed designed for the gliding of souls rather than the clambering of men. We half-slid, half-jammed our way down its slope. Why were there no steps? Had some kind of carts or sleds once ascended or descended here? Had the builders never expected to come this way? Or had these shafts been built for creatures or transport that we couldn't imagine? In the first thirty meters we passed three voids in the shaft's ceiling. When I lifted my torch I could see blocks of dark granite, suspended above. What were these ceiling pockets for?

We continued our descent. At length the man-made blocks gave way to walls of slick limestone, still perfectly straight and dressed. We'd passed beneath the pyramid proper and entered the bedrock of the limestone plateau it was built on. Down we went, deeper into the earth's bowels, far below the descending passage I'd explored with Jomard and Napoleon. The passage began to twist. A hint of air left a curl of torch smoke behind us. The smell was dusty rock.

Suddenly the passageway leveled to a tunnel so low we had to crawl on hands and knees. Then it opened up. When we stood and lifted the torch, we found ourselves in a limestone cavern. A worn channel showed where water had once run. High above were the stumps of stalactites. While the ceiling was made by nature, the walls had been chiseled smooth and covered with hieroglyphs and inscribed drawings. Once again, we couldn't read a word. The carvings were of squat, snarling creatures that obstructed twisting passageways filled with tongues of fire and drowning pools.

"The underworld," Astiza whispered.

Standing like reassuring and protective sentinels along the wall were statues of gods and pharaohs, the faces proud, the eyes serene, the lips thick, the muscles powerful. Carved cobras marked the doorways. A line of baboons made a crown molding near the stone roof. A statue of ibis-headed Thoth stood near the far doorway, his beak poised like the reed pen he held, his left hand holding a scale to weigh the human heart.

"My god, what is this place?" I murmured.

Astiza was tight to my side. It was cool in the cave, and she shivered in her diaphanous rags. "I think this is the real tomb. Not that bare room in the pyramid you described to me. The legends of Herodotus, that the true burial chamber is under the pyramid, may be true."

I put my arm around her. "Then why build a whole mountain atop it?"

"To hide it, to mark it, to seal, to mislead," she theorized. "This was a way to keep the tomb forever hidden, or to hide something else within it. Alternately, maybe the ancients always wanted to be able to find where the cave was by marking it with something so huge it could never be lost: the Great Pyramid."

"Because the cave was the real resting place of the pharaoh?"

"Or something even more important."

I looked at the ibis-headed statue. "You mean the prize everyone wants, this magical, all-knowing Book of Thoth."

"This may be where we find it, I think."

I laughed. "Then all we have to do is find our way back out!"

She looked at the ceiling. "Do you think the ancients hollowed this space out?"

"No. Our geologist Dolomieu said limestone gets carved by flowing water, and we know the Nile is close by. Sometime in the past, the river or a tributary probably flowed through this plateau. It may be sieved like a honeycomb.

When the Egyptians discovered this, they had an ideal hiding place—but only if it could be kept secret. I think you're right. Build a pyramid and everyone looks at *it,* not what's underneath."

She held my arm. "Perhaps the pyramid shafts Bonaparte explored were simply to convince the ordinary workers and architects that Pharaoh would be buried up there."

"Then some other group built the shaft we just came through and carved this writing. And they came down here and returned, right?" I tried to sound confident.

Astiza pointed. "No, they did not."

And ahead in the gloom, just past the feet of Thoth, I saw a carpet of bones and skulls, filling the cave from one side to the other. Death grins and blank sockets. With dread, we walked to inspect them. There were hundreds of human bodies, laid in neat rows. I saw no mark of weapons on their remains.

"Slaves and priests," she said, "poisoned, or with their throats slit, so they couldn't carry secrets out. This tomb was their last work."

I toed a skull. "Let's not make it ours. Come. I smell water."

We picked our way across the bone chamber as best we could, the dead rattling, and passed to another cave chamber with a pit in the middle. Here a ledge skirted the pit, and when we gingerly looked down it, our torchlight caught the reflection of water. It was a well. Rising out of the well and into a narrow hole in the ceiling was a golden shaft identical to the one I'd seen when we entered the pyramid. Was it the same? The cave could have twisted to lead us directly under the secret door, so that this shaft was the one that controlled the weight of the block we had entered past.

I reached out and touched the shaft. It rocked gently up and down as if floating. I looked more carefully. Down in the well, the shaft stuck straight up from a floating golden ball the diameter of a man. The shaft would push up or drop down depending on the level of the water. On the side of the well was a chiseled water gauge. I grasped the cool, slick coating of the shaft and pushed. The ball bobbed.

"Old Ben Franklin would have loved to guess what this is."

"The markings are similar to those on Nile meters used to measure the rise of the river," Astiza said. "The higher the rise, the richer that year's crops, and the greater the tax assessment the pharaoh would impose. But why measure down here?"

I could hear running water somewhere ahead. "Because this is connected to an underground branch of the Nile," I guessed. "As the river floods, this well would rise, and with it the shaft."

"But why?"

"Because it's a seasonal gate," I reasoned. "A lock that is timed. Remember how the calendar pointed to Aquarius and today's date, October 21? Whoever created the stone door that we came through designed it so it could only be opened at the time of maximum flooding, by someone who understood the secret of the medallion. As the river rises, it lifts that globe, pushing this shaft upward. It must lift a mechanism above which can hold the weight of the stone block so that, with the medallion key, it can be opened. In the dry season this cavern is locked tight."

"But why must we enter only when the Nile is high?"

I jiggled the shaft uneasily. "Good question."

We went on. The cave snaked so that I no longer knew what direction we were heading. Our first torches burned to stubs and we lit the next. I'm not a man afraid of tight spaces, but I felt buried down here. Underworld of Osiris indeed! And then we came to a large room that dwarfed any we'd seen so far, an underground chamber so large that our torchlight could not illuminate the far side. Instead, it made a path on dark water.

We stood on the shore of an underground lake, opaque and still, roofed by stone. In its middle was a small island. A marble pavilion, just four pillars and a roof, occupied its center. Heaped about its periphery were chests, statues, and shoals of smaller things that even at this distance gleamed and sparkled.

"Treasure." I tried to say it casually, but it came out as a croak.

"It's as Herodotus described," Astiza breathed, as if she still did not quite believe it herself. "The lake, the island—this is Pharaoh's real resting place. Undiscovered, never robbed. What a gift to see this!"

"We're rich," I added, my state of spiritual enlightenment not quite a match for commonsense greed. I'm not proud of my commercial instincts, but by heaven I'd been through hell the last few months and a little money would be just compensation. I was as transfixed by the valuables as I'd been by the riches in the hold of *L'Orient*. Their value to history didn't occur to me. I just wanted to get at the loot, bundle it up, and somehow sneak out of this sepulcher and past the French army.

Astiza squeezed my hand. "This is what the legends have been hinting at, Ethan. Eternal knowledge, so powerful that it had to be hidden until men and women were wise enough to use it. In that small temple, I suspect, we'll find it."

"Find what?" I was transfixed by the glint of gold.

"The Book of Thoth. The core truth of existence."

"Ah, yes. And are we ready for its answers?"

"We must safeguard it from heretics like the Egyptian Rite until we are."

I touched the water with my boot. "Too bad we don't have a spell to walk on water, because it looks like a cold swim."

"No, look. There's a boat to take Pharaoh to the sky."

Sitting beside the lake on a stone cradle, pretty as a schooner, was a narrow and graceful white boat with the high prow and stern of the type I'd seen in temple wall paintings. It was just big enough to float the two of us, and had a gilded oar to scull with. And why hadn't it rotted? Because it was not built of wood at all, but rather of hollowed alabaster with ribs and thwarts of gold. The polished stone was translucent, its texture velvet.

"Will rock float?"

"A thin pot will," she said. Handling the craft carefully, the two of us dragged it down to the opaque water. Ripples fanned out across a lake as smooth as a mirror.

"Do you think anything lives in this water?" I asked uneasily.

She climbed aboard. "I'll tell you when we get to the other side."

I boarded, the boat delicate as glass, and pushed off with Bin Sadr's staff. Then we glided toward the island, sculling and looking over the side for monsters.

It was not far—the temple was even smaller than I would have guessed. We grounded and got out to gape at a pharaoh's horde. There was a golden chariot with silver spears, polished furniture set with ebony and jade, cedar chests, jeweled armor, dog-headed gods, and jars of oil and spices. The hummock sparkled with precious gems like emeralds and rubies. There was turquoise, feldspar, jasper, cornelian, malachite, amber, coral, and lapis lazuli. There was a red granite sarcophagus, solid as a bunker, with a rock lid too heavy to lift without a dozen men. Was anyone inside? I'd little interest in finding out. The idea of grubbing into a pharaoh's grave didn't appeal to me. Helping myself to treasure did.

Yet Astiza had eyes for none of this. She barely glanced at the spectacular jewelry, dazzling robes, canopic jars, or golden plate. Instead, as if in a trance, she walked up a path sheathed in silver toward the little temple, its pillars carved with baboon-headed Thoths. I followed.

There was a marble table under the marble roof. On it was a red granite box, open on one side, and inside this a golden cube with golden doors. All this for a book or, more accurately, rolls of parchment? I pulled the small door handle. It opened as if oiled.

I reached inside . . .

And found nothing.

I felt with my hand in all directions and touched only slick gold lining. I snorted. "So much for wisdom."

"It's not there?"

"The Egyptians had no more answers than we do. It's all a myth, Astiza."

She was stunned. "Then why this temple? Why this box? Why those legends?"

I shrugged. "Maybe the library was the easy part. It was the book they never got around to writing."

She looked around suspiciously. "No. It's been stolen."

"I think it was never here."

She shook her head. "No. They would not have built that granite-and-gold vault for nothing. Somebody's been here before. Somebody high-ranking, with the knowledge of how to enter this place and yet the rage and pride not to respect the pyramid."

"And not take all this gold?"

"This prophet didn't care for gold. He was interested in the next world, not this one. Beside, gold is dross compared to the power of this book."

"A book of magic."

"Of power, wisdom, grace, serenity. A book of death and rebirth. A book of happiness. A book that inspired Egypt to become the world's greatest nation, and then inspired another people to influence the world."

"What other people? Who took it?"

She pointed. "He left his identity behind."

There, propped in one corner of the marble temple, was a shepherd's crook, or staff. It had the practically curved end to snare a sheep's neck. Its wood seemed marvelously preserved, and unlike a normal crook it was remarkable in its polish and tasteful carving, with a winged angel at the curved end and the blunt head of a serpent at the other. Midway down were two golden cherubim with wings extended to each other, a bracket holding them to the staff. Yet it was still a modest object in the midst of a pharaoh's horde.

"What the devil is that?"

"The rod of the most famous magician in history," Astiza said.

"Magician?"

"The prince of Egypt who became a liberator."

I stared at her. "You're saying *Moses* was down here?"

"Doesn't that make sense?"

"No. It's impossible."

"Is it? A fugitive criminal, spoken to by God, comes out of the desert with the extraordinary demand to lead Hebrew slaves to freedom, and suddenly he has the power to work miracles—a skill he's never shown before?"

"Power given by God."

"Really? Or by the gods, under the guise of the one great God?"

"He was *fighting* the Egyptian gods, the false idols."

"Ethan, it was men fighting with men."

She sounded like a bloody French revolutionary. Or Ben Franklin.

"The savior of his people did not just take the enslaved Hebrews and destroy Pharaoh's army," Astiza went on. "He took the most powerful talisman in all the world, so mighty that migrant slaves had the power to conquer the Promised Land."

"A book."

"A repository of wisdom. Recipes of power. When the Jews reached their Promised Land their armies swept all before them. Moses found food, healed the sick, and struck down the blasphemers. He lived past a normal span. Something kept the Hebrews alive in a wilderness for forty years. It was this book."

Once more I tried to remember the old Bible stories. Moses had been a Hebrew slave baby rescued by a princess, raised as a prince, who killed a slave overseer in a fit of rage. He fled, came back decades later, and when Pharaoh refused to let his people go, Moses called down ten plagues upon Egypt. When Pharaoh lost his oldest son in the tenth and worst calamity, he gave up at last, releasing the Hebrew slaves from bondage. And that should have been the end of it except Pharaoh changed his mind yet again and chased Moses and the Hebrews with six hundred chariots. Why? Because he discovered that Moses had taken more than just the enslaved Hebrews. He had taken the core of Egypt's power, its greatest secret, its most feared possession. He had taken it and . . .

Parted the sea.

Had they carried this book of power to Solomon's temple, supposedly raised by the ancestors of my Freemasons?

"This can't be. How could he get in here and back out?"

"He came to Pharaoh shortly before the Nile was at its height," Astiza said. "Don't you see, Ethan? Moses had been an Egyptian prince. He knew sacred secrets. He knew how to get in here and back out, something no one else had dared. That year Egypt lost not just a nation of slaves, a pharaoh, and an army. It lost its heart, its soul, its wisdom. Its essence was taken by a nomadic tribe that after forty years transported it . . ."

"To Israel." I sat on the empty pedestal, my mind reeling.

"And Moses, thief as well as prophet, was never allowed by his own God to enter the Promised Land. Maybe he felt guilt at unleashing what was meant to remain hidden."

I stared at nothing. This book, or scroll, had been missing for three thousand years. And here were Silano and me, chasing an empty vault.

"We've been looking in the wrong place."

"It may have become part of the Ark of the Covenant," she said excitedly, "like the tablets of the Ten Commandments. The same knowledge and power that had raised the pyramids passed to the Jews, who rose from an obscure people to tribes whose traditions became the source of three great religions! It may have helped bring down the walls of Jericho!"

My mind was tumbling over itself. Heresy! "But why would the Egyptians bury such a book?"

"Because knowledge always carries risk as well as reward. It can be used for evil as well as good. Our legends say the secrets of Egypt came from across the sea, from a people forgotten even when the pyramids were raised, and that Thoth realized such knowledge had to be safeguarded. People are creatures of emotion, cleverer than they are wise. Maybe the Hebrews realized that too, since the book has disappeared. Perhaps they learned that to use the Book of Thoth was dangerous folly."

I didn't believe any of it, of course. This mixture of gods was patent blasphemy. And I'm a modern man, a man of science, an American skeptic in the Franklin mold. And yet was there some divine force that worked through all the wonders of the world? Was there a chapter to humankind's story that our revolutionary age had forgotten?

And then there came an echoing boom, a long roll of

thunder, stirring the air with distant wind. The rocky cavern quivered and rumbled. An explosion.

Silano had found his gunpowder.

As the sound reverberated through the subterranean chamber, I got up off the pedestal. "You didn't answer my other question. How did Moses get back out?"

She smiled. "Maybe he never closed the door that we entered, and got out the way he came in. Or, more likely, there is more than one entrance. The medallion suggests there is more than one shaft—one west and one east—and he closed the western door behind him but exited the east. Certainly the good news is that we know he did. We found our way in, Ethan. We'll find our way out, too. First step is to get off this island."

"Not until I help myself."

"We have no time for that!"

"A pittance of this treasure, and we can buy all the time in the world."

I had no proper sack or backpack. How can I describe the king's ransom I tried to wear? I draped enough necklaces on my chest to give myself a backache and jammed on bracelets enough for a Babylonian whore. I belted gold around my waist, fastened anklets above my feet, and even took off Moses' cherubim and jammed them in my drawers. Yet I barely scratched the treasure trove that lay under the Great Pyramid. Astiza, in contrast, touched nothing.

"Stealing from the dead is no different than stealing from the living," she warned.

"Except that the dead don't need it anymore," I reasoned, torn between sheepishness at my own Western greed and the entrepreneurial instincts to not let a once-in-a-lifetime opportunity slip by. "When we're outside we'll need money to finish finding this book," I reasoned. "For heaven's sake, at least put a ring or two on your fingers."

"It's bad luck. People die when they rob from tombs."

"It's simply compensation for all we've been through."

"Ethan, I'm worried there is a curse."

"Savants don't believe in curses, and Americans believe

in opportunity when it is staring you in the face. I'm not going to leave until you take something for yourself."

So she put a ring on with all the pleasure of a slave slipping on its manacle. I knew she would come around to my
way of thinking once we were out of this catacomb. That
ring alone, with a ruby the size of a cherry, was a life's income. We jumped in the boat and quickly sculled to the
main shore. Once on the ground we felt shudders in the
grand structure above, and a continued creaking and groaning as an aftereffect of the explosion. I hoped that fool Silano hadn't used so much gunpowder that he'd bring the
ceiling down.

"We have to assume Bin Sadr and his assassins are going
to be coming in the same way we did, if that keg of gunpowder worked," I said. "But if the medallion showed a V with
two shafts, the other path out must be the eastern shaft.
With luck we can pop out that way, shut the eastern door,
and be well on our way before the villains figure out where
we've gone."

"They'll be transfixed by the treasure too," Astiza predicted.

"So much the better."

The disquieting grinding continued, accompanied by a
hiss, like a cascade of falling sand. Had the explosion triggered some kind of ancient mechanism? The building felt
alive, and disapproving. I could hear distant shouts as Silano's henchmen descended toward us.

Still holding Bin Sadr's staff, I led Astiza to a portal on
the eastern end of the lake. It had two tunnels, one going
down and another up. We took the upper course. Sure
enough, it soon led to an ascending shaft opposite the one
we'd come down. This shaft rose at the same angle, aimed
for the pyramid's eastern face. Yet the higher we climbed,
the louder the hiss and groan.

"The air is feeling heavier," I said worriedly.

Soon we saw why. The overhead voids I'd noticed in the
western shaft were repeated here, and from the mouth of
each one a granite plug was descending like a dark molar
from a stone gum. They were steadily sliding down to seal

the passage and any escape. A second was coming down behind the first, and a third beyond that. Sand, somewhere in the pyramid's workings, must have worked as a counterweight to balance these stones in place. Now, with Silano's disturbance, it had been triggered to leak away. No doubt the portals were closing on the tunnel we'd entered through, as well. We might be trapped down here with Bin Sadr's gang.

"Hurry! Maybe we can slip beneath before they shut!" I started to wriggle forward.

Astiza grabbed me. "No! You'll be crushed!"

Even as I struggled against her grasp I knew she was right. I might make it past the nearest, and even the one beyond that. But the third would surely crush me, or more likely trap me for all eternity between it and its brother behind.

"There has to be another way," I said with more hope than conviction.

"The medallion showed only two shafts." She dragged me backward with my necklaces like a dog on its collar. "I told you all this was bad luck."

"No. There's that descending tunnel we haven't followed. They wouldn't just cork this off for all time."

We hurriedly descended back the way we came, coming out again to the underground lake with its island. As we neared we saw a glow of light and soon confirmed the worst. Several Arabs were on the isle of gold and silver, shouting with the same glee I'd felt, wrestling for the best pieces. Then they spotted our torches. "The American!" Bin Sadr cried, his words echoing across the water. "The man who kills him gets a double share! Another double for giving me the woman!"

Where was Silano?

I couldn't help but wave his staff at the bastard, like a cape at a bull.

Bin Sadr and two of the men leaped into the little alabaster boat, almost capsizing it but also sending it skittering toward us with their momentum. The other three leaped into the cold water and began swimming.

With no other choice, we ran down the descending tunnel. It too seemed to lead vaguely east, but deeper into the limestone bedrock. I dreaded a dead end, like the descending corridor we'd seen with Napoleon. Yet now another sound was growing, the deep, throaty roar of a running underground river.

Maybe that was the way out!

We came to a scene out of Dante. The tunnel ended on a stone landing that jutted into a new cave chamber, this one faintly lit by a lurid red glow. The source of the illumination was a pit so deep and foggy that I couldn't make out its bottom, even though a glow like banked coals seemed to be coming from its depths. It was an unworldly light, dim yet pulsing, like a navel of Hades. Rock scree and sand sloped down the pit's sides toward the light. Something mysterious was moving down there, ponderous and thick. A stone bridge, cracked, pockmarked, and without railings, arched across the pit. It was enameled blue and covered with yellow stars, like an upside-down temple roof. Slip from its course, and you'd never get back out.

At the far end of this chamber the bridge ended on a broad set of wet, glistening, granite stairs. A spilling sheet of water ran down them and into the pit, possibly the source of the swirling steam. It was from the direction of the stairs that I heard the roar of a river. While impossible to see, I guessed there was an underground diversion of the Nile there, running in a channel across the far side of the chamber like an irrigation canal. The channel must be at the top of the wet stairway, higher than the platform on which we stood, and was so brimming with water that some was spilling over.

"That's our exit," I said. "All we have to do is get there first." I could hear the Arabs coming behind as I trotted out on the bridge.

Suddenly a block bearing one of the inscribed stars gave way and my leg plunged down into the gap, almost toppling me off the archway and into the pit. Only with luck did I catch the edge of the bridge and regain my footing. The archway block made a bang when it hit, far below. I looked down into the reddish fog. What was writhing down there?

"By the timber of Ticonderoga, I think there are snakes down there," I said shakily, pulling myself up and retreating. At the same time I could hear the shouts of the approaching Arabs.

"It's a test, Ethan, to punish those who enter without knowledge. There's something wrong with this bridge."

"Obviously."

"Why would they paint the sky on the bridge deck? Because the world is upside down here, because . . . the medallion disc! Where is it?"

After Astiza had retrieved it from its fall down the face of the pyramid, I'd tucked it into my robes. Souvenir, after all this trouble. Now I pulled it out and gave it to her.

"Look," she said, "the constellation Draco. It's not just the north star, Ethan. It makes a pattern we have to follow." And before I could suggest we consider the matter, she hopped past me onto a particular stone in the archway. "Only touch the stars that are in the constellation!"

"Wait! What if you're wrong?"

There was the boom of a musket and a bullet whined into the chamber, bouncing off the rock walls. Bin Sadr was coming at full charge.

"What choice do we have?"

I followed Astiza, using Bin Sadr's staff for balance.

We'd barely started when the Arabs came boiling out of the tunnel and stopped at the lip of the pit as we had, awed by the peculiar menace of this place. Then one of them rushed forward. "I've got the woman!" But he'd gone only yards when another star block gave way and he fell in surprise, not as lucky as me. He struck the bridge with his torso, bounced, screamed, scrabbled at the lip of the arch with his fingers, and fell, striking the side of the pit and sliding down into the gloom in a tumble of rock. The Arabs moved to the lip of the ledge to look. Something down there moved, quickly this time, and the victim's scream was cut off.

"Wait!" Bin Sadr said. "Don't shoot them! See? We must step where they do!" He was watching me as carefully as I watched Astiza. Then he leaped, landing where I had. The bridge held firm. "Follow me!"

It was a bizarre, mincing dance, all of us mimicking the hops of the woman. Another Arab missed and fell shrieking as still another block gave way, transfixing us all for a moment. "No, no, *that* one!" Bin Sadr shrieked, pointing. Then the deadly game commenced again.

At the center of the span I couldn't see a bottom at all. What kind of volcanic throat *was* this? Was it this navel that the pyramid had been built to seal?

"Ethan, hurry," Astiza begged. She was waiting for me to make sure I stepped on the right star stones, even though it gave Bin Sadr time to spy them as well. Then she was finally at the wet stairs, swaying from the tension, and I made a final leap, landing on the polestar. With a triumphant stride I made the granite stairs and turned, holding Bin Sadr's snake staff in readiness to stab him. Maybe he'd make a mistake!

But no, he came on implacably, eyes gleaming. "There's nowhere left to run, American. If you give me my staff, I'll save you to watch while we have the woman."

He was only steps away, his three surviving men bunched behind him. If they rushed me, it was over.

The Arab stopped. "Are you going to surrender?"

"Go to hell."

"Then shoot him now," Bin Sadr ordered. "I remember the last stars to touch." Muskets and pistols began to be leveled.

"Here then," I offered.

I threw the staff up in the air, high, but so he could catch it. His eyes widened, gleaming. Instinctively he stretched, leaned, snatched it with the quickness of a reptile, and in the course of doing so unthinkingly moved his left foot for balance.

A keystone piece at the end of the bridge gave way.

The Arabs froze, listening to it smash as it ricocheted into the pit below.

Then there was a groan, a sound of rock splintering, and we looked down. The missing block had begun a disintegration. The bridge's connection with the granite stairs was dissolving as blocks popped out, the untethered end beginning to dip remorselessly into the pit. Bin Sadr had made a fatal misstep. The Arab's henchmen cried out and began to stampede back the way they had come. As they did, heedless of where their feet were, more stones gave way.

Bin Sadr leaped for the wet granite stairs.

Had he let go of his staff, he might have made it, or at least gotten a hand on me and dragged me down with him. But he held his favorite weapon too long. His other arm was still wounded and weak, his hand slipped on the wet rock, and he began sliding down into the abyss, trying to hold both himself and his staff. Finally he let go the rod in time to grip a knob of stone to arrest his slide. The staff fell out of sight. He was dangling at the precipice, a skein of water streaming down past him to dissolve into steam, his legs kicking. Meanwhile his companions behind screeched in terror as the bridge rotated downward with a roar, collapsing toward hell, taking them with it. They plummeted, limbs flailing. I watched them disappear into the fog.

Bin Sadr hung grimly, looking at Astiza with hatred. "I wish I'd butchered this whore like I did the one in Paris," he hissed.

I took out my tomahawk and crept down toward his fingers. "This is for Talma, Enoch, Minette, and every other innocent you'll meet on the other side." I lifted the hatchet.

He spat at me. "I'll wait for you there." Then he let go.

He plunged down the side of the pit, struck a steep slope of sand, and tumbled, soundless, into the dim red mist below. Small rocks rattled with him, tracing his slide. Then there was silence.

"Is he dead?" Astiza whispered.

It was so quiet that I feared he'd somehow find a way to climb back out. I peered over. Something was moving down there, but for a while we could hear nothing but the roar of the water at the top of the wet stairs. Then there came, faint at first, the sounds of a man beginning to scream.

By this time I'd heard more than my share of screams, both in battle and among the wounded. There was something different about this sound, however, an unworldly scream of such absolute terror that my stomach clenched at whatever unseen thing or things were prompting it. The screams went on and on, rising in pitch, and I knew with grim certainty that it was the voice of Achmed bin Sadr. Despite my enmity for the man, I shuddered. He was experiencing the terror of the damned.

"Apophis," Astiza said. "The snake god of the underworld. He is meeting what he worshipped."

"That's a myth."

"Is it?"

After what seemed an eternity the screams sank to an insane gibbering. Then they stopped. We were alone.

I was shivering from terror and cold. We hugged each other, all retreat impossible, the pit's red glow our only light. Finally we started up the wet staircase, its waterfall smelling of the Nile. What underworld test would we face next? I didn't have the energy—the will, as Napoleon would say—to go much farther.

We reached a trough that ran across the top of the stairs. Nile water was racing from a pipelike opening in the cave wall to fill the stone canal to the brim, and then disappearing in another tunnel at the other end of the stairway. The current was pouring out with such force that there was no possibility of ascending it. Our only exit would be to go the direction the water was running, into a dark drain.

There was no room, I saw, for air.

"I don't think Moses came this way."

CHAPTER TWENTY-FOUR

"Moses was an Egyptian prince who knew how this chamber was constructed," Astiza said. "He didn't trigger the granite plugs like foolish Silano. He left by one of the shafts."

"And at low water, this trough might be a possible escape route," I said. "But at high water, the only time that door to the pyramid would open, it's full to the brim. There's no air. If you get in you have to use the correct exit to get out or it's a trap."

"But why, then, a bridge that tests your knowledge of the constellation?" Astiza asked. "It must be possible to leave this way, but only for men who know its perils. Maybe this was a last resort for the architects, in case a mistake left them trapped. Perhaps it's a test of faith that we can get out of here."

"You can't be planning to try to ride this sewer to the Nile."

"Worse than waiting for a slow death in here?"

She did have a way of getting to the heart of things. We could sit on the wet stairs for eternity, contemplating the broken bridge and the granite plugs high above, or take our chances in the sluiceway. Maybe Thoth had a sense of humor. Here I was, fugitive, the medallion used and broken, beaten to a fabled book by a desert prophet some three thousand years before, tired, sore, in love, and—if I could ever use the metal hanging on my body—fabulously wealthy. It's a wonder what travel will do for you.

"Suffocation is quicker than starvation," I agreed.

"You *will* drown if you don't get rid of most of that treasure."

"Are you joking? If we're supposed to jump into this sluiceway, maybe the ceiling opens up ahead. Maybe the outlet to the Nile isn't that far away. I haven't come this far to come away with nothing."

"And what do you call nothing?" Her smile was mischievous.

"Well, except for you." It seemed we were a couple; you can always tell when you start tripping over what you say. "I just meant it's nice to have a financial start in the world."

"We have to save the world, first."

"Let's start by saving ourselves." I looked at the dark rushing water. "Before we try, I guess I'd better kiss you. Just in case it's the last time."

"A sensible precaution."

So I did.

She was so good at returning the favor that it gave me all kinds of ideas.

"No." She pushed my paws aside. "That will be your reward on the other side. Believe in me, Ethan." And with that, she vaulted herself over the low wall, dropped with a splash into the water, pointed her feet downstream, and let go. In a flash she was where the ceiling touched the water. She took a last breath, dipped her head, and was gone.

By the spurs of Paul Revere, the woman had pluck! And damned if I was going to stay in this tomb alone. So before I could philosophize about it further I plunged in myself—but instead of floating like a cork I sank to the bottom of the trough like a lead sinker.

It was the treasure, you see.

I was helpless as a rat in a pipe, or a bullet in a barrel. My hand reached up to scrape a wet ceiling, looking for air, and couldn't touch it. I was bouncing along the bottom as if I'd tied on an anchor. Cursing my luck, or stupidity, I began clawing at golden pendants, emptying my pocket of precious gems, and shedding my arms of bracelets. Off came a belt worth a king's ransom, an anklet I could buy a country estate with. Rings I dropped like bread crumbs. As I tugged each one off it was lost forever, or at least lost to the mud of the Nile or the belly of some crocodile. Yet with each frantic discard I became more buoyant. Soon I was off the bottom and slithering near the top of this insidious culvert, hands scraped raw, hoping against hope for a pocket of air as my lungs began to squeeze and burn. *Don't breathe!* I silently screamed at myself. Just one moment more. And one moment more . . .

And more.

And still more as I thrashed to rid myself of wealth.

The last treasure came off.

My lungs burned, my ears felt close to bursting, and I was sightless in the dark.

One thing I especially feared was colliding with the lifeless body of Astiza, which would have caused such despair that I'd suck the Nile into my lungs. Conversely, it was the thought of her waiting ahead that kept me determined to stick it out. *Believe!*

I put my arm up one last desperate time, expecting to feel wet rock, and encountered . . .

Nothing!

My head burst the surface just as my breath burst from my mouth. Air! It was still pitch black but I gasped for a lungful. Then I collided with the ceiling again with a painful bang and was sucked further down the seemingly endless, relentless, underground pipe. Air, air, just one more lungful, lord, how I ached, I couldn't take much more . . . and then I was weightless, pitched into nothing, the water falling away beneath me. I gasped in surprise and terror, tumbling as I fell, my stomach gone, before crashing into a dark pool. I came up sputtering, eyes blinking, seeing I was again in a limestone cavern. I could breathe! Even more amazing, I could faintly see. But how? Yes! There was light coming from the water at the far end of the cave, a glimmer of outside! I dove and kicked to swim with all my might.

And surfaced at the edge of the Nile.

There was Astiza, floating on her back, her dark hair in a fan, her wet clothes translucent, her body pale, in a shallow of papyrus reeds and lotus blossoms. Was she dead, drowned?

She rolled and treaded water, looking at me with a smile.

"You shed your greed, and the gods gave you air," she teased.

Trading breath for the wealth of Croesus. Thoth does have a sense of humor.

We paddled into a shallow by some reeds, resting on the muddy bottom with just our heads above water, considering what to do next. Somehow the entire night had passed and it was just after dawn, the warming sun on our faces and a haze of smoke over Cairo. We heard the pops and bangs of skirmishing. The city was still in open revolt and Bonaparte was still determined to suppress it.

"I think I've overstayed my welcome in Egypt, Astiza," I wheezed.

"The pyramid is locked and the Book of Thoth is gone. We can do no more here. But what was lost remains a potent weapon. I think we still need to learn its fate."

"Wasn't it last seen with a fugitive Jew named Moses three thousand years ago? With no mention of it since?"

"No mention? And yet Moses raised his arm to part the sea, healed the sick with a bronze snake, found food from the sky, and talked with God. Everyone knew he was a magician. How did he learn such powers? And was it solely the Ten Commandments the Hebrews carried in the Ark of the Covenant that won them their victories, or did they have another aid as well? Why did they spend forty years in the desert before invading their promised land? Perhaps they were mastering something."

"Or perhaps they had no magic at all and had to do things the old-fashioned way, by building an army."

"No. What is the book but another source of the same knowledge you and the other scientists are seeking to uncover right now? That book could give the savants of any nation the knowledge to dominate the world. Do you think

Silano and Bonaparte haven't guessed that? Do you think they don't dream of a sorcerer's powers or an angel's immortality?"

"So you want us to spend forty years in the desert looking for it?"

"Not the desert. You know where the book must be, just as the Romans and the Arabs and the Crusaders and the Templars and the Turks knew, and always looked: Jerusalem. That's where Solomon built his temple, and where the Ark was kept."

"And we're supposed to find what they could not? The temple was destroyed by the Babylonians and Romans three or four times over. This Ark, if not destroyed, high-tailed it into the wilderness. It's as mythic as the Holy Grail."

"Yet we know what we are looking for. Not a grail, not a treasure, not an ark."

You know how women are. They grab an idea like a terrier and won't let go unless you can figure a way to distract them. They don't understand the difficulties, or they figure that you'll do the heavy lifting if you run into a snag. "Capital idea. Let's look for it, right after we settle my affairs in America."

Our philosophic discussion ended when the crack of a musket shot sent up a little geyser of water just feet from our heads. Then another, and another.

I looked up the riverbank. On the crest of a dune was a patrol of French soldiers and, lively as a stag in heat, Count Alessandro Silano. While his henchmen had run down into the pyramid of death, he'd prudently decided to stay outside.

"The magicians!" he shouted. "Get them!"

Well, hell. The bastard seemed indestructible—but then he was probably thinking the same thing about us. And of course he had no idea what we had, or rather hadn't. Astiza still had the medallion's disk, and I realized I still had the cherubim from Moses' staff, if that's what it was, tucked uncomfortably in my loincloth. Maybe I'd make a dollar out of this after all. We launched ourselves into the river and began swimming hard for the Cairo bank, letting the current widen the distance. By the time the soldiers had run down to the edge of the riverbank to take better aim, we were out of effective range.

We could hear Silano ranting. "To the boats, you fools!"

The Nile is half a mile wide at the pyramids, but it seemed like half an ocean in the condition we were in. The same current giving us some distance from Silano was carrying us closer to the fighting in downtown Cairo. As we thrashed the last weary feet across the river's breadth I could see a battery of artillery deploying outside the city's walls, and one of Conte's balloons hovering a few feet off the ground. It was being inflated to be used again as an observation post. It was a pretty thing, a patriotic red, white, and blue, with stones hung from bags on the side for ballast. The balloon gave me an idea, and since I was as winded as a Virginia congressman invited to give a few remarks, it might be our only chance.

"Have you ever wanted to fly away from your troubles?"

"Never more than now." She looked like a half-drowned kitten.

"Then we're going to take that balloon."

She blinked water from her eyes. "You know how to operate it?"

"The first French aeronauts were a rooster, a duck, and a sheep."

We dragged ourselves from the Nile and crept along its bank, working downstream toward Conte. I looked back. Silano's soldiers were pushing hard on the sweeps of their boats. The count was shouting and pointing to call attention to us, but all eyes were focused on fighting in the city. It would be a close thing. I took out my tomahawk, the other piece of metal I'd saved in my long sluiceway tumble. It was starting to look hard-used.

"Now!"

We charged. If anyone had bothered to look in our direction, we would have looked like two half-naked lunatics: wet, sand-plastered, wild-eyed, and desperate. But the fighting gave us the moment we needed to cross the verge and interrupt Conte just as his gasbag reached full inflation. An artilleryman was climbing into the wicker basket.

Astiza distracted the famed scientist by bounding up into his view like a disheveled harlot, more of her charms on display than either of us would have preferred. Conte was a savant, but he was also a man, and he gaped in stupefaction as if Venus herself had popped from the half-shell. Meanwhile, I darted by and collared the artilleryman, somersaulting him backward out of the rising basket. "Sorry! Change of assignment!"

He reared up to argue the point, obviously confused by my remnants of Egyptian clothing. To settle the issue, I clouted him on the forehead with the butt of my tomahawk and climbed into the basket in his place. Several French soldiers had disembarked from their boat and were lining up to give me a volley, but their aim was blocked by a charging Silano.

"I'm sorry, Nicolas, we must borrow your airship," Astiza said to Conte as she jerked the peg holding its anchor rope out of the ground. "Bonaparte's orders."

"*What* orders?"

"To save the world!" The balloon was rising, the rope skidding along the ground, and I was already too high to reach her. So she jumped and grabbed the tether, hanging below the basket as we rose off the earth. Conte, running after us with arms waving, was butted aside by the sprinting Silano. Just as the writhing rope kicked up a last tendril of dust and climbed into the air, the count leaped and grabbed too. The sudden weight sent us sagging, the basket only fifty feet off the ground. Silano began climbing the tether with sheer arm strength, tenacious as a bulldog.

"Astiza! Hurry!"

The ground was slipping beneath us at an alarming speed.

Her ascent was painfully slow, given her weariness. Silano gained on her, teeth gritted, eyes slit with hatred. I reached down. Just as Astiza's hand neared mine, he grabbed her ankle. "He's got me!" She kicked, he cursed and swayed, holding the tether, and then clutched her leg once again. "He's like a leech!"

I leaned over the basket rim to haul. "I'll get you in and cut the rope!"

"Now his other arm is on me! He's hanging on me as much as the tether!"

"Kick, Astiza! Fight!"

"I can't," she cried. "His arms are locked around me."

I looked down. The demon was squeezing her legs like a constricting snake, his face bitter with determination. I pulled, but couldn't lift both of them. Combined, they weighed three hundred pounds.

"Tell me what you learned, Gage!" he shouted. "Let me in, or we all go down!"

The balloon continued to lumber along less than a hundred feet off the surface. We passed over the edge of the riverbank and drifted along the shallows of the Nile. Conte was running along the river after us. Ahead I saw a company of French infantry turn and look at this scene in amazement. We'd pass so close that they could kill us all with a volley if they chose.

"It's the ring!" Astiza cried. "The ring you made me wear! I forgot to take it off! It's the curse, Ethan, the curse!"

"There is no curse!"

"Take it off me!"

But her hands were grasped like iron on the rope and out of my reach, and I could no more slip the silly ring off than I could chop off her hand. Meanwhile Silano, clutching her legs, was even farther from me.

That gave me an idea.

"Take my tomahawk!" I said. "Crack his head like a nut!"

Desperately she released her right hand, the one without the ring, caught my weapon as I dropped it, and chopped down at Silano. But he'd heard us and as she swung he dropped until his arms were clamped like a vise around her ankles, his head out of range. The blade whistled by his hair. With just one arm holding on she slid down the rope a few feet, palm burning, out of my grasp. I hauled on the tether, but couldn't lift it.

"Astiza!" Silano shouted. "Don't! You know I still love you!"

It was as if the words paralyzed her for a moment, and

they shocked me as well. Her eyes flickered with memory and a thousand questions roared in my end. He loved her? She'd said she didn't love him, but . . .

"Don't believe him!" I cried.

She thrashed the tomahawk at air, her look frantic. "Ethan! I can't hold on! Pull up the rope!"

"You're too heavy! Shake him off! The soldiers are aiming! They're going to shoot us all unless we can climb!" If I somehow climbed down over her to get to Silano, we'd probably all tumble off.

She jerked but the count was like a barnacle. She slid down another foot.

"Astiza, they're about to fire!"

She looked up at me in desperation. "I don't know what to do." It was a sob. We lumbered along, too heavy to rise, the Nile glittering below.

"Astiza, please," the count pleaded. "It's not too late . . ."

"Kick! Kick! They're going to shoot us all!"

"I can't." She was gasping.

"Kick!"

Astiza looked at me with tears in her eyes. "Find it," she whispered.

Then, swinging viciously, she swung the tomahawk against the tether. The line snapped with a crack.

And in an instant, she and Silano were gone.

With their weight released, the balloon popped up like a champagne cork, soaring so quickly that I lost my footing and toppled into the bottom of the basket. "Astiza!"

But there was no reply, just screams as the pair fell.

I scrambled up just in time to see a titanic splash in the river. Their fall had distracted the soldiers for a moment, but now the muskets swung in unison back to me. I was soaring away. There was a sharp command, a flash of muzzles, and a huge plume of smoke blew out.

I heard the hum of bullets, but none arced high enough to hit.

In despair, I studied the surface of the receding river. The rising sun was in my eyes and the Nile was a dazzling platter of light, every wavelet a mirror. There, was that a head, maybe two? Had one or both of them survived the fall? Or was it all a trick of the light?

The harder I strained, the less certain I was of what I saw. The soldiers were shouting excitedly and milling on the riverbank. Then all became impossibly blurred, my hope gone, my ambitions dust, my heart profoundly alone.

For the first time in many years, I was crying.

The Nile was molten silver, and I was blind.

I kept rising. There was Conte far below, staring in stupefaction at his lost prize. I was high as a minaret, with a panorama of Cairo's smoking rooftops. The world was shrinking to toys, the sound of battle receding. The wind was taking me north, downriver.

The balloon climbed higher than the pyramids, and then as high as a mountain. I began to wonder if it would ever stop and if I, like Icarus, would be burned by the sun. Through morning haze I saw Egypt in all its serpentine glory. A snake of green stretched south until lost in the distance, like a ship's wake in an ocean of brown desert. To the north, the direction we were drifting, the green opened like a fan to the Nile Delta, the brown flood waters creating a vast lake that was thronged with birds and dotted with date palms. Beyond was the sea glimmer of the Mediterranean. There was a hushed silence, as if everything we'd just experienced was some dark and noisy dream. The wicker creaked. I heard a bird cry. Otherwise, I was alone.

Why had I made her wear the ring? Now I had no treasure, and no Astiza either.

Why hadn't I listened?

Because I needed Thoth's bloody book to pound some sense into my own thick head, I thought. Because I was the worst savant in the world.

I slumped in the wicker basket, dazed. Too much had happened. The pyramid was locked, Bin Sadr gone, the Egyptian Rite defeated. I'd had a measure of revenge for the deaths of Talma and Enoch. Even Ash was reunited with his people in a struggle for Egypt. And I had resolved nothing, except to learn what I believed in.

The woman I had just lost.

The pursuit of happiness, I thought bitterly. Any chance of that had just fallen into the Nile. I was furious, heartsick, deadened. I wanted to go back to Cairo and learn Astiza's fate, whatever it would cost me. I wanted to sleep for a thousand years.

The balloon permitted neither. Its bag was sewn tight. It was cold this high, my clothes still wet, and I felt dizzy from vertigo. Sooner or later this contraption had to come down, and what then?

The delta was a fairyland below. Date palms made stately rows. Fields formed quilted patterns. Donkeys trundled on ancient dirt lanes. From the air everything seemed clean, tidy, and untroubled. People pointed and ran after my progress, but I soon left them behind. The sky seemed a deeper blue. I was having, I thought, a glimpse of heaven.

I kept drifting northwest, at least a mile above the earth. In a few hours I spied Rosetta at the Nile's mouth, and Abukir Bay where the French fleet had been destroyed. Alexandria was beyond. I crossed the coast, the surf a rim of cream, and drifted out over the Mediterranean. So, I would drown after all.

Why hadn't I given up the medallion a lifetime ago?

And then I saw a ship.

Ahead on the Mediterranean was a frigate, cruising the coast near Rosetta where the Nile debouched with its long tongue of chocolate. The tiny vessel sparkled in the sun, cutting a foamy wake. The sea was dotted with whitecaps. Flags snapped in the wind.

"It has an English ensign," I muttered to myself.

Hadn't I promised Nelson I'd return with information? Despite my sorrow, dim thoughts of survival began to beat into my brain.

But how to come down? I grabbed the ropes holding the basket and shimmied to the bag overhead. I no longer had either rifle or tomahawk to pierce it. I looked down. The frigate had changed course to intercept my own, and sailors the size of insects were pointing. But I'd easily outrun him if I didn't descend to the sea. Then I remembered I still had a stub of candle and a scrap of flint. There was a steel collar to hold the ropes under the gasbag. I peeled some strands of hemp and struck my flint against the collar, generating enough spark to ignite tendrils of rope, which in turn lit peeled strips of wicker, which gave me flame for my wick. Shielding my candle, I reached up toward the gasbag.

Conte had told me hydrogen was flammable.

I held the flame to the silk, saw it smolder, a wink of light . . .

Then there was a whoosh and a clout of hot air punched me straight down into the basket, singed and terrified.

The bag had exploded with fire!

Flames ran up a seam like a train of gunpowder, boiling skyward. The balloon didn't burst, the eruption was not that violent, but it burned like a dry pine bough. I began a sickening plunge, much faster than I wanted. The flames gathered force and I threw all the rock ballast off to slow my descent. It hardly helped. The basket rocked madly as we spiraled down, trailing fire and smoke. Too fast! Now the whitecaps became individual waves, a gull skittered by, the burning bag was falling down around me, and I could see spray whipping off the swell tops.

I braced, and the basket hit with a jarring crash. A huge fountain of water shot up and the bag fell just past my head, hissing as its heat hit the Mediterranean.

Fortunately, the fire mostly consumed what might otherwise have been a soggy anchor. The wicker basket leaked, but slowly, and I'd given the frigate a beacon it could hardly miss. It was steering straight for me.

The basket went down as a longboat was being lowered. I treaded water for only five minutes before being picked up.

Once again I was deposited soaked and sputtering on launch floorboards, crewmen gaping, a young midshipman peering at me like I was a man from the moon.

"Where the bloody hell did you come from?"

"Bonaparte," I gasped.

"And who the bloody hell are you?"

"An English spy."

"Aye, I remember him," one of the crewmen said. "Picked

him up when we was at Abukir Bay. He pops up like a bloody bobber."

"Please," I coughed. "I'm a friend of Sir Sidney Smith."

"Sidney Smith, eh? We'll see about that!"

"I know he's not the navy's favorite, but if you just put me in touch . . ."

"You can put your lies to him right now."

In short order I was standing dripping on the quarter-deck, so sore, singed, hungry, thirsty, and heartsick that I thought I would faint. The grog they gave burned like a slap in the face. I learned I was a guest of Captain Josiah Lawrence, HMS *Dangerous*.

I didn't like that name at all.

And sure enough, Smith materialized. Dressed in the uniform of a Turkish admiral, he came bounding up on deck from some cabin below when the news of my rescue was passed to him. I don't know which of us looked more ridiculous: me, the drowned rat, or him, gussied up like an Oriental potentate.

"By God, it *is* Gage!" exclaimed the man I'd last seen in a gypsy camp.

"This man claims he's your spy," Lawrence announced with distaste.

"Actually, I prefer to consider myself an observer," I said.

"Heart of oak!" cried Smith. "I had word from Nelson that he'd contacted you after the Nile, but neither one of us really believed you'd make it out again." He slapped my back. "Well done, man, well done! I guess you had it in you!"

I coughed. "I never expected to see you again, either."

"Small world, is it not? Now then, I hope you got rid of that damned medallion."

"Yes, sir."

"I sensed nothing but trouble from that. Nothing but trouble. And what's the word on Bonaparte?"

"There's a revolt in Cairo. And Mameluke resistance in the south."

"Splendid!"

"I don't think the Egyptians can beat him, however."

"We'll give them help. And you've flown like a bird from Boney's nest?"

"I had to borrow one of their observation balloons."

He shook his head in admiration. "Damn fine show, Gage! Fine show! Had enough of French radicalism, I hope. Back to king and country. No, wait—you're a colonial. But you *have* come around to the English point of view?"

"I prefer to think of my view as American, Sir Sidney. Put off by the whole thing."

"Well. Quite, quite. Yet you can't capitulate to indecision in desperate times, can you? Have to believe in something, eh?"

"Bonaparte is talking about marching on Syria."

"I knew it! The bastard won't rest until he's occupied the sultan's palace in Constantinople! Syria, eh? Then we'd best set course for there and give warning. There's a pasha there, what's his name?" He turned to the captain.

"Djezzar," Lawrence replied. "The name means 'butcher.' Bosnian by birth, rose from slavery, supposed to be unusually cruel even in a region known for its cruelty. Nastiest bastard in five hundred miles."

"Just the man we need to face off against the French!" Smith cried.

"I've no more business with Napoleon," I interrupted. "I simply need to learn if a woman I was with in Egypt survived a terrible fall, and reunite with her if she did. After that, I was hoping to arrange passage to New York."

"Perfectly understandable! You've done your bit! And yet a man of your pluck and diplomatic acumen would be invaluable in warning the wogs about this damned Bonaparte, wouldn't you? I mean, you've seen his tyranny firsthand. Come on, Gage, don't you want to see the Levant? Scarcely a stone's throw from Cairo! That's the place to learn about this woman of yours! We can send word through our damned oily spies."

"Perhaps an inquiry through Alexandria . . ."

"Go ashore there and you'll be shot on sight! Or worse, hanged as a spy and a balloon thief! Ah, the French will be sharpening their guillotine for you! No, no, that option is foreclosed. I know you're something of a lone wolf, but let the king's navy here give you some help for a change. If the woman is alive, we can get word through Palestine, and organize a raid with a chance to really get her back. I admire your courage, but now's the time to use a cool head, man."

He had a point. I suppose I'd burned my bridges with Napoleon, and charging back into Egypt alone might be more suicidal than brave. My balloon ride had left Astiza at least a hundred miles to the south, in Cairo. Maybe I could play along with Sir Sidney until I learned what had happened. Once ashore in a nearby port like El Arish or Gaza, I'd pawn the cherubim in my crotch for money. Then a card game, a new rifle . . .

Smith was going on. "Acre, Haifa, Jaffa—historic cities all. Saracens, Crusaders, Romans, Jews—say, I know just the place you could give us a hand!"

"A hand?" I wanted their help, not the other way around.

"Someone with your skills could slip in and have a look about while making inquiries about this woman. Perfect place, for your purposes and mine."

"Purposes?"

He nodded, plans building in his head like a thundercloud, his grin wide as a cannon's mouth. He grasped my arms as if I'd dropped from the sky to answer all his prayers.

"Jerusalem!" he cried.

And as I contemplated the will of the gods and the luck of cards, the bow of our ship began to turn.

HISTORICAL NOTE

Napoleon Bonaparte's 1798 invasion of Egypt was not just one of the great military adventures of all time, it was a turning point in French, Egyptian, and archeological history. For Bonaparte, Egypt would prove to be both defeat and springboard, giving him the desperation and fame to seize absolute power in France. For Egypt, the French invasion was the beginning of the modern era after centuries of Ottoman and Mameluke domination. It not only opened the door to Western technology and trade, but also began a turbulent era of colonialism, independence, modernization, and cultural tension still playing out today. For archeology, Napoleon's inclusion of 167 savants in his invading force was a watershed. Early in 1799, French soldiers discovered a stone at Rosetta with Greek, Demotic, and ancient writing that would prove the key to deciphering hieroglyphics. That, coupled with publication of the savant's monumental *Description de l'Egype,* in 23 volumes between 1809 and 1828, gave birth to the science of Egyptology. It started the Romantic era's enchantment with Egyptian fashion and ignited a global fascination with ancient Egypt that continues to this day. Almost everything we know about ancient Egypt has been learned since Napoleon's invasion.

The idea that the Great Pyramid of Giza functioned as something other than a simple tomb, and that its pharaoh may be buried elsewhere, dates as far back as the ancient Greek historians Herodotus and Diodorus. The puzzle increased when ninth-century Arab grave robbers found no mummy, no treasure, and no inscriptions when they broke into the tomb. In the last two centuries there has been unending fascination with, and debate about, the pyramid's dimensions, mysteries, and mathematical meaning. While some of the most speculative theorists accuse mainstream Egyptologists of being close-minded, and while some academics have labeled the zaniest of the crackpots as "pyramidiots," there is serious scholarly debate about the pyramid's structure and purpose. New mysteries are still being discovered by robotic explorers, and hidden chambers are still suspected. The Giza pyramids rest on a limestone plateau that could contain caves, and Herodotus reported an underground lake or river beneath the structure.

The Great Pyramid's precise geographic placement, its mysterious relationship to the size of our planet, its relationship to pi, and the fascinating correlations between the dimensions of its chambers and intriguing mathematical concepts are all true. The Fibonacci Sequence is a real phenomena, seen in nature in spiral patterns as Jomard describes, and the pyramid's embodiment of the golden section, or golden number, is also true. Pascal's triangle is a real mathematical concept and it yields many more number games than are mentioned in this novel. It does produce a value close to that of the Egyptian value for pi, though I won't promise the pattern really leads to a secret door. I've taken the liberty of allowing my French savants to guess more about pyramid mathematics than was immediately apparent during Napoleon's invasion. While Jomard really did publish intriguing theories, some of the concepts in this novel came from later scholars after more precise measurements could be made. A fascinating and controversial introduction to these concepts and an exhaustive analysis of pyramid mathematics can be found in the 1971 book *Secrets of the Great Pyramid* by Peter Tompkins and Livio Catullo Stecchini.

This novel closely follows the early history of Bonaparte's military invasion of Egypt. Most of the characters are real people, including ten-year-old Giocante Casabianca, whose death at the Battle of the Nile inspired the famed nineteenth-century poem, "The Boy Stood on the Burning Deck." One historical liberty is that I place Desaix's presence at the temple of Dendara three months earlier than the general actually arrived there. The army paused in late January 1799, and the weary artist Vivant Denon was so entranced by the temple's glories that he wrote, "What I saw today has paid me back for all my misery." A few days later, when the French division first saw the ruins of Karnak and Luxor, the troops spontaneously came to a halt, applauded, and presented arms.

Many historical details used in this novel, including the presence of Conte's balloons, are true. There is scholarly disagreement about whether Napoleon actually entered the Great Pyramid, and what happened to him if he did, but the author has lain in the granite sarcophagus as Bonaparte may have, and found it a remarkable experience.

This story weaves together military and political history, Masonic lore, biblical scholarship, mystic speculation, and information about ancient Egypt. For a general history of the invasion I recommend J. Christopher Herold's 1962 prize-winning book *Bonaparte in Egypt.* Fascinating eyewitness accounts of the expedition include those by the artist Vivant Denon, French captain Joseph Marie Mouret, and the Egyptian Al-Jabarti. Some of the quotes attributed to Napoleon in this novel are taken from real life, though not all were spoken during the Egyptian campaign. His own words reveal a man of fascinating complexity.

There are hundreds of scholarly and popular works on scientific Egyptology. Speculative and historical literature on the pyramids, ancient gods, and Egyptian magic is also vast. A good recent introduction to alternative theories about ancient Egypt is the 2005 book *Pyramid Quest* by Robert Schoch and Robert McNally. A book that mentions the birth of the Egyptian Rite of Freemasonry and gives a sense of mystical yearnings in the Age of Reason is Iain McCalman's 2003 biography, *The Last Alchemist,* about Cagliostro. A sprawling, sometimes incoherent, but truly monumental work of mysticism is Manly P. Hall's 1928 classic, *The Secret Teachings of All Ages.* It summarizes what enthusiasts label

Hermetic lore, after the god Hermes, the Greek adaptation of the Egyptian god Thoth.

I'm indebted to dozens of nonfiction authors for the facts behind this novel, as well as the guide Ruth Shilling of All One World Egypt Tours; Egyptian guides Ashraf Mohie el-Din and Galal Hassan Marghany; and Egyptologist-in-the-making Richard Mandeville of the United Kingdom. What is true in this novel is to their credit, while the fictions are all mine. As always, praise must go to the support and insights of my editors at HarperCollins: Michael Shohl, Jill Schwartzman, and Jonathan Burnham; senior production editor David Koral; copy editor Martha Cameron; and my agent, Andrew Stuart. Special appreciation to my wife and helpmate, Holly, who crawled through the pyramids with me. Finally, thanks go to the hospitality of the people of Egypt, who are so proud of their heritage.

BOOKS BY WILLIAM DIETRICH

THE EMERALD STORM—COMING SUMMER 2012!
An Ethan Gage Adventure
ISBN 978-0-06-198920-9 (hardcover)

Action and adventure from around the world, with a magical Spanish treasure, the fate of England, and the first successful slave revolt in history hanging in the balance.

THE BARBARY PIRATES
An Ethan Gage Adventure
ISBN 978-0-06-219141-0 (paperback)

Swashbuckling hero Ethan Gage finds himself in a desperate race with the Barbary Pirates, a powerful band of Muslim outlaws from North Africa.

THE DAKOTA CIPHER
An Ethan Gage Adventure
ISBN 978-0-06-219143-4 (paperback)

Ethan Gage is sent by newly-elected Thomas Jefferson on a mysterious and perilous quest to the edge of the American frontier.

THE ROSETTA KEY
An Ethan Gage Adventure
ISBN 978-0-06-219157-1 (paperback)

Our beloved hero continues his pursuit of Napoleon and a precious Egyptian relic whose owner has the power to rule the world.

NAPOLEAN'S PYRAMIDS
An Ethan Gage Adventure
ISBN 978-0-06-219148-9 (paperback)

In the first installment, American adventurer Ethan Gage travels with Napoleon's great expedition to solve a 6,000 year old riddle.

BLOOD OF THE REICH
ISBN 978-0-06-198919-3 (mass market)

Two American adventurers must stop the Nazis from acquiring a mythical substance that promises them immortality and world domination.

HADRIAN'S WALL
A Novel of Roman England
ISBN 978-0-06-056372-1 (mass market)

William Dietrich evokes a lost world of Roman ideals and barbaric romanticism in this novel about the final great clash of Roman and Celtic culture.

THE SCOURGE OF GOD
A Novel of the Roman Empire
ISBN 978-0-06-073508-1 (mass market)

On the plains of Hunuguri, Attila the Hun gathers the most menacing army the Roman Empire has ever faced.

Available wherever books are sold, or call 1-800-331-3761 to order.